ISHMAEL
AND THE
HOOPS
OF
STEEL

ISHMAEL and the HOOPS of STEEL

MICHAEL GERARD BAUER

templar

A TEMPLAR BOOK

First published by Omnibus Books,
an imprint of Scholastic Australia Pty Ltd, 2011

Published in the UK in 2013 by Templar Publishing,
an imprint of The Templar Company Limited,
Deepdene Lodge, Deepdene Avenue, Dorking, Surrey, RH5 4AT
www.templarco.co.uk

LONDON BOROUGH OF WANDSWORTH	
9030 00003 0905 1	
Askews & Holts	24-Jan-2013
JF TEENAGE 11-14	**£6.99**
	WWX0010703/0119

ISBN 978-1-84877-738-5

Printed and bound by CPI Group (UK) Ltd,
Croydon, CR0 4YY

To my son Joe –
for all your input
into the Ishmael books,
but mostly just for liking them.

CONTENTS

PART ONE Term One

1. Calling Ishmael!   13
2. The Awesome Light Bulb of Total Braininess   18
3. The Short, the Tall and the Cuddly   25
4. The Fab Five   34
5. Uncle What's-his-face and Auntie Thingo's Daughter   43
6. The Lifesaver of Love   51
7. Let's Get Ready to Ruuuuummmble!   55
8. Kiss Me, Stupid!   63
9. A Turbo-charged Cobra   71
10. Deceased Piece of Solid Bodily Waste   79
11. Show Me the Suncream!   85
12. Bill and Razz's Excellent Sun Safe Adventure   96
13. Final Answer (a) Hell, Yeah!   103
14. A Killer, Petrol-driven, Motorised Hamburger   110
15. Talking about *Talk* Talk   115
16. A Prairie Dog on a Caffeine High   121
17. A Gross Invasion of Piracy   126

Term Two

18. The Alcoholic Dane   135
19. The Accelerated Jedi Course   140
20. That Smokin' Elf Chick   146
21. Well and Truly Newtoned   150

22. Watch Your Back, Billy Shakespeare 155
23. Focusing is for Wimps! 159
24. Did I Mention I Was an Idiot? 171
25. Here, Pass Me One of Those Knives 176
26. Fatal Flaw Thingies 182
27. The Return of the Brainiacs 190
28. Windy Perspiration of Horse Breath 199
29. Don't Disturb the Piranhas, Dude 206
30. The Grimmest of His Grim Days 212
31. Hmmmmmm 218
32. Advanced Self-pity Wallowing 401 225

PART TWO Term One

1. The Last of the Lasts 234
2. You Had Me at 'Data' 243
3. Standby Eyes 250
4. Drowning in a Straight Line 255
5. Sledgehammer Meets Soft-boiled Egg 262
6. The Pi Man Delivers! 273
7. The Brown Undies Effect 279
8. The Razzman v The Mudman 287
9. The Pride of Goroka 291
10. Prindabel's Butt Ball 295
11. That's What I'm Talking About 302
12. Words in the Blood 307
13. Operation Get Razz into Uni 316

14. The Poor Suckers Are Us   319
15. Airy-fairy, Tree-hugging, Cheesecloth-wearing,
    Incense-sniffing Hippy Twaddle   324
16. The Razzinator   328
17. A Heavily Drugged Giraffe   334
18. OMG! OMG! OMG!   342

Term Two

19. Male Chauffeuring Pigs   348
20. Grace Under Pressure   355
21. A Razzman Masterclass   361
22. Dying in Key   367
23. A Tsunami Brainwave   374
24. Spawn of Bjorn   384
25. Hot Geek Chicks   393
26. Kabooooooooooooooooooooom!   400
27. The Dugongs of Steel   406
28. Reverse Cool   410
29. You Da Bomb! Da Bomb-bomb!   418
30. You Are to Me   424
31. Three Phone Calls and a Decision   429
32. Play or Party?   438
33. Lines 116 to 119   442
34. A Show Tunes Superman   447
35. Perfect, Just Perfect   453
36. There's No Easy Way to Put This   465
37. Just in Case You're Interested   472

PART ONE

Term One

How weary, stale, flat and unprofitable
Seem to me all the uses of this world!

William Shakespeare, *Hamlet*,
act 1 scene 2, lines 133–134

1.
Calling Ishmael!

Iclicked on my inbox. I had three emails. The first one said *Calling Ishmael!* My heart shot up like it had launched itself off a springboard. I think it nailed a perfect reverse triple somersault in the full pike position.

I had an email from Kelly Faulkner.

Did you hear what I said? Kelly Faulkner, who could stop the world with her ice-blue eyes and kick-start it again with her smile had sent an *actual* email – to me. *Me!* Ishmael Leseur – the world's one and only sufferer of Ishmael Leseur's Syndrome. And if you've never heard of Ishmael Leseur's Syndrome (ILS for short), consider yourself lucky. It's been known to destroy the 'normal behaviour' gene and expose a person's innermost idiot to the world. And I should know, because I *am* that person. If you don't believe me, maybe you should read my last two journals. Just a warning though, they're not for the faint-hearted.

But don't worry, you're safe. ILS is not contagious. In fact, in order to get it, you actually have to have the surname 'Leseur'. Then, following some sort of bizarre birth ritual, your parents have to decide to call you 'Ishmael' after the narrator of Herman Melville's old whaling novel, *Moby Dick*. So basically, what all that means is, you're pretty much in the clear unless you happen to be *me*. Then you're in big trouble.

But maybe things were looking up. Surely a personal email from Kelly Faulkner was a clear sign that I was finally cured of ILS and from now on my life was going to pretty much totally rock. It certainly rocked the last time we were together.

That was about six weeks ago at the end of last term – the night of the big reunion concert for my dad's old rock band, the Dugongs. That was the night my life catapulted from pretty pathetic to potentially perfect. It was the night Kelly Faulkner accidentally found a poem I'd written about her and kissed me – right on the lips. I still had those lips and they still tingled every time I thought about that kiss (which averaged around ten times a day, give or take a few – mostly give). After that Kelly and her family left for New Zealand to visit relatives and I hadn't seen or heard from her since.

But now her name sat before me on my computer in thick, bold font, like a big, chunky Christmas present, the best I was ever going to receive, screaming out to be opened. But I didn't open it. Not then. I wanted to save the best till last so I shifted the cursor to the email below, the one that said *Urgent Message*, and clicked on that instead.

It was from a Mr Mbootu in Nigeria. Huh? Mr M-*who*-tu? I read on. Wow, it was my lucky day! Even though I didn't know Mr Mbootu from a Thomson's gazelle, apparently he was going to give me half of the fifty million dollars he'd found lying around in a bank vault somewhere. Talk about *generous*! And it just got better and better, because all I had to do was send him my name and address. Bargain! Oh, and some silly little bank detail-y things. Hey, no probs! I could give him Mum and Dad's. I'm sure they wouldn't mind. Just wait till Kelly Faulkner found out that I was going to be a multi-millionaire. I bet she'd be impressed. Maybe I could use some of the money to help find a cure for ILS. Thanks heaps, Mr M! What an awesome guy!

I hit *Delete*.

My twenty-five million dollars vanished into the ether. What did I care about money when I had an email from Kelly Faulkner? I was dying more than ever to read it, but first I had to get rid of all other distractions. Kelly and I needed to be alone. I checked out the next email down. This one said *Think BIG!* I clicked on it.

Someone wanted to enlarge my 'Pennis'.

Hmmmmmmmm... tempting. But was I willing to put my 'pennis' in the hands of someone who was so careless with their spelling? I DON'T *THINK* SO! (Miss Tarango, my English teacher, would be *so* proud of me.)

I gave the *Delete* button another jab.

Only one email remained – Kelly's. I moved the cursor over it and watched the little I-shape on the screen morph into a chubby pointing hand. My heart had abandoned the springboard and had climbed right to the very top of the highest of high-dive towers. It was now peering down at a teensy-weensy square of water far, far below. As I clicked on Kelly's email, my heart lurched forward and plunged into free fall.

A bunch of purpley-coloured words leaped into view. The first two were *Hey Ishmael*. It was the best thing I'd ever read. I wanted to pump the air with my fist but I didn't have time. My eyes were already ripping back and forth across the screen.

I tried to make myself slow down. I wanted to take my time so that I could enjoy every letter, every syllable and every punctuation mark that Kelly had written for me. I failed – miserably. With my heart still doing that 'plummeting-off-the-top-of-the-highest-of-high-dive-towers' thing, the words just whooshed past.

... holiday going well... sorry didn't email sooner... bad internet connection... lots of snow... skiing... fun... freezing... staying with relatives... heaps of places... Lord of the Rings... the not-so-good news... father... new job... change in plans... can't believe it... parents have decided to...

Whaaaaaaaaaaaaaaaat!

I read that last bit again.

And again.

Then I forced myself to read it one last time.

My heart wasn't racing in free fall any more. It had come to a shuddering HALT.

Someone had emptied all the water from the high-diving pool.

2.
The Awesome Light Bulb of Total Braininess

"*Bummer*, man. Bum-*mer*. I mean, that's, you know..."

"A bummer?"

"The mumma of all bummers, dude. The mumma bummer!"

Just in case you may have missed it, my best friend Orazio Zorzotto, more commonly known as Razz, Razza or the Razzman, was pointing out in his own delightfully subtle way that the news about Kelly Faulkner and her family deciding to stay in New Zealand permanently (yes, you heard it here first!) was, in fact, a 'bummer'.

Razz blew out a long breath before presenting his final, concise summary of the situation.

"*Epic* bummer!"

We were in my room the day after Kelly's email had

arrived and two days before we were due to start a new school year. Razz screwed up his face.

"So the Kelster's family is staying in New Zealand because her dad got offered some kind of a hot shot new job or something?"

I didn't really feel like talking but I did anyway.

"Yep. He gets to be head of some big weather station. Kelly's not very happy about it."

"Yeah, Sal's cut up too, man."

Razz was talking about Sally Nofke. She's Kelly's best friend, and ever since the night of the Dugongs' reunion concert, I guess you could say she was also Razza's girlfriend.

"Man," Razz said as he gave his head one last, slow shake, "all aboard the Bummer Express. Next stop – Bummer Central."

I had to hand it to Razz. He was really hitting the bummer nail right on its bummer head. And to think I actually thought this year was going to be different. I thought I might have kissed goodbye to Ishmael Leseur's Syndrome for good. After all, hadn't Barry Bagsley (chief tormentor and expert make-my-life-miserable guy) kept his promise about leaving me and my friends alone? And hadn't Kelly Faulkner (supreme goddess and expert make-my-life-awesome girl) walked straight out of my dreams and into my real world? Do those sound like the sorts of things that would happen to a victim of ILS? No way! I was over all that! This was going to be *my* year! I was going to totally *own* this year!

WUH-WAAAAAAAAAA! *Incorrect. The correct response is:* 'This year is going to suck big time!' *Thanks for playing. Next contestant, please!*

For a while it went quiet in my room. I lay on my bed staring at the ceiling and Razz sat at my desk twirling a pen in his hand.

I guess we were both trying to comprehend just how seriously bummer-like the whole situation was. We stayed that way until Razza grabbed the pen in mid-twirl and snapped his head up.

"Well, it's gonna be a bit tricky, so we better get to work."

"Get to work? Get to work on what?"

Razz looked at me as if it should have been blindingly obvious exactly where his thoughts had just that second transported to in hyperspace.

"On finding you a new girlfriend, dude."

"What?"

"Don't get me wrong – I really like the Kelster and everything – she's way cool – but she's left the building, man. So it's game back on. No use putting all your eggs in one basket and crying over spilt milk."

"Whaaaaaat?"

"Seriously, you gotta move on, dude."

I really wasn't in the mood for another dip into the well of Razza's bottomless enthusiasm.

"Move on? Why? What's the point? Wherever I go, whatever I do, I'll still be me and that means everything's always going to turn out like crap."

"*That's* the spirit, Leseur!" Razz said, leaping off his chair and grabbing me by the arm. "Come on! It's only 11.45. If we hurry we'll make it to the train station just in time for you to throw yourself under the 12.06."

I shrugged my arm free and lay back down. "Hilarious, Razz. No, really, I'm actually cracking up big time – on the *in*side."

"Hey, I'm just trying to help, man. I know this whole Kelly thing's a real…"

"Bummer? Yeah, you know, I'm *fairly* sure we've established that much already."

Razz moved to the end of the bed. "Look, man, you can't just give in. Just think of it like you've had this killer wipeout on your bike, see. And you know what you gotta do when that happens, right?"

"Aaah, let me guess. Seek immediate medical attention, get plenty of rest, drink lots of fluids and whatever I do, don't, I repeat *don't*, under any circumstances, let my psycho friend talk me into getting on anything that looks even remotely like a bike, ever again in my entire life?"

"Hi-*laaaar*-ious, Ishmael. No, really, I'm cracking up big time – on the *in*side," Razz said in a pathetic imitation of me. Then he switched on his serious face.

"Come *on*, man, this was gonna be the big year, remember? What about all the stuff we talked about doing together, you and Kelly, and me and Sal? You know, parties, movies, dances… the Semi-formal. We can still do that stuff, dude. We just have to hook you up with a new chick now that Kelly's out of the picture."

"What, just like that? Razz, it took me two *years* to 'hook up' with Kelly – that's if you can even call a three-second kiss 'hooking up'. You don't think you're being just a touch… *ambitious*?"

"No way, man! Now you've got two years of valuable chick-chasing experience behind you. You're love match-fit. We just need to step it up a bit, that's all. You know, eliminate the middleman, go straight to the source and play our cards close to our chest."

"Riiiiiiiiiiiiiight… And when exactly did you swallow the *Cliché Dictionary*?"

Razz's eyes went for a bit of a roll.

"All I'm saying is that we should concentrate our efforts on chicks who are… soft targets."

"Soft targets? What the hell does that mean?"

"You know, chicks you already have some connection with, like chick friends of Sally… or sisters of guys in our class… or maybe someone's rela—" Razz froze. His eyes widened. A final syllable dropped from his mouth. "…tive."

He turned to me shaking his head in disbelief.

"I'm a genius. I am your *actual* genius. No, seriously, man, it's true. I've just had a brainwave – a Razzman special. Stand *well* back, Ishmael. And cover your eyes too, dude, before they're burned out by the awesome light bulb of total braininess that must be glowing above my head."

"Razz, what are you talking about now?"

"What am I talking about? I'm talking about me maybe having the answer to all your chick-drooling prayers, Ishmael. *That's* what I'm talking about."

"Really? And what exactly *is* the answer to all my chick-drooling prayers?"

Razz opened his mouth to speak. Then he closed it.

"Nah, you'll have to wait. Got to check a few things out first to make certain. Don't want to get you all fired up for no reason. I'll tell you when I'm sure."

That was all I could get out of him. Later on when Razz was leaving he said, "Just you wait, Ishmael. If I can pull this off it'll be huge!" He looked about as excited as a barber at a werewolf convention.

Would you be at all surprised to hear that I had a very bad feeling about all of this?

3.
The Short, the Tall and the Cuddly

There wasn't much time to worry about what terrifying surprise Razz might have in store for me, because two days later the new school year started and my life lurched into overdrive.

Back at St Daniel's everything was pretty much the same except for a new Creative Arts Centre that was finished over the holidays… and us. We were different because for the first time we were wearing the Senior uniform – long grey trousers and a light blue shirt with a navy and gold striped tie. In winter and on special occasions, we added a blazer.

I didn't like to admit it, but my new Senior uniform made me feel a bit special. Mum said I looked like a "real man". Even my near-genius little sister Prue agreed. Kind of. What she actually said was that "From a distance, in suitably low light and through a soft-focus lens,

I might make a very passable approximation of a real man". High praise indeed! Dad reckoned I had been "straitjacketed in the uniform of the Establishment", whatever that meant.

Our first day back started with a meeting for our whole year group in the gym.

I caught up with Razz on the way there. He was pretty hard to miss. His tie was dangling around his neck like a noose and his new blue shirt was hanging out and blotched all over with sweat. It also had a couple of buttons missing and a big grass stain on one side that kept on going right down to his trousers.

"Man, do you know how these things work?" Razz asked, grabbing and yanking at his tie like he was fighting off a blue and gold striped anorexic python. I was about to rescue him from almost certain self-strangulation when a familiar voice hit us both from behind like a piece of four-by-two.

"Mr Zorzotto. Please inform me. I *need* to know. Which one was it, exactly?"

Razz and I turned and were confronted by Mr Barker's face. It didn't look overjoyed. One eyebrow was raised.

"Sir?"

"I'm fascinated to know which one it was, Mr Zorzotto.

Were you dragged here behind a pack of runaway horses or have you been the unfortunate victim of multiple lightning strikes?"

"Been playing football, sir."

"Football?" Mr Barker raised his other eyebrow and stared at Razza's uniform. "Football?" he said again before completing a Razz circumnavigation.

"Did the grandstand fall on you, Mr Zorzotto? Were you trampled in a mass pitch invasion? Did someone set off a large incendiary device near where you were standing?"

Mr Barker was still the undisputed Sultan of Sarcasm.

Razz screwed up his face like he was seriously considering these possibilities. "Nah, nothing like that, sir. Just had a bit of a kick around, that's all."

"Just a bit of a kick around?" Mr Barker said as a disturbing smile died on his face. "Well, Mr Zorzotto, I *strongly* suggest you have 'just a bit of a tidy up' before you even *think* about joining your fellow Seniors in the gymnasium this morning. I hope I make myself *perfectly* clear."

He had. Mr Barker was *excellent* at making himself perfectly clear. We watched as he strode off towards the gym, clicking his fingers at bits of rubbish on the ground and sending boys scurrying after them.

"Do you reckon maybe he's got one of those split

personality things?"

I knew exactly what Razz was getting at. Last year we discovered that Mr Barker was a big fan of my dad's old band, the Dugongs. He even stepped in as manager for the reunion concert when the real guy ran off with all the band's money and gear. For a while there he seemed... almost human. He actually smiled sometimes. He even *danced* with Razz's mum during the Dugongs' concert. Now the band were trying to get their old album remastered and rereleased and get back into performing, and Dad said if they did, they wanted Mr Barker to be their full-time manager. But here at school, he'd totally morphed right back into Deputy Principal Barker – the man most likely to make your life hell.

"Must be a Batman and Bruce Wayne thing," I said. "You know, two identities but one person, so they can never be in the same place together."

"Maybe. 'Cept I can't see Barker jumping about in tights and a cape, can you?"

While I tried unsuccessfully to imagine that, Razz gave a few half-hearted tucks and pulls at his uniform and then we followed the crowd into the gym. It didn't take long to spot who we were looking for.

"Ah, here they are," Razz said cheerfully. "The Short,

the Tall and the Cuddly."

Three faces looked our way. They belonged to James Scobie, Ignatius Prindabel and Bill Kingsley. Razza's description was pretty spot on.

Even with his trademark stoop Ignatius Prindabel was almost a head taller than Bill and about three heads taller than Scobie. Add to that a high forehead that seemed to be chasing his hairline back, and about 20 centimetres of wrist extending out past each cuff, and you could swear he was growing as you watched.

James Scobie, on the other hand, looked like his new uniform was attempting to swallow him – and succeeding. His shirt was bunched around his little chubby belly and his trousers, due to James's acute leg shortage, were backed up like a concertina above his perfectly polished shoes. He was the human equivalent of one of those wrinkly Chinese dogs.

But it was Bill Kingsley that had Razz and me gawking.

"Geez, Billy Boy. Is the rest of you being shipped in later or something?"

What Razz was so tactfully pointing out was that Bill didn't seem quite as 'cuddly' as he'd been at the end of last year. Don't get me wrong, there was still *plenty* of him to go around, but when you looked closely at the way he filled out his new blue shirt, there was definitely not as much as you expected.

Bill answered Razza with his usual shrug.

"Come on, Billy. Spill the low-fat beans. Let us in on your secret before you disappear completely."

Bill shrugged again but managed to mumble, "It's nothing… just… you know… stuff I've been doing… just food… and stuff."

"Just food and stuff? Geez, Kingsley, could you be a little *less* specific? What kind of stuff? A jungle commando course? An all-you-can-eat-low-cal-steam diet? A close encounter with some kind of flesh-eating virus? Out with it, Bilbo."

Bill looked around at all of us, then at Razza.

"Just been hooping."

"Hoping for what?"

"Not *hop*ing – *hoop*ing."

"Hooping? What, you've had whooping cough?"

"No, I got a hoop."

Razz looked totally lost for a moment then he slapped his forehead.

"Aw, man, no! You didn't, did you? You didn't get one of those rubber hoop things tied around your stomach to squish it into the size of a pea?"

"No, I got a hoop – just a normal hoop."

Razz frowned. "A normal hoop… as in…"

Bill swallowed. "As in… hula."

"A normal hoop," Razz repeated slowly, "as in… *hula*? What, one of those big round plastic things that… *chicks*… used to wiggle around their stomachs way back in the past before anything *good* was actually invented?"

Bill opened his mouth but didn't get the chance to answer.

"Did you know that the record for the most hula hoops spun by a single person at the one time is one hundred and five? Someone from China, as I recall. And did you know that the circumference of the largest hula hoop ever spun was fifty-one and a half feet? That's approximately sixteen metres. An American did that."

Razz kept the same gaze of disbelief on his face but shifted it slowly from Bill to Ignatius.

"*How*, Prindabel? Please tell me. How do you *know* stuff like that? And what's even more scary and freaking-me-out-ish is *why* do you know stuff like that?"

"Simple. At last year's Extreme Science camp we were investigating the properties of wave motion and centripetal force and in order to assist our understanding of the topic we were required to undertake detailed research into a variety of examples of—"

Razz placed his hand on Prindabel's shoulder and

patted it reassuringly.

"That'll do, Prindabuddy, that'll do. I knew there *had* to be a perfectly geekish explanation."

"They're sort of making a comeback… Hula hoops, I mean."

This was Bill. Scobie and I nodded encouragingly. Razz just stared.

"They have these big hula-hooping conventions all around the world. My mum read about it. Then there was this notice at the church hall for a hooping class, so she joined up and really liked it. Bought her own hoop and everything and started practising at home all the time. Got really good too. And she lost heaps of weight. Mum wanted my father to have a go. But he wouldn't. Reckoned it was just for women and kids."

"You *don't* say?" Razz offered.

"Yeah, well, anyway Mum said I should try it. So I did. I was hopeless but Mum gave me some good tips. Like where to put my feet and about my 'thrust points' and everything and I sort of got the hang of it. I started practising every day. And I lost a bit of weight too. Now I'm learning some tricks. I can already do the 'lasso', the 'vortex', the 'helicopter', and the 'ninja pass' and I'm working on the 'revolving door', the 'corkscrew', and the 'booty bump'. I reckon I…"

Razz squeezed his eyes shut and held up a hand in front of Bill's face.

"Bilbo, stop, please. I don't feel very well. We must *never* speak of this again, okay? It's awesome that you're killing the kilos, man, but some things should definitely stay in the closet. That's what we got closets *for*."

Bill looked at Razz but said nothing as Mr Barker's voice sliced through the gym.

"All right, let's get moving, gentlemen. I want everyone up the front and seated – now. We've got a lot to cover this morning."

We shuffled our way with the rest of the year group to the rows of seats set out at the front of the hall. Mr Barker was on the assembly stage.

"Come on, you lot. Rise and shine. Holidays are over. I need you all seated and paying attention. Oh, and I'll also need two volunteers to join me up here. So let me see… Yes, could I have *you* come up, Mr Carlson-Steele… and could I also have… *you*, Mr Zorzotto? Between the two of you we are going to demonstrate the right and the wrong way to wear the Senior uniform."

"Gee whiz," Razz whispered to us excitedly. "I wonder which one *I'm* going to be!"

4.
The Fab Five

In the end I'm sure Mr Barker regretted choosing Razza as the 'wrong way' school uniform guy.

Gerard Carlson-Steele just stood in the middle of the stage like a shop dummy and turned red while Mr Barker pointed out to us all the perfect features of his perfect uniform.

With Razza it was *slightly* different.

When Mr Barker called him forward Razz slipped right into supermodel mode, gliding across the stage and posing with his arms folded, glaring at the audience. Then he pranced to the edge of the platform, loosened his tie and slowly undid another button on his shirt before twirling around dramatically and slinking back across the stage with his hips thrusting wildly from side to side.

It was quite a performance, and at just on eight minutes into the new school year, it earned Razz the distinction of receiving the fastest detention in St Daniel's history. It was probably all the cheering and wolf-whistling that finally pushed Mr Barker over the edge.

After the fun of Razza's catwalk capers died down, the real business of the day started. Our Principal, Brother Jerome, spoke to us first, followed by Mr Barker. They basically said the same kind of things: how this year was important; how they expected a lot more from us because now we were Seniors and school leaders; how we needed to show maturity (glares from Mr Barker directed at Razz); how we needed to be thinking seriously about our future careers (what future careers?); how we should involve ourselves in all aspects of school life; and how it was crucial that we apply ourselves to our studies and stay totally focused at all times (supersized glares from Mr B at the Razzman). Mr Barker said this year was all about "making informed and mature choices".

Beside me, Razz pushed out his bottom lip and nodded. Then he whispered out of the side of his mouth.

"Speaking of choices, who would you choose – a good-looking chick with a not-so-hot bod or a not-so-good-looking chick who was really, really built?"

As much as I wanted to demonstrate my brand new Senior School maturity by totally ignoring Razz's question, I found myself giving it serious consideration. Eventually I was brought back to reality when Miss

Tarango appeared at the side door of the gym and headed for the stage.

A murmur of approval ran through the year group. Miss Tarango had that effect on people. Even Brother Jerome and Mr Barker seemed to spark up when she joined them. It was hard not to. Miss T was so bright and full of energy she probably glowed in the dark. Up on stage Mr Barker and Miss Tarango spoke together for a bit before Mr Barker clicked the microphone back on.

"Thank you. Quieten down, gentlemen. We've got a truckload of administration details to get through. But first I have an important announcement. As you know, our long-serving Senior Coordinator, Mr Carver, retired last year so we've had to appoint a replacement, and I am very pleased to be able to tell you that Miss Tarango has generously agreed to step into that role."

Cheers, clapping and a rumble of talk filled the gym. Miss Tarango gave us one of her best double-dimpled smiles and took over the mic.

"Thank you, boys. I'm really looking forward to being your coordinator for the next two years. I appreciate your support and I'm certainly going to need it. I know I have very big shoes to fill."

That comment earned Miss Tarango a big laugh. Mr Carver was an ex-international rugby front row forward. His nickname at school was 'Andre the Giant'. Miss Tarango could probably have parked her little red and black Mini in one of his shoes.

Anyway, after telling us what she hoped we could all achieve in the year ahead, Miss got down to tackling some of the "truckload of administration details" that Mr Barker had warned us about. First up, we found out that the good news about Miss T being our coordinator was balanced by the bad news that therefore she wouldn't be taking one of the tutor groups. We also found out that last year's groups had been totally reorganised. We all knew what that meant. There was virtually no chance Razz, Scobie, Bill, Ignatius and me would all end up in the same group again. And it got worse. Apparently the tutor groups were also going to double as English classes, which meant we wouldn't be together there either. I mentally added another couple of 'bummers' to my rapidly expanding collection.

If we weren't all together in Tutor Group or English it meant we wouldn't be together much at all. This was because of our different subject choices. According to Razz's definitions, Scobie was doing the 'Future World Dictator' course because he'd chosen subjects like Legal Studies and Economics, Ignatius had taken the 'Extreme Nerd' course because he'd picked heaps of science subjects as well as 'Mega-brain' Maths, Bill and I were down for the 'Mixed Grill' course because we had a bit of everything, and Razz had himself enrolled in 'Senior for Dummies' because he'd taken Media Studies, Health and Physical Education and 'McHappy' Maths.

Up on stage Miss Tarango began to read out the four English classes. She started with hers. The names were in alphabetical order. We all held our breaths, waiting and hoping as Miss worked her way through the list. None of us was on it. We all slumped a little lower than normal in our seats. Beside me, Razza slumped so low he almost disappeared.

Then Miss read out the second list – Ms Verity's class. None of us was in that one either. There were only two classes left. Mr Slattery's and Mr Krueger's. Miss Tarango started on Mr Slattery's group. She was about halfway through when Bill's name came up. Then a few names later mine was read out. Then Prindabel's. Then Scobie's. It was unbelievable!

We all looked at Razz, who had pulled himself forward and was perched on the edge of his seat drumming his fingers nervously on the chair in front of him. There was still a chance. We knew 'Zorzotto' would be right at the end – if it was there at all. Miss read out three more names.

"Jared Wilson. Matthew Wozniaki. Melvin Yip."

Then she placed the sheet of paper she was reading on the table. Razz stopped drumming his fingers and thumped his head down on them. He let out a low moan. Miss poured herself a glass of water and took a couple of sips. She cleared her throat.

"Sorry, boys – not used to all this talking. Now, where was I?" She picked up the class lists again. "I think we've finished with Mr Slattery's class, haven't we? No, wait. Sorry. One name to go… and that would be… let's see… Oh, Orazio Zorzotto."

Razz let out a wild whoop and shoved the chair in front so hard that Ryan Babic was sent sprawling to the gym floor. Brother Jerome and Mr Barker glowered at Razz in stereo. Miss Tarango glanced up as Ryan Babic climbed back to his seat, cursing Razz not quite under his breath. I could swear Miss was fighting to keep her dimples under control.

After the meeting we all headed straight to the Senior noticeboard to check the class lists to make sure it was true. We couldn't believe our luck. But there it was in black and white – all of us were together in Mr Slattery's English class and, not only that, we'd scored Mr Guthrie as our tutor group teacher.

"Hope you're not too disappointed with your new class, boys."

We spun round to see Miss Tarango standing in a patch of sunlight. Her short jaggy blonde hair was glowing and her teeth and her eyes looked backlit. If it was a movie you'd swear someone had gone a bit overboard with the airbrush and special effects. She looked like she'd swallowed summer.

"Nah, it's awesome, Miss!" Razz said. "We're all in the same tutor group. What are the chances of that?"

Prindabel's face lit up.

"Well, if you wanted to calculate the exact probability, you'd have to consider that there are four separate class groups so therefore the chances of any one of us being in a particular group is one in four, but then because there are five of us you'd have to multiply the…"

Ignatius found Razz's hand wrapped around his mouth. "Don't worry about him, Miss. Some of his sound cards are playing up."

Miss Tarango laughed. Then she stepped a little closer. She looked like summer but she smelled like spring. Dangling from her lobes were gold earrings in the shape of tiny books.

"Well, just between you and me, boys, *chance* didn't play much of a role. You see, the Senior Coordinator gets to draw up the class lists – in consultation with her colleagues of course – and I thought it made perfect sense for me to keep the debating team together. Easier to arrange meetings and maybe use some Tutor Group or English time for last-minute preparation."

"Brilliant, Miss, thanks," Scobie said. "That'll be a big help. We seem to have a bit of trouble getting everyone together. *Some* of us are a little unreliable."

"Hey, what are you looking at me for?" Razz said. Then his forehead creased into a frown and he looked back at Miss Tarango. "But Miss, if you made up all the lists, how come you didn't put us in your English class?"

"Well, Orazio, tempted as I was, I thought it might be prudent to wait a while before totally abusing my newfound power and getting the other English teachers off-side by hogging all the star pupils."

Razz nodded in agreement. "Yeah, I get it, Miss. I guess they were all hoping to score me in their English class, hey? Even if it meant putting up with the rest of these losers."

Miss Tarango smiled sweetly. "No comment, Orazio."

"I understand, Miss – don't want to hurt these guys' feelings, right?"

Scobie gave an exaggerated clearing of his throat then twisted his mouth to one side and back again. "Congratulations on the year group coordinator appointment, Miss."

"Thank you, James. I think they thought I was

the only one mad enough to take it on. It's a big responsibility, especially following a St Daniel's legend like Mr Carver. And I've taken over his old position of Charlton House Patron as well."

"Charlton House Patron? You'll be awesome, Miss, but you'd better practise up on your *There's no shame in coming last* speeches."

"Well, I'm hoping to turn that around, Orazio, so I'll be really relying on you guys to help me out, okay?"

We all nodded eagerly. Hell, we'd coat ourselves in honey and dance in front of a pack of bears if Miss Tarango asked us to.

"Great. Thanks, boys. I knew I could count on the Fab Five to watch my back."

Then Miss Tarango flashed some bright orange fingernails at us in a quick wave before twirling round and walking briskly back up the path.

We were watching her back already.

Well, sort of.

5.
Uncle What's-his-face and Auntie Thingo's Daughter

There was no way you could mistake our new form room. It had Mr Guthrie written all over it. Not literally, of course. Teachers weren't allowed to write all over classrooms. That's the students' job.

Just joking. All I'm saying is, you could tell Mr Guthrie lived there because every centimetre of wall and noticeboard space was plastered with posters and articles covering every issue, concern and injustice known to humankind. There was stuff on climate change, recycling, homelessness, refugees, anti-whaling, political prisoners, deforestation, binge drinking, pollution, poverty, nuclear waste, third world debt, child labour, endangered species, carbon footprints, renewable energy, land rights, women's rights, gay rights, workers' rights and animal rights. Then on the *next* wall there was... Well, you get the picture.

Our sports master, Mr Hardcastle, liked to call Mr Guthrie 'St Daniel's resident tree-hugging hippy'. That's when he wasn't calling him 'Mr Cheesecloth' or 'Mr Tie-dye'. Brother Jerome's description was better. He said Mr Guthrie was 'St Daniel's Patron Saint of Lost Causes'. It seemed just about everyone had their own name for Mr Guthrie. Two years ago Razz and I nicknamed him 'Pele' after he scored a truly freaky winning goal for the Charlton Chiefs in the big inter-house football competition. Then we found out later that most of the other teachers called him 'Woody'. I thought it was because he wore a bracelet with wooden beads on it. But one day I heard Dad talking about some famous old singer called Woody Guthrie, so I figured that's where the name came from.

Mr Guthrie did actually have a proper name. It was Emerson. Emerson Guthrie. Not exactly catchy. But I guess it was different; a bit like Mr Guthrie himself. With his mop of short, springy dreadlocks and his wispy beard he looked like a tall, thin elf. And then there were his clothes. Mr Guthrie wasn't really into designer labels unless they turned up in charity shops or they were marked *Fair Trade*.

It was in Mr Guthrie's form room that I finally got to find out what Razz's solution to my 'chick-drooling' prayers actually was. It began with him sliding into the seat beside me and grinning madly.

"Ishmael, my man. Awesome news! It's all done and dusted, dude."

"What's all done and dusted?"

"The thing we talked about at your house."

"Oh right, that would be the 'answer to all my chick-drooling prayers'."

"That's it!" Razz said, thumping the desk and causing Mr Guthrie to look up from the register and frown.

"Well, what is it, Razz? What is the answer to all my chick-drooling prayers?"

A crazy look took over Razza's eyes. It was the same crazy look that usually appeared just before even crazier words began exploding out of his crazy mouth. I prepared myself for the worst. He leaned closer and spread his hands like he was making a rabbit appear from a hat.

"Cindy Sexton!" he said, with a grin that would have frightened off a pack of hungry sharks.

I stared a while at the maniacal face with the beaming eyes hovering in front of me.

"Razz, I don't think my parents would approve of me hooking up with a porn star."

Razz jerked back and pointed an accusing finger at me.

"Hey, that's my *cousin* you're talking about!"

"Your *cousin*?"

"Yeah, and you better not let Uncle Henry and Auntie Carla hear you say stuff like that about their daughter."

"So you want me to hook up with one of your *cousins*? Is *that* what you're saying?"

Razz nodded enthusiastically.

"One of your relatives?"

He nodded again.

"Someone related by birth... to *you*?"

He stopped nodding.

"Dude, is your brain still in holiday hibernation mode or something? *Yes*, she's my cousin, okay? Her family's moving up here from down south in a few weeks. I didn't want to tell you until it was definite, but now they've got a house and everything is sweet. Don't you see the beauty of it, man? Kelly moves out, Cindy moves in. It's the Circle of Luuuuuuurve! It's fate, dude, fate!"

"Razz, I don't really think me hooking up with your cousin is such a terrific idea."

Now *that* was definitely going to be my official entry in the Understatement of the Year Competition. As far as I was concerned, me hooking up with a cousin of Razza's was the idea equivalent of a rotting corpse. Not only did it stink, it frightened the life out of me.

"What are you talking about, man? It's perfecto. It's all the planets lining up. Look, don't you get it? Cindy's worried about moving and being new in town and not knowing anyone; my uncle and auntie are worried about her being unhappy; my mum's worried for them; I'm worried because I'll have to hang out with Cindy and show her around when I'd rather be hanging out with Sally; and you're Mr Misery anyway because you've turned into a Kelly-Faulkner-free zone. *But...* if you and Cindy hook up, everybody's happy!"

This was all starting to sound disturbingly familiar.

"Waaaaait a minute. This isn't another one of your famous 'win, win, win, win situations', is it? You know, like the one last year when you talked me into reading Kelly's private diary to find out if she liked me or not? Didn't you reckon that was going to make everyone happy too? Remember how *that* one turned out, Razz? Remember how Kelly ended up hating my guts because she walked in while I was reading her private stuff after someone – i.e. *you* – decided it was a good time to go for a leak even though someone – i.e. *you* – *promised* me they would be guarding the door? Remember *that*?"

Razz hunched up his shoulders. "Yeah, well, there might have been some *slight* technical hitches along the way, *but* it turned out all right in the end, didn't it?

I mean, as I recall, someone – i.e. *you* – did end up engaging in some serious saliva-swapping action with someone – i.e. Kelly Faulkner. I bet *you* remember *that*, man. Anyway," Razz said, "you can't compare the two things. This is *way* different."

"How?"

"Well, if you go out with Cindy it'll make *six* people happy – Uncle Henry, Auntie Carla, Cindy, Mum, me and you. We'll all be thrilled. So technically it's not a win, win, win, win situation. It's a win, win, win, win, win, win situation, which makes it even better."

I squeezed my eyes closed. Maybe if I couldn't see him he'd just disappear.

"And another thing, dude…"

Unfortunately not.

"… just wait till you get a look at her, man. She might be a Sexton but she's got Zorzotto blood in her from her mum's side, so naturally, she's *smokin'*. I'm not kidding. If I didn't have Sal I might try to pull her myself."

I opened one eye.

"*You?* But she's your *cousin*."

"*Third* cousin. I'm not *that* sick."

"But… didn't you just say Cindy was your Uncle What's-his-face and Auntie Thingo's daughter?"

"Uncle *Henry* and Auntie *Carla*. Yeah, that's right.

But they've got two *other* daughters, haven't they – *older* ones – so that makes Cindy my *third* cousin – duh!"

I opened both eyes and locked them hard on Razz. I waited for him to crack so I'd know that he was just joking. He held my stare.

"O-kaaaaaaaaaaay, then," I said. "Moving right along. What makes you think she'd be interested in me anyway? If she's as hot as you reckon, she'll probably say no."

Razz scrunched up his forehead and squinted off into the distance. "Cindy say *no*?" Then he squinted even harder like he was trying to see a speck of dust on the surface of the sun. "Well, I guess it's… *possible*."

Something about Razz's response worried me but I let it go. I was hoping if we stopped talking about it, the whole 'Cindy and me' thing might just blow over. All I told Razz as the bell rang for first lesson was that I'd "think about it".

That night an email arrived from thebigZ@hypermail. com. It said, *Check out the piccie, dude!*

I groaned. Why couldn't Razz just leave me alone so I could be miserable and depressed and slowly waste away to nothing in peace? Was that too much to ask of your best friend? Why couldn't he get it through his thick skull that I didn't want Cindy or anyone else for that matter? I just wanted Kelly. I wanted Kelly, with her ice-blue eyes and her heart-attack smile. I wanted Kelly, with her killer laugh and her electric-shock lips. I wanted Kelly… who was hundreds of kilometres away… in another country… and who wasn't coming back… ever.

A big stale lump of emptiness invaded my body and started growing and mutating there. I groaned again but scrolled down the page to the photo. I recognised the Zorzotto kitchen straight away. Razz and his mum were sitting at the table. A large woman was sitting between them. I figured it was Auntie Carla. I guess Uncle Henry had taken the shot. Sitting at the end of the table, closest to the camera, was a girl with curly black hair. She was wearing a blue and white striped top and white shorts. Short white shorts. Everyone in the photo was smiling. The black-haired girl was smiling the most. Under the photo Razz had written,

"Time to vote, dude: HOT or NOT?"

I zoomed in on the black-haired girl until just her face and the top half of her body filled the screen and studied her closely. I clicked on *Reply*, typed a three-letter word and hit *Send*. There are some things that are so obvious you don't even need to be a near-genius like my little sister Prue to figure them out. One of those things was this:

Cindy Sexton was definitely *not* a 'NOT'.

6.
The Lifesaver of Love

In Tutor Group the next morning, Razz was a one-man Cindy Sexton publicity campaign in full swing. While Mr Guthrie was busy taking the register and doing admin stuff, Razz was buzzing in my ear.

"Didn't I tell you, man? Didn't I? Is she smokin' or what? I told you. Was I right or was I right? Just wait till she gets up here, man. You'll see. You and Cindy. It'll be awesome!"

Luckily I was saved from permanent hearing loss by Miss Tarango making an appearance at our form room door.

"Sorry for interrupting, Mr Guthrie, but may I just have a moment to speak to the boys?"

Mr Guthrie jumped from his seat and knocked some papers onto the floor. "Yes. Yes, of course. All right, listen up, everyone," he added as he gathered up the sheets and then almost tripped backwards over his chair. There was no doubt in my mind that if Mr Guthrie really had a poster stuck up in our form room for everything he cared about, then the biggest one would have Miss Tarango's face plastered all over it.

"Okay, boys, I have important information for you about the rapidly approaching Arts Fair," Miss said as she passed around some handouts.

The rapidly approaching Arts Fair was a big celebration the school had planned for the official opening of what everyone at St Daniel's very creatively referred to as '*the* extensions' or '*our* extensions'. These consisted of the brand new Creative Arts Centre plus some extra classrooms. Their official opening was going to be combined with the annual school fair in the last weekend of the first term. According to Miss Tarango, my year group were being asked to act as guides on the day and a volunteers' rota was going up later on in the week.

After Miss finished talking to us she stayed to help Mr Guthrie sort out the boys who had timetable problems. With Miss Tarango standing so close, Mr G looked like a drowning man who was too afraid to ask for a life jacket. I knew exactly how he felt. I'd drowned plenty of times within reach of Kelly Faulkner.

"You know, I reckon Woody could do with some of

my expert help. Maybe it's time I started to weave some of my magic."

I shuffled around in my seat to get a good look at Razz.

"Your *magic*? And exactly what *magic* would that be?"

"My matchmaking magic obviously, dude. You know, like the way I got you and the Kelmeister together."

"Razz, I don't want to appear critical or ungrateful here, but you didn't actu—"

"And now how I'm fixing you up with Cindy. Man, I'm like… I'm like… the Lifesaver of Love. Yeah, that's it. That's exactly what I am, man," Razz said, gazing dreamily into the distance. "The Lifesaver of Luuuuuuurve… always on duty… to rescue the broken-hearted… from the Undertow of Rejection."

My stomach churned a little and it wasn't *just* because of that "rescuing the broken-hearted from the Undertow of Rejection" line. It was also because of the mention of Cindy. As 'hot' as she was, I'd been kind of hoping that Razz had forgotten about trying to hook me up with his cousin.

"So yeah, I'm thinking maybe I could work my awesome magic and get Woody and Miss T together, 'cause I'm telling you, that dude needs all the help he can get."

Even though I knew that Razz messing in Miss Tarango's and Mr Guthrie's personal lives was a bad idea, I didn't say anything. I figured that if Razz got distracted thinking about that project, then maybe he wouldn't have any time left to come up with some crazy scheme involving me and Cindy. That way I might avoid the near-certainty of becoming the star act in another humiliating disaster. But hey, guess what? I was totally and completely wrong.

And I was about to find out exactly how totally and completely wrong at the rapidly approaching Arts Fair.

7.
Let's Get Ready to Ruuuummmble!

A few weeks later Scobie called an early planning meeting for the upcoming debating season. All of us were sitting around a table in one of the library discussion rooms. Well, when I say 'all of us', I mean all of us except Razz. When he finally did roll up, he ignored the others completely and bounded in beside me.

"Hey, Ishmael! Wait'll I tell you the awesome news, dude. It's *awesome!*"

"What is it?"

"Cindy's arrived and she's coming to the Arts Fair!"

I didn't have time to reply before Prindabel jumped in.

"Cindy? Cindy who?"

"Cindy Sexton," Razz shot back at him as if it was obvious. Scobie, Bill and Ignatius exchanged confused looks.

"So... is this *Cindy* person something to do with

the entertainment Miss Tarango said the school was organising for the fair?" Scobie asked.

"Hope so," Prindabel said. "She sounds like a stripper."

Ignatius was so pleased with himself over this comment that he did that thing of his that was supposed to be laughing but was more like bobbing his head up and down and making jerky hissing noises through his teeth. Bill snorted. Scobie stretched his mouth into a perfect horizontal line.

Razz looked at them all in disgust.

"What is the matter with you people? Get your behinds out of the gutter. Cindy Sexton just happens to be my cousin. And I'm hooking her up with Ishmael here. Cindy is the new Kelly!" he announced proudly.

Three necks twisted my way like they were compass needles and I was the North Pole. Thanks to Razz they already knew all about me and Kelly and about her staying in New Zealand. But so far I'd managed to keep the whole Cindy thing off the radar. Up until now, that is.

Ignatius leaned across the table at me and held up a long, bony index finger.

"Ah, point of clarification, Ishmael," he said. "Did I just hear our *learned* colleague Mr Zorzotto say that you are going to be… 'hooking up'… with his… *cousin?*"

"No, well, maybe. I'm not sure. Look, this is all…"

"But you're *considering* it? You're actually contemplating the possibility of going out with Orazio's *cousin*?"

"I'm not sure. I might be. I don't know. I haven't really…"

But Prindabel was on a mission. He usually only got this excited over advanced quadratic equations and toad dissections. He hunched even closer and tapped his finger on the tabletop as he spoke.

"Just to be absolutely sure I understand the situation, let me rephrase it for you. You're seriously entertaining the possibility of going out with… a female offspring… of a brother or sister… of one of Orazio's parents?"

This was *waaaaay* too much for Razz.

"Yes! Yes! Yes! Enough already! He gets it! We *all* get it! She's my cousin! What's the matter with you, Prindabel? Were you sick the day they did Happy Families at nursery? Did you contract some kind of computer virus from using your flash drive as a dummy? Or didn't they teach you about 'human stuff' like family trees at the cyborg factory where they put you together?"

Prindabel held up his hands and said no more. He just sat back in his seat and continued to stare wide-eyed at me as if I was volunteering to bellyflop naked into a pit of loaded mousetraps.

"Right. Well, anyway, dude, like I was *trying* to say

before I was interrupted by Professor Von Looney here, Cindy's coming to the Arts Fair – so's Sal – but the best bit is when I told Cindy all about you and showed her your photo in the school magazine, she was keen as, man. She was keen-on-growth-hormones keen, man!"

The image from my computer screen flashed into my head. "Really?"

"Yeah, really. So it's totally sweet, man," Razz said, then added as an afterthought, "just as long as Uncle Henry doesn't find out about you, of course."

"What? Why not? What's wrong with me?"

Razz laughed and slapped my back.

"Geez, Ishmael, how much time have we got? No, seriously, man, Uncle Henry'd go mental if he found out you were fooling around with his daughter."

"What? I'm not fooling around with his daughter!"

"Not *yet*."

As he said that, Razz made his eyebrows jump up and down like little pistons while I imagined myself ripping them off and inserting them up his nose.

"Besides," he said when he had finished with the eyebrow pumping, "for Uncle Henry, just 'looking' is fooling around. He's a *teensy-weensy* bit overprotective."

"What? You didn't tell me that. What about all that stuff about the win, win, win, win, win, win situation? One of those winners was supposed to be Uncle Henry. You said everyone would be 'thrilled' if Cindy and I hooked up."

"*Did* I?" Razz said as a wave of astonishment broke briefly over his face before vanishing without a trace. "Yeah, well, that might have been a *slight* exaggeration. You know, like one of those persuasive argument techniques Miss Tarango taught us about last year."

"Slight exaggeration? So when you said Uncle Henry would be 'thrilled', you *actually* meant he'd be completely off his brain, did you?"

"I wouldn't say *that* exactly."

"How about 'enraged to the point of criminal homicide'?"

That was Prindabel's suggestion. Scobie nodded his approval. Bill snorted again. Razza shook his head at them then turned back to me.

"Look, it doesn't matter, anyway. I've got it all covered. When I introduce you, Sal's gonna pretend to be your girlfriend. What Uncle Henry doesn't know won't hurt him – or you, hopefully."

"Razz, this is getting a bit crazy. I think we better forget the whole thing."

"What? We can't! I've already told Cindy. What do you want me to do now? Tell her she's been dumped? I can't do that. You know what chicks are like. They're fragile, man. They're not like us guys. You want to break Cindy's heart and like totally destroy her self-image? You want *that* on your conscience?"

"Course not, but I don't think…"

"Great, then it's set for take-off. You and Cindy at the Arts Fair. Let's-get-ready-to-ruuuuummmble!"

Right on cue the warning bell for the end of lunch blared out like the start of the next round.

"Gotta go," Razz said, already turning and heading for the door. "Just remembered, I think I might have had a homework detention from Mr Rameesh or something."

Before anyone could reply, Razz was charging like a maniac through the library, neatly sidestepping and weaving his way through the mass of boys already stampeding their way out. It was only when he attempted to beat them all by taking a short cut to exit via the entrance that disaster struck. Apparently those little gates at the entrance and exit are made to swing only one way. As we watched, Razz hit the arm of the gate, somersaulted forward, completed a full body rotation in mid-air and thudded back first onto the carpet. An appreciative mob of boys at the exit laughed, cheered and applauded wildly while the head librarian, Mr Fitler, glared at Razz like a deranged killer who'd just discovered someone tampering with his private axe collection.

Inside our discussion room Scobie pushed back his chair with a long screech and stood up.

"Right then," he said, collecting the various sheets of paper he had spread out before him and shuffling them back into a folder. "Thank you one and all for your attendance here today. It's been a very fruitful and informative discussion. Maybe next planning meeting we might even consider breaking with tradition a little and actually do some planning."

Then he twisted his mouth to one side of his face and left it there as he strolled from the discussion room. Bill followed him out.

That just left Ignatius and me. Outside, Mr Fitler was standing in front of Razz waving his hands about. His face was bright pink. Razz had dragged himself off the floor and was attempting to straighten out the bent gate. He was doing pretty well until a part of it broke off in his hands and the rest collapsed onto the floor. Mr Fitler's face turned from bright pink to a worrying shade of volcanic eruption-red. Prindabel's voice floated in from behind me.

"She's *his* cousin."

"Well, *third* cousin," I corrected without turning round.

"What? But didn't he say..."

I held up a hand. "Just joking," I informed him.

But for some reason I didn't really feel too much like laughing.

8.
Kiss Me, Stupid!

The Sunday of the big Arts Fair rolled around pretty quickly. It ran from two to six, finishing up with the official opening ceremony for the new extensions. Razz and I spent the first hour in the Creative Arts Centre acting as guides. We'd arranged to meet Sally and the Sextons after that.

I still wasn't sure about the whole Cindy thing, but I decided that maybe it was time I stopped moaning and moping about Kelly not being around and just got on with my life. After all, I couldn't change anything and who knew, perhaps a little bit of Cindy Sexton was just what I needed.

I had no idea how those words would come back to haunt me.

As soon as our guide duty shift was over, Razz and I grabbed a cold drink from one of the stalls and waited for Sally to turn up. It didn't take long.

"Hey, guys, looking sharp. James Bond, watch out."

As guides we had to wear our full Senior uniform with our navy jackets. I guess we looked all right. We were no match for Sally Nofke though. She was wearing jeans with a strappy yellow top and her long dark hair was braided and pulled back. She gave Razz a quick hug and then me. Some things end too soon. After talking for a bit, we headed off to the front of the main admin building where we were meeting Cindy and her family. They were waiting when we arrived. Razz did the intros.

There was a lot of smiling and hello-ing from everyone. Except for Uncle Henry, who barely managed a nod. While Razz was talking away at a million miles an hour, I took the chance to get my first serious up-close look at Cindy Sexton. She was even better in the flesh than she was on my computer screen. Her black hair curled around her face framing her big brown eyes and she had the kind of lips that looked like they were built to be kissed.

I might have been looking a little too closely at those lips, because I suddenly realised Uncle Henry was staring at me. Uncle Henry was kind of tall and big. His head was shaved. He was wearing a dark suit. He would have made a good undertaker, and the way he was staring at me I think he might have been very keen to be *my* undertaker.

Sally must have thought so too, because she moved in closer beside me. Her arm pushed against my arm and she slid her hand in mine. It was warm and it fitted perfectly. She smiled at Uncle Henry and rested her head on my shoulder. It worked. Uncle Henry stopped measuring me up for a casket and let Auntie Carla know with just a lift of an eyebrow and a flick of his head that it was time to go. As Cindy waved goodbye to her parents and brother and promised 'to be good', I felt Sally's hand slip from my fingers. Yep, some things definitely ended too soon.

Then Cindy swung round and her face exploded into a smile.

"Oh, my gawwwwwd! Free at last! I thought they'd *never* leave," she said as she fiddled with her dress and belt until like magic her skirt was so short it was barely doing its job. "And look at youse two couple of hotties," she squealed at Razz and me, placing a hand full of bright red fingernails on each of our chests. "Oh, my gawd, *suits*! Never seen you looking so sexy before, Razta. And *yoooou*," she said, hitting me full force with those big brown eyes, a dazzling array of teeth and her kiss-me-now lips, "Dishy Ishy, that's what I'm gonna call you. Oh, my gawd. What do you reckon, Sal?"

Sally laughed and opened her mouth to speak but she was too slow.

"Ooooo, I just *adore* your braids. They are so sweeeeeeet. I can't do anything with my hair. It just goes mad. And your skin is a*maaaaz*ing! What do you use? Something expensive? No chocolate for you, I bet. I break out if I just *look* at chocolate. Prob'ly because if I look, I eat. Big time! I am *such* a guts! And oh, my gawd, where did you get that top from? It's adorable. Perfect for you. Wouldn't suit me but. No way. Boobs way too big. Not that I'm complaining. Or anyone else, eh!" she said, digging a finger into my ribs and winking.

I smiled stupidly and tried desperately to keep my eyes directed above the level of her chest. I failed. Cindy caught me. She wagged her finger in my face and started to sing, "Ishy's a bad, bad boy." I think my ears were flashing red but I was saved by her phone ringing. Cindy fished into her bag and pulled out a sparkling mobile.

"Rach! Hi! Yeah, yeah, I'm there now. True! Yeah, yeah, he's right here. He *is*! Right in front of me. I *am* serious. It's truuuuue! Wait, wait, wait I'll show you." Cindy pointed her mobile at me and clicked. She checked the screen, stabbed a few buttons and put the phone back to her ear and squealed. "Rach, you idiot! Get out! You're awful! No! No way! No! Well, *maybe*." She squealed again, only louder. "Gotta go. See ya, babe. Yeah, I will. Yeah, yeah, I will. I WILL! Later, gorgeous."

Cindy's finger flew around her phone some more. "There. Just posted you on my Facebook page. Hope you don't mind," she said, clicking the phone shut and pushing it back in her bag. Then she grabbed my arm and held onto it like we were about to jump out of a plane together.

"Right, what are we waiting for? What's first? I think it should be either the Turbo Twister or the dodgem cars? What do you all reckon? But we gotta go on everything and I mean everything – even the merry-go-round, you guys. Right, Sal? Come on, let's do the Turbo first. And you'd better hold on tight and protect me, Ishy, because I'll be totally packing it. Oh, and I better warn you, I might scream a bit. Come on, you guys. Let's go! Wooohooo!"

Dragged along by Cindy we all set off in the direction of the swirling arms of the Turbo.

"So tell me about yourself, Ishy. Do you like music? What's your favourite band or singer? I luuuurve music! I'd just die without my iPod. Oh, my gawd. I'm always singing. Aren't I, Razta? Do you read? Are you into the Vampire School series? I'm a big fan. Massive! Oh, my gawd. You wouldn't believe it. You should see my bedroom. Bet you'd like *that*, wouldn't you, you cheeky devil!"

Another fingernail attack speared into my ribs.

"Anyway, I reckon the books are pretty good, 'specially the first one, *Love Sucks*, but the films are *way* better, because in the films you get to *see* Tyson Woods with his shirt off but in the books it's just like all these words and stuff. What a bod eh, Sal! Such a hunk! He is so cute! Wouldn't mind him changing into a wild animal with me! Are you into sport, Ishy? I'm not much but I dance loads. That's how I keep fit. What about you, Sal? How'd you get such a great bod? I bet you're some kind of a super-athlete or something. Or have you and Razz maybe been 'working out' a bit together, eh? Oh, my gawd! Come on, you guys. Turbo time!"

One thing about Cindy Sexton was, she was really easy to talk to. Mainly because you didn't have to say anything. Being with her was like being on the Turbo – permanently. It was kind of fun and terrifying at the same time, but after a while it made your head spin.

In the end we did go on every ride and Cindy wasn't kidding about her screaming. I finished up with ringing in my ears and fingernail puncture marks in my arm that looked like a row of little smiles.

It had just started to get dark when it was time to head back for the opening ceremony. All Seniors were expected to attend. We were almost there and just about to pass the alleyway between the old school block and the new extensions when Razz and Sally suddenly veered into it.

"Razz, where are you guys going?"

"Umm, just thought the girls might like a quick tour around the extensions before we go in."

"But it's starting already. Anyway, you won't see anything down there. That just leads around to the back."

"Ooooo, sounds fascinating," Cindy purred.

Razz and Sally shared a smile and disappeared in the shadows. Cindy pulled me after them. A little way in she stopped and yanked me to the side.

"This is soooooo interesting. What's *that*?" she said, pointing at a downpipe.

"It's a downpipe. You know, for water."

"A-maaaaaazing," she said. "Why is it called that?"

"Ah, I guess because it's a pipe and water comes down it."

"Wow! You are soooo smart," she said as she placed her hands on my chest and pushed me back until I felt the cool of the brick wall behind me. Then she moved slowly forward and her body began to press against mine. Her chest was the first part of her to arrive – by a clear margin. Big brown eyes looked up at me. Cindy had a strange smile on her face. Her lips opened slightly and I could see a row of her perfect whiter-than-white-toothpaste-advertisement teeth.

As Cindy Sexton's face moved closer, images of Kelly

Faulkner flashed through my mind. I remembered our kiss – the soft touch of Kelly's lips and the electric shock that shot through my body as they melted gently into mine. Now I was staring at other lips. They were big and red. And they seemed to be screaming out, 'Kiss me, stupid!' It sounded like an excellent idea. I aimed my own puny lips at Cindy's supersized ones and hoped for the best.

I just wasn't quite prepared for what happened next.

9.
A Turbo-charged Cobra

Cindy's lips met my lips. They squished together. Something detonated in my chest and shock waves zinged throughout my body. Some parts were zinging more than others.

Cindy moaned and wrapped her mouth around mine. She tasted like strawberries. The outside world was melting away and so was most of me. I was just a mouth and a pair of lips. That's all that mattered. Cindy opened hers wider and pushed in harder. Suddenly I found myself with a mouth full of tongue and the vast majority of it didn't belong to me!

For a second, having Cindy Sexton's tongue take up residence in my mouth felt like a very good thing indeed. But that was before it went berserk and began thrashing around like a turbo-charged cobra, slithering and slipping everywhere and poking and prodding every gap and cavity in my teeth. Not even my dentist was this thorough!

I desperately tried to subdue Cindy's manic tongue by counter-attacking with my own. But it was hopeless. I was fighting a tongue way out of my league. Hers was bigger, stronger, faster and obviously match-fit. It was an Olympic Champion tongue! Mine was easily and quickly out-manoeuvred, body-slammed and counted out. Cindy moaned again and pushed her mouth harder against mine. The killer tongue slid in even further. It had my tonsils in its sights!

I pulled away. Cindy and I slurped apart. I gulped in some air. I made a mental note to remember to breathe through my nose. Cindy licked her lips. They seemed to have doubled in size. Maybe she had them fitted with a special pump mechanism like in those trainers. Okay, now I was being ridiculous. I needed to calm myself down and prepare for Round Two. I looked at Cindy. Was that a mad glint in her eye or just a reflection from the moon? There was no time to decide. She began zeroing in again. I took a deep breath as we edged closer together. I kept thinking, *If I could just get her to calm down a bit and take it a little slower, then this could be really, really goo—*

AAAAAAAAAARRRRRGH!

Turbo-tongue was back with a vengeance! I could

have sworn a giant salamander was throwing a fit in my mouth. I pulled back again and we slurped apart once more. Cindy frowned a little but she was soon moving in for another assault. I tried to keep it together. I tried to be cool and hold my nerve but when her teeth parted and I saw that psycho tongue poised to strike like a big pink moray eel I couldn't help it – I flinched and at the last moment I turned my mouth away.

AAAAAAAAARRRRRGH!

Cindy had latched onto my neck and was sucking like a leech on steroids! A riot of shivers torpedoed down my arms and legs. It was worse than being held down and tickled. I was on the verge of hysteria. I told myself to *calm down, calm down, calm down, calm down*, while I struggled frantically to keep my hyperventilation under control so I could assess the situation.

My neck felt hot and wet. My pulse was throbbing. Cindy was still clinging on like a sucker fish. I could feel her tongue tickling my skin. She'd gone right for the jugular. That's one of the four big veins in the neck, you know. We learned all about it in Science with Mr Kalkhovnic. It supplies blood to the brain. Hey, wait a minute. What if all that sucking was stopping my circulation? What if my brain was being starved of blood? Little spots began to blink and float in front of my eyes like tiny silent fireworks.

I was feeling light-headed. Maybe Cindy was crazy? What did I really know about her, anyway? Maybe she'd seen too many Vampire School movies. Maybe she *was* a vampire. Oh my god, and it was a full moon tonight! Of course! Didn't vampires come out when there was a full moon? Or was that just werewolves and goths? Wait a minute, did I just feel teeth on my neck? Was my pulse getting weaker? Was she drinking my blood right now? Wait, nobody said it was my shout! I pulled my neck away. *SHWWWUUCK!* She was off.

Cindy giggled. I had a quick check. Thank goodness for that – no blood dripping from her fangs. All right, I guess I might have been getting a little hysterical there. Probably a result of lack of blood to the brain. Or possibly lack of brain. I tried to smile but Cindy was coming for me again. My god, she was a female Terminator. She was the Terminatrix! Or possibly the Tongue-inator! Whatever she was, you couldn't stop her. Her mouth began to open. Wait, were her teeth always that pointy? She was jugular-bound again. I felt her hot breath on my wet skin and I panicked. I scrunched my shoulder up and tilted my head down in a last ditch attempt to save my neck.

AAAAAAAAAARRRRRGH!

She was devouring my ear lobe! She wasn't a vampire at all! She was a cannibal on a diet! She was having a lobe linguine! In Science Mr Kalkhovnic made us compare our lobes with other students to illustrate personal differences. I have detached lobes. And now one of them felt like it was about to be detached *permanently*! It was in Cindy's mouth being sucked and mauled and nibbled around the edges. Hey, actually, to tell you the truth, that nibbling was starting to feel pretty goo—

AAAAAAAAARRRRRGH!

A huge slug had begun burrowing into my ear canal! Ewwwwwwww! When was the last time I'd cleaned that canal? I couldn't remember. I couldn't think. I couldn't *hear*! It was no wonder. There was a tsunami in my head! Cindy wrapped her arms more tightly around my neck and pulled herself higher. She was on her tippy toes. Her tongue was probing and poking its way deeper. Was she drilling for oil or what?

Wait! The tiniest most delicate and fragile bones in the entire body were found in the inner ear. Isn't that what Mr Kalkhovnic said? And they had these weird names. What were they called again? The hammer, the anvil and the shifting spanner? No wait, not spanner, stirrup. That's it! The hammer, the anvil and the stirrup. They were all incredibly small and they balanced together in some amazing way so you could hear sound. And now mine were about to be slobbered on by the Godzilla of the tongue world! I twisted my head around and pulled away. *SLUUUUURP!* My de-tongued ear felt cold and clammy but at least for the moment my hammer, anvil and stirrup were safe.

Cindy was grinning at me. She was saying something but my right ear was still making strange popping and crackling noises. Was someone munching breakfast cereal in my inner canal?

"What? Sorry?"

Cindy looked around, then repeated her words slowly with a crooked smile, "I *said*... would you like me to..." *SNAP! CRACKLE! POP!*

What did she say? What was the end of her question?

> *Would you like me to:*
> *...jab my tongue with a tranquilliser dart?*
> *...suck out another pint of your blood?*
> *...reattach your lobe?*
> *...regurgitate your hammer, anvil and stirrup?*

I didn't have a clue what Cindy had just asked, but at least for the moment I wasn't being probed, sucked or eaten, so I just sort of smiled and half-nodded, half-shook my head at her.

Cindy pushed out her lips and winked at me. Then

she poked me in the stomach with her finger and gave it a twist before trailing it lower. I had no idea what was going on, so I just smiled back at her again. She wrinkled her nose up as she stepped closer and whispered something. All I heard was another round of full-volume cereal crunching – *POP! POP! SNAP! POP! CRACKLE! SNAP!* – as the grin on her face spread wider.

Just then a light came flashing down the alleyway. It bounced around the walls before landing on my face. Cindy leaped back and squealed. Almost immediately another squeal came from further down the alley. The light jumped from my face to Cindy's. Then it shot past us and caught Razz and Sally just as they sprang apart.

The light came from a torch.

The torch was held by Mr Barker. His voice ground its way down to us like one of those tunnel borers eating its way through a rock wall.

"Would you mind explaining *exactly* what you're doing down there, Mr Leseur, when our opening ceremony is about to commence?"

My mind went blank. But somehow I automatically came up with the perfect stock answer for an occasion like this.

"Nothing, Mr Barker…"

And of course *that's* where I should have stopped.

That's where I should have shut my mouth and taken whatever Mr Barker was going to dish out. But did I do that? Oooooh, no! I had something *more* to say, didn't I? Something *brilliant*. Something that would win me my very own entry in St Daniel's folklore. Yes, that's right, I had to add *this*:

"We were just showing the girls our extensions."

10.
Deceased Piece of
Solid Bodily Waste

"But wait, wait, wait, wait, wait. I haven't told you the *best* bit yet."

Monday morning Tutor Group went quiet and the crowd of eager faces clustered around Razza huddled even closer.

"The best bit is… he looks up at Barker and he says… he says, 'Aw, sorry, sir, we were just showing the girls our *extensions*'!"

That last word barely blurted out of Razz's mouth before he collapsed forward choking with laughter and banging his fist on the desk. Around him the crowd erupted in a mixed chorus of groaning, hooting and guffawing. And then rare gems of observation and wit were showered down upon me.

"*Good* one, Ishmael."

"Legend Leseur… *NOT!*"

"What a (take your pick, folks):

(a) dork!

(b) clown!

(c) idiot!

(d) berk!

(e) deceased piece of solid bodily waste! (or words to that effect)

(f) All of the above."

"Wouldn't need a building permit for *your* extension, Leseur."

"Microscope might help."

"I didn't even know Leseur *had* a dick."

That last one was Aldo 'Boggo' Bogola's contribution. The subtlety and brilliance of the razor-sharp witticisms tapered off somewhat after that. Only the appearance of Mr Guthrie saved me.

"All right, come on. Grab a seat and quieten down. I need to see anyone who hasn't returned those excursion forms."

I grudgingly sat down beside Razz.

"Thanks a lot… *mate*," I told him. "Now I know who to go to if I need someone to keep a secret."

Razz was sprawled back in his chair still recovering from his laughing fit. He was sucking in air and patting his chest as if he was trying to get his heart to slow down. After a minute or two his head flopped sideways and he looked at me.

"Sorry, man. But there's just too much pain and misery in the world not to share gold like that. 'Just showing the girls our extensions'. Totally rigid, dude!" Then he threw back his head and shook with silent laughter for quite a while before wiping his eyes with the back of his hands and lurching forward onto his desk.

"But anyway, man, what about Cindy? Didn't I tell you? She's awesome, eh? What about we all go to the pictures or something this weekend?"

"I don't know, Razz."

"Don't know what?"

"About Cindy and me and everything."

I knew that Razz would be gawking at me like my head had just sprouted spaghetti so I just kept staring at the school diary on my desk.

"Whatdya mean, you don't know about you and Cindy? What's not to know, man? You guys got on great."

"Yeah… sort of."

"Sort of! Sort of! I hook you up with a smokin' chick, you do an advanced tongue tango together and then she's all over you like Prindabel with a new motherboard. Dude, if that's your idea of 'sort of' getting on, I can't *wait* to see what happens when you really hit it off with someone."

"I just don't think she's my type."

"Not your type! What is *wrong* with you, man?"

I stopped studying my diary and studied Razz instead. "What do you mean, what's *wrong* with me? Nothing's *wrong* with me, okay? Why do you think there's something *wrong* with me?"

"Well, let me put this as delicately as I can. You know how Miss Tarango reckons guys need to get in touch with their feminine sides? Well, dude, I think you might have jumped the fence and set up camp there."

"What?! What are you getting at?"

"Settle down, Ishmael. No need to throw a tissy-fit. I wouldn't want you smearing your mascara now."

"Oh, that's a riot, Razz. Look, there's nothing *wrong* with me, OK? Cindy's great, but she's just... I don't know... she's just..."

"...not Kelly Faulkner?"

"No, it's not just that. We're different, that's all. Cindy's too...she's too...she's just too... *much*... for me anyway."

"Too much? Geez, sorry, dude. Next time would you like me to fix you up with some weird-looking chick who thinks you're a total loser? Would *that* be more fun for you?"

"That's not what I mean and you know it."

"What I *know*, man, is that every guy in this room would chew through a brick wall to go out with Cindy, 'specially after your extension story."

Those last words stuck in my head but I didn't reply. I was through arguing. Beside me Razz rocked back on his chair.

"All right, man, all right," he said, closing his eyes and shaking his head. "Back to the drawing board, I guess. Just hope Cindy doesn't take it too hard."

I was wondering about that when Mr Guthrie called for attention.

"Thanks, boys. Look, before we run out of time I just wanted to say well done to all of you for helping out at the Arts Fair on the weekend. Top effort. I've only heard glowing reports, particularly about this year group's tour guides."

"Aaaah, sir? I heard one complaint."

Everyone turned around to Danny Wallace who had his hand up at the back of the class.

"Really, Danny? I'm very surprised by that."

"Yeah, sir, me too, but apparently someone wasn't very happy with Ishmael."

Mr Guthrie threw a worried look at me.

"Ishmael?"

"Yeah, well, she was complaining that his personal

extension tour… was way too *short*."

The rest of our tutor group cracked up. I sat there with a 'yes, yes, very funny – I *don't* think' sort of smile smeared on my face. Mr Guthrie gazed around at us like we'd all gone mad.

When I left our form room that day something was playing on my mind and it wasn't Danny Wallace's joke. It was that bit Razz said about how all the other guys in the class would chew through a brick wall for the chance to go out with Cindy. If that was true, then why was I different? Was it just because of Kelly Faulkner? Or was there some other explanation?

Like maybe there really was something wrong with me.

11.
Show Me the
Suncream!

Following our painful break-up, Cindy somehow managed to pull herself together and struggle on with her life. Just two days after the Arts Fair she met a guy at a shopping mall and they became what Mum likes to call 'an item'. Or, as Razz put it, "She was all over him like melted cheese on a hot beef patty."

Back at school, I didn't really have time to think about Cindy or Kelly or anyone else for that matter. This year was last year on steroids. It was all homework, assignments, tests and study – then repeat the dose. And just to add to the fun, the start of the debating season was only two weeks away.

As soon as Mr Fitler lifted Razz's library ban for 'destroying school property' and 'behaving like a savage', Scobie booked the discussion room again for another meeting. Mr Fitler still didn't seem that sure about it. Every few minutes he'd wander past the door and peer in at us. Razz had too much other stuff on his mind to even notice.

"Man, what was the Wreckin' Ball *thinking*? I mean, is she crazy or what?"

The Wreckin' Ball Razz was going on about was actually Ms Heckenvaal, our Modern History teacher. She wasn't called the Wreckin' Ball just because it sort of rhymed with her name. Ms Heckenvaal was slightly on the 'biggish' and 'roundish' side, a bit like a top-heavy barrel with legs. She was also one of the best teachers in the school.

"I mean, I get all the World Wars stuff we did last term. Some of that was pretty cool. But the History of Feminism? Is she nuts? What do we need that for? I mean, can you *see* any chicks around here?" Razz said, spreading out his arms wide and looking around crazily. "Can you? She does realise this is an all-*guys* school, doesn't she?"

"Perhaps," Scobie said, peeking over the top of his little round glasses, "*that's* the point."

"Point? What point?"

"Well, because we *are* an all-boys school, it could be that Ms Heckenvaal feels it might be a good thing for us to have some understanding and empathy for the struggles and challenges of the other half of the population."

Prindabel immediately held up his official 'objection' finger.

"Correction. The other fifty point two per cent of the population, to be precise – at least according to the most recent census. You see, the life expectancy of women is approximately—"

"Yes, thank you, Mr Google. Can I just stop you there?" Razz interrupted. "Maybe you could rest your search engines for a while before you give us all a boredom overload, okay?"

Razz turned slowly back to Scobie, pulling his eyes off Ignatius only at the last second.

"Yeah, well, that's all fine and dandy, Scobes, but how come we always have to learn about *chick* stuff when they never have to learn about *guy* stuff? What about *our* struggles and *our* challenges?"

"Such as?"

"Well… stuff like how if a guy says that a chick's got a hot bod, some chicks love it but then some chicks think that guy's a sexist pig or something and they want to scratch his eyes out. How do you know what you're supposed to say? What about *that* challenge? I mean, if chicks don't want us perving at them, man, how come they wear stuff that gives us so much to perve *at* in the first place? Where's the study unit on that?"

Scobie twisted his mouth back and forth for a moment. "Maybe you should raise those points with Ms Heckenvaal. I'd be very interested to hear her response."

Bill, Ignatius and I smiled. Razz spat out a laugh.

"Do I look like the kind of guy who would volunteer for a suicide mission?" Then he turned to the rest of us. "You guys agree with me about all this feminism stuff, don't you?"

Ignatius and I worked up enough enthusiasm to shrug. Bill mumbled out a few words.

"I think some of it's pretty interesting."

Razz gave him a patronising smile and patted him on the back.

"Yes, yes, of *course* you do, Hoop Boy, and we *all* know why *that* is, don't we?"

Bill opened his mouth to respond but Razz had already moved on.

"And another thing, what about that crap song she keeps torturing us with? I'm telling you, it's unnatural cruelty, man. I bet there's something in that Geneva Connection thing about it."

"Correction – Con*ven*tion, not Con*nec*tion," Ignatius threw in with another raised digit.

"Correction, Prindababble – who cares!" Razz threw

straight back at him with a slightly different raised digit.

The 'crap song' Razz was referring to was 'I Am Woman' by someone called Helen Reddy. I guess it was fair enough having to hear it once, because according to Ms Heckenvaal, it was the 'call to arms' and the 'anthem' of the women's movement in the 1970s. But recently she'd started to use it more as a weapon against us.

It was probably just revenge for all the groaning and laughing and smart comments that went on the first time she tried to play it. Now whenever the class gets a bit noisy or isn't working hard enough Ms Heckenvaal just says, "Sounds like we're in the mood for a sing-song, boys!" and she belts out the opening lines, all about her being a woman and roaring in numbers too huge to ignore or whatever it is, and everyone starts working furiously so she'll stop.

(Of course the real lyrics shouldn't be confused with the ones that Danny Wallace wrote, which went more like, *I'm a woman in the raw, my bum is too big to ignore/ When I eat too much it goes on my rear end.*)

Back in the discussion room Scobie tried to get the meeting back on track.

"Well, we're only doing feminism for this term, so maybe you'll like the next topic more. Now about our first debate…"

But Ms Heckenvaal wasn't Razz's only problem.

"And what about Media Studies? Mr Nelson gave us this big assignment on the first day of term and it's due in a few weeks and there's loads of work to do. An *assignment* for Media Studies! What's going on? I thought we'd just be watching movies and stuff. What a rip-off!"

"What's the assignment about?" I asked, although Scobie didn't look too pleased with my enquiry.

"Gotta make a community service advertisement thing for TV. Bill and me are doing it together. Ours is on sun safety. We've got to film it and write a report and everything. Sal and one of her friends are supposed to be in it except they reckon I have to change my script otherwise they won't do it."

"*You* wrote the script?"

"Yes, Prindabella, I did. And it's pretty rigid even if I do say so myself. It's epic."

"If it's so *epic*, then how come the girls don't like it?"

"Haven't got a clue. Who knows what goes on in chicks' heads? When I asked Sal what was wrong with it she wouldn't tell me. She just said, 'If you don't know, there's no hope for you.' What am I supposed to do with that? I can't read minds. I'm not cyclic."

Prindabel's finger went up but Razz had already disappeared under the table and he missed it. When he resurfaced he held up a folder with a fringe of loose sheets desperately trying to escape from it.

"Got it right here," Razz said, extracting some crumpled A4 paper. "This is the bit they're going on about."

Razz flattened the script out on the table and began reading.

"Scene: Outside. Beside a swimming pool. A girl (Britney Parker) is sitting on a towel. She is wearing a bikini. A second girl (Amber Jackson) joins her."

"Britney and Amber?" Ignatius said with a smirk.

"Yes, Prindabelly. They're chick names. You remember chicks? They're those ones who run away screaming whenever you turn up."

Ignatius lost his smirk. Razz continued with his reading:

AMBER: Hi, Britney!

BRITNEY: Hi, Amber!

AMBER: Hey, Britney, you look so hot in that new micro bikini! But with all that yummy flesh showing, I think you'd better get some suncream on.

BRITNEY: Suncream? No way! I'm working on my gorgeous golden tan. That's what all the guys like.

Bill, Ignatius, Scobie and I looked at each other. Razz beamed a grin around the table. "Pretty good eh? Just wait. It gets even better!"

AMBER: Britney Parker, I know the guys will only like you if you look hot, but how can you look hot if you end up all dry and leathery and you have loads of skin cancer?

BRITNEY: Hey, I never thought of that! What should I do, Amber?

AMBER: Do what I do, Britney. Always wear a hat, use a thirty-plus suncream and don't stay out in the sun for more than fifteen minutes. That way you'll have beautiful skin like mine and the guys won't be able to keep their hands off it.

BRITNEY: You mean, if I wear a hat, use a thirty-plus suncream and don't stay out in the sun for more than fifteen minutes at a time, all the guys will want me?

AMBER: That's right. If you wear a hat, use a thirty-plus suncream and don't stay out in the sun for more than fifteen minutes at a time, you can have the pick of any guy you want.

"Did you notice how I used a bit of repetition there to emphasise our sun safety message?"

We all nodded.

"Ingenious," Ignatius said.

"Inspired," I added.

"Subtle," Scobie concluded.

"Cool!" Razz said and grabbed up the script again.

BRITNEY: Awesome, Amber! Well, what are you waiting for? Show me the suncream!

AMBER: I've got the thirty-plus right here.

BRITNEY: Great. Why don't I lie down on this towel and undo my bikini top and you can rub some of that thirty-plus all over my back?

AMBER: Cool!

BRITNEY: Mmmmmmmmm, that feels so goooooood!

AMBER: Feels good and it's good for you!

BRITNEY: When you're done, I'll do you!

AMBER: Awesome!

Just then a couple of guys walk past and whistle at Britney and Amber.

AMBER: See, Britney? Just like I told you. Guys just love chicks who are sun safe.

BRITNEY: Hey, you're totally right, Amber! I guess
I learned a valuable sun safe lesson today,
didn't I?

AMBER: What valuable sun safe lesson was that,
Britney?

BRITNEY: Well, I learned that you don't have to *burn* to
be *hot*!

Britney and Amber both laugh and start rubbing loads of suncream on each other. Then they start wrestling. Fade. End.

When he'd finished reading, Razz slapped the script on the table. "Apparently *that's* supposed to be 'offensive'. Can you believe it? How can that be offensive? There's not a single swear word anywhere in it."

Razz glanced around at the four pairs of dazed eyes directed his way.

"What?" he asked.

At the end of the table Scobie cleared his throat. Then he closed his eyes and bowed his head.

"Let us all now join hands and together offer up a silent prayer of support for Ms Heckenvaal in the hope that it might sustain her in this time of great sorrow and in the torturous and trying months that must surely lie ahead."

"Amen," Bill, Ignatius and I answered together.

"What?" Razz asked again looking around bewildered.
"No, guys, seriously, *what?*"

12.
Bill and Razz's Excellent Sun Safe Adventure

A couple of weeks later we'd won our first debate of the year against Concordia High School and the filming of what became known as *Bill and Razz's Excellent Sun Safe Adventure* had been completed. I caught up with Razz before school on a Monday morning to hear about how the weekend's shoot had gone.

"Not bad. Got it all done, anyway. Haven't had a chance to go through any of it yet. I've got a computer booked in the media room after school. I'm checking it out then. Bill did the filming and I'm doing the editing."

"Did Sally end up being okay with it?"

"Yeah. And we filmed it at her place so we could use the pool as a backdrop. Her friend Jess came along too. Remember her from Sal's party last year?"

"Yeah, sure."

How could I forget? An image of Jess in a certain yellow bikini had been permanently seared into my retinas.

"And let me guess, Razz; did you just happen to cast Jess in the role of Britney 'Ooooooo! Why don't I just slip off my bikini top' Parker?"

"Yeah, well," Razz said, looking glum, "The girls sort of made us cut that bit out. Reckoned their characters sounded like a couple of 'randy airheads' or something. Unbelievable. Then they wanted that whole scene rewritten. Wouldn't let me touch it. They made Bilbo do it."

"Actors can be highly strung," I told him.

"You're not wrong there," Razz said with a roll of his eyes. "Anyway, Billy Boy got stuck in and totally changed it. Took out all the best bits, I reckon. But at least the girls liked it. Sally went on about him being a 'New Age man'. Puuuuuh-leeeeease! Hoop Boy a New Age man? Are we even sure he comes from this *planet*? Anyway, at least it's all in the can, as we film dudes say. Now it's up to me to get it edited and finished by next week."

Razz looked a bit daunted by that thought, so following a brief Amnesty meeting with Mr Guthrie after school, I wandered over to the media room to see how he was going. I found him alone in one of the cubicles with a video camera hooked up to a computer.

"Where's Bill? I thought he was going to stay back with you."

"Had to head off. His mum rang. An emergency in Hoopville apparently. Some appointment he'd forgotten about."

"So how's it looking?" I asked, nodding at the computer where an image of Sally's garden and pool was frozen on the screen.

"Yeah, not bad so far. I'm doing a quick run-through first up to pick the best takes. Hey, you want to hang around? Got some scenes coming up pretty soon with Jess *almost* wearing a bikini."

Then Razz threw back his head and slapped the desk.

"Aw no, wait, I forgot. You're not really into that kind of thing. Might be like Cindy, eh? A bit 'too much' for you, right, dude?"

I shot him a pained smile. "Shove over."

I wedged a chair in beside Razz and he hit *Play*. After only about ten minutes of viewing, four things became crystal clear to me.

The first was that Bill and his rewrite of the script had performed a complete brain and personality transplant on Britney and Amber. They actually seemed like real people. The second was that Sally and Jess could really act. The third was that Razz and Bill really couldn't.

The fourth was that no matter what the quality of the finished product, Jess in a bikini was worth the price of admission alone.

It took about half an hour to get through all the takes. Then after a final scene featuring Sally and Jess, Razz jumped in front of the camera and yelled, "Cut. That's a wrap, people!" This was followed by a bit of general cheering and whooping and Sally saying, "Let's eat! Just put all your stuff in my room."

On the screen the image began to tilt and shake like an earth tremor had just hit and there were flashes of Bill's chubby hands as they worked to unscrew the camera from the tripod. Beside me Razz was shaking his head.

"No way, not again. Geez, how many times did we have to remind him? Turn it off first, Bilbo!"

Back on screen there was a wild blur of colours and lights, then flashes and streaks of the pool, of the sky, of Sally, Razz and Jess and finally jerky, bouncy images of Bill's joggers heading down a path towards the house. Razz began shouting at the computer.

"Shire to Bilbo! Shire to Bilbo! This is Star Fleet Command. Do you read me? Turn off the camera! I repeat. TURN OFF THE CAMERA!"

Strangely enough, Bill didn't respond to Razz's pleas and the jerky images continued until the screen plunged into darkness as he entered the house. When the camera finally adjusted to the lower light, there was a bit more of the blurry, category-five cyclone-type stuff and then everything stopped. Slowly the edge of a quilt, some walls, a desk, a chair, a mirror and a few posters crawled into focus.

"Hey, that's Sal's room. He's just dumped the camera on her bed. Wait! Hoop Boy! Look at the little green light! It's right in front of you! It means the camera is still on! Open your eyes. It's right there on top! You couldn't *possibly* miss it, unless you're the biggest..."

Suddenly Bill's backside appeared in close-up on the screen.

"Wooooooo! Notify NASA! I think we've discovered a new planet!"

Bill moved further away across the room. He stood in front of Sally's desk. He was looking at a big poster on her wall of a football player striking a ball.

"Liverpool!" Razz said in disgust. "Where's the AC Milan one I got her? Didn't know Bilbo was that into football."

Bill stayed in front of the poster for a few seconds then turned and left. All that remained was the empty room. It looked like a really boring screen saver. Beside me Razz broke into raucous applause.

"Bravo! Bravo! Well done, Bilbo! Stupendous!

A masterpiece! Never before have I seen such inspired cinematography. A tour of force. The movement! The angles! The colours! The light and shade! The drama! I felt like I was *right* there! And now *this*. The piece of resistance. Never in the history of film-making has a *room* been captured with such... honesty... such sensitivity... such passion... such *truth*. I'm lost for words. It's just so... so... *room*-like!"

Razz and I were killing ourselves laughing.

"How could he not see the *On* light?" Razz shouted at the heavens. "Is he blind?"

Just then some movement on the screen caught our eyes. Someone else had come into Sal's room. It was Razz. He was carrying a sports bag. He walked over and stood directly in front of the camera then tossed the bag on the bed. The image on the screen bounced around for a bit before settling. Then Razz checked himself out in the mirror on Sally's dressing table, and left.

"Yeah, well, that *On* light is pretty small, you know, and..."

Back on screen, Jess had now entered the room. She was still in her bikini with a towel wrapped around her waist. She was shoving some things into a carrier bag. Razz leaned forward.

"That's right. Jess couldn't stay for lunch. I passed her

in the corridor. Had to run off straight away. Hardly said goodbye. Going to the cinema or something with her boyfriend *Brad*. Apparently they…"

Razz stopped talking, because Jess had moved to the centre of the room and was standing there brushing her long blonde hair. The automatic focus blurred slightly then locked in on her. She filled up the screen. The camera didn't just love her, it totally had the hots for her. She bent forward, brushed all her hair down over her face, then flicked it back as she stood up. Razz groaned. I knew exactly what he meant. Jess certainly made a bikini top earn its keep. It was the first time I'd ever felt jealous of fabric.

"Ishmael, my friend, that's what we Film and Television nerds call your classic medium shot. You see how it gets in most of the body from about the…"

Jess had taken off her towel and flung it on to the bed. Now she was reaching with both hands behind her back and biting her bottom lip with the effort. There was no mistaking her intention.

Jess Hambleton was about to unclip her bikini top.

13.
Final Answer (a)
Hell, Yeah!

Razz's nose was almost touching the computer screen when Jess's image froze. Immediately he began swearing, shaking the computer and frantically checking the connections. He only stopped when he spotted my finger on the *Pause* button.

"Are you crazy? What are you *doing*, man?"

"Razz, maybe we need to think about this a bit first."

Razza's eyes drilled into me for a moment and then began to wander around the room.

"Yeah. Yeah, you're absolutely right. Good one, Ishmael!" he said before jumping up from his chair, shutting the door to the editing room, drawing the curtains closed on the window beside us and rotating the computer screen so that it couldn't be seen from the main teaching area. "Wouldn't want to be interrupted, would we? Okay, push the button, dude!"

My finger stayed where it was.

"What're you waiting for?" Razz said, twisting his head around. "Did I miss something?"

"Razz, I don't think we can watch this."

'Sure we can. Look, it's easy. Give it here, I'll show you. You just push *Play*."

Razz reached over for the camera but I moved it away.

"I know we *can* watch it. What I mean is we *shouldn't*. It's not right. It's… wrong."

"Wrong? We've got Jess Hambleton about to take off her clothes. We've got *Pause*, *Rewind* and even *Slow Mo*. Man, this is so right, it's not funny. It's like we've won first prize in the chick-perving lotto! The only thing wrong, man, is you if you don't push that button!"

"So you'd be happy to sit there and gawk at Jess while she gets undressed?"

"What, is that like a trick question or something, dude? No? Okay then. Final answer: (a) *Hell, Yeah!*"

"I don't believe it. What, are you a peeping Tom or something now?"

"Peeping Tom? What are you on about? This isn't like *that*. I'm not creeping around in the dark like some scumbag trying to spy on Jess. I didn't *plan* this. It's just a lucky accident, man. The best and luckiest accident *ever*."

"That's rubbish, Razz. It's just wrong and you know it."

"Well, what are you, my conscience? Anyway, what's

so wrong about it? It's not gonna hurt anyone. Jess'll never know and it certainly ain't gonna hurt me. So how about you just push the button."

"No. It's wrong."

Razz threw up his hands and slumped down in his chair with his head resting on the back, gazing up at the ceiling.

"*Why* is it wrong? Why? Tell me that. Go on... educate me. Better yet, you're a debater. Convince me. Go on. Let's just say the topic is: *That watching Jess get naked is wrong* and you're arguing for the Affirmative. Go on, give me the outline of your case."

"This is stupid."

"What's the problem, Ishmael? You keep going on about how wrong it is. Haven't you got anything to back it up?"

Razz smirked at me and twiddled his fingers on his stomach as he waited.

"All right. You want my case? Is that it? Well, here it is. *First* of all, watching that video is a gross invasion of privacy, and personal privacy is one of the most basic and essential rights human beings have. *Secondly.* Just because it's accidental and you didn't plan it doesn't make it right. That would be like saying if you came across an open bank vault it would be okay to take the money because *you* weren't the one who unlocked it. *Thirdly.* You reckon it's okay to watch the video because Jess wouldn't know about it. Well, if it's okay for you and me to watch it then I guess you'd have no problem with someone like Danny Wallace or Bagsley watching it if they were the ones who *accidentally* found it. And what about if it was someone else in the video? Someone like... *Sally*? You'd be okay with that too, would you? *Fourthly.* Even if Jess never finds out about it, it's still wrong, because you *know* if she had a *choice* she wouldn't want people to watch her undress, otherwise she wouldn't have bothered going into Sally's room in the first place to get some *privacy.* And if you're doing something that you *know* would hurt or embarrass someone, then that *must* be wrong. And *finally*, it's even *worse* when the person you are doing the *wrong* thing to is a *friend.* A friend who's only *on* the stupid video in the first place because she's helping *you* out with your Film and Television assignment. You're not supposed to take advantage of your friends, Razz. And you know why? Because it's WRONG!"

All the time I'd been speaking Razz had been sitting there studying the ceiling. Now he turned his head lazily to the side and frowned at me.

"*That's* it? *That's* your case? That's all you got?"

"What?! Well, what have *you* got, then? Go on,

let's see how you'd go. Give me the Negative case."

"All right, I will."

Razz pushed back his chair and moved to the centre of room.

"Madam Chair. Ladies and Gentlemen. I would like to outline in *detail* the case for the Negative team."

Then he paused thoughtfully to find just the right words.

"Jess Hambleton," he said finally, "NAAAAAKEEED!"

Razz flopped back down.

"Admit it, Ishmael. I win in a landslide. Now push *Play*."

I stood up and headed for the door.

"Hey, wait up! What're you doing? Where're you going?"

"You were right, Razz. I'm not your conscience. So if you think it's fine to watch it, then go ahead and watch it. It's totally your call. But *I* think it's wrong and that's my call. So I'm leaving. Just so long as we agree on one thing. After you finish watching it, you delete it for good. Okay?"

I was reaching out for the door handle.

"No, wait, man! I'm not watching it without you."

"Why not?"

"Well… if you don't watch it… and I do… that makes me look like a bit of a sleaze bag."

"Well gee, Razz, if the coat fits…"

"What?!"

Razz bent forward and began slowly pounding his head on the desk in time to his words. "DO-NOT-BELIEVE-THIS. CAN-NOT-BE-HAPPENING. JUST-BAD-DREAM."

"That's it, I'm leaving."

I turned to go but Razz reached out and grabbed hold of the back of my shirt.

"Waaaaaaait," he said, squeezing his forehead like he had a mega-migraine. Then he passed me the camera. "Here, take it. You'll have to do it, man. I haven't got the heart."

I took the camera from Razz and pushed *Rewind*. On the screen, a towel flew off the bed and snaked itself around Jess's waist. Then she frantically messed up her hair with a brush, jiggled around a bit (accompanied by groaning from Razz) and scuttled backwards out of view. I pushed *Stop*, put the lens cap on the camera and pressed *Record*.

Beside me Razz picked up a ruler from the desk and clasped it in two hands like a samurai sword. He turned one end towards himself, jabbed it in his side and drew it swiftly across his stomach. As his eyes rolled back into his head he collapsed in a silent heap on the floor. The only sound left in the room was the low hum of the video camera and the words that floated up from the crumpled form on the carpet.

"What is *wrong* with you, man?"

14.
A Killer,
Petrol-driven,
Motorised
Hamburger

That was the second time Razz had asked what was wrong with me. First because of Cindy. And now because of Jess. That night I lay in bed with all sorts of questions squirming around inside my brain.

Was I really that different from other guys my age? Would every other sixteen-year-old male have jumped at the chance to go out with Cindy Sexton again? Would they all have happily pushed the *Play* button on Jess Hambleton? Those questions kept me awake for ages. Or maybe I'd just eaten a bit too much of the takeaway we'd had for dinner.

Anyway, it felt like I'd been awake for hours when I rolled over to check the time on the clock radio.

That's when I found myself staring at a big heart monitor machine. A green line ran across a black screen. It was jumping up in sharp peaks in time with my heartbeat. On the top of every peak a little image of Kelly Faulkner's face appeared for a moment then popped liked a bubble.

Okay, I thought to myself, maybe I did finally get to sleep, and this *could* be a dream.

I checked out the room more carefully. It looked like a hospital and my bed was now suspiciously like an operating table. On closer examination I found that I was wearing pink pyjamas. They were covered in lots of little white whales. A doctor entered. Or to be *slightly* more accurate, it was Ronald McDonald in a white coat. There was an oversized badge on his chest. It had *Ronald McDoctor – Surgeon to the Clowns* printed on it in bubbly rainbow letters. He had a hamburger in one hand and a chainsaw in the other.

Yep, I was almost one hundred per cent certain now that I was dreaming.

"What's going on?" I asked.

"I have some very McSad news to tell you," Ronny said. "I'm afraid you have the worst case of Ishmael Leseur's Syndrome I've ever encountered and it's mutating out of control. I'll have to operate immediately – otherwise you're a goner."

I jumped off the table and yelled, "I'm not going to let some clown who can't buy the right-sized shoes operate on me!" (I think I might also have suggested that he should go for a more natural hair colour and apply a lighter touch with the make-up.)

He began chasing me around the table. I shouted over my shoulder, "Ishmael Leseur's Syndrome's not real! It's just some stupid thing I made up when I was a little kid as an excuse for all the times I messed up! There's nothing wrong with me! I'm perfectly normal!"

Ronny stopped in his tracks and smiled (It's painted on. What else can he do?). "Oh, well, that's all right then," he said, chucking away the chainsaw.

How easy was that? What a pushover. I was feeling pretty proud of myself, but then RM held out his hamburger. It was huge. It also had a strange cord hanging from it that I hadn't noticed before. Ronny grabbed it and yanked down. Deadly blood-covered blades shot out and rotated in a blur. Only looking back, I think those deadly blood-covered blades might have actually been beetroot slices. That was the clincher for me – a killer, petrol-driven, motorised hamburger. No way! This was *definitely* a dream and I wanted out!

I tried to wake myself up but I might as well have been sleeping inside a block of cement. Next thing

I knew, the killer hamburger was gone and in its place Ronny Mac was holding up Prue's old Ringo peg person and cooing, "Remember what happened with this way back in our first debate? Was *that* normal?" Then he pointed to a plastic bottle of cordial on the floor. He jumped on it and squished it flat. Yellow liquid sprayed all over me. "Last year?" he said, "Sally's pool party? You haven't forgotten that, have you? Are you telling me *that* was normal?" Then he reached into his pocket and pulled out... Wait, was that what I thought it was? He held out his hand. There was a tongue the size of a baby elephant's trunk thrashing about on his palm. "And *this*? Do you honestly believe this kind of thing happens to *normal* people?"

Now Ranga Ronny was standing right over me and I was cowering in a corner. From that angle, with his crazy hair and that maniac smile, he looked just like a more colourful version of Razz. It was quite a comforting thought. Except for the giant, glinting knife he had in his hand.

"*Dude*," he said McScarily, "there's nothing to worry about, *dude*. I'm just gonna slice you open, *dude*, and see what's wrong with you, *dude*. We think you might be a dud *dude*. Hey, dud dude. That's McAwesome!"

Then the room was crammed with all these weird people with three eyes or their heads on backwards or bodies like fish or toads or something. It was like a mutants' convention. They pushed in beside Ronny and began poking me with sticks and spears and sesame seed buns and quarter pounders and chanting, "WHAT'S *WRONG* WITH YOU, MAN! WHAT'S *WRONG* WITH YOU, MAN! WHAT'S *WRONG* WITH YOU, MAN!"

I lurched awake. I was back in my normal room. Hey, what do you know? It was all just a dream! (Please don't tell Miss Tarango I wrote that. She'd kill me.) But right then I didn't care. I was just so happy. There was nothing wrong with me after all. I was the same as everyone else. I was completely normal. I didn't have Ishmael Leseur's Syndrome. How could I? It never even existed in the first place!

Of course I was wrong.

Ishmael Leseur's Syndrome certainly does exist. And just to illustrate the point, soon I'd be hearing the 'What's wrong with you?' question directed my way again in real life. Only next time, the person asking the question wouldn't be Razz.

It would be me.

15.
Talking About Talk Talk

Our second-round debate was now less than two weeks away and with Bill and Razz rushing to get their Film and Television assignment completed in time it was decided that Ignatius, Scobie and I would make up the team. It was also decided that Razz and Bill wouldn't need to be involved in the preparation.

With just the three of us attending meetings, they seemed to run more smoothly and we achieved a lot in a short space of time. Of course, without Razz they were nowhere near as much fun. I was on my way home from our final after-school meeting when I spotted Razz sitting under a tree down by the Fields. He'd been to football training but it was all over now and he was the only one left. As I got closer to him I could see that he didn't look happy. I figured it had something to do with the sun safe assignment.

"Hey, Razz, here's a tip for you. When they take down

the nets and everyone packs up and goes home, that's usually a subtle sign that football training is over for the day."

He glanced up half-heartedly.

"What? Oh yeah… Yeah, I guess so."

Then he returned to picking at grass shoots and staring at his hands.

"Razz, it was a joke. You remember jokes, don't you? One person says something hilarious and the other laughs his guts up."

This time he couldn't even manage a half-hearted glance.

"Yeah… Yeah, right… Sorry."

Now I was worried. I plonked myself down beside him.

"Are you okay? Something up with the assignment?"

He flicked a bit of twig away with his finger and pushed his hand through his hair.

"Nah, it's not that… It's Sally."

"What about her?"

"Something she said."

"What?"

"She told me we had to… talk."

I waited for more. Razz stared back at me with desperate eyes.

"*Talk*," he repeated, as if Sally had asked him to base jump into an active volcano.

"So? You've never had any trouble with that before."

"No, you don't get it, man. She wasn't just talking about normal talk talk. She was talking about *talk* talk."

"Oh yeah, right, I get it now. It's obvious when you put it that way. Talk talk as opposed to *talk* talk. Good job of clearing that up, Razz. Ever thought of writing your own dictionary?"

But something had stolen all Razz's funny bones and left him a lifeless blob of seriousness.

"It's bad, man. She wasn't kidding around. She didn't sound happy at all. Just kept saying we had to... talk... like it was super-important or something."

As I listened to Razz an uneasy question was uncurling in my mind.

"Razz, you don't think... I mean, Sally wouldn't be... you know... like, have you guys..."

Razz looked across at me blankly for a second before a light switched on in his eyes.

"No... No way, man... No, she couldn't be. Sally's been pretty straight with me from the start. She doesn't want anything too heavy before she finishes this year. School and study come first. She told me that. I don't mind, I guess, 'cause she's worth it. 'Cept sometimes it gets pretty hard."

"Geez, Razz, too much information!"

When even that didn't register a smile, I gave up.

"Okay, so what do you think she wants to talk about?"

Razz drew in a breath.

"Can only be one thing, man. She wants to dump me. I knew she was too smart for me. Too good for me." Razz picked up a stone and hurled it out of sight. "Too *everything* for me."

I hadn't seen him this miserable since last year when he made a stupid joke and accidentally hurt Sally's feelings. It was weird. He was so thick-skinned he could take every insult, every put-down that Barry Bagsley or anyone else hurled at him, and laugh it off. But with Sally just a look or a word could slice him to pieces.

"I *really* like her, man… *more* than like."

Razz turned his head away and blinked up at the sky.

"But I don't get it. Why would she want to break up anyway? Have you said or done anything bad?"

"I haven't had time to do anything."

"What about the last time you saw her?"

"That was when Bill and me did that filming at her place. She was great all day – laughing and joking around. After that she was flat out with exams,

then she was away on a camp for a week. We were going
to do something together as soon as she got home. She
was really keen. So I rang her straight after my football
game on Saturday, to see what she wanted to do. But she
sounded really down. Reckoned she was just tired. Then
I said what about next weekend and that's when she said
it. First we had to… talk. Said we couldn't discuss it over
the phone – we had to do it face to face."

Face to face? Razz was right. This was sounding bad.

"So when's it going to happen? When are you two
going to… talk?"

"She's coming to the debate tomorrow night. I'm
seeing her there. That's when I'll get the flick."

"But if you two were getting on great a couple of
weeks ago and nothing's happened since, why would she
suddenly want to dump you?"

"Well, I think I figured that out too. Something must
have happened on the camp."

"Like what?"

"Like she met someone else."

"On a school camp with a bunch of other girls? Who
could she meet?"

"Sometimes there are other schools there as well
– boys' schools. They're supposed to stay in separate
areas but you can't trust some of those scumbags.

Remember that camp we went on three years ago and some guys got busted for trying to sneak around to the girls' showers?"

"Yeah, I do…Weren't you one of them?"

"That's totally beside the point, Ishmael. The thing is, it shows that Sally could have easily met up with some guy on camp. And now she's dumping me."

"Well, it just doesn't sound like Sally to me. You're probably worrying about nothing."

That's what I said to Razz anyway, but I wasn't sure if I really believed it myself.

"Hey, man, do me a favour and sort of hang around after the debate when I have to talk to Sally? You know, just in case I need you."

"Need me? But what can I do?"

"Don't know. Just… be there, I guess."

I had no idea what kind of help I could be, but I said yes anyway. When your best mate was going head to head in a serious *talk* talk, the least you could do was be in his corner and try to patch him up when it was all over.

16.
A Prairie Dog on a Caffeine High

All the next day Razz wasn't quite himself. That meant he was sort of quiet and serious and merged into the background. A bit like a normal person. It was scary. But by the time our second-round debate was due to get under way that night, Razz had gone from 'sort of quiet' to hyper-jumpy.

He was sitting in the audience on the lookout for Sally. From out the front I could see his head bobbing around like a prairie dog on a caffeine high. Sally didn't arrive till after the debate had started. Jess was with her. They slipped in quietly between speakers and grabbed a seat right by the door. Sally shot a tight smile at Razz and then a not-so-tight smile at Scobie, Ignatius and me out the front. My hopes for Razz were fading fast.

Just for the record, we ended up winning. That made it two out of two. At the end there was the usual congratulating and commiserating and everyone milled around chatting for a while before heading off. When Scobie, Bill and Ignatius left to support our younger debating team there was just me, Razz, Sally and Jess in the room.

Sally's eyes were a bit puffy, like she'd stayed up all night. Both girls looked tense. Razz struggled to get the conversation going, but he was fighting a losing battle.

"Great debate, hey? Don't know how the boys did it without my help."

The girls pushed out a couple of weak smiles.

"Of course, it's a little known fact that I write most of Scobie's stuff for him. He'd be nothing without me."

The girls' weak smiles weakened.

"On his own this time though. I've been too busy editing the sun safe epic to make you two look even hotter."

The girls' smiles died stone dead. Sally levelled her serious dark eyes at Razz.

"Can we talk now?"

Razz tried to stay upbeat, but his upbeat looked like it had been beaten to a pulp.

"Talk… Sure, right…Yeah… No problem. In there okay?"

Razz pointed to the next classroom. Sally nodded and went through the connecting door with Razz tagging along behind. If his shoulders had been slumped any lower he'd be sliding along the floor. They closed the door behind them and I was left alone in an empty room with Jess. I stood there feeling stupid until she sat down and patted the chair beside her.

"Have a seat. Might be a bit of a wait."

It crossed my mind that being seen sitting next to Jess Hambleton might do wonders for my shattered post-'extensions' reputation. I was hoping someone from my Tutor Group might wander down the corridor.

"Great debate," she said. "I could never do that. I can talk all right. Mum says I can talk under wet cement. I just can't say anything smart enough, that's the problem. Scobie was awesome. I'm listening to him speak and I'm like 'Wow!' You were great too."

"Thanks. It helps a lot when I don't pass out."

Jess's mouth opened in a big 'O'. "That's right! It was *you* that time, wasn't it? You ended up on top of Kelly. We heard all about it back at school and I'm like, *Oh my god, that is soooooo funny!* Not for you, of course. Or Kelly." Jess's smile turned down. "Gosh, I miss her."

"Me too!" I wanted to say, but didn't. Then Jess bit her bottom lip and went quiet. She sat staring ahead at the whiteboard as if she had X-ray vision and could see through it into the next room.

I followed her gaze. "Wonder what's going on in there."

Jess didn't answer, but when I looked across at her, she had her head down and was wiping dampness from under her eyes.

"Jess? What's up? You okay?"

Her face just crumpled up.

"I've wrecked everything for Sal. It's all my fault. I should have kept my big mouth shut."

"What do you mean? What did you do? What happened?"

Jess shook her head and dabbed at her eyes with a tissue.

"I wasn't going to say anything. I totally wasn't. But we were on camp and Sal's like 'What's wrong? You don't seem happy.' And I'm like, 'No, it's nothing. I'm fine, really.' And she's like, 'No, you're not. You have to tell me what's wrong. I'm your friend.' And she's right but I don't want to tell her because she *is* my friend and I know it will just stuff everything up for her. But she keeps saying, 'You have to tell me. I'm your friend. I can help.' And I'm still totally like, 'No, really, I'll be fine. It's no big deal.' But she can tell it totally is and she won't let up till I say what's bugging me. So I do. I didn't want to, I didn't mean to, but I do. And now I wish I could take it back, because it's going to ruin everything for Sal just like I knew it would. God, I'm such an *idiot* sometimes!"

Beside me Jess blinked up at the ceiling as big tears pooled in her eyes and overflowed down her cheeks. I know Razz would probably say that there was something wrong with me, but I couldn't help thinking that Jess Hambleton didn't really need a micro bikini to be beautiful.

"But what was it? What did you tell her?"

Jess dug into her bag and wiped her nose with a big wad of tissues.

"I told her…"

But just then Razz burst in on us and grabbed me by the arm.

"Come on, dude! I need you!"

"Why?"

"'Cause you're the only one who can save me, man!"

17.
A Gross Invasion
of Piracy

Razz grabbed a hold of Jess as well and we were both dragged through the door and up to the front of the next classroom where Sally was looking confused.

"Go on, tell him. Tell Ishmael what you just told me."

The confusion on Sally's face deepened along with the colour in her cheeks.

"But this isn't Ishmael's problem. It's got nothing to do with him."

"It has. Just tell him… *please*."

Sally pushed her hair back behind her ears and took a deep breath.

"Okay. When Jess and I were on camp she told me… that on the day we did that filming at my place… someone had set up the video camera in my room… to film her while she got changed. And she said the person who was in the room just before she went in… was Razz."

Razz's eyes were fixed on me like satellite dishes. "See! See! Tell 'em, Ishmael! Tell 'em!"

I told them.

"Razz didn't put the camera there. It was Bill."

Sally and Jess looked at one another. They each pulled a weird face and laughed a bit.

"Bill?" they said in unison before Sally took over. "From what I know of Bill, I'm *pretty* certain he wouldn't do something like that. Anyway, he wasn't the one who was going to see it. Only the person doing the editing would. And we all know who that was."

"Tell 'em, Ishmael! Tell 'em!"

That seemed to be the only thing Razz appeared capable of saying any more.

"Bill didn't mean to put the camera there. It was an accident. He just left it on the bed and forgot to turn it off. I saw him do it when I was looking through the other shots with Razz."

"That's right. What Ishmael said. That's exactly what happened. And I still got that shot of Bill doing it."

The girls exchanged a frown.

"But if you saw Bill you must have seen me too."

Razz and I nodded at Jess.

"Then Razz... how come you didn't say anything to Sally or me straight away after you watched the video?

Why didn't you defend yourself then?"

Now it was our turn to frown.

"Defend myself?" Razz said. "Against what?"

"Against all the things I called you when I saw that little green light on top of the camera and worked out it was still on."

"You *saw* the green light?"

"Yeah, you'd have to be an idiot to miss it. I saw it just in time. Then I totally gave you a gob-full before I switched it off."

Sally was really frowning hard at Razz now.

"How could you guys not know that? If you watched all the tape, you *must* have seen Jess do that."

"We only saw her come in. We didn't see the rest," Razz said. "Not the very last bit."

"How come?" Sally asked.

"Because we stopped it. As soon as we saw Jess was about to whip her top off, we stopped the video."

Both Sally and Jess were studying Razz now like he'd just claimed that not only was Elvis still alive, he was actually working part-time at the local supermarket – along with his friends John Lennon, Kurt Cobain and Michael Jackson.

"You're telling us you *stopped* watching the video just *before* Jess took off her top?"

Razz was nodding now like his life depended on it. Both girls kept their eyes speared on him waiting for him to crack. He didn't. So they plunged their eyeball spears into me. I felt like breaking down and confessing even though I was innocent.

"It's true, Sal. I was there. We stopped the video when we saw what was going to happen, you know with Jess and the top and everything... and then we recorded over it."

Lucky the ceiling was there, otherwise Jess and Sally's eyebrows would have been heading into deep space by now.

"You guys *stopped* the video... and then you recorded *over* it?"

This time I gave Sal the good old 'life-depending -on-it' nod. The girls seemed too stunned to speak. Razz, on the other hand, had no such trouble.

"Yeah, of *course*. What do you think we are? Perverts or... peeping Toms or something?"

I shot Razz a quick warning glance. He completely ignored me and charged on.

"I mean, if Jess wanted us to see her undress she would have got changed in the lounge room, right there in front of us, while we all just sat back and watched."

This concept seemed to derail Razz's concentration

and he wavered a bit before finally reboarding his train of thought.

"Ummmmmm… So… like I was saying… of course we stopped the video and recorded over it. Watching it would have been so *wrong*, man. It would have been, like a, like a… a gross invasion of piracy."

"Ah, I think that would be 'privacy', Razz."

"What? Oh yeah, yeah, of course… privacy," Razz said, sending me a warning look of his own. We were involved for a moment in a silent eye-to-eye battle before Jess let out a moan that startled us out of it.

"Awwwwwwwww," she wailed like she was in pain. "That is so sweeeeeeeeeeeeeeeeeeeeet! You guys are amaaaaaaaaaaaaaaaaaazing! You are both totally made of awesome!"

Jess rushed at Razz and wrapped him in a bear hug. Then she flung her arms around my neck and squeezed her body so tight against mine we could have been two Lego blocks clicking into place. When Jess finally levered herself off me, she stepped back and looked around at the rest of us with an uber-sad clown face.

"I'm really, *really* sorry. I've been such a dumbo blonde. What a klutz! I should've known you guys wouldn't do anything sicko like that. Ooo! That reminds me. I better ring Brad and tell him. He's like totally planning to punch your lights out, Razz. Isn't he sweeeeeeeeet!"

Jess pulled out her mobile and headed for the corridor. Sally took Razz by the hand.

"I'm really sorry too."

Razz shook his head sadly.

"I just don't understand how you thought I'd *do* a thing like that. Me? I mean, even if Jess got filmed accidentally I can't *believe* you'd think I'd watch it. Man, that'd be like… like… finding a bank vault open and stealing the money and saying it was okay because *you* weren't the one who opened it. It just wouldn't be right. It'd be… *wrong*."

I fought the urge to roll my eyes in case Sally saw me.

"It's like I said before, Sal, we're talking about *privacy* here. And I reckon privacy is one of the most *basic* rights any…"

"It was Ishmael's idea not to watch the video, wasn't it?" Sally said flatly.

"Absolutely," Razz answered immediately.

"Probably had to twist your arm, right?"

"Posssssibly."

Razz grimaced and squinted at Sally as if he was bracing for a punch. But Sally didn't come out swinging. Instead she stepped forward and planted on Razz's lips the biggest, juiciest, most lingering-est kiss ever.

When they finally separated Razz looked like he'd had most of his energy and a good portion of his brain sucked from him.

"What was *that* for?" he said like he'd just woken up.

Sally smiled her best heart-melter smile at him.

"Your reward… for letting your arm be twisted."

"Yeah, I did, didn't I? Which was an awesome effort on my part. Huge. So I was thinking maybe I deserve…"

"Don't push it, Orazio," Sally said with all the finality of a guillotine. Then she turned to me.

"Thanks, Ishmael. I'm *so* glad you're Razz's friend. I don't know what he'd do without you."

Then she gave me a big hug.

I was glad I was Razz's friend too. But later that night as I walked alone behind Razz and Sally and watched them holding hands and laughing together, I couldn't stop myself imagining what it would be like to swap places with the Razzman. Even just for a little while.

Yeah, right, I thought as I shook the idea from my head, like that'd ever happen.

Term Two

This above all: to thine own self be true,
And it must follow, as the night the day,
Thou canst not then be false to any man.

William Shakespeare, *Hamlet*,
act 1 scene 3, lines 78–80

18.
The Alcoholic Dane

Our first term of Senior School finished in the usual blaze of assignments and exams. A few people were warmed by the glow, many suffered minor burns and some perished in the inferno.

Debating-wise, the second term didn't start too well. Our third-round contest resulted in an unexpected loss. Miss Tarango diplomatically described the judge's decision that night as "just a little curious and hard to fathom". Razz described it as "totally mental, man!" When Miss reminded him that we must never criticise the adjudicators he said, "Yeah, you're right, Miss. You should never speak ill of the brain-dead."

The loss meant that our hopes of making the debating finals now hinged on us winning the fourth round. We had gathered in the library to prepare for just that, but as usual Razz wasn't quite with us.

"*Hamlet*? We're doing *Hamlet*? I still don't get why

Slattery's making us do *Hamlet* when all the other classes get to do *Macbeth*, which is loads better 'cause it's way shorter."

Razz and Mr Slattery had already had a discussion on this very issue in a previous lesson. It went something like this:

"*Hamlet*? How come we're doing that, Sir? Everyone else is doing that *Macdeath* one."

Mr Slattery hoisted up his trousers by the belt to make sure they remained unfashionably high on his thin waist. Everything about him was neat and precise, from the razor-sharp creases on his trousers and shirt, to his never-out-of-place, slicked-back, straight-from-a-bottle, fiery red hair. He waltzed across to Razz's desk. Literally. As well as teaching English and French, Mr Slattery was apparently an enthusiastic ballroom dancer. He posed in front of Razz with one hand on his hip. If you threw in a cape and a couple of those swordy things, he would have made a pretty good bullfighter.

"That would be *Macbeth*, Mr Zorzotto, and while that is a very fine play indeed – a masterpiece in fact – we are doing *Hamlet* because I believe it shows Shakespeare's genius at its most… sublime."

Razz didn't look like he was that into 'sublime'.

"But how come we're doing some play written

thousands of years ago anyway? Why can't we do something relevant?"

After twenty years of teaching, Mr Slattery was fully prepared for this and his eyes lit up. "Oh, *Hamlet is* relevant, Mr Zorzotto. It's all about the conflict between thought and action. You see, Prince Hamlet – or the Melancholy Dane as he has become known – is a thinker, philosopher and poet and *yet*," Mr Slattery said, shooting his finger into the air Prindabel-like, "he is called upon by his father to be a warrior, an action hero if you will. As such, Hamlet finds himself torn between thought and action, between thinking about the deed and the doing of it. I'd say the issue of thinking before you act is relevant to everyone, *particularly* teenage boys like yourself, Mr Zorzotto, who tend to be somewhat *impetuous* in their actions from time to time."

Razz wasn't impressed.

"What, so the play's just about some prehistoric prince dude who sits around thinking about doing stuff but doesn't actually do anything?"

Mr Slattery tapped his fingers together like a spider bouncing on a mirror. "Well, yes… that… and murder, revenge, incest, betrayal, death, madness, suicide, love, lust and the supernatural."

Razz stared back, unimpressed.

"What? No car chases?"

Mr Slattery pretty much gave up trying to convince Razz of the benefits of studying *Hamlet* after that.

Back in the debating meeting Razz scrunched up his hair in frustration.

"And can someone tell me why those dudes didn't speak English back in Shakespeare's time? I haven't got a clue what they're talking about most of the time. And another thing, old Willy's supposed to be a genius, right? Well, instead of all that talking, why not just have Hamlet's old man come back from the dead and say, 'Hey, Hammy, that Claudius dude knocked me off so he could be king and pinch my wife. Kill him for me, will you?' And then just have Hamlet say, 'Sure, Dad. You bet I will. Watch me go.' That way at least something would *happen* and we'd get to see some action. Plus it would be way shorter."

"Interesting theory," Scobie said. "You don't think it might undermine the complexity of Hamlet's character just a touch?"

"Aw, man, don't talk to me about Hamlet's character. I've had a gutful of old Slats rabbiting on about the Telescopic Dane or whatever he calls him."

Prindabel had his head buried in a *New Scientist* magazine, and without lifting his eyes off the page he raised a crooked finger into the air and mumbled, "Melancholy Dane."

"Yes, thanks for your input, Professor Pointer. Okay, yeah, right, the *Alcoholic* Dane, whatever."

Prindabel's finger rose up again in silent protest before losing interest and sinking back down to the desk.

"All I'm saying, Scobes, is, wouldn't it be better if Hamlet forgot about everything else and just got on with it?"

"Perhaps we could discuss that at some other time, Orazio," Scobie suggested, "because what *we* really need to get on with is preparing this debating topic. We're up against Claremont and they're easily one of the best teams in the competition. If we can't come up with some very solid arguments to match theirs, then we will certainly lose this next debate and then we'll be out of the finals again."

Unfortunately, to put it simply, we couldn't, so we did, and we were.

19.
The Accelerated
Jedi Course

A few days after our fourth-round debating defeat, Scobie scheduled his usual debriefing and review meeting to find out what we did right, what we did wrong and how we could improve for next year. We didn't know it, but we were about to find out something a lot more than interesting than that.

As usual, Razz was the last to arrive.

"Sorry I'm late, Herr Scobemeister. Uniform detention. Hey, by the way, any of you guys seen my tie? Or my Senior badge? No, forget it, doesn't matter. Listen up. You know how I'm going to the Lourdes Semi-formal with Sally?"

How could we not? Razz had been talking about it non-stop for weeks.

"Yeah, well, some chicks still haven't got partners so they're looking for volunteers. Just going to draw names out of a hat and match people up. You guys wanna be in it? Come on, it's two weeks from this Saturday."

"That rules out Ignatius and me," Scobie said, checking his student diary. We're away on the Accelerated Science Course that weekend. It's live-in."

Razz let out a high whistle. "A two-day science slumber party, eh? Wicked! You guys must be nearly bursting your Bunsen burners with anticipation. Now make sure you pack plenty of clean lab coats, you hear? Oh, and at dinner time, be sure to remember your Periodic Table manners."

Scobie gave an exaggerated Cheshire Cat-type smile. "We'll take *lots* of notes and photos and post them on your Facebook page, Orazio."

"Peachy, Scobes. I am fighting *so* hard to contain my excitement, and hey, what do you know? I have. So okay, you guys are definitely out. But what about you, Ishmael? You might get lucky and draw out another Kelly Faulkner."

"I don't think so, Razz. I don't want to be matched up with someone I've never met."

"What are you worried about, dude? Stranger Danger? Well, never fear. The Razzman will come to your aid if some chick refuses to take advantage of you."

"Gee, thanks, but I think I'll be fine."

"Come on, man! Hey, maybe I can get Sally to pull some strings. You know, make sure you're not lumped with one of those brainy chicks who look like the Bride of Frankenstein or something."

"So how did that *History of Feminism* unit work for you, Orazio?"

"What?"

"Doesn't matter," Scobie said and began humming a few bars of what sounded suspiciously like 'I Am Woman'. Razz ignored him.

"So what do you reckon, Ishmael?"

I shook my head. I was sick of being talked into stuff I wasn't sure about. I didn't care if Razz thought there was something wrong with me. For once I wanted to go out with someone *I* chose.

Razz rolled his eyes at me. "All right, dude, yeah, whatever." Then he waved across the table at Bill.

"Hoop Boy! Looks like it's left to you, Billy, to fight off all those desperate chicks. Better bring the light sabre along."

Bill shifted his eyes around the table and mumbled, "Sorry, Razz… I don't want to go either."

Razz slapped his forehead.

"You too, Bilbo? What's *your* excuse, man? Got the Accelerated Jedi Course on or something? Or are you too busy moping over some chick who's a million miles away like Ishmael here? Come on, dude, what's *your* problem?"

The vague clouds seemed to shift from Bill's eyes a little as he focused them on Razz.

"I haven't got a problem. Just don't want to go, that's all."

"Well, why not?"

Bill shook his head. "Not really… interested."

"Not interested? Not interested? How can you not be interested? There's gonna be food, dancing and chicks," Razz said, holding up a finger for each item. "I'm thinking that's gotta be pretty close to three out of three for you, big guy."

Bill stared hard at Razz then down at his own chubby hands.

"Two out of three… if you really want to know."

"Well, forget the dancing then. Just feed your face and hit on the chicks. It'll still be a top night."

Across the table Bill gave Razz's words some serious thought before he replied.

"It's not the dancing. I like dancing," he said. "I used to dance all the time when I was little. Mum and me used to dance to her old tapes. The ABBA ones were the best."

"Are you watching what you eat then, Bill?" I asked.

"Not really," he said. "Cutting back a bit maybe, and hooping."

"Well," Prindabel said, "if it's not the dancing and it's not the food, then by a simple process of elimination, you mustn't be interested in…"

Ignatius stopped in his tracks as it dawned on him where his logical process of elimination was about to wind up.

Bill finished the journey for him. "Girls," he said.

There was a bit of a gap in the conversation at that point and then Ignatius ventured, "Not interested in girls… at the *moment*?"

"Not interested… ever."

Bill kept his eyes trained intently on his fingers. "You might as well know. I wanted to tell you all for ages anyway."

Silence. Stony cold, what-the-hell-do-we-say-now kind of silence.

Prindabel frowned. "So… you're telling us… you're one of the very roughly estimated 2.1 per cent of the population who claim to be…"

Bill nodded.

Silence. The Extended Version. I tried to process what Bill was telling us but it kept getting blocked by a confusing image in my mind.

"But Bill… last year at my dad's concert… you danced with Sally… and you looked… pretty *happy*?"

Bill smiled without looking up. "I was. She's really nice. And she's a great dancer too. It was like when I used to dance with Mum."

"So it wasn't because…"

Bill shook his head.

"Right."

Silence. The Director's Cut this time, with extra embarrassment and never-before-seen awkwardness. As always, it was left to Scobie to build a life raft of words and come to our rescue.

"Well, Bill," he said, thrusting his hand forward, "I'd say congratulations are in order. You definitely win the award for Best and Most Original Excuse for Not Going to the Lourdes Semi-formal with Orazio."

Relieved laughter spilled around the table as Scobie and Bill shook hands and Bill at last found the strength to lift his eyes and smile. But it was only a second before his face collapsed in worry and doubt.

Scobie, Ignatius and I followed the path of Bill's gaze across the table. It led to Razz. His face was distorted with disgust and the full force of it was levelled at Bill Kingsley.

"Razz?" Bill said, just barely managing to get the name out. "Razz… you okay?"

Everyone at the table held their breath and waited for the reply. Razz shook his head slowly and twisted his mouth into an ugly, bewildered sneer.

"You like… *ABBA*?" he said.

20.
That Smokin'
Elf Chick

After Bill's surprise announcement any thought Scobie had of running a debating season review meeting pretty much went out the window.

As for Razz, apart from the fact that according to him it showed a "complete lack of taste", he insisted he was "totally cool" with Bill "going for the other team". To prove his point he added, "Geez, I've even got friends who support Manchester United. Can you believe it? Manchester *United*!"

The rest of us looked at him vaguely while he continued.

"And you should meet my Uncle Georgiou. Man, he didn't just *come* out of the closet – he cartwheeled out in high heels! He does this act down at the Italian Club every month called 'Show Tunes Serenade'. A couple of times I've filled in on drums. You should see his costumes. Mum says they'd make a peacock weep with envy.

Uncle Georgiou is my dad's brother. He's helped my mum and me a lot. He's a great guy." The smile that was on Razz's lips hardened. "*Loads* better than my dad ever was."

But just because Razz was "totally cool" with Bill's announcement, it didn't mean that it made sense to him.

"Bilbo, you're totally into *Lord of the Rings*, right? So tell me this, if you had a choice between, like, that Aragorn dude you keep going on about and that smokin' elf chick he had the hots for in the movie…"

"You mean Arwen? Actually she was only half elfin. She and Aragorn met when…"

"Yeah, terrific, anyway, *her*. My question is, are you honestly telling me, man, that if you had your choice between the two of them, you'd pick *him*?"

Bill pushed out his bottom lip. "Might be a bit old… but if I had to choose… Yeah."

"Man, oh man," Razz said. "Unbelievable. So are you Team Jacob or Team Edward?"

"Well," Scobie said, picking up his pen and tapping it on the blank sheet of paper in front of him, "as *fascinating* as all this is, can I remind everyone that we are in fact gathered here for a debriefing meeting and…"

"Yeah, hang on, Scobes. I just got one more question, okay?"

Scobie placed his pen on the empty sheet and

flopped back in his seat, waving a weary hand at Razz to go ahead.

"Cool. Okay, Bilbo, tell me this. You said you liked dancing with Sally that time, right? So, if you had a chance to dance up close and personal with someone, who would you choose, Sally or... me?"

"Definitely Sally," Bill said immediately.

Razz pointed a finger at him. "AAAAA-HA!" he shouted as if he'd caught Bill stealing his lunch. Then his face snapped into a frown. "Wait up. What's wrong with me?"

"Now's *there's* an excellent discussion topic for an episode of *Doctor Phil*," Scobie said.

"Might require a *double* episode," Ignatius suggested helpfully.

Razz grabbed his stomach.

"Oh, ho, ho. You guys should form a comedy team," he said, "but here's a little tip – just make sure neither of you is in it, OK?"

Then he turned his attention back to Bill.

"Come on, Hoop Boy. How come you'd pick Sally over me?"

"She can dance better than you... and I don't see you like *that*... at all."

"What?! Why not? Not good enough for you, is that it? Not *attractive* enough? You guys are all the same.

You don't give two hooters about brains or personality. It's all just looks, looks, looks to you lot. Well, I've got feelings too!"

Razz threw himself forward onto the table and sobbed silently.

"We can still be… friends," Bill said with a smile.

"Oh yeah, sure. The old 'just friends' brush-off, is it?" Razz said, dragging himself upright. "Well, it looks like I'll just have to go to the Lourdes Semi-formal without you, Bilbo, and Sal will get me on the rebound. Your loss, her gain."

As it turned out, things didn't go *quite* the way Razz had planned.

21.
Well and Truly Newtoned

When the day of the Lourdes College Semi-formal arrived, Razz found it harder than ever to concentrate in class. However, he did end up learning something that day. Ignatius described it as "a painful but valuable lesson in Newton's Third Law of Motion".

It happened at lunchtime in the gym. Razz was playing in the annual inter-house indoor football competition. He was captaining our Charlton House team and we were well ahead with only a few minutes to go. This was mainly because Razz was easily the best football player in the school and pretty much untouchable on the pitch. Or he was until Liam Bannerman touched him.

To be fair it wasn't really Liam Bannerman's fault. It's just that at one point in the match when Liam and Razz leaped to head the same ball, they collided in mid-air and Liam's substantially larger bulk caused Razz to be propelled rapidly towards the side wall. The result wasn't pretty. According to Prindabel this was entirely due to Newton's Third Law of Motion.

Ignatius explained it very nicely this way: "When object A (Razz's head) applies a force to object B (a solid masonry wall), then B (the solid masonry wall) applies an equal and opposite force to A (Razz's head)." Or in even more simple terms – when Razz's head hit the wall, the wall hit him back. The wall won. Poor Razz ended up well and truly Newtoned.

Mr Guthrie and Mr Hardcastle were the first ones on the scene. Mr Hardcastle held three fingers in front of Razz's eyes.

"How many fingers do I have, Orazio?"

Razz blinked his eyes and leaned forward. "You mean *apart* from those six?"

"Boarders' infirmary," Mr Hardcastle concluded. "Now!"

Mr Guthrie let Scobie and me hang around while the infirmary sister looked Razz over. She didn't waste any time with her diagnosis. "Bad case of concussion. Outside chance of a fractured skull."

But for Razz there was even worse news to come.

"He'll need to go to the hospital straight away for X-rays. Even if there's no fracture they'll probably want to keep him in overnight for observation."

"Whaaaat?" Razz slurred. "I can't do that. Can't. I gotta go to a Semi-normal tonight."

"He means Semi-*formal*," I explained, "at Lourdes College."

Razz turned a pair of glassy pinprick eyes to me. "Yeah, yeah, that's right, Prindabuggle. What *you* said. Tell 'em I can't go to hostipal… ah, hopstacle… um hot… I can't go there. Gotta take Sal to the semi-trailer."

Razz lost his appeal right then.

Mr Guthrie rang Mrs Zorzotto and arranged to meet her at the hospital. Scobie and I volunteered to go too but Sir said there wasn't much we could do, so he took my number and said he'd give me a ring when there was some news.

A couple of hours after I got home I finally got the phone call. Mr Guthrie said the X-ray showed there was no fracture and that Razz was much better but the doctor insisted he stay in overnight just to be on the safe side. About ten minutes later I got another call. I recognised the voice straight away.

"Razz! How're you feeling? You okay?"

"Yeah, yeah, I'm okay now, apart from the guy setting off landmines inside my head. But listen, man, you gotta help me. You gotta do me a massive favour."

"Yeah, sure, Razz, anything. Just name it."

Even as the words were coming out of my mouth I was wondering what I was getting myself into.

"Thanks, man. You're the only one who can do it. And I wouldn't ask you if it wasn't really important. I'll owe you big time, dude, big time."

Now my imagination was working overtime on horrendous possibilities. Had the collision somehow caused Razz to lose bladder control? Would he need someone to empty his bedpans? Or worse?

Razz's voice came pleading through the earpiece to put me out of my misery.

"You gotta take Sally to her Semi-formal for me, man."

I have to admit, compared to changing Razz's bedpan, taking Sally to the formal was quite a step up. I was still a bit surprised though.

"Me? Why?"

"Because she won't go otherwise. You gotta do it, man. Sal's been hanging out for this thing for ages. She's got a new dress and she's had her hair all done specially. She reckons she doesn't mind missing out on it, but she does, man. She'd be gutted. Her mum brought her up to visit me and I could tell she'd been crying. And it's all my stupid fault."

"Razz, you hardly head-butted the gym wall on purpose."

"Yeah, I know, man, I know, but I've still stuffed it up for her anyway without even trying. So come on, will you do it, Ishmael? It's her big night."

"But what does Sally think?"

"She wasn't going at all until I suggested you. You're the only other person she'll go with. That's what she said. Come on, man. She *really* wants to go. I can't take her. Will you do it? Please."

There was really only one answer I could give.

"Well, if you're absolutely *positive* Sally's okay with it. Then yeah, no problem."

"Awesome! That's great – thanks, man! You're a legend, dude, a real hero!"

That was a first. Razz calling me a hero. It certainly felt a lot better than him wanting to know what was wrong with me all the time. Ishmael Leseur – hero. It had a nice ring to it.

But I was about to find out whether it was true or not.

22.
Watch Your Back,
Billy Shakespeare

As soon as I got off the phone to Razz everything went into fast forward. Mum started ironing some clothes and I wolfed down half a sandwich then threw myself in the shower. Just as I was finished getting dressed Mrs Zorzotto arrived with a pretty cool jacket Razz had bought specially for the night as well as some roses he'd got for Sally. Then, less than an hour after agreeing to the whole thing, I was being dropped off by Razz's mum at the Nofkes' house.

Mrs Nofke met me at the door and took me into the lounge room. I was there talking to her and Mr Nofke about Razz's accident when Sally came in. I could tell you plenty of things about her. I could tell you the colour of her dress and what it looked like. And I could tell you about her long dark hair and how it was lifted up off her shoulders. I could tell you all that kind of stuff. But none of it would come close to telling you how beautiful she looked.

"Hey," she said with a smile.

Her smile was beautiful too. But there was something missing from it. And it was missing because of me. It was missing because I wasn't the one that Sally Nofke really wanted to be smiling at right then. I wasn't the one she wanted to look beautiful for.

I 'hey'-ed her back and handed over Razz's flowers. I told her how great she looked but it sounded pathetic and I frantically searched my mind for something better. I came up with "Really great". Genius! Watch your back, Billy Shakespeare. There's a new kid on the block! Sally blushed a little bit, then Mr Nofke left to get himself "organised" to drive us to the dance and Mrs Nofke said she'd better "pop those roses in some water" and then Sally and I were alone.

As soon as her parents were gone, a little crease formed in the middle of Sally's forehead as if she was feeling a pinprick of pain and her smile went all crooked. "Thanks for doing this, Ishmael," she said. "You don't mind *too* much, do you?"

"Mind? Are you kidding? I went to all the trouble of putting a contract out on Razz and hiring a hit man to throw him head first into a wall, didn't I?"

I know what you're wondering – *How does he come up with them?* At least Sally was nice enough to manage a laugh.

"Thanks, Ishmael. But really, I'm sorry for dragging you into this. You probably had loads of other things you wanted to do."

The amazing thing was that Sally seemed to actually believe there was a possibility this could be true.

"Well, Mum did want me to clean out the bottom of the budgie cage, so I was pretty disappointed about missing out on that. Anyway, I'm the one who should be saying sorry to you."

"You? Why?"

"For not being Razz."

Sally shook her head.

"Well then, I guess I should apologise to you too, shouldn't I? You know, for not being Kelly."

We both smiled then and I tried to imagine Kelly Faulkner standing there in front of me, but the image kept fading into Sally.

"You know what I think we should do?" she said. "I think tonight we should forget about who we're *not* and stick with who we *are* and just have fun. What do you think?"

"Sounds like a plan to me," I told her.

"Then here's to our plan and here's to us," Sally said, holding out an imaginary glass. I followed her lead and we clinked two invisible drinks together.

And for quite a while that night, our plan worked just fine. In fact I was enjoying myself so much that I started to feel a bit guilty. Here I was dancing, laughing and chatting with Sally while Razz was stuck in hospital thinking I was a hero.

I didn't deserve that title. True heroes had to face big challenges. They had to be put to the test. How could I be a hero then? Spending time with Sally Nofke at the Lourdes Semi-formal was easy. I wasn't being tested at all.

But I was about to be – and severely.

23.
Focusing is for Wimps!

The trouble started towards the end of the evening when Sally and I took a break from dancing. It was a muggy night and we were both melting, so we headed outside to a courtyard scattered with tables and benches to cool down. While Sally found a seat, I went to get us some drinks.

There was a big crowd ahead of me with the same idea. While I was queued up an elbow nudged me in the back. When I turned round I discovered it was connected to Danny Wallace. I'd spotted him a couple of times during the night but had managed to keep my distance. Now he was standing in front of me with a styrofoam cup in each hand.

"Hey, Leseur, got a couple spare lemonades here if you want 'em."

Now normally I'd avoid Danny Wallace not just like the plague but like any one of a number of contagious diseases capable of wiping out huge tracts of humanity. But right then my throat and mouth were so dry I was worried that if they didn't taste liquid soon, they might never talk to me again.

"Where'd they come from?"

"Got 'em for some friends, but they've gone off somewhere. Look, Leseur, you want 'em or not? Otherwise I'll dump 'em."

I checked out the mass of bodies ahead of me, then glanced over at Sally, who was flapping a hand in front of her flushed face, then back at the cups of cool, clear liquid.

"Yeah, all right, okay. Thanks."

Danny handed them over.

"No problems, Leseur. Us St Daniel's guys have to stick together and look out for each other, right?"

Not quite the words I ever thought I'd hear coming from Danny Wallace's mouth, but hey, maybe Mr Barker's "mature and responsible Seniors" talks were actually sinking in. Anyway, before I had a chance to reply, Danny Wallace was making his way over to a tight cluster of people in the far corner of the courtyard.

I looked at the two drinks. There were beads of condensation on the outside of the cups and they felt cool and moist in my hands. My throat, on the other hand, felt like it was coated with a mixture of dirt and roughly ground glass. I wove my way quickly to Sally.

"That was fast," she said as I handed her a cup.

All I could summon was a quick smile and a nod before I threw mine to my mouth and guzzled half the contents in one gulp. The remaining half was already sloshing its way down behind the first when a chain reaction of sensations shuddered through my body.

First up, the soothing serpent of liquid goodness that I had imagined snaking its way down my throat suddenly transformed itself into a roasting river of sizzling lava. After searing its way through my intestines and exploding in a fiery ball in my stomach, it rocketed straight up to my head, implementing a 'search and destroy' policy on my brain cells before finally bursting from my mouth in a wall of flames. To be totally honest, I didn't actually *see* flames shoot from my throat as I wheezed and choked like a misfiring jet engine, but I definitely *felt* them.

Sally must have had a similar experience, because when I finally stopped spluttering enough to look at her, she was puffing like she was trying to blow out those trick birthday candles and her eyes were watering. Luckily she hadn't gulped down all her drink like me.

She was huffing and blinking at a half-full cup in her hand.

"Where did you... get this from... This is... vodka... straight... vodka," she managed to gasp out between puffs of air.

I looked over at Danny Wallace and his friends. It wasn't easy. My eyes and brain seemed to be operating in wildly different time zones. But even through the blur I could see them pointing at Sally and me and doubling over with laughter. They were still cracking up as they all filed past us on their way back into the hall. Danny Wallace slapped me on the shoulder and said, "Smoooooooooooth, eh, Leshhhuer?" before laughing and tripping his way after his friends.

"Sorry, Sally. Supposed to be lemonade... My fault... Should have known Wallace... would do something stupid...like that."

I really should have. Razz once famously said that if Danny Wallace had three-quarters of his brain removed he'd still be overqualified at being himself. To which Danny retorted even more famously that if Razz had three-quarters of *his* brain removed he'd be a half-wit.

"Wouldn't be surprised... if Amanda Duggan put him up to it," Sally said, eyeing the blonde girl with Danny. "She'd just *love* to get me in trouble." Then Sally blew out a long breath, shook her head and blinked her eyes a couple of times. "Now I *really* need some water."

"I'll get it," I said, jumping to my feet.

Bad move. I didn't realise that my brain was just rolling around inside my skull like a blob of blancmange. After my head went for a wild spin and my eyes took a little wander about all by themselves, I landed back on the bench with a thump. I guess that's the sort of thing you have to expect when you only have half a sandwich for dinner, then proceed to totally dehydrate yourself on a dance floor before topping it all off by chugging down a large, full-to-the-brim cup of straight vodka.

"Whoa," Sally said, grabbing me by the shoulders to stop me from wobbling. "You wait here. I'll be right back. Try to stay upright."

I sat there by myself and concentrated on the challenging task Sally had set me. I was pleased that I succeeded in not face-kissing the paving, but no matter what I did my eyes just flatly refused to behave themselves. The only message getting through to my pupils seemed to be, 'Focusing is for wimps!'

"Here, drink this," Sally said, handing me a big styrofoam cup when she returned. "I've had one already."

I opened my mouth and poured. Never had a couple of hydrogen atoms with a single side order of oxygen tasted so good. Sally sat down beside me and popped the top off a can of cola. She took a long slow drink and sighed before passing the rest to me. "You might need this as well." I took it from her and showed remarkable restraint in not swallowing the can whole.

"Feeling better?"

I nodded and everything around me – the people, the lights, the tables and chairs and Sally – swirled and smudged before separating and settling back into place. I moved my head from side to side a little more slowly this time and watched the world blur and regroup. It was a bit like shaking up one of those snowglobes. It was kind of cool. I focused on the coloured lights around the entrance to the hall and swayed my head from side to side. They left little rainbow trails behind them.

"Ishmael, are you okay?"

"Huh?"

I turned to Sally. I was seeing her through a pair of soft-focus lenses. She was glowing. God, she was…

"I said, are you okay? I'm feeling a bit woozy and you had twice as much as me."

"No, no, I'm fine. Really. I was just checking out the lights. They're all swirly-whirly," I told her.

For some reason I found this highly amusing and had to stifle a laugh. Sally was looking at me strangely.

Or maybe I was looking at her strangely. Anyway, while all this strange looking was taking place, the music started up again in the hall and everyone else began wandering back inside.

"It might be a good idea if we stay out here and try to sober up a bit. What do you think?"

I nodded again. There was less swirly-whirly this time, just my head floating around like a fuzzy hotair balloon and everything slowing down a notch or two. I kept my eyes anchored on Sally to stop myself from drifting away. It felt like I wasn't really there. Like I was watching her on TV or at the movies or something. I looked closely at her face.

She really had great eyes – the colour of dark chocolate. I liked how they twinkled and how the skin at the side crinkled up when she laughed. I liked her twinkle and her crinkle. I tried not to giggle. I really liked her eyebrows too. I liked how dark they were and how they changed shape when she frowned or laughed or when she was sad or surprised. And her teeth. They were great. I liked the way they crept out from behind her lips when she smiled and how they weren't perfectly straight or even, but somehow still looked perfect.

And you know what else I liked? I liked the little strand of hair that had fallen from her braids and was hanging down against her cheek. And I liked that bit on the back of her neck, where it was pink from too much sun. Oh, and the one teeny freckle on the side of her nose. And the little 'M' shape that the middle of her top lip made. And the way…

"What? What is it?" Sally said, brushing her fingers across her mouth.

"Sorry?"

"What's the matter? What have I got on me? Is it something gross?"

"No, sorry, no, it's nothing. You're fine. There's nothing there, honest. It's nothing."

"You sure? You'd tell me if there was something wrong with me wouldn't you, Ishmael? You wouldn't let me walk around looking like a complete idiot, would you?"

"No, of course not. And there's nothing wrong with you…nothing at all."

"Then what were you staring at?"

"Nothing. I didn't know I was staring. I was just…"

"Just what?"

I knew how that sentence ended of course. *I was just … thinking how amazing and beautiful you are.* And that was the truth. I admit it. That's all I could think about as I stared at Sally Nofke. How amazing and beautiful she was. But there was no way in the world I was ever going to say those words to her.

"I was just thinking how amazing and beautiful you are."

What? I hadn't said that out loud, had I? No way! I looked at Sally. She was staring back at me. She gave a nervous laugh and fidgeted with her necklace.

"Yeah, right. I think that vodka might have knocked out more brain cells than we thought."

"No, no, it's true. You are. You're great. Really great."

Suddenly it was like my mouth had a mind of its own and it didn't care what it said.

"Everything about you is great. You're... incredible."

Sally's dark eyes were drilling into me like surgical probes. But even that wasn't enough to stop me.

"You're beautiful. You really are. You're so beautiful, it hurts."

All right, could someone put their hand over my mouth right now? How about masking tape? Anyone got any of that handy? A couple of spare socks, perhaps?

Sally's dark eyebrows pushed together in a frown and her nose wrinkled.

"Hurts? What do you mean?"

Nothing. Nothing at all. I don't mean anything. This isn't really me talking. No way! Some babbling lunatic has taken my vocal cords hostage and is forcing them to say crazy things.

"It's what my mum said once. She was talking about when Prue was born. You remember Prue, my little sister? You met her at my dad's concert."

"Scobie's number one fan."

"Yeah, that's her. She's a near-genius, you know. I'm not, by the way. Just in case you were wondering."

I giggled. Great! Now I was laughing at my own pathetically unfunny jokes. How cool! Luckily for me Sally was too nice not to smile.

"Well, I did have my doubts about your genius status after you had to drink a litre of vodka before you worked out it wasn't lemonade."

"Yes," I said, waving a finger at her, "but it's only my stupidity that gives me away."

Sally laughed this time and showed a little glimpse of her perfectly imperfect teeth before pressing her lips back together. God she had nice li—

"What were you going to say about Prue, and your mum?"

"What? Oh yeah, well, when Prue was born she was really premature. She was tiny and it didn't look like she was going to make it. For ages she was in one of those plastic cribby things with all the tubes and everything and all Mum and Dad could do was just watch her from the outside."

"How awful."

Sally's face folded and her eyes became little pools of sadness. She had so many ways of being beautiful.

"Mum told me one day it was the hardest thing she'd ever had to do. She said that it hurt just to look at Prue."

"Because she was so tiny and helpless?"

I glanced up at Sally Nofke. The light from the hall was shining in her eyes. She began to push that loose strand of hair behind her ear again but stopped when she saw me watching her.

"Yeah… and because she was so beautiful…"

Don't say it! Don't say it! DON'T SAY IT!

"… just like you…"

The corners of Sally's mouth crept up slightly then fell back down.

"… and because she was right there…"

OK, that's enough. You've made your point. You can SHUT UP NOW!

"… and she was so close…"

The rest of the world was just some fuzzy, muffled place. There was only Sally and me.

"… but you weren't allowed to touch her."

Don't do it! Don't do it! DON'T DO IT!

I did it.

I moved closer and I leaned forward.

My best mate, the one who thought I was a legend and a hero, was at that very moment lying in a hospital bed – suffering from concussion. And I was kissing his girlfriend.

What was *WRONG* with me!

24.
Did I Mention
I Was an Idiot?

As I kissed Sally Nofke that night, every atom in my body was screaming out, "See, Cindy, now *that's* what I'm talkin' about!" I was hoping it would never end, but it did, and only after a few seconds. That's when Sally pulled away and her eyes clouded over.

She was shaking her head and staring at me like I was one of the walking dead – and obviously one of the least appealing ones.

"What am I *doing*? This *can't* be happening."

"Sal, I'm sorry. That was wrong. I shouldn't have done that. I'm an idiot. I am. I really am. I'm sorry. I'm an idiot."

The look of horror was swamped by confusion and Sally just sat gazing at the ground and shaking her head.

"But it wasn't just you," she said.

"Doesn't matter. I started it. I'm an idiot. It was wrong. It was stupid. Did I mention I was an idiot?"

We sat without speaking for quite a while, every now

and then catching each other's eyes. Finally I worked up the nerve to say something.

"I think maybe you were right about the vodka killing off a whole bunch of my brain cells. And I didn't have that many to spare to begin with. They should have been on the endangered species list."

A little scrunched-up smile came to Sally's lips.

"I feel awful."

"Sal, it wasn't your fault. Nothing would have happened if it wasn't for me."

"Maybe. But I didn't stop you, and it's not just the… kissing thing," she said, and shot a shy look my way.

"What do you mean?"

"Well… at the start of the night, all the time I was with you, I was thinking about Razz and wishing I was with him and not you. Sorry, that sounds really terrible, doesn't it?"

"Don't worry about it."

"Anyway, after a while I decided I was going to have the best night I could, so I tried not to think about Razz."

"Nothing wrong with that."

"No, but then I sort of stopped thinking about him without really trying."

Sally looked away and picked at the hem of her dress.

"And then... when I did think about Razz again it was because I was wondering... who I'd rather be with... you or him."

I couldn't really believe what I was hearing. Sally turned to me with all her painful beauty on show.

"I even wondered what it would have been like if Razz and I hadn't met and there was just you and me. Maybe that's why I didn't stop you."

Sally placed her hand on mine.

"I *really* like you, Ishmael. I do. You're a great guy. Any girl would be lucky to have you... but..."

She didn't have to say anything more. That "but" said it all.

"Sorry," she whispered.

"Hey, no problem," I told her. "If I had to choose between Razz and me, I'd choose Razz too."

Sally smiled with her lips together and squeezed my hand.

"I've had such a lovely night. I don't want anything to spoil it. Do you mind if we just rewind and edit out that last bit?"

"Sure. And I know my head would be really grateful if we could go right back and edit out Danny Wallace and the vodka as well."

"Good idea. And make sure you cut out Amanda

Duggan too. Oh, and that bit where I looked like a cat coughing up a fur ball."

"Ah yes. That would be the same bit where I looked like I was coughing up an entire cat."

It wasn't really that funny but Sally and I both laughed. And then we couldn't stop. Every time we looked at each other we started up again. In the end we were both bumping our shoulders together and wiping tears from our eyes. When I recovered enough to form decipherable words, there was only one question I wanted to ask.

"Sal, you know when I do that editing?"

She nodded.

"Can I leave just one little bit in?"

"Which bit?"

"The bit where I tell you how amazing and beautiful you are?"

Sally's bottom lip pushed up and a little crease appeared in her chin. I thought for a minute she was going to cry. But she leaned forward, kissed my cheek and hugged me. Then she sat back and pointed a finger at me.

"Ishmael, if you try to edit *that* bit out," she said, "I will personally break your face." She sounded like she meant it too.

The Semi finished in a bit of a rush after that. The highlight came when Danny Wallace (who had obviously over-indulged in the 'lemonades') threw up impressively all down Amanda Duggan's back during a passionate embrace on the dance floor. That more or less brought an end to the night and Sally and I walked together to the front gate where Mr Nofke was waiting to pick us up.

Back home I lay in bed replaying every minute of the Semi-formal in my mind. When I came to the kissing bit I even did what Sally asked. I edited it out. But I didn't throw it away. I couldn't. Instead I played it on a continuous loop in my mind. And as I did, one thought kept slinking into my head. It was this. *If Razz wasn't around, my life could be perfect right now.*

I had finally figured out what was wrong with me.

I was a total scumbag.

25.
Here, Pass Me One of Those Knives

"**Y**ou're a total legend, man!"

It was before school. I was in our form room finishing off some English homework when Razz grabbed me by the shoulders and gave me a friendly shake.

"Sally reckons you were awesome on the weekend. I owe you big time, dude. You really stepped up to the plate."

"It was no big deal, Razz. Really. Forget it."

"Don't you 'no big deal' me, man! If it wasn't for you, Sal would've missed out on wearing her new dress and getting all done up and hanging out with her friends and everything. Plus she reckons she had a lot of fun. Not *too* much fun, I hope, or I'll have to kill you!"

He already was. After what happened with Sally, every nice thing Razz said about me felt like a knife in the gut. (Not that I've ever had a knife in the gut, but I'm guessing it wouldn't be one of my favourite things.)

Razz patted me on the back again and climbed into the next seat.

"Hey, how's the head?" I asked him.

"Not bad – a bit tender. They let me out of hospital on Sunday morning. Just said to take it easy for a bit."

"Well, you'll be thrilled to know that the wall is expected to make a full recovery."

"So humorous. Have you been working on that one all weekend?" Then he peered at my workbook. "Whatcha doing, anyway?"

"*Hamlet*. You know, we had that Claudius soliloquy to go through before today's lesson."

"Guess you would've got it done on the weekend if you weren't helping me and Sal out. Sorry, man. I really owe you one."

Anyone for another knife in the gut?

"It's okay, Razz, really. It was nothing. Just forget it."

I figured it was time to change the subject, so I pointed to my open copy of *Hamlet*.

"You looked at this yet?"

"Nah, but I got a rolled-gold excuse, man. Concussion, hospital, doctor's certificate, letter from my mother – it doesn't get much better than that. Even Slats will be impressed."

Razz pulled my play book towards him and began

reading. '*O, my offence is rank, it smells to heaven.*' Man, what's old Claudius going on about there? Hasn't had an accident in his pants or something, has he?"

"Not quite. He's talking about him killing Hamlet's father and marrying his mother. He's feeling guilty."

Get in line, Claudius.

"Yeah, and so he should, man. Those two dudes were brothers, eh? Hamlet's dad should've been able to trust his brother. Some brother he turned out to be."

The old gut was starting to feel like a pincushion now.

"Geez, and what's he on about here? '*My stronger guilt defeats my strong intent, and like a man to double business bound, I stand in pause where I shall first begin*'."

"Not sure, but Claudius is praying, so I think he wants to be forgiven, but he feels too guilty to ask for it. Something like that."

Here, pass me one of those knives, I'll save you the trouble and just stab myself for a while.

Luckily, before Razz had the chance to ask more questions, I was rescued by Scobie, Bill and Ignatius wandering into the room.

"Orazio, welcome back to the land of the living. How's the head?"

"No worries, Scobes. Tried to tell 'em there was nothing wrong with me at the hospital but they wouldn't listen."

James and the other two dragged some chairs in and sat around our desk.

"Did they do any tests?"

"Sure did, Prindabuddy. They were poking me and shining things in any opening they could find and tapping my knees and elbows with these crazy little hammers. It was wild. They even did some kind of a brain scan thingy on me."

"Really?" Ignatius said, "and did they find one?"

Razz twisted his mouth up Scobie-style and waited while Bill and Ignatius snorted and hissed and bumped their fists together in celebration of Prindabel's joke. Scobie just clamped his mouth closed in a thin smile and gave it his customary nod of approval.

"You know, P-buddy, for *you* that actually wasn't too bad. That was *almost* mildly humorous. What's happening, man? You haven't gone and downloaded a personality off some dodgy internet site, have you?"

Ignatius brushed Razz's comments aside and sat bathing in the warmth of his rare witticism.

"What was the food like, Razz?"

"Not bad, Hoop Boy. They did a very nice range of 'bland' with some delightful and creative side dishes of 'What the hell *is* that?' Hey, but you guys want to hear something *really* interesting?"

No one had an objection to this.

"Okay. Because I couldn't go to the shower alone in case I passed out or something, one of the nurses had to give me… a *sponge* bath. You know what that is? It's where you're naked in the bed… and then they wash you… with a *sponge*. That's why it's called… a *sponge* bath."

Glances bounced and ricocheted around the group and everyone automatically crept in closer.

"Yeah, that's right," Razz continued, "and guess who gave me my *sponge* bath? One of the really young nurses… maybe only about twenty or so… good-looking… and *really* built."

Razz stopped and sat back.

"Yes, *and*?"

"And *what*, Prindabuddy?"

"And what was it *like*?"

"Not bad, but *personally*, I would have preferred to have one of the *female* nurses do it."

Groans filled the air and the tight circle pushed back.

"You guys are making it too easy," Razz said. "Where's the challenge? And Billy, stop drooling, man. It's not a good look."

That afternoon in English, Mr Slattery went through the Claudius soliloquy in painstaking detail. While I wasn't *quite* in the Big C's league (after all, kissing your best friend's girlfriend didn't quite match up with murdering the king and stealing his wife), I could certainly relate to the feeling guilty thing as well as the 'wanting to do something about it' part.

I carried that feeling around inside me for the next few weeks. Razz was still Razz, and I was still me, but it felt like there was a shadow or a curtain between us that only I could see.

It wasn't until the very last day before the holidays that I finally decided I had to try and make it go away.

26.
Fatal Flaw
Thingies

The second term concluded with a full school assembly in the gymnasium. After we were dismissed Razz and I hung around for a while helping Miss Tarango carry some boxes of "holiday marking" to her car. "The joys of being an English teacher" she called it.

By the time we were finished we'd missed the first buses. We were sitting on the brick fence out the front of the school with about a twenty-minute wait ahead of us. I didn't really mind. I'd been looking for a chance to talk to Razz all day. But it still took me a while to work up the courage to speak, and even longer to find a break in the usual avalanche of words that was pouring from Razz's mouth. Eventually a rare pause appeared and I pounced.

"Hey, Razz, we're going down to the beach for most of the break, so I probably won't see you till next term…

and there's um… some *stuff*… I think you need to know."

The mop of black hair beside me stopped bobbing to some inner beat and a serious face turned my way. "If this is about the birds and the bees, I'm totally cool with all that already, man."

"Razz, I'm serious. This is important. There's something I have to… Something I *want* to tell you… about me."

Razz looked worried. "Wait, you're not going to pull a Bill Kingsley on me, are you?"

"What? What?! No! Why would you even *think* that?"

"Well, let me see," Razz said. "First we had the Cindy thing and then we had the Jess thing…"

"Hey, I explained about Cindy! *And* I seem to recall that 'Jess thing' worked out pretty good for you with Sally."

"Okay, forget Cindy and Jess then. But what about the time we saw that smokin' chick jogging around that oval in those little shorts and top?"

"What about it?"

"Well, *you* said you liked the way her ponytail went from side to side while she was running. You said it looked *cute*. Remember?"

"Yeah, so what?"

"So *what*?" Razz said, staring at me in disbelief.

"Of all the awesome parts of that chick that were moving and wobbling about, you were watching her *ponytail*?"

"Look, this is stupid. I'm not like Bill and you *know* it. If I was there wouldn't have been any 'Kelly thing', would there? And we wouldn't even be having this stupid conversation because I wouldn't have this... *other* thing... I have to tell you... which I wish I didn't... but I do."

I guess even Razz could tell from my voice that this might be serious.

"Okay. Sorry, man. Go ahead. Let me have it."

"Well, it's just... something happened and I think you should know about it. I sort of *did* something and I didn't really mean to... or maybe I did, I don't know any more... But anyway, it was wrong and I feel bad and if I could take it back I would because it was all my fault. No one else's. Look, it's just that..."

Razz squinted hard at me.

"Is this about you kissing Sally at the Lourdes Semi-formal?"

"What?! You *know* about that?"

"Yeah."

"But how?"

"Sally told me."

"When?"

"The weekend after the Semi. She came over to watch some videos. She was really quiet. I asked her what was wrong. That's when she told me about it. Said she felt bad. Didn't like having secrets. Except then, she told me not to tell you, about her telling me. So go figure."

I looked at Razz's face. I couldn't work out what was going on behind it.

"And when she told you… you were… *okay* with it?"

"Are you jokin', man? I wanted to smash you. I really did."

"Then what changed your mind?"

"Changed my mind? Who said I changed my mind? I've just been waiting for a chance to get you alone without any witnesses…" Razz stopped suddenly and did a 360-degree sweep of the deserted horizon. "Hey, waaaaaaaaaaaait a minute…"

Then he laughed. But not very much.

"Razz, I'm sorry. I really am. I don't know what happened. I didn't mean it to happen. It just did. I wouldn't blame you if you did smash me."

"Nah, it's all right, man. Sal told me about Wallace and the booze and everything. Man, that guy gives morons a bad name. She explained everything. I'm totally cool with it all now. Besides, I still owe you for saving my neck in that whole Jess thing."

"I still feel like crap about it. You're my friend. My best friend. I shouldn't have done it. Ever. Even if I had a dozen vodkas."

"A dozen vodkas? You? Dude, if you had a dozen vodkas even Danny Wallace would've got a snog. That's if they didn't have to give *you* the kiss of life first."

We both smiled. Then we ran out of things to say for a while. It was Razz who came up with something first.

"If you want to know the truth, man, when Sal told me about what happened, I was more scared than angry."

"Scared? Scared of what?"

"Of loads of stuff. Scared that Sal would choose you instead of me. Scared I'd lost her. Scared that it would muck everything up. Muck *us* up."

Razz looked away into the distance.

"There's no way you're going to lose her, Razz. Sally likes you a lot. It's a real failing on her part, but she does. You got nothing to worry about. Nothing at all."

"Yeah, maybe." He didn't seem too convinced so I decided to convince him.

"You know what she said to me that night?"

Razz turned a little my way.

"She told me… that all the time she was with me, even when she was having fun… all she was thinking about… was you."

Razz's eyes lit up.

"Really, man? You're not just saying that?"

"Her exact words."

Some of her exact words anyway. Things went quiet again after that until I noticed a smile creeping its way onto Razz's face.

"What? What is it?"

"I can't believe you told me. I can't believe you actually 'fessed up, about you and Sally, even when you didn't have to. Anyone else would've kept their mouth shut. But not you, man."

Razz was grinning and shaking his head.

"Yeah, yeah, go on. Let's hear it. I know what you're going to say. There's something wrong with me, right?"

"Oh, there *is*," Razz said. "There *definitely* is. And I think I've just figured out what. You're like Hamlet, dude. You are. You both think too much about stuff and you've both got one of those 'fatal flaw' thingies that Slattery keeps going on about."

"Fatal flaw thingies? Wow, Razz, I'm impressed. Don't tell me you've actually been listening in class."

"Sometimes I just can't help it."

"So what's my fatal flaw then?"

"Isn't it obvious, man? You're too nice. That's your big problem. You always have to do the right thing all the time. That's why you need me around to sort of balance things out."

"I knew there had to be a reason for putting up with you," I said.

"Yeah, we make a good team," Razz said. Then he clicked his fingers and pointed at me. "Hey, I just thought. If you're Hamlet then that makes me that Horatio dude."

"My good friend, I'll exchange that name with you."

"Huh?"

"That's what Hamlet tells Horatio – that he's happy to call him a friend."

"Cool! How do you remember that stuff? I'm hopeless."

"Don't know. I guess it just gets stuck in my head. But anyway, I don't know about you being Horatio. I got a feeling he wasn't quite as 'out there' as you."

"Really? Well maybe I'm the extreme version. Or maybe I'm like one of those cyborgs. You know, part Horatio, part Orazio."

"Horazio?" I suggested. I didn't think it was that funny but Razz slapped his knees and almost busted a gut laughing.

"Horazio! Man, I'll pay that, Ishmael! That is gold!"

Just then a bus pulled around the corner at the end

of the street. It was Razz's. He hopped off the fence and threw his bag over his shoulder.

"See ya, man. Give us a call when you get back from the beach."

"Yeah, okay. And Razz… Thanks… You know…"

"Forget it," Razz said and jumped on the bus. He swiped his card, found a seat then stuck his head out the side window and shouted, "Farewell, sweet prince! May ummm… like, heaps of angels… ummm… do really good stuff to you!"

Razz's fellow passengers gawked at him. Since they were gawking already I thought I might as well make it worth their while.

"Farewell, Horazio!" I shouted back, "I will keep thee in my heart's core, in my heart of hearts."

As I waited for my bus, I wondered how Razz was going to go with the assessment we had coming up after the break. I mean, if he really did have trouble remembering quotes, then our *Hamlet* orals were probably going to cause him a fair amount of grief.

For once I was right. I just had no idea how right.

27.
The Return of
the Brainiacs

We had finally made it into the last term of the year and the teachers weren't about to let us forget it. They kept going on about how important it was and how short it was and how much our final assignments and exams would affect our overall grades. All that was true, of course. But apart from the *Hamlet* orals, what I was most concerned about was our Semi-formal.

Unlike the Lourdes Semi-formal, ours was traditionally held in the last week of school when exams were over. As well as a dance and a celebration of the year, it also marked the moment when our year group officially took over as school leaders. It was still a couple of months away, but the pressure to find someone to take was already starting to build.

The thing is, if you were going to go to the Semi-formal you had to have a partner. No exceptions. If you were so embarrassingly hopeless that you couldn't get your own partner, you were paired up with one of the girls invited in bulk from one of the local colleges. This provided you with the unique opportunity of being seen as a total loser. Now that very real possibility was looming ever larger for me. All I could think of was how brilliant my life would have been if Kelly hadn't left and I was taking her to the Semi.

But what was the point in torturing myself? Kelly was gone. And every day that passed, she was drifting further and further away. It was ages since I'd got an email from her and the last one she sent didn't really say much. Even Sally reckoned she wasn't getting any news. As much as I could, I tried to push the whole Semi-formal, no-partner, total-loser thing out of my mind. But one lunchtime, thanks to Razz, it became the main topic of discussion.

Scobie, Bill, Ignatius and I were eating at one of the tables in the Seniors' quadrangle when the man himself bounded in to join us.

"Hey, guys, I was just thinking we better get in early and organise a table for the Semi-formal so we can all be together. It'll be massive."

"I'm not going."

A table full of eyes rotated to Bill.

"No point," he said with the regular Kingsley shrug.

"I've got no one to take. And even if I did…"

"Why don't you get yourself matched up with some chick for the night, Billy Boy? You just have to talk and dance. You don't have to marry her. And we'll all be there."

Bill shook his head. He wasn't about to change his mind.

"Well, what about you, Prindabundle? You don't mind being matched up with some chick and making her miserable for a night, do you?"

Ignatius looked at Razz blankly.

"I have my own partner."

Razz reared back like he'd taken the full impact of a bazooka to the body.

"What?! Geez, Prindabudster," Razz said, grabbing his chest, "I thought you were serious for a minute there. You know, you shouldn't joke about stuff like that. You could've given me a heart attack. There are certain basic laws of the universe that we human beings have grown to trust. Stuff like gravity and the sun being the centre of our solar system and you being a total no-go area for chicks."

"Then prepare yourself for possible acute myocardial infarction, Orazio, because it's true. I do have a partner for the Semi-formal."

Razz leaned in close to Ignatius and gave him an understanding smile.

"Prindabubbles. P-bud. You do realise that when we talk about 'partner' it doesn't include your laptop, even if you *have* gone to all the trouble of downloading a screen saver with a chick's face on it. And I'm pretty sure that it's also against the school rules for your Semi 'partner' to be anything you have either built in a laboratory, cloned, inflated or brought back to life using electrodes attached to the brain."

Ignatius listened patiently then said, "Well, I think I'm fine then."

Razz was about to say something else but Scobie beat him to it.

"Who is she, Ignatius?"

"Maude Everingham. She's from Morley Girls' College. You met her, James. She was at the Accelerated Science Course weekend we went to."

We all turned to Scobie. He raised his eyebrows.

"Outstanding."

"What?" Razz broke in. "Really? The P-man has actually landed a genuine real live chick-type person *without* the use of chloroform or a spring-loaded net?"

"Absolutely," Scobie said.

"Prindabuddy, you legend! How'd you do it, man? Come on, tell us all about it."

"Well," said Ignatius, becoming almost animated, "it was during the Accelerated Chemistry class. We were doing a quantitative chemical analysis involving a diprotic acid titrated with a strong base to establish equivalence points."

"Just keep talking, P-bud," Razz said. "Eventually, just on the law of averages, you'll accidentally say something that I understand."

"We were doing a titration experiment, Orazio."

Razz stared blankly ahead.

"Well, anyway, at the end of the analysis," Ignatius continued, "we had to compare our results with someone else. Maude was working at the bench beside me so I asked if I could see her titration curves and she said yes."

"What?! You've only just met and already she's showing you her titration curves! You don't waste any time, do you? You da man, Prindabuster! You da man!"

Ignatius looked confused but kept going.

"Anyway, I examined hers and then she had a look at mine…"

"Oh my god, cover your ears, Ishmael!"

"… Then we talked a bit while we washed out our pipettes and burettes…"

"Stop it, man! There are children present!"

"… And that's how we met. At the end of the course

we exchanged emails. Last weekend we went to the Da Vinci exhibition at the museum. That's where I asked her about coming to the Semi-formal. She said yes again."

Ignatius linked his spidery fingers together and smiled at us.

"Excellent work," Scobie said as Bill and Ignatius exchanged a dangerously off centre high-five and I managed to hide my 'Oh-my-god-even-Ignatius-has-got-someone-to-take-to-the-Semi-so-what's-wrong with-me?' face behind a cheesy grin.

"Prindabundle, you rock! I was wrong about you, dude. You are smooth, man. Super-smooth! You are so smooth they could lay you down and use you for a golf tee."

Ignatius thought about that for a second and then held aloft the infamous objection finger.

"Or," he said, "I'm so smooth... my coefficient of friction is zero."

"P-buddy," Razz said with glazed eyes and a shake of his head, "you are the undisputed king of geek humour."

Ignatius obviously thought so too. It took quite a while for him to control his fit of hissing laughter. When he did, Razz turned his attention to James.

"Well, that's me and Sally and P-buddy and the Titration Queen. What about you, Herr Scobmeister – got a fraulein lined up?"

Scobie shifted in his seat. His mouth did a bit of a twist-a-thon and his cheeks were dabbed with two pink blobs.

"Wait a minute," Razz said with an ever-widening smirk. "What am I thinking? Of course Scobes has someone lined up. Someone's hot little sister, perhaps?"

Scobie's cheeks laid down another coat of crimson.

"Aha! I thought as much. Scobes and Prudles back together – *The Return of the Brainiacs!*"

Scobie glanced my way. "Well, actually, now that Orazio has brought it up, I *was* thinking… as long as you were all right with it, Ishmael… and your parents agreed… and of course if Prue wanted to in the first place… that maybe…"

"I'm sure Mum and Dad will be okay with it. And it's fine with me," I told him. (Except of course for that bit where now even my little sister in the year *below* had a partner for *my* Semi-formal while *I* didn't. I could almost feel the big capital 'L' sizzling into my forehead.)

"And we *all* know that Prudles will be raring to go," Razz said. "Cool! So we got Sal and Me, Mr and Mrs Chemical Analysis and the Mensa Twins all signed up. That just leaves you, Ishmael. You got any ideas yet?"

The spotlight swung round and fell on me. Great.

"About what?"

"Ah, about how to reverse the disintegration of the polar ice caps, of course," Razz said brightly before adding with an impatient sigh, "About who you could invite to the Semi-formal."

"I haven't really thought much about it."

Liar.

"Anyway, there's plenty of time to work something out."

Liar.

"Besides, I'm a bit like Bill, I don't even know if I really want to go to the Semi or not yet."

Pants on fire!

"Don't be stupid, man, of *course* you gotta come. And don't worry, dude. There's still time. I'll figure something out. Rest easy, because the Razzman is on your case, working his magic."

As I stared at the ridiculously over-confident face before me, I couldn't help thinking how Razz's 'magic' often had the potential to go horribly wrong and when it did, I usually ended up being the one who got sawn in half. As it turned out, it wasn't me, it was the Razzman who was headed for trouble. He didn't get cut in two or blown up or anything (not literally anyway), but he was about to get king hit with ten straight days of after-school detentions.

And it was all because of Bilbo, the Bard and the Melancholy Dane.

28.
Windy Perspiration of Horse Breath

Scobie was really the one who started the whole thing rolling. After all, it was his idea to use the room we'd pre-booked for possible debating finals meetings to work on our *Hamlet* orals together. For the orals we had to choose a passage from *Hamlet*, perform it in front of the class, explain it in detail and then analyse its relevance to the overall play and to society today. A piece of cake! Except for that bit about performing the passage in front of the class, explaining it in detail and analysing its relevance to the overall play and to society today. That part was going to be tricky.

Anyway, we all thought Scobie's idea about practising together was great. Mainly because James was the expert on Shakespeare and we would be able to pick his brains. At first we concentrated on the performances. We didn't have to use props and costumes if we didn't want to, but we had to know our lines off by heart. As I predicted that afternoon at the bus stop, Razz struggled a little with this.

"What extract are you doing, Orazio?"

Razz flicked through his play book then placed it in front of Scobie and pressed it flat.

"That bit there, Scobes. Hammy talking to his mum."

"Okay. Fine. I'll read a couple of the queen's lines to lead you in and then you start."

Razz set himself up and posed with a steely gaze. Scobie and I were down the back of the classroom to check volume. Bill and Ignatius were up the front. Prindabel was prompting and Bill was finishing off his lunch. Scobie started reading.

"Thou know'st 'tis common; all that lives must die. Why seems it so particular with thee?"

Suddenly Razz leaped forward and angrily smashed his fist down hard on Bill's desk. The rest of us jumped. Bill spilled iced coffee down his chin.

"SEEMS, madam! Nay it IS! I know not 'SEEMS!'"

After the initial shock passed, we were all pretty impressed. We waited to hear more, but Razz stood motionless out the front like a very cross shop dummy.

Prindabel's whispered voice crept in from the side. *"'Tis not alone my inky cloak, good mother…"*

Razz sprang into life like someone had released the

Pause button. "Yeah, that's right, I know, I know, don't tell me, don't tell me. 'Tis not alone this stinky cloak, good mother."

"*Inky* cloak, not *stinky* cloak," Prindabel interjected.

"Inky? You sure? What's he got ink on his cloak for?"

"There is no ink," Scobie said patiently. "His coat is black – the *colour* of ink. He's wearing black because his father, the king, has died recently, remember."

"Okay, okay, okay. I got it."

Razz steadied himself and focused.

SLAM! His fist hit Bill's desk again. We all jumped again. Bill dropped his iced coffee into his lap.

"*SEEMS*, madam! Nay it *IS*! I know not '*SEEMS!*'... Ummmm... Aw, yeah, it's not just my *inky* cloak, good mother or... um not just my umm... is it something about his *pants*?"

Prindabel shook his head. "*Nor my customary suits of solemn black.*"

"Yeah, right. Nor my cassowary shoes of swollen cats."

Ignatius jerked his head up from his play book but Scobie signalled for him just to keep going.

"*Nor windy suspiration of forced breath.*"

"Ah yeah, of course. Nor windy perspiration of horse breath."

Scobie held up his hand to Ignatius like a traffic cop.

"Orazio, have you even tried to learn any of this?"

"Yeah, of course – sure, Scobes."

"That's not how it seems."

SLAM!

"*SEEMS*, Scobie! Nay it *IS*! I know not '*SEEMS!*'"

Bill dried his face with his shirt sleeve.

"Orazio, we appreciate that you've nailed that first line, but what about the rest of it?"

"I tried, Scobes, but how can you remember something that doesn't make any sense to you?" Razz grabbed the play book from Ignatius. "Like, what's 'windy suspiration of forced breath' anyway?"

"Heavy sighing," Scobie said.

"Yeah, okay, I started off with an easy one, but what's 'the fruitful river in the eye' or 'the dejected 'havior of the visage'?"

"First one's tears and the second one is a sad face. Look, Orazio, Hamlet's just explaining to Gertrude that he's not putting on a show or pretending to be sad by sighing and crying and wearing black. He's saying that he doesn't merely *seem* sad, he actually *is* sad. His sorrow is real. All those other things are just like accessories a person could wear to make themselves *appear* sad. They are the 'trappings and the suits of woe'. It all ties into one of the major themes of the play – appearance versus reality."

"Yeah, well, Slattery should have explained all that to us."

"I think you'll find he did," Scobie said.

"Oh."

"Anyway, why pick that passage in the first place if you couldn't understand it?"

"Well, we had to choose one that was at least ten lines long, didn't we? This one's cool 'cause it's only got eleven."

"That's all right then," Scobie said. "For a minute there I was worried you didn't have a good reason."

Razz took a break after that to work on memorising his lines and the rest of us had our turns. Ignatius was next up doing a pretty fair job as the ghost of Hamlet's father, "*Doomed for a certain time to walk the night*". Razz considered this an excellent choice because he said that Ignatius wouldn't need much make-up to play a dead person. I followed Ignatius with the Claudius guilty speech. At least it was something I could relate to. I think I went okay. Nowhere near as good as Scobie, of course, who was word-perfect and as brilliant as always with the classic '*To be or not to be*'.

The last one up was Bill. He was playing Polonius in the scene where he gives advice to his son Laertes. Bill started off well.

> "... *Give thy thoughts no tongue,*
> *Nor any unproportioned thought his act.*
> *Be thou familiar, but by no means vulgar.*
> *Those friends thou hast, and their adoption tried,*
> *Grapple them unto thy soul with hoops of steel.*"

"What?" Razz interrupted, looking up from his lines and completely breaking Bill's train of thought. "Who has this guy adopted and wrapped up in heaps of steel?"

Scobie threw his head back and muttered something at the ceiling. Bill, as always, didn't seem to mind that much.

"It's just Polonius telling Laertes that if he finds really good friends, then he should hold on to them and keep them close. That's what 'grapple them unto thy soul with hoops of steel' means, doesn't it, Scobie? Sort of like they're so important you should tie them to you with the strongest thing you can find."

Scobie nodded.

"Carbon nanotubes would be better," Ignatius said.

Everyone looked at him.

"Carbon nanotubes. They're these tiny particles that they think might be hundreds of times stronger than steel. If you wanted something *really* strong, that would be the material to make it out of."

"Grapple them unto thy soul with hoops of carbon nanotubes," Scobie said. "I think perhaps we should stick with the original text just for the present. You want to take it from the top, Bill... before I scream?"

"Scream? I KNOW NOT 'SCREAM'!" Razz shouted.

On his second go Bill made it right through without forgetting a word. He was good too, especially when he got to the last part.

> *"This above all: to thine own self be true,*
> *And it must follow, as the night the day,*
> *Thou canst not then be false to any man."*

Bill really put a lot of feeling into that bit. When he finished we gave him a burst of applause. I guess I wasn't the only one who could relate to their chosen *Hamlet* passage.

We had three more practices in the few weeks after that. Razz got a lot better at remembering his lines once Scobie explained them all to him. But in the end it wasn't the acting part of the *Hamlet* orals that would cause Razz grief. It wasn't even his presentation.

It was Bill's.

29.
Don't Disturb the
Piranhas, Dude

We had one more practice together before the *Hamlet* orals commenced. We'd all run through our talks a couple of times over the previous sessions. All of us, that is, except Bill.

Bill was fine with his Polonius speech but was having trouble with some parts of his analysis. In our last practice session he was finally going to try a full run-through. The rest of us were spread around the room. Razz was sitting beside me with his head propped on the back of his chair and his body stretched forward in a straight line at an angle of about thirty degrees to the floor. His eyes were closed. He could have been asleep. Or in a coma. Listening to other people talk took a lot out of Razz.

Bill got under way. His explanation of the passage and its importance to the overall play was good. Then he went on to the very last part where he tackled the issue of the relevance of the extract to society today. He looked up from his sheets of paper and hesitated a moment before continuing.

"I feel that the major relevance of Polonius's speech to society today is found in the line, 'To thine own self be true'. Even though in many ways the world today is more open and tolerant than it was in the past, there are still many areas where people are discriminated against or persecuted because of their beliefs, background or culture, or for just trying to be true to who and what they are. This can be seen particularly in the issue of sexual preference."

Beside me Razz raised his head slowly off the back of the chair.

"For example, many gay men and women today are still unable to be true to who they really are because of the prejudice and discrimination that unfortunately still exist in today's world. I can personally relate to this—"

Beside me, a body catapulted forward like it had been expelled from an ejector seat. Razz snatched Bill's speech from him and his eyes did high-speed laps back and forth across the page. Then he stopped and looked at Bill in horror.

"Are you mad, Bilbo? You can't say this!"

"Why not? It's true."

"Lots of things are true, man. Like Ms Heckenvaal's got a backside the size of a small country, but if you've got any brains at all you don't say it out loud."

"What, so I should go around hiding and pretending I'm something that I'm not?"

"Now you're getting the idea, Billy Boy!" Razz said, jabbing his arm. "Just till we leave school for good, man. Then you can jump out of a cake in a tutu if that's your idea of a good time."

"Why should I wait till then? I'm not ashamed of what I am."

"It's not about being ashamed. It's about self-preservation, dude. You think my Uncle Georgiou got around in his Show Tunes costumes when he was at school? Billy, listen to me. School is like… like crossing a big stream, okay? On the other side of the stream is life after school and that's where you're headed, see. But first you have to get *all* the way across the stream safely. Are you with me?"

"I think so," Bill said, looking about as convinced as the rest of us.

"Cool. But here's the thing. In the stream – which, remember, is really *school* – there are these flesh-eating piranha. Not loads of them, but enough. So Billy, all I'm saying is, while you're crossing the stream – don't disturb the piranhas, dude. Just wait till you get *out* of the stream and then you can find a nice safe pool where you can splash around and practise your synchronised swimming moves as much as you like."

"Well, thanks, Razz I'll be sure to keep that in mind next time I'm in the Amazon."

"No, Bilbo. You don't understand. See, it's not a *real* stream or *real* piranha, it's actually…"

"Yes, I get it, Razz. But you guys know and it didn't make any difference."

Razz draped an arm around Bill's wide shoulders.

"That's because we're all wonderful human beings. But sadly there are some people in our happy school community here at St Daniel's – the ones with calluses on their knuckles from too much scraping along the ground when they walk, for example – who are different. Geez, Billy, you should know that. Remember how Bagsley and those other guys gave you a hard time for being overweight? How do you think they'd react to your latest status update?"

"It'd only be some."

"But it'd be enough, man, same as the piranhas."

"But what about being true to myself?"

"Look, I know everyone thinks old Shaky is some sort of a god or something, but let's just get real for a second. If big Willy turned up here at St Daniel's and started spouting all that flowery language and thee-ing and thou-ing all over the place, I'd give him less than one of Prindabel's nanoseconds before he'd be experiencing the joys of a head flush in the Senior toilets. I'm trying to help you here, man, that's all. So I'm telling you as a friend, Billy, *don't* do it."

Bill raised his confused face and looked around the room.

"Scobie, what would you do if you were me?"

I think everyone else in the room knew what James 'No Fear' Scobie would do. What we wondered was what he would say to Bill.

"It doesn't matter what I would do if I were you, Bill, because I'm not. So all that matters is what feels right for you to do."

"But I'm not sure any more."

Scobie kept his eyes on Bill like he was X-raying him.

"Do your parents know yet? Have you told them?"

"Mum does. I told her but I think she knew already." Then a miserable expression took over Bill's face. "My father doesn't know. Mum said she'd tell him for me. But I have to do it."

As Scobie nodded, the bell for the end of lunch started ringing.

Bill took his speech back from Razz. "I guess I'll just have to think about it some more," he said, and wandered out of the room.

Razz shook his head. "We can't let him do it, Scobes. We just can't."

"If it's what he decides," Scobie said, "we have to."

30.
The Grimmest of His Grim Days

The *Hamlet* orals were scheduled for the following Monday. So were all the sports photos for the magazine. Razz was involved in quite a few and he had to report straight to the gymnasium before school. He wasn't in our form room when Bill told us about his decision.

"I'm not doing it," he said.

I didn't know if I felt relieved or disappointed for him. I don't think Bill knew how he really felt either.

"How come?" I asked. "It wasn't just what Razz said, was it?"

"No. The piranhas didn't scare me off," Bill said with a half-hearted smile. "It was more what you asked me, James. You know, about whether my parents knew yet. Like I said, I haven't told my father and I don't think I should go blurting it out to everyone else until I do that. Don't know when I'm going to tell him, though."

"You'll find the right time," Scobie said.

"Not that easy. He's hardly at home. He's always overseas somewhere building stuff. He's got about six months away in Egypt coming up. And we don't talk much even when he's home. We don't do anything much."

"He'll be all right with it, won't he?"

Bill's face made me wish I'd never asked that question.

"No," he said.

Once again it was Scobie, as always, who had the words to put things right.

"Well, Bill, for what it's worth, I think you made the correct decision, waiting till after you've spoken to your father. That's what I would have done if I were you. And Bill," Scobie said, "I would be proud to be you."

It wasn't exactly a smile that came to Bill's face, but at that point in time I think it was the most we could have hoped for.

Everything happened pretty quickly after that. Our English lesson followed Tutor Group and Bill was the first of us scheduled to speak. After a great acting performance as Polonius, he was just about to commence the analysis part of his presentation when Razz appeared at the door. Mr Slattery waved at him to come in quickly and take one of the vacant seats at the back. I was in the second row from the front beside Scobie and

I caught a flash of Razz's tense face as he went past.

Bill started his analysis. I turned round a couple of times and tried to catch Razz's eye to let him know not to worry about what Bill was going to say. But Razz was concentrating too hard on the presentation. Then Mr Slattery came over and tapped me on the shoulder and told me to pay attention, so I gave up. I figured Razz would find out for himself soon enough anyway. But what I *thought* would happen and what actually *did* happen were so far apart they might as well have existed in different dimensions.

Everything was going smoothly enough until Bill arrived at the last part of his talk – the relevance of Polonius's speech to today's society. I risked a quick glance over my shoulder at Razz. He was shifting around like his seat was on fire. I shook my head at him. Mr Slattery scowled at me. I faced the front. Oh well, it'd all be over in a minute. (Quick, someone text Nostradamus and tell him his job is still safe.)

I turned my attention back to Bill. From the practice sessions I knew he was nearing the end.

"… For example, many gay men and women today are still unable to be true to who they really are because of the prejudice and discrimination that unfortunately still exist in society today. I can…"

The screech of a chair being pushed back more or less drowned out the remainder of Bill's last sentence which I just made out as, "… only describe this situation as unjust and intolerable."

Overlaid on the soundtrack of the screech was Razz clapping wildly and calling out, "Bravo, Billy! Couldn't agree more. Hear hear! Down with discrimination! We have suffered enough already!"

The whole class swung round. Danny Wallace woke up for the first time in the lesson. Mr Slattery struck a dramatic pose.

"Mr Zorzotto, resume your seat immediately!"

Bill looked horrified. "Razz, it's all right. I…"

But Razz was on a mission not to let Bill speak and he was determined to succeed. He climbed onto his chair shouting, "We will not be held down! We've been repressed too long! We must all stand up and end inequality now!"

Mr Slattery's face now matched the colour of his hair. I'm pretty sure you could have roasted marshmallows on it.

"Mr Zorzotto, this is your final warning. If you do not get off that chair and resume your seat, the consequences for you will be dire!"

But Razz was totally committed to the cause and there

was no turning back. He stepped on to the desk and began chanting, "What do we want? Equality! When do we want it? Now!"

Some of the class started to join in, clapping and shouting out in response to Razz's calls. Hold the marshmallows. Mr Slattery's face was going into meltdown. And then, when I thought it couldn't get any worse, what do you know? It did! Razz threw his arms out and started singing. It was a song everyone from Ms Heckenvaal's history class knew only too well.

"I AM WOMAN," Razz bellowed out, and even though he numbered only one, there was no way he was ever going to be ignored.

Why he thought this was an appropriate song to burst into at that particular moment I will never know. At least he had the brains to steer clear of Danny Wallace's version.

While Mr Slattery shouted to be heard, Razz kept belting out verse after verse of the feminists' anthem. Ms Heckenvaal would have been so proud. He was just informing us, at the top of his lungs, something about him being an embryo and having a long way to go, when Mr Barker appeared at our classroom door and stood there like the Grim Reaper. Every sound, every word, every note, every shuffle, every murmur, died.

Our Tutor Group was a morgue. We all stared zombie-like at our Deputy Principal's face.

Even on the grimmest of his grim days, the Grim Reaper had never managed to appear quite *that* grim.

31.

Hmmmmmm

Mr Barker didn't shout when he told Razz to get down off the desk and go to his office. In fact his voice didn't rise much over a whisper. But it was still the scariest thing I'd ever heard.

Of course I'd seen Mr Barker angry plenty of times before. We all had. He was Deputy Principal. 'Angry' was what he did. And Mr Barker was a true professional. Sometimes I'm sure he made himself *seem* angrier than he really was, just for effect. I guess Hamlet would say that sometimes Mr Barker's face and voice were just the 'trappings and the suits' of anger. But that's not the way it was the day he stood in the doorway with Razz fiercely locked in his sights. That day, everything about him said, 'I KNOW NOT "SEEMS"!'

After he was trudged from Tutor Group like a prisoner for an appointment with a high-voltage recliner, Razz wasn't sighted at all for the rest of the day. I was half-expecting the police to arrive any minute and charge Mr Barker with some unspeakable rage crime.

Eventually Razz showed up after school while I was waiting at the bus stop.

"Razz, what happened? What did Barker say? What did you get?"

Razz rattled off his punishment with little emotion.

"A written apology for Mr Slattery, one for Bill and one for the class, ten days of afternoon detentions, working outside Barker's office every English lesson until the orals are over and if I mess up again just once, no Semi-formal."

"Geez, that's a bit much. Mr Barker must have been pretty mad."

"Possibly. Apparently I'm 'immature and self-centred' and I 'lack respect for my school, my teachers, my fellow students and myself'. I also have 'no idea of appropriate behaviour', I 'treat life as a joke' and seeing how I obviously went out of my way to make a 'complete mockery' of Bill and his talk, I'm 'totally insensitive to anyone else's feelings and views' as well."

"What? That's rubbish. Didn't you explain why you did it?"

"I'm trying to *stop* people finding out about Bill. Why would I go and shoot my mouth off to Barker? I just said I did it for a bit of fun. What's it matter, anyway? Barker already thinks I'm a loser. He's been on the phone to my mum most of the day and now she's got an appointment to see him after school tomorrow while I'm doing my first detention."

"Your mum is meeting with Mr Barker?"

"Yeah, what about it?"

"Nothing," I said as casually as I could.

Razz ran his fingers through his hair.

"Anyway, I don't care about that stuff. It was worth it to stop Bilbo shooting himself in the foot."

"Ah, Razz… there's something I think I should tell you."

Razz turned a pair of weary eyes my way.

"If you're going to tell me that you pashed Sally again, I'll really have to kill you this time. You know that, don't you?"

"Right, thanks for the warning. I'll just keep that to myself then and tell you this other thing instead. Razz, Bill decided not to say anything. Not until he could work up the nerve to tell his father. We found out in Tutor Group when you were getting your sports shots done."

Razz's chin slumped to his chest and he groaned. Talk about your 'suspiration of forced breath' and your 'dejected 'havior of the visage'.

The following morning when Bill found out about the detentions he said he was going straight to Mr Barker, but Razz wouldn't let him. He reckoned it was all "just water under the carpet". As it turned out, detentions weren't the Razzman's only worry.

"So now your mother and Mr Barker have an *appointment* together? Hmmmmmm."

Razz's eyes narrowed.

"What do you mean, 'Hmmmmmm', Prindabel?"

"Nothing."

"Didn't sound like a nothing 'Hmmmmmm' to me. People don't 'Hmmmmmm' for no reason."

"They don't?" Ignatius said. "Hmmmmmm."

Razz looked around suspiciously at the rest of us. Everyone except Scobie tried to avoid eye contact.

"What is it with you guys? What's the matter? Come on, Scobes, tell me."

"Well, Orazio, perhaps Ignatius is *alluding* to the fact that your mother and Mr Barker *did* seem to get on *quite* well at the Dugongs' concert last year."

A second passed before Razz's face crumbled like it had been hit by a massive earth tremor.

"What? You guys don't think… that my mum… and Mr Barker…" Razz's half-finished question hung in the air. "That's crazy talk!"

"Yes, you're probably right," Scobie said reassuringly, "*Although* you did mention that your mother and

Mr Barker had already spoken *all day* on the phone. So one might be inclined to wonder *why* a face-to-face meeting would be deemed... *necessary*."

Razz looked at us like we were all members of some bizarre sect that worshipped tapeworms.

"You're all mad, you know that? You've been reading way too much *Hamlet*. You've all gone psycho like him. There's nothing happening between my mother and Barker. Not now, not ever. They're just having a meeting about *me*, that's all."

"Are you going to be there?" Ignatius asked.

"Well... no... but..."

That was as far as Razz got. I think some disturbing images had overwhelmed him. Ignatius added a couple more.

"Orazio *Barker*. It has a nice ring to it, don't you think? You might even be able to do future detentions at home with the family. Very convenient."

Razz performed a commendable impression of Mr Barker's grimmest of grim, Grim Reaper looks and directed it with laser-like intensity at Prindabel.

Over the next few days the remaining *Hamlet* orals were completed without further incident. The closest we came to anything vaguely exciting was when Danny Wallace included a brief ventriloquist routine involving

Yorick's skull in his, and when Melvin Yip, with some expert assistance from Xiang Chu, staged the Hamlet and Laertes sword fight scene in a way that was more samurai than Shakespeare. Scobie christened it "Crouching Hamlet, Hidden Poison".

The rest of the performances were more traditional. Scobie delivered a powerful and moving portrayal of a more than usually height-challenged Hamlet. Ignatius showed everyone that as a dead guy he could be remarkably convincing. And I ended up being happy with my Claudius. Yes, you heard right. Me, happy with an oral presentation. That's something I never thought I'd say. Three years of debating was finally paying off.

The last presentation was Razz's. It had to be held over until his official return to English class. And he surprised everyone. He didn't joke around or muck up a line in his speech and he looked pretty impressive dressed all in black including a leather jacket. Even Mr Slattery said he was "pleasantly surprised" by the "depth and understanding" of Razz's analysis, particularly the concept of "appearance" versus "reality".

In a strange coincidence, that was the same concept that Scobie and I had a long discussion with Mr Barker about in his office the day after Bill's speech. You know, how a person can 'appear' one thing but 'really' be nothing like that. And in another strange coincidence, on that very day Mr Barker decided to let Razz spend all his detentions helping the Junior Dormitory Supervisor Mr Murphy run after-school activities for the younger boarders.

Apart from a few afternoons spent with the boarders at Mr Slattery's ballroom dancing classes, Razz mainly got to organise and play sport. For once it was a win-win situation that actually worked. Mr Murphy said Razz was a "godsend" and Razz liked helping with the junior boarders so much he kept doing it even after his detentions were over.

The other thing Mr Barker did was to schedule another meeting with Mrs Zorzotto to discuss Razz's 'progress'.

Hmmmmmm.

32.
Advanced Self-pity Wallowing 401

After the excitement of Razz's 'coming out', the year ground its way to the finish line. Soon a tsunami of final exams and assignments loomed large on the horizon and we all scrambled to reach the high ground of knowledge so that the waters of ignorance wouldn't drown us in a bottomless sea of failure. (Did I mention our short English unit on Figurative Language?) When Senior exam week finally ran its course, only the dreaded Semi-formal remained.

Razz really did try to work his 'magic' and help me find a partner. He dragged me along to a couple of parties and dances with him and Sally, but I didn't end up meeting anyone. It wasn't Razz's fault. I'm pretty useless in those make-a-quick-impression situations. They're fine if you're a Brad type like Jess's boyfriend. Girls just take one look and say, "Great, I'll have one of those!" But if you're like me, it's more, "Hmmmmmm, haven't you got anything else?" I need time to grow on people. A bit like mould.

But that was the problem. As far as finding a partner went, my time had completely run out. The last day finally arrived for anyone who needed to put their name down on the I'm-so-crap-with-girls-they-basically-have-to-force-someone-to-be-my-partner list that Miss Tarango put up on our year group's noticeboard. So I wrote mine down. I thought about adding LOSER. Then I remembered what Mr Slattery said about avoiding redundant words when you write.

A week or so later I found out that my chosen partner's name was Raychell Taylor and she went to Claremont College. That's all I knew about her. Of course I spent the next week and a half wondering what a Raychell Taylor would look like and what she'd *be* like. If you believed my mum, it didn't matter anyway. Apparently my only job was to make sure that whoever my partner was, she "enjoyed herself" and didn't feel "left out or neglected" on the night. Mum only told me that about a hundred times so I guess she thought it was pretty important.

Our Semi-formal took place in the Old Hall. On the night all we loser-list people had to meet Miss Tarango in the foyer so we could be introduced to our partners. We looked about as relaxed as a herd of cattle milling around outside an abattoir. I think for most of us that would have been the more appealing option.

Then I saw Raychell Taylor. I'd been given a reprieve from the slaughterhouse. She looked great – except for the 'Hmmmmmm, haven't you got anything else?' expression that flashed across her face when we were first introduced. At least she was kind enough to try to hide it. But I knew it was still lurking there somewhere behind Raychell's big smile and I was fairly certain that the night wouldn't be anywhere near long enough for me to make it go away.

I'm not saying that the Semi was a disaster or anything. It wasn't. Raychell had a great personality and had no trouble fitting in with everyone – even if her eyes did seem to drift away to the other tables and to her mobile more than I hoped. And we had a fun group. Apart from me and Raychell there was Razz and Sally (who finally got to wear a new dress and be heart-achingly beautiful for the right person); Ignatius and Maude (who was really nice and made everyone laugh, except when she said things that sounded exactly like Prindabel – then she was scary); Scobie and Prue (who wore lace-up boots and a dress she'd cut down from one that used to belong to our grandmother and yet still managed to look more like a supermodel than my little sister); a good friend of Sally's called Alyce (who was super-nice) and Gerard Carlson-Steele (who as well as still being the undisputed champion of perfect uniform wearing, was a good guy). I just wished that Bill could have been there with us.

Overall it was a pretty good night and it even contained one thing that I'd definitely place in the awesome category. It happened towards the end of the Semi when I wandered outside to the foyer area. Don't worry, I wasn't 'neglecting' Raychell. She was doing juuuuust fine. She'd sort of drifted off and attached herself to another table with a bunch of her Claremont friends. And Mum would be happy. The last time I checked she was certainly 'enjoying' herself with Gary Horsham. Razz and Sally and everyone else were up dancing.

I made my way over to one of the big foyer windows. Outside it was pelting down with rain. On the other side of the main yard I could just make out the gymnasium. At almost exactly the same time last year, that's where I was – in the school gym at the Dugongs' reunion concert.

A bit had changed since then. The band had played a few more gigs together and now there were definite plans to remaster and re-release their old album, maybe with some new songs on it.

Things had changed for me too. But none of it was an improvement. A year ago, instead of staring out a window by myself while all my friends were having a great time without me, I was with Kelly Faulkner. And she was kissing me and everything was perfect. After that I couldn't wait for this year to start so Kelly and I could be together and go the movies and parties and school dances.

But none of that happened.

Now the year was over and what did I have to look forward to next year? Let's see...

- More exams and assignments
- More pressure
- No clue about a future job or career
- No Kelly
- No anybody
- No nothing.

How's that for your 'slings and arrows of outrageous fortune'?

It was around about this time while I was immersing myself fully in Advanced Self-pity Wallowing 401 that I was distracted by a call from behind.

"Ishmael! I've been looking everywhere for you, man.

Brother Jerome wants us all inside and sitting down, *plus* I've got some gooder-than-good news for you, dude. You're gonna love it."

"Good news? I'll believe that when I hear it."

"Sal sent a text to Kelly, you know, to tell her how the Semi was going and everything."

"Super." (No doubt about it. I was totally aceing Advanced Self-pity Wallowing 401.)

"But that's not the good part, dude. The good part is Sal just got a reply and guess what?"

"Surprise me."

He did. He came out with the night's 'one awesome thing'. It made my year.

"Kelly's coming home, dude. She's coming back with her mum and little brother. She's gonna be boarding at Lourdes next year. The Kelster is back in the building, man!"

A déjà vu thing was happening in my chest. My heart was shooting up like it had launched itself off a springboard. It was in the process of nailing a perfect reverse triple somersault in the full pike position – with a twist!

"Well, what do you reckon, dude? You and Kelly back together. Was I right or was I right? That seems like pretty good news to me!"

"Seems?" I said, grabbing Razz by the front of his shirt. "Seems! I KNOW NOT 'SEEMS'!"

And this is how my year at St Daniel's ended: with Razz and I racing each other back inside the Old Hall just in time to hear Brother Jerome announce the name of next year's College Captain to a cheer that almost lifted the roof clean off.

James Scobie tended to have that effect on people.

Next year?

BRING IT ON!

PART TWO
Term One

Doubt thou the stars are fire;
Doubt that the sun doth move;
Doubt truth to be a liar;
But never doubt I love.

William Shakespeare, *Hamlet*,
act 2 scene 2, lines 116–119

1.
The Last of the Lasts

Across from me, a head bobbed rhythmically and a blur of fingers drummed out a furious beat on the tabletop. Then everything ceased and a pair of eyes blinked open like torches.

"Hey, do you guys realise that this is the last 'first day back' we'll ever have?"

It was morning break. We were sitting around one of the tables in the Senior courtyard. Scobie, Bill, Ignatius and I took time out from demolishing our lunches to contemplate Razz's observation.

"This is it, man," Razz said, taking in all the buildings and the riot of students in the playground. "The last time. We'll never be on holidays ever again, and think like, 'Aw, man, school tomorrow! What a total bummer!'"

"I've never thought that."

Razz threw a sympathetic look at the lanky figure

chewing on a muesli bar and poring over a *Science World* magazine.

"Sorry, my bad, Prindabel. I was actually just talking about us humanoids. Should have made myself clear."

"But what you said about the last first day back might not be true anyway. What if you had to repeat the year?"

"Me? Why should I have to repeat?"

"I wasn't referring to *you* specifically, Orazio... *Although*..."

Razz glared. Ignatius backed off.

"I'm just saying that if *anyone* had to repeat the year, then for that person it wouldn't be his last first day back, would it? He'd only *think* it was, but in reality it would be just the *first* of his last first days back, because he'd have one last, last first day back to go the next year."

Razz looked around at the rest of us. Then he jerked a thumb towards Ignatius.

"You see. Here's my problem with trying to recreate human life in the laboratory. What do we do with the experiments when they fail?"

Unperturbed, Ignatius returned to his magazine.

"Orazio does have a point though."

This came from Scobie, of all people.

"My genius is recognised at last! Thank you, Mein Capitan and Ruler Over All the Lands!"

Ever since the Semi-formal, when Brother Jerome announced that Scobie was this year's College Captain, Razz had showered him with countless titles. 'He Whose Feet I Am Not Worthy to Lick Clean' was one of my personal favourites.

"Tell us more, Your Highest of All Highnesses, so that these ignorant donkeys may see the light."

"Well," Scobie said with a trademark twist of his mouth, "this will be an entire year of lasts for us, won't it? Last swimming carnival, last athletics carnival and last assembly and then it will come right down to the last Tutor Group, last lesson in each of our subjects, last assignment, last exam and finally the last day."

"Last lesson, last exam, last assignment. Scobes, you sure know how to cheer me up!"

The smiles around the table said that he wasn't alone there. Razz clicked his fingers at us.

"And I got another one. Last time we'll have to be here when Charlton House finishes last in the College Cup. The last of the lasts!"

None of us from Charlton House would miss the annual humiliation that went with the announcement of the final College Cup point totals.

"This year's just looking better and better," Razz said.

There was quite a bit of head nodding and smiling

then, but Bill wasn't looking quite as convinced as the rest of us.

"Yeah, but there'll be other stuff as well, won't there?" he said. "Like our last debate together."

The smiles subsided a little. Then Ignatius had a thought to share.

"Last time we'll have to wait around for Orazio to turn up to a debating meeting," he said with a sly smirk.

"Yeah," Razz shot back, waving his index finger about, "and the last time I'll have to put up with the Prindabel Power Pointer wagging in my face whenever I open my mouth."

"Last time Scobie will have to bang on the table and call out, 'Debating meeting? Remember?'" I said.

It went a bit quiet then. Maybe like me, the others were thinking about some of the more memorable moments from our meetings over the past three years. We returned to the present when Scobie threw in another debating 'last'.

"Last chance to win the debating championship."

Razz slapped the table. "Man, we should've at *least* got to the finals last year," he said. "I'm telling you, if that adjudicator we had against Claremont had any less brains he would have been a potato."

"Can't do anything about that now," Scobie said.

"But we can do something about this year. We made the finals back in our first year of debating, so there's no reason we couldn't do it again and then maybe go all the way. Of course, we'd need to be really serious about it."

"Ah, what exactly do you mean by *serious*, O Supreme Being and Jumbo Storehouse of All Wisdom?"

"Well, Orazio, for a start it would be good if we could all get to the meetings on time. And it would also be very helpful if once we got there we were *organised* and *focused* and we didn't waste time discussing totally irrelevant *personal* issues, like problems we might have with certain *teachers* and *assignments* or even the love life of another member of the debating team – or lack thereof."

Razz pointed at Bill, Ignatius and me in turn. "Are you guys listening to what our Glorious All-knowing Leader is saying here? If we wanna win the big one, you guys have gotta cut *all* that stuff out, okay?"

Then Razz turned back to Scobie.

"Don't worry, O Captain, My Captain, I'll keep them in line. And look, don't be too hard on them. Hey, I've probably been guilty of some of those things myself."

"Surely not," Scobie said. Then he thrust his hand forward, palm down, with his chubby fingers spread out. His eyes swept around the table. "What do you say? Senior Debating Champions?"

We all pancaked our hands on top of his.

"Senior Debating Champions," we replied.

We were just disentangling ourselves when Miss Tarango weaved her way through the yard, setting a course for the staffroom. She was carrying an armful of folders. We all watched as she disappeared inside. I think the same thought was going through each of our heads, but it was Bill who turned it into words.

"Last year with Miss Tarango."

That put a bit of a dampener on how everything was shaping up.

"We'll have to get her something really nice when we leave."

"Nice idea, Billy Boy!" Razz said with a soft punch to Bill's arm. "And not the usual stuff like flowers or chocolates. Gotta be something special."

We all agreed with that. But what?

"Hey, I know what we can do," Razz said. "It's simple, man. We're winning the Debating Trophy, right? Well, why don't we just win the College Cup for Miss Tarango while we're at it?"

We joined with Razz in laughing at the sheer ridiculousness of his suggestion.

All of us, that is, except James Scobie.

"Maybe we should look into it."

We all waited for the punch line. It never came.

"Forgive me, My Lord of Humungous Heaps of Grey Matter, but are you *nuts*?"

"It would be the perfect present for her," Scobie stated calmly. "She's always been Charlton House's number one supporter even before she was made Patron. She supports everything, she gets dressed up in the house colours, she always cheers the loudest even when we lose – which is normally the case – and she's by far the hardest working of all the house Patrons. It's about time she got some reward. And I can't think of a better reward for all that effort than winning her the College Cup. I'm just suggesting we should consider it, that's all."

Razz screwed his face up in disbelief.

"Consider it? Look, Your Know-It-All-Ness, I think there are some pretty basic things you're missing. Like, for a start, *this*, Scobes," Razz said, thumping on the table and stamping on the ground, "is reality. It's where the rest of us here are living. Why don't you forget about Charlton ever winning the College Cup and come join us?"

"I'm happy to deal with reality, Orazio. That's why I think before we dismiss the idea we should do some hard research into our previous performances, assess our strengths and weaknesses, study the points table and see what the *reality* of our situation is."

At the mention of the words 'research' and 'points table' Prindabel lifted his nose slightly off his *Science World* magazine and glanced up.

"Well, if you want research," Razz said, "just take a look at how we went last year in the Big Three. Athletics Carnival – last place. Swimming Carnival – last place. Cross-country – hey, what do you know? Last place. You won't go changing that all around in just one year. It's impossible."

"*Seems* impossible," Scobie said and held up his hand just in time to stop Razz from shouting *I know not 'seems'!* "But not all the points that contribute to the College Cup come from just those three events. What we really need is for someone to *analyse* all the available *statistics* on last year's competition and then prepare a detailed *breakdown* – perhaps a *spreadsheet*, even – of the points-scoring system and *report* back to us."

Prindabel's head had crept a little higher and his eyes had opened a little wider with each of the words Scobie had stressed.

"What we *need*," Scobie said finally, tapping the point of his finger on the table, "is for someone to do the *maths*."

The Prindabel Power Pointer shot up into the air.

"I could do that."

"Really, Ignatius? Would you?" Scobie said, actually

managing to look genuinely surprised. "That would be excellent. At least then we would have a better picture of where we stand."

"Well, yeah, sure, Prindabuddy, why not? Go ahead. Knock yourself out. Write a report on Charlton's chances of winning the College Cup. And to save time, do your conclusion first. Just type in 'zero'."

That's where the discussion ended. Even though I couldn't think of a better thank you present for Miss Tarango than winning her the College Cup, I had to agree with Razz. It was never going to happen.

The remainder of morning break was spent throwing up other 'lasts' for the year. We came up with plenty too. Some good, some not so good. The one that got the biggest laugh was 'last detention for Razz'.

But there was one 'last' that I kept to myself. One that I couldn't stop thinking about.

The last day without Kelly Faulkner back in my life.

2.
You Had Me at 'Data'

I'd spent most of the holidays thinking about meeting Kelly Faulkner again; wondering where and when it would all happen and what it would be like. I also spent a bit of time trying to hose down all my spot-fire doubts, which threatened to take hold and rage out of control.

Things like, that maybe Kelly had changed, or met someone else. I mean, all we really had was that night at the Dugongs' concert and one short, amazing, mind-blowing kiss. If she really did like me, then why did she stop sending emails? When we finally met again she'd probably just stare at me with those beautiful ice-blue eyes and say, "Do I *know* you from somewhere?"

All right, I was just being stupid with that last bit. Kelly would remember me. After all, how many other Ishmaels did she know? *I* might be forgettable, but unfortunately my *name* certainly wasn't. I decided to remain positive and focus on what I knew rather than what I didn't know. And I knew from Sally Nofke via Razz that Kelly and her mother and brother Marty were back, I knew that she'd been really busy getting set up in the boarding house at Lourdes College and I knew that Razz and Sally were working on getting Kelly and me together. I was daydreaming about that very get-together one lunchtime when Ignatius Prindabel presented his report on the College Cup. When he did, the course of the entire school year changed.

With Mr Guthrie's permission we were all gathered in our form room to hear the official findings. Some were gathered more enthusiastically than others.

"Welcome to Fantasy Island, kiddies, where Uncle Iggy Wiggy will now waste our time."

Ignatius ignored Razz and pulled some sheets from a folder. We each received two pages. They were filled with charts, diagrams, lists, tables, figures, percentages and bullet points.

"You really do have a very bad case of chronic nerdism, don't you, P-buddy?"

"Thank you, Orazio," Scobie said. "Now I've already studied the report in detail, so Ignatius, why don't you just run through the highlights for everyone else?"

"Well, Pie Graph 1.0 shows the breakdown of all the various sources of points for last year's College

Cup, obviously expressed in percentages."

"Obviously," Razz repeated.

"As you can see, the Big Three – the Swimming Carnival, the Athletics Carnival and the Cross-country – accounted for approximately 56 per cent of the total points allotted. The remaining points came from a range of other minor events, which I have labelled Miscellaneous and spelled out in more detail in Pie Graph 1.1 as well as Table (A). These include the various inter-house competitions such as the indoor football competition and the talent quest as well as points for participation in certain school activities.

"Now I've also completed a breakdown and analysis on each of the Big Three events to see where the individual houses gained their points, with a particular focus, via James's instructions, on what proportion came from performance compared to participation. You can see the results of that in Charts 1, 2 and 3 and Tables (B) and (C). In addition, Table (D) shows the points difference between the losing houses and the eventual winning house expressed both in raw numbers and as a percentage of the total winning score. On the second page…"

"Prindabel, stop!" Razz said, waving the handouts at him. "I'm sure this is brilliant, man, and you'll probably win the Nobel Geek Prize, but before my head explodes, just tell us what it all means."

Ignatius placed his two sheets of paper together, tapped them on the desk in front of him and laid them down.

"It means, Orazio, that based on the evidence of last year's results… it's mathematically possible for Charlton House to not win *any* of the Big Three and still win the overall College Cup."

"You're joking."

"No, I'm not. Of course the more successful we are in the Big Three, the smaller the percentage of points we need to win in the Miscellaneous section and therefore the better our chances of winning the cup will become."

Razz blew out a long breath. "What about you, Your Way-Better-Than-Us-ness? Do you agree with Professor Pie Graph here?"

"Absolutely," Scobie said. "And I've come up with a Three-point Plan to help us achieve our goal."

Scobie waddled to the front of the classroom and wrote OPERATION TARANGO on the whiteboard.

"The madness begins," Razz said with a shake of his head.

Then Scobie added:

I. MOTIVATION

"The first thing we have to do is motivate everyone in Charlton House to get involved, to train hard and to do their best. We certainly need to lift our game as much as possible in the Big Three."

Scobie returned to the board and wrote:

2. PARTICIPATION

"This will be our secret weapon. In the cross-country, for example, as long as you finish within a set time, you get a point for your house. Same with some events in the swimming and athletics. This is an area that has never been fully exploited. We'd need to aim at what I like to call *Saturation Participation*."

Scobie added the final point of his Three-point Plan.

3. DIVERSIFICATION

"We definitely need to spread our points-earning potential away from just the big three. We need to specifically target the long list of miscellaneous items. We need to make sure that *when*ever and *where*ver College Cup points are up for grabs, Charlton House is there, in numbers and ready to compete."

Scobie clipped the lid on his whiteboard marker and walked back to the cluster of desks where the rest of us were sitting.

"Motivation, Participation and Diversification," he said. "That's what can win Charlton House the College

Cup. I think we should give Operation Tarango a go. Who's with me?"

Just as he did with the debating challenge, Scobie held his hand out in front of us.

"What about you, Ignatius? A lot of data would have to be continually collated and analysed once we got under way. We'd need someone who could give us accurate, detailed, up-to-date reports on our progress and coordinate our plan of attack. Would you be willing to do it?"

Ignatius immediately placed his spider-like hand over Scobie's.

"You had me at 'data'," he said.

"Excellent. And what about you, Bill? Surely a *Lord of the Rings* devotee wouldn't turn down the opportunity to join an unlikely quest with a ragtag band of companions to bring back a legendary golden cup for a fair damsel."

Bill had a Shire-sized smile on his face as his big hand engulfed Prindabel's. "You had *me* at 'quest'," he said.

"And Ishmael, your namesake was a bit of a quest man too, wasn't he? Can't promise you an adventure on the high seas, but it should turn out less dangerous than tackling the great white whale. Will you answer the call, Ishmael? Can we pipe you aboard?"

"Aye, aye, Captain," I told him and added my hand.

That just left Razz.

"So, you're all off on a *biiiiiiig* quest now, are you?" he said, like he was talking to pre-schoolers.

We all nodded back at him like pre-schoolers. Razz rolled his eyes but clamped his hand firmly on top of the stack.

"Well, there's no way I'm gonna let you four lunatics have all the fun while I'm stuck here by myself in Hobbitville."

There was a moment of communal grinning before we began to withdraw our hands.

"Hold on," Razz said. "Isn't this the bit in the movies where some dude says something way cool and meaningful to get us all psyched up?"

I automatically looked towards Scobie. So did Razz. So did Ignatius.

But it was Bill who spoke.

"The quest for the College Cup stands upon a knife edge," he said, catching us all off guard. "Stray but a little… and it will fail. Yet hope remains while the company is true."

"I take it that was a Lord of the Ringy thingy, Bilbo?"

Bill nodded.

"Terrific," Razz said. "We're all headed for Mount Doom. This could end in tears."

3.
Standby Eyes

Kelly Faulkner and I finally caught up at exactly the same place I'd first seen her way back – at a debating seminar at Moorfield High. It was kind of appropriate, I guess, but also kind of weird.

This time the talks and workshops were specifically for Senior debaters. To show we really were 'serious' about our last year of debating, all our team agreed to attend. Sally and her Lourdes College team, which included Kelly, were also coming. Everything was set. At Moorfield on the Saturday morning there was a big turnout. We were milling around outside the main venue waiting for the first talk to start when Sally and Kelly found us.

I can't remember much about what anyone said. I just remember my first sight of Kelly in over a year. Her hair was shorter and darker. And she might have been a little bit thinner. But she was as beautiful as I remembered her. And as always, it was Kelly's eyes that stayed with me. But for a different reason this time. They were still pale blue and clear like ice. But some of the light seemed to have gone out in them. Now they looked like they were on standby, waiting for some button to be pushed that would bring them back to life.

It wasn't until lunchtime that Kelly and I really had a chance to talk. Scobie, Bill and Ignatius were already queueing up to get something to eat and Sally and Razz volunteered to get our lunch for us. I watched as they headed towards the tuck shop. I was dreading the moment I lost sight of them, because I knew then I'd have to look at Kelly and say something and I didn't have a clue what that should be.

"Looks like we may have been conveniently left alone," Kelly said with a half smile. "Maybe we should wait over there, out of the sun."

We moved to a bench under a tree.

"It really is nice to see you again," Kelly said.

Out of the vast recesses of my magnificent brain I conjured up a "You too".

She smiled. I smiled. Okay, my turn to keep the conversation from dying now.

"Your hair's different."

Gosh, really? I bet Kelly hadn't realised. Maybe she'd been the victim of some crazed hairdresser who broke in and dyed and style-cut people while they slept.

"I like it," I added, which saved me from sounding like a complete moron. Barely.

"Thanks," Kelly said, flicking at her fringe. "You haven't changed much, except you're taller. All you guys are. Even Scobie. Wish I could add a few centimetres."

"You don't need to be taller. You're fine. You're… perfect."

Kelly looked off into the distance. "No. I'm not," she said.

It didn't sound like something she was willing to debate. It took a little while for her to move her eyes away from the horizon and back to me.

"Sorry I was so slack with emails and everything. I meant to write. I was going to. But it all went a bit… crazy… over there."

"That's all right. No problem. You probably had tons of other stuff to do."

Kelly looked at me for a second and then down at her hands.

"My parents look like they're going to get a divorce."

I sat there with my mouth half-opened, trying to think of what to say.

"Mum and Dad were… having trouble… for a while. I didn't really know. But that's why Mum agreed with Dad taking that new job and all of us going to live in

New Zealand in the first place. It was supposed to help, supposed to fix things. It didn't."

"Kelly, you don't have to talk about this…"

"It's all right. I want to. There are some things I think you need to know. Not just about Mum and Dad. About me too. And… us."

My heart began bracing itself for a pounding.

"I didn't cope too well when all that stuff was happening with my parents. My school grades were hopeless, but I didn't really care. I guess I was angry at my mum and dad and trying to get back at them in some stupid way. I don't know. I think they call it 'going off the rails'. My counsellor told me it was a natural response."

Kelly glanced up at me with a tired smile. "Counsellor," she said. "All we *perfect* people have them." Then she looked down and bit her lip.

"And then… there was this boy…"

Braced or not, my heart reeled from the blow.

"… And maybe it was because of all the stuff with my parents… or maybe I'm just not as smart as I thought I was, but… things happened, things I wish I could take back or undo… and then I had to deal with that too."

Kelly closed her eyes and shook her head as if she was trying to make the memories disappear.

"He's gone now, that boy. He was nothing like

you, Ishmael. He never wrote me a poem."

The tight smile that came to Kelly's lips was just movement without feeling. Then it vanished.

"I really like you and I'd never do anything to hurt you. So you need to know how I feel."

She looked directly at me.

"I just haven't got time for a boyfriend. I couldn't handle it. Not now. I just want to put all last year behind me. I want to get my grades back so I can do journalism at uni. I want to get my life back. I want to get *me* back."

Her ice-blue standby eyes were melting.

"I haven't got room in my life for a boyfriend right now. I'm sorry. And I know this sounds so lame, but… I do have a vacancy for a friend… if you're interested."

I was.

When I came away from Moorfield College that day I promised myself that somehow I would put the lights back on in Kelly Faulkner's eyes. I had another quest.

This time it was personal.

4.
Drowning in a Straight Line

At our first house meeting for the year, Operation Tarango began in earnest. As Charlton House Captain, James Scobie got up and proudly announced that this year we were aiming to win the College Cup. It took quite a while for the laughter and general hilarity to settle down.

Scobie wasn't fazed at all. He just stood behind the lectern until an awkward silence took hold and gripped tight. Then he waited a bit longer.

"That, gentlemen," he said, "is why, for the past seventeen years, we have been unsuccessful in our bid to be House Champions. Not only do the other houses laugh at us – we laugh at ourselves. Not only do the other houses think we're losers – so do we. Other houses don't defeat us – we defeat ourselves."

Scobie thumped the lectern and it echoed through the microphone.

"But not any more. From this day on, I say we stop thinking like losers and we start acting like winners. I believe we can win the College Cup, and not only that, St Daniel's top mathematical brain has proved that it's do-able."

Scobie nodded at Ignatius, who clicked a remote at the big screen beside him. The two pages of Prindabel's detailed notes, diagrams and calculations appeared in giant form. Of course, no one had the slightest idea what any of it meant, but for the few seconds it was up there, it looked mightily impressive.

Scobie nodded again at Ignatius and the words MOTIVATION, PARTICIPATION and DIVERSIFICATION filled the screen, and for the next few minutes he gave an impassioned sales pitch on the MPD formula for College Cup success before summing up.

"Gentlemen, with your support, I believe Charlton *will* be this year's Champion House. And we will do it…"

Scobie's chubby index finger rose Prindabel-like above his head.

"… One point at a time!" he said.

Scobie hadn't succeeded in converting all of Charlton House into 'true believers', but at least nobody was laughing. It was a good sign.

The other thing on the house meeting agenda that

day was the election of our Sports Captain for the year. As expected, Jimmy 'The Main Event' Mainwaring, vice-captain of the rugby Firsts and St Daniel's discus and javelin champion, was nominated and enthusiastically seconded. The second person nominated, Clinton Turner, tennis champion and a senior member of the college Cross-country team, was also no great surprise. But for some people, the final nominee was.

"I nominate Orazio Zorzotto."

It was Scobie who'd put up his hand. A murmur rose from the rest of the house. Razz sat up like he'd been jabbed by a cattle prod.

"What?"

"Any seconders?" Scobie said.

I stuck my hand up.

"Do you accept the nomination, Orazio?"

"Well… I don't… I *guess* so," Razz said, looking around bewildered.

"Good. Any more nominations?" Scobie asked. "No? Okay, let's vote."

Beside me Razz slid down in his seat. "Man, this'll be embarrassing."

It was – for Clinton Turner. He received two votes. The remaining votes were split almost evenly between Razz and "The Main Event", with Jimmy winning by only three. Razz looked like he'd just witnessed some magic trick that he couldn't fathom.

"Wow," he kept saying and looking around the meeting room, "I did all right."

He did too. I wasn't that surprised. Razz was always helping Mr Hardcastle coach and train the younger kids, particularly in football. And a couple of days a week he was still helping Mr Murphy organise and run the afternoon activities for the junior boarders. I reckon if just the Eights, Nines and Tens had voted, Razz would have romped it in.

A couple of weeks later Operation Tarango faced its first challenge – the annual Swimming Carnival. Traditionally this was by far our worst event. None of the school's top swimmers were in Charlton House and we always came last by a very comfortable margin. But with points up for grabs for anyone who just made it to the end of the pool in the 50 metres freestyle, it was Saturation Participation time and Scobie led the way.

Razz described James's freestyle technique as "drowning in a straight line". By the time he touched the wall, Scobie was almost on the bottom. When they dragged him from the pool his lips were blue and he couldn't speak. But it didn't matter. He had just enough strength left to hold up a wobbly index finger. Everyone in Charlton House got the message loud and clear. 'One point at a time'.

The goal we'd set ourselves was modest and achievable – just not to finish up last. So with Scobie inspiring the troops Charlton House put in a massive effort. And… we finished up last.

We tied with Radley House. It ended up being the best thing that could have happened, because it proved Scobie's 'One point at a time' theory.

"One more point. That was all we needed to come third," he said when he addressed our next house meeting. "One measly point. One more person to have a go. One more person to try a little bit harder. One more person to do something they could have done for the team, but didn't. We should all ask ourselves this. Could it have been me?'

It was pretty stirring stuff, and after the disappointment of the result it was exactly what we needed. It was supported by Prindabel's analysis, which revealed that, compared to last year, we'd increased our points tally by a whopping 30 per cent and we were much closer to the leading two houses. Plus there were some real positives to come out of the day. We came first in the total number of participation points earned (mainly due to Razz's encouragement and organisation of the younger kids) and we took out quite a few of the novelty events. We also annihilated the other teams in the 'best supporters' competition.

We had Miss Tarango to thank for that. She led our cheering dressed in Charlton House colours including gold plimsoles, long gold football socks, gold face paint and gold hair ribbons. She was practically gold from head to toe – as if we didn't know *that* already. And she kept it up all day, bouncing around like crazy and screaming herself hoarse. When Mr Guthrie brought home the teachers' race for us, I thought she was going to bounce into the pool.

Prindabel's analysis also revealed that it was a Charlton swimmer who had contested more events on the day than anyone else. We gave him three rousing cheers and Scobie presented him with a special 'Top Saturation Participation' certificate with his name on it. That name was *Orazio Zorzotto*. I'm not quite sure what award Jimmy 'The Main Event' Mainwaring was going for on the day. The Looking Good in My Bathers prize perhaps.

Not long after the Swimming Carnival, something happened that gave Operation Tarango an unexpected boost. Jimmy 'The Main Event' Mainwaring got drunk one weekend and gatecrashed a party where he successfully offended every female he came in contact with in more and more creative ways (usually involving 'pointed' references to himself being a 'javelin' champion). Sadly for Jimmy, it was all captured on someone's mobile and posted on YouTube. Then it went viral. 'The Main Event' had finally managed to become the main event. When Brother Jerome eventually caught the virus, Jimmy found himself faced with a last warning notice, a long suspension and the permanent loss of his Sports Captain's badge.

At Charlton House we didn't mourn very long over the demise of our leader. Luckily we had a ready-made replacement. And when asked if he was willing to take over the job, our ready-made replacement told us that he was "totally cool with that". He also mentioned on numerous occasions that it was "awesome, man!".

And so it was.

5.
Sledgehammer Meets Soft-boiled Egg

What James Scobie was doing for Charlton House, he was also doing for the whole school, only on an even bigger scale.

Every fortnightly assembly he preached the gospel of Participation. And when Scobie spoke, people listened. In some ways it worked against Operation Tarango as the rising tide of school spirit overflowed into the inter-house competition. But as James kept telling us, 'It's all good.'

And Scobie wasn't just empty words. It wasn't long before it was pretty clear to everyone that when it came to school captains, James Scobie was as good as it was ever going to get. Only one person at St Daniel's thought he could possibly do any more – James himself. We were all at our regular lunch table one day when he explained how.

"Orazio, I really need your help."

Bill, Ignatius and I lapsed temporarily into a state of mild shock. Razz, however, seemed completely unfazed.

"At last! So you've finally seen the light, hey, Scobes. I knew you'd eventually recognise my superior brain power. Start taking notes, Prindabuddy, you're about to witness a master at work. So what can I help you with, O Great One? Having a few probs with the old theory of relativity? The origins of the universe? Bantam physics?"

Before Ignatius could jump in with a bony-finger protest, Scobie answered. "I want to play a sport for the school. I need you to help me find one I can do."

"You? Sport? Why?"

"I'm always telling everyone else in assembly to get involved in school life. I have to lead by example, and sport is about the biggest thing there is at St Daniel's."

At least now it made sense why Scobie was asking Razz for help. When it came to anything that even remotely involved throwing, running, jumping, catching, hitting or kicking, Razz knew all about it and could do it without even trying.

"But you do tons of other stuff already," Razz said, counting them out on his fingers. "Debating, Public Speaking, Chess Club, Amnesty, Student Council *plus* you lead the cheering and write all the war cries for the rugby Firsts and *then* there's all your House and School Captaining stuff, for crying out loud. Geez, Scobes, no one does more than you. You're practically running the joint."

"Except I don't do sport."

"True. But there's a *very* good reason for that, My Honourable Stupendousness."

"What?"

"You totally *suck* at sport, dude."

Cruel but fair.

Over the last two years Scobie had tried a number of sports at St Daniel's, all of which ended up being considered too risky. It had a bit to do with that brain tumour operation he had when he was younger, but it was mostly due to Scobie's almost total lack of size, strength, fitness, vision, speed, agility and coordination.

"There has to be *something* I can do. I'll try anything."

Razz blew out a long puff of breath.

"Well," he said. "Let's see. Cricket's out."

A murmur of general agreement rose from the rest of us.

Scobie had attempted cricket in his first year here. As a bowler he wasn't *too* bad. He was actually quite tricky to score runs off. This was because very few of his deliveries ever landed anywhere near the batsman.

Quite a few of them did, however, land on his own close-in fieldsmen; usually on the back of their heads, much to their surprise, annoyance and pain. Once, in a feat of bowling that almost defied the laws of physics, a wayward ball from Scobie knocked out a fielder who was standing *behind* him.

As far as batting went, it would be fair to say that Scobie had certain… limitations. One was that after he got fitted out with a helmet, pads, box and every other form of cricket protection known to man, he could barely move. He practically had to be carried out and placed on the pitch like some kind of chubby, soft-toy version of a white knight. That's when it got even trickier for him. The smallest set of pads still came up to his stomach. This made it almost impossible for him to run. The only way for Scobie to counteract this problem was for him to hit fours or sixes. That was about as likely as me dating all the Miss Universe contestants at once. Not only did Scobie lack hand–eye coordination, it didn't seem like his hands and his eyes had ever actually been introduced to each other before.

After a couple of games it was unanimously agreed that Scobie should resign from cricket before he either got killed or killed someone else.

"And rugby's *definitely* out."

The murmur of agreement increased another notch.

Last year Scobie shocked everyone by announcing he was trying out for rugby. We all did our best to talk him out of it, of course, by explaining there was a definite down side to spending the rest of your days in a full body cast on life support, but he wouldn't listen. Nothing ever scared James 'No Fear' Scobie.

The person who *was* afraid was Mr Hardcastle, the sports master. He insisted that Scobie get medical clearances before he played, and even then Mr Hardcastle made Scobie wear two sets of headgear and the biggest shoulder pads he could find. Then he made James play on the wing, "well out of harm's way".

Word spread pretty quickly about Scobie's first rugby trial. On the day itself it looked like half the school was packed around the sidelines. When Scobie shuffled onto the field he was greeted with raucous cheers, a stirring rendition of the school song and laughter. Mainly laughter. Apart from his hands and a squished-up portion of face, the only other part of James Scobie that was actually visible was a brief flash of pale knees between the top of his socks and the bottom of his circus-tent shorts.

Amazingly, for the first twenty minutes of the trial game Scobie did pretty well. This was because the ball didn't come within ten metres of him. Then, tragically, it did. Someone on the opposition team miscued a kick and the ball tumbled and spun across the grass and came to rest right at his feet. Scobie picked it up, tucked it under one arm, gritted all of his little white teeth, and ran.

Well, when I say 'ran', I mean that Scobie's feet moved *quicker* than they normally did and his knees pushed up *higher* than they normally did and his little arms pumped *harder* than they normally did. But the only problem was, Scobie didn't actually go any *faster* than he normally did. A James Scobie run was everyone else's dawdle. He looked like he was one of those mimes trying to run against a strong wind – and failing.

Of course the lethal combination of Scobie's complete lack of speed and his total inability to change direction to avoid an opponent made him the easiest target ever to grace a rugby field. He wasn't just shooting-fish-in-a-barrel easy. He was more like totally-nuking-fish-that-were-already-filleted-and-on-display-in-the-deli-section-of-the-local-supermarket easy.

To make things even worse, the first person to confront Scobie that day as he gamely took his maiden 'run' with the football was Tommy 'Flatliner' Manu. Tommy Manu loved to tackle. It's what he was born and built to do. In fact, Tommy just loved to run into things

,period – people, trees, walls, buildings, large animals. I'm pretty sure that Tommy would have tackled his great-grandmother if she was on a rugby field carrying a ball. Maybe even if she wasn't.

People still talk about that day Tommy 'Flatliner' Manu tackled James Scobie at the rugby trials. Razz described it as "sledgehammer meets soft-boiled egg". Amazingly there were no broken bones, although Scobie did come out in so many purpley-blue bruises that for the next week or so everyone called him Mini-Avatar. Mr Hardcastle said the school couldn't afford to pay for Scobie's funeral expenses and promptly banned him from the rugby field.

"And I think we all agree, after recent evidence, that we can also give swimming a big swerve."

That was a no-brainer too. Scobie hadn't earned the nickname 'The Stone' at the Inter-house Swimming Carnival for nothing.

"Basketball?" Razz said, raising his eyebrows. "I think not. Some people are 'height-challenged', Scobes, but you're more like 'height-totally defeated', dude."

Razz pulled at his mop of hair. "So what have we got here? We need to find something that doesn't require too much speed, height, strength or any actual sporting talent of any kind whatsoever."

We all waited as Razz became lost in deep contemplation. Then his eyes twinkled and he clicked his fingers. "Is sleeping a sport?"

Scobie hung his head. I'd never seen him like that. He looked beaten.

"There has to be *something*. I don't have to be any *good* at it. Just as long as I can convince Mr Hardcastle I won't fatally injure myself... or anyone else."

"Well, let's do a Prindabel here and look at this logically using a process of elimination. First up, it can't be anything to do with water, so there goes water polo and your synchronised swimming dreams, Scobes. Secondly, you need all the help you can get. That means it should be a team sport. Thirdly, you can't run very fast... or very far... or very well. So forget stuff like cross-country, athletics or anything on a big field. Fourthly, we need to avoid anything where you have to catch, hit, kick or possibly just see something too small. So bye-bye hockey, tennis or badminton. Fifthly, for obvious reasons, it can't be a contact sport or one requiring strength or endurance. So no wrestling, boxing or weightlifting for you, I'm afraid, my liege."

Razz drew in a deep breath.

"What else do we have at St Daniel's?" Scobie asked without much enthusiasm. "Is anything left?"

"Only one I can think of," Razz said. "And you know what, man? It just might work. Six guys on a team – so plenty of help. Small court – so not much running. Fairly big ball – so easier to see. Opposition on the other side of a net – so no body contact. Hey, Scobes, I think we might have cracked it, dude. You just might be able to survive a game or two of... volleyball."

Scobie and Razz were in the process of congratulating each other when Ignatius poked a tentative finger into the air.

"Ah, just one *minor* point. Aren't volleyball nets fairly... high?"

"I see what you're getting at, P-man. But not everyone on a volleyball team needs to be tall. Like, here's your classic play. The opposition serves the ball and then your team has a max of three hits to get the ball back over the net without anyone hitting it twice in a row and without it touching the floor. Simple as that. So the guy who receives the ball from the serve 'digs' it out. That means he controls the serve and knocks the ball up in the air with his hands or arms. The second dude gets under the ball and 'sets' it. That means he tries to push it up high into the air so that it comes down nice and easy, close to the net. The third guy leaps up and 'spikes' it – which basically means he thumps it as hard as he can – into the opposition court. Dig. Set. Spike. Three hits. Scobes could be the setter dude. They're normally shorter than the spikers anyway so they can get under the ball and push it up into the air for the easy put-away."

Scobie was now grinning widely and showing all of his little pointy teeth.

"There's only one problem though. And it's a pretty big one."

Scobie's row of little pointy teeth slowly disappeared behind his thin lips.

"The volleyball season starts Saturday week, so they've already had the open volleyball trials and they picked all the teams last weekend. They wanted to get five teams of six players plus two reserves for the inter-school comp, but only enough guys turned up to scrape together four teams. I know because Melvin Yip trialled and he missed out. Hardcastle made him the reserve, reserve for the Fourths. Yippy wasn't too happy about it."

"Well then, all I have to do is get a Fifths team together."

"Don't like your chances, Your Supreme Leadership," Razz said with a shake of his head. "Hardcastle tried and couldn't. I mean there's you and Yippy, but even if you don't have any reserves, you still gotta come up with four other guys."

"Four other guys?"

Scobie's gaze moved from Razz to Ignatius to Bill. By the time he got to me, his little pointy teeth were well and truly back on show.

6.
The Pi Man
Delivers!

Us, Scobes? You want *all* of us to be in the team? You do realise, don't you, that the closest Prindabel's ever got to playing sport was last year when he got beaten up by a junior nerfball team?"

"If you all join up I can tell Mr Hardcastle we've got a team. He'd have to let me play then. What do you say? Please? I wouldn't ask you if it wasn't important to me."

"Well, I got nothing till football starts up, so it'd be fine by me," Razz said.

Now Scobie was looking right at me. What could I say? It was James Scobie. How many times had he been there when I needed him? How many times had he stood up to Barry Bagsley? How many times had he rescued us all from debating disasters?

"Well, if you really want to do it, then, yeah, me too I guess."

Razz draped an arm over Bill Kingsley's shoulder.

"And what about you, Big Bill the Man Hill? Feel like throwing your hoop into the ring with us?"

"Sure." Bill shrugged. "Why not?"

I'm fairly certain that would have been Bill's answer if Razz had asked him to join the Mount Everest downhill skiing team.

That just left Ignatius. Everyone turned his way. Two terrified eyes stared back at us.

"No, no, you don't understand," he said, holding up his hands. "For once in his life Orazio's right. I don't do sport. I'm sorry, James. I don't. I *can't*. Sport and me, we're... mutually exclusive. We're binary opposites. I'm the natural enemy of sport. I've tried – I have, honestly. I just end up getting laughed at or yelled at or both. I'm hopeless. I'm not just the last one picked. I'm the one who's *never* picked. You'd be better having a player short than have me on your team. Ask anyone."

"Awwwwwwwwww, Prindabubbles! Snookems!" Razz said, spreading his arms wide. "Come here. What you need is a great – big – hug!"

Ignatius reeled back in horror.

"Okay," Razz said, "maybe later. But dude, don't you see, you *are* being picked. *We're* picking you, man. And not *just* to make up the numbers or because we've got no hope in hell of getting anyone else – although that's totally, like, ninety-nine point nine per cent of the reason – but *also* because we actually *need* you, dude. We need your height. You and Billy can be our net guys, our main 'go to' spikers."

"But I don't know anything about volleyball."

"Are you kidding me? You knew the net was high. That's a great start. I can teach you how to play. And I even promise not to laugh or yell. Well, maybe I'll laugh a bit – I'm only human. Come on, dude. It'll be great! And you'll get to do other exciting stuff as well, like help keep score, analyse the match statistics, double-check the dimensions of the court and calculate the optimum velocity and trajectory for serving the ball over the net."

The worried look on Ignatius's face actually eased a little.

"Look, we don't want just another guy on the team, Prindabuddy. We want *you*. We're the Fab Five, like Miss T says. It wouldn't be a proper team without the Pi Man."

I could tell Prindabel was wavering as he rubbed a palm across his large expanse of forehead.

"You don't have to do it if you really don't want to, Ignatius," Scobie said, "but it would be great if you could."

Prindabel took us all in with a sweep of his eagle eyes.

"You do realise, don't you, that once I'm placed within the set parameters of a sporting arena, there is a very real possibility that it may result in a fatal fracture of the space-time continuum leading to the collapse of the universe and the imminent destruction of all life as we now know it."

"For you, Ignatius, it's a risk we're willing to take," Scobie told him.

"All right. If you really need me, I suppose I'm in," Ignatius said as if he was volunteering himself for a full body wax.

"Awesome!" Razz shouted. "The Pi Man delivers!" Then he thrust his hand high above his head and left it hanging. Ignatius stared at it for a moment before a flash of understanding swept across his face. Then he drew back his own hand, focused his eyes and carefully lined up Razza's open palm for a high five.

"Well, Scobes," Razz said, after just managing to avoid getting slapped in the head, "looks like you got your dream team. Now all you need is a coach."

Scobie twisted his mouth about.

"But you're going to coach us, aren't you?"

"Sure. I can be your *actual* coach, but you have to have a teacher on board as well. Hardcastle's rules. No teacher, no team. Might be tricky too. The Hard Man has already bribed and threatened every teacher he could to get a coach for the Fourths. In the end he had to do it himself and he's already got the Firsts."

"What does the teacher have to do?"

"Nothing much. For starters they don't have to know a thing about volleyball. We can take care of ourselves. They just sort of have to be there, you know, when we train and play. Hey, what about Miss Tarango?"

"She'd do it," Scobie said "but I don't think we should ask her. Not on top of her year coordinator role. It wouldn't be fair."

"What we really need is someone who's a soft touch," Razz said. "Someone who'd do it even if they were way too busy. Someone who'd feel bad if they turned us down."

Just then Mr Guthrie strolled into our form room and greeted everyone with a warm "Good morning, boys!" He dropped his canvas bag on the teacher's desk, pulled out a poster and began pinning it up on the noticeboard.

Scobie kept his eyes on Mr G but directed his next question at Razz.

"Someone who wasn't afraid of taking on seemingly hopeless causes?"

Razz nodded solemnly. "Dude, have you seen our team? That would be the *minimum* requirement for the job."

Mr Guthrie pushed a final pin into the bottom of the poster and stepped back. *END WORLD HUNGER NOW!* shouted at us from the noticeboard.

Scobie performed one of his classic mouth twists then smiled.

"Come the moment, come the man," he said.

7.
The Brown Undies Effect

Even though he had his hands full trying to save the planet, Mr Guthrie came to our rescue as well and agreed to become our volleyball 'coach'. I guess some superheroes get their tights and capes from charity shops.

As soon as Mr G signed on, Scobie and Razz met with Mr Hardcastle and soon the St Daniel's Open Fifths volleyball team was officially alive and kicking. Well, alive anyway. As a sporting unit we weren't exactly a well-oiled machine. More like the remains of a rusty, broken-down tractor bogged in an overgrown paddock somewhere – with chickens roosting in us. Don't get me wrong. I'm not saying that we were the worst team in St Daniel's long and proud volleyball history. (We were, of course. But it's just that I'm not saying it. Not out loud anyway. I've got some pride.)

On the plus side we had two things going for us. One was Razz and the other was Mr Guthrie. As far as

Razz was concerned, we all knew that he'd be a natural at volleyball and our best player, but what we didn't know was what a great coach he would be. But after just two sessions he'd transformed us from a totally hopeless, incompetent rabble into what could only be described as a well below average volleyball team. And he made training fun. It was a minor miracle.

Mr Guthrie was our second plus because for him, winning wasn't *everything*. In fact sometimes I wondered if it even registered on his radar. This, of course, made Emerson Guthrie a perfect match for the mighty Fighting Fifths, because it was pretty obvious that we were never going to win *anything*.

So much for our pluses. On the minus side was... well... the rest of us, basically.

First up there was Bill and me. I'd say that on a very good day, if we reached the extreme outer limit of our abilities, we *almost* made it to okay. Bill was better than me. He actually had good ball control and not a bad serve. I think hooping helped, and Bill hooped a lot. On the other hand his mobility wasn't great because there was still plenty of him to move around. To his credit though, he was quite fast over about two steps.

Next there was Ignatius Prindabel. Seeing Ignatius on a sporting arena of any kind was as startling as seeing a flamingo on the polar ice caps. Seeing him in sports clothes bordered on the disturbing. Razz described him as a cross between a giraffe in fancy dress and a scarecrow minus the straw. And Ignatius was absolutely right when he said he was the natural enemy of sport, because the volleyball appeared to be on a mission to kill him.

No matter how Ignatius positioned his hands, the ball always found a way to avoid them and hit some part of his body. Often his groin. I had a theory that because Prindabel's arms were so long, it took more time than normal for messages to travel between his brain and his hands and by the time they did, it was too late. Razz had another theory involving Ignatius having "excessive levels of the extreme nerd hormone".

Next in our stellar line-up was James Scobie. I've already described Scobie's prowess in various sporting arenas, so all you have to do is transfer most of that to a volleyball court. By far his biggest problem was receiving serve, and his decision not to wear his glasses for safety reasons didn't help. As the ball hurtled towards him, Scobie squinted on the baseline, desperately trying to get it into some sort of focus. From what I could figure out, this didn't actually happen until just before the ball thudded into the floor for a winner or into James himself.

Last in our long list of negatives was Melvin Yip. At least Melvin looked the part. This was because he owned every item of brand-name sporting clothing and equipment ever made and he liked to have as many of those items on his body at one time as humanly possible. His sport shoes were something else again.

As well as being all the colours of a fluorescent rainbow, Melvin's footwear featured every sort of pump, gel, stripe and brand-new-adjust-to-any-surface-straight-from-the-latest-space-programme-ultramodern-cutting-edge-technology that you could possibly imagine. One day as a joke Razz asked Yippy if he could check his emails with his shoes. Melvin just frowned a bit and said, "Not sure. I haven't read through all the instructions yet." It would have been a good comeback if he wasn't being serious.

As well as having all the right gear, Yippy was short, wiry, keen and super-fit, with rock-hard calf muscles that bulged from his bandy legs. There was no doubt that on a volleyball court he looked like a million dollars. Sadly he played like loose change. This, however, didn't bother Melvin in the least. Not only did he firmly believe that he was the best volleyball player in the entire school, somehow he had managed to convince himself that he was descended from either a long line of Japanese samurai or some secret society of ninja. This was despite the fact that the Yips originally came from Malaysia, not Japan, and that Melvin himself was a second-generation Australian. Reality wasn't exactly Melvin Yip's strong suit.

The big problem for us was that Melvin liked to display his ninja and samurai moves on the volleyball court whenever possible. This meant that when the ball came his way, he would leap into the air, scream "Yeeee-aaaaaa!", thrash his arms at it and then land back on the court, where he would pose for a few seconds, crouching ninja-like, before springing nimbly backwards into position. The rest of us, meanwhile, had to try to figure out where the ball had gone. It was hardly surprising, therefore, that Melvin Yip was known in volleyball circles as the Psycho Samurai or the Nutcase Ninja. He wore both titles with great pride.

So that was our team. Just the six of us. But this was about to change. It was at the end of our second training session that Razz informed us of his awesome brainwave.

"Hey, listen up, guys. I just had this awesome brainwave."

Everyone glanced in Razz's direction, but no one stopped getting changed or shoving stuff into bags. Given his track record with 'awesome brainwaves', our expectations weren't that high.

"Look, we need to get at least one extra guy to join the team so we've got a reserve, right?"

We nodded.

"Well, I've been thinking about who we could get. So here's my question. What does our team lack?"

There was quite a pause then as each of us tried to decide which of the countless possible answers he should choose. Fortunately Razz came to our rescue.

"I'll tell you. The Intimidation Factor. Hardcastle's always going on about it. Personally, I like to call it 'the Brown Undies Effect'."

"Intimidation?" Scobie said. "This is volleyball, not football."

"Doesn't matter. It still works, Your Humungousness. We need some guy who can stand right up at the net and stare down the other team. Someone to put their blockers and servers off their games. Now, while I'd be the first to admit that Prindabel in his volleyball shorts is pretty terrifying, we need more than that. We need someone who can give the opposition… the Look."

"The Look?"

"That's right, Scobes. The Look. The one that says, 'If you win this point I'm gonna come over there and force-feed you the ball followed by a tasty side dish of your own trainers'."

"I see," Scobie said. "And who have you got in mind for such a *commendable* role?"

"Well, just think about it for a minute. Who've we got in our year that could pull that off?"

It didn't take me long to come up with a name.

"Not Bagsley?"

"Yeah, I thought of him too. But he'd never play with us. Anyway, the dude I'm thinking of makes Bagsley look about as intimidating as a Teletubby with a balloon sword."

What followed was a few seconds of group frowning followed by growing expressions of disbelief as each of us figured out exactly who Razz was talking about.

Scobie performed an extreme mouth twist.

Melvin Yip narrowed his eyes in a vain attempt to look inscrutable.

Ignatius gave a nervous laugh. "You can't be serious?"

Bill lost a little of the colour in his face. "You don't mean…"

All I managed to squeeze out was, "Not…"

Razz addressed each of us in turn. "I *am* serious, Prindabudster. I *do* mean, Bilbo. And yes, Ishmael, my man… *him*. If we're talking intimidation, we might as well set our sights on the Grand Poobah, right? What do you say, Scobes? This whole show is your baby."

James Scobie slowly released his mouth from its twist and adjusted his glasses. His two beady eyes focused in on the question. Then he pushed out his bottom lip and nodded.

"All right!" said Razz, picking up a volleyball and spinning it effortlessly into a twirling blur on the tip of his index finger.

"Time to pay a call on the Mudman."

8.

The Razzman v The Mudman

The Mudman's real name was Theodore Bungalari. He had come to St Daniel's last year from Papua New Guinea. That wasn't such a big deal. We had plenty of boarders from overseas and quite a few of those were from PNG. But none of them were quite like Theodore Bungalari.

When Theodore was introduced to our Tutor Group we learned that he was from Goroka in the Highlands. Mr Guthrie had been there on one of his trekking holidays, and he told us the region was famous for its spectacular festivals and ceremonies, and especially for the Goroka Mudmen – locals who wore big headdresses and covered their bodies entirely in mud. Theodore got his nickname a couple of days later when a boy came around looking for him and saying, "Hey, if anyone sees that mudman guy, tell him he's wanted at the office." A name like that couldn't really do anything else but stick.

But it wasn't where he came from or his nickname that set Theodore Bungalari apart. As Razz rightly pointed out, Theodore had the intimidation factor. Even the other boys from PNG seemed in awe of him. He was only around sixteen like the rest of us, but with his hair shaved close to his skull and his face looking like it had been chiselled roughly out of dull black marble, he probably could have passed for thirty-six. And he was big. Not tall-big, just solid-muscle-and-heavy-chunky-bones-big. If you were careless enough to bump into Theodore in a crowded corridor, it was pretty much the same as bumping into a wall. The only thing that rebounded was you. After you did, you would be confronted by Theodore's perfectly still eyes peering at you like two cannons from the shadows of a cave. Right from day one everyone automatically gave Theodore Bungalari a very wide berth.

Of course the cannibal thing only added to his mystique.

That came about one day when we were waiting for our maths teacher, Mr Xiang, to arrive to class. That's when Danny Wallace thought it would be a good idea to start firing questions at the new boy.

"Hey, Mudman, what's it like up in the Highlands? Come across any good mud lately? You and the pigs must really hit it off, eh? Is it true that you rub all the mud on your skin to help fight the seven signs of ageing?"

The whole class sat there in stunned silence. Even Barry Bagsley had the sense to leave Theodore Bungalari alone. But not Danny Wallace. Apparently you had to have a certain minimum level of grey matter before the self-preservation response kicked in.

And Danny was only warming up.

"Hey, you guys got *Mud*Donald's up there? I reckon you could put away a few quarter pounders. You'd like your *meat*, wouldn't you, Muddy? Didn't all you mudmen used to cook people up and eat them?"

While all these questions were flying his way Theodore sat quietly at the back of the room filling out his school diary. Then he put his pen down and calmly lifted his head. He folded his arms and hunched himself forward on the desk to get a better look at Danny Wallace. His blue school shirt strained under the pressure from his shoulders and biceps. Theodore ran his dark eyes slowly over Danny Wallace from the top of his head to the tip of his shoes and back again. Then he locked on to Danny's eyes and frowned.

"What do you mean... *used* to?" he asked in his deep, rolling voice.

We all knew he wasn't being serious, of course.

He was obviously just kidding. Except Theodore Bungalari didn't look like your typical 'just kidding' sort of guy. Anyway, Mr Xiang came striding into the room at that point and the whole thing was pretty much forgotten. But not by Danny Wallace. He kept shooting glances at Theodore throughout the lesson, and whenever he did, Theodore's eyes would widen and the tip of his pink tongue would slip slowly across his lips.

After that day everyone, including Danny Wallace, just left Theodore Bungalari alone. He didn't seem to mind. As far as I could tell, Theodore was 'an island, entire unto himself'. That comes from one of Mr Guthrie's form room posters.

But the Island of Theodore Bungalari was about to be invaded. And leading the charge was none other than Orazio Zorzotto.

It was the Razzman v the Mudman.

9.
The Pride of Goroka

The day after Razz's awesome brainwave and just two days before our first volleyball match we set out to recruit Theodore Bungalari. We'd been looking for him half of lunchtime. We finally tracked him down to an empty classroom on the top floor of the Senior Block.

He was sitting in a desk at the back corner near a window taking notes from his history textbook. Theodore always completed every assignment and every piece of school work to the minutest detail. And he did it in the neatest handwriting I'd ever seen. His exercise books were works of art. Teachers gushed over them. I kid you not. There was actual real-life gushing involved.

"Hey, here's the guy we want. The Pride of Goroka! Mud… ah… Theodore, my main man! Looking good, dude! How're they hanging, Bunga?"

Razz slapped the the Mudman heartily on the shoulder. It was like he was whacking a block of concrete.

Theodore stopped writing and looked around slowly at each of us. He wasn't smiling. Suddenly this seemed like a very bad idea. But Razz wouldn't be put off.

"Muddy," he said, "it's your lucky day, pal. Believe it or not, I am offering you the chance to join our very exclusive volleyball team! No, please, no need to thank me."

Theodore stared back at Razz. I tried to remember if I'd ever seen him blink. Razz cleared his throat and ploughed on.

"Please, contain your excitement for just a moment longer, TB, and let me explain. We want you, yes *you*, to be part of the mighty Fighting Fifths. As such, you will be joining an elite band of athletes – all these fine specimens you see here before you and… um… *that* guy."

Razz was pointing out the window to where down in the yard Melvin Yip was facing up to an incoming fast bowler and waving his cricket bat around like a sword. We all waited to watch the delivery. It came. We all winced. Everyone except for Theodore Bungalari. Melvin Yip lay doubled over and clutching some now extremely tender parts of his body.

"I guess that's why they call him the Nutcase Ninja," Razz said. Everyone smiled. Everyone except for Theodore Bungalari.

"Aaaaanyhoo," Razz said, "as I was saying, this is the

chance of a lifetime, Muddy Buddy. You could have it all, man – sporting glory, multi-million dollar merchandising deals and really hot groupie chicks throwing themselves at you. Too good to be true? I think not!"

All the while Razz was speaking, Theodore hadn't moved a muscle or changed his expression. I was tempted to poke him to see if he was real. I want you to know that I had no trouble at all resisting that particular temptation.

"Aaah, Theodore," Scobie said, stepping forward and joining Razz, "I would just like to *clarify* a few things that my… *learned* friend… has said to avoid any possible *misunderstanding* and *disappointment* later on. I'm afraid that in his undoubted enthusiasm to have you on board he might have been guilty of some *slight* exaggeration."

Theodore shifted his eyes slowly from Razz to Scobie.

"Firstly, apart from Orazio here, none of us can really play volleyball. And I feel justified in saying that, because I am undoubtedly the worst in the team. You, however, if you were to join us, would most certainly be at *least* the second best. Secondly, there will be no sporting glory. None whatsoever. We will probably not win a game. Taking these two things into account, I think you can safely draw your own conclusions about both the 'multi-million dollar merchandising deals' and the 'really hot groupie chicks'. Theodore, the truth is, we need another player. We'd really like that player to be you."

Razz leaned down and whispered to Scobie behind his hand.

"Nice going, Scobes. Way to totally ruin our chances. Oh, and here's a little tip. You know those forms we're filling out for career choices? You might like to put a big black line through sales assistant, public relations guy and motivational speaker."

The next voice we heard was Theodore's. It always made me think of thick rich syrup pouring slowly out of a can.

"I will play in your volleyball team."

"Yeah, well," Razz said, "can't say I blame you. After the build-up the Scobster gave us you'd be cra— *What?* What did you say?"

"I said I will play in your volleyball team."

There were smiles all round. Well, at least from us.

"That's awesome, dude," Razz said, scratching his head. "But I gotta ask you, man. Why? I mean, why would you want to play for our team?"

Theodore Bungalari gave us all the once-over.

"You fellows make me laugh," he said without a single atom of a smile anywhere within a light year of his face.

10.
Prindabel's Butt Ball

We played our first game that Saturday morning against Harrisville High. Theodore hadn't had a chance to train with us at all. It was probably just as well. It might have scared him off.

All matches were best of three sets. Two sets to fifteen points and if it was one-all, a final, first to seven, set. For a while there against Harrisville, we were holding our own. But then the warm-up finished and the actual game started.

We lost 15–3; 15–5.

Believe it or not, the score actually flattered us. Four of our massive eight points came from the other team serving into the net. Another three of them were won by Razz virtually on his own. Our final point came when Ignatius tried to spike a ball, missed it completely and it rebounded off his big forehead over the net for a winner. That was one of our match highlights. It was celebrated with high fives all round.

Additional highlights included Melvin Yip leaping

into the air, performing a 360-degree ninja spin and whacking the ball with a wildly swinging arm – straight into the umpire's face, and Bill losing his balance while going for a low serve and landing on top of me. I thought the roof had caved in.

On the up side, we did have our Intimidation Factor. At least for a while. Razz was spot on about the Mudman. When we stuck him up at the net at the start of the game the Harrisville net guys took a couple of steps back and their server sent his first wobbly ball straight into the back of a team mate's head. It was 1–nil. We were winning! If there had been a massive meteor strike right then that wiped out all life on Earth, victory would have been ours. But no such luck.

After our brilliant start, Harrisville won the following six points in a row. Then Theodore managed to work the Brown Undies Effect again on another one of their servers. That brought Ignatius into the server's position. We didn't know it then, but he was about to totally ace our Intimidation Factor.

Ignatius steadied himself behind the baseline and threw the ball up above his head. His long arm flapped through the air. To everyone's surprise Prindabel's hand actually made contact with the ball – but only just.

Instead of sailing over the net, the ball rocketed to the left and down – right into James Scobie's little round backside.

This set off an unfortunate chain of events. Scobie, who had been crouched over and totally unprepared for what became known as the Prindabel Butt Ball, was propelled forward like a swimmer from the blocks of the Olympic 50 metres freestyle final. It all ended horrifically, when James, in a vain attempt to save himself, grabbed desperately at the only thing within his reach – the back of Bill Kingsley's shorts. As Razz said afterwards, it was the only time a full moon had ever appeared inside the St Daniel's gymnasium.

It was just after Bill's rump made its grand appearance that we heard the squeaking noise. It was like someone was strangling a hyperventilating guinea pig. Both teams looked in the direction of the sound. It was coming from Theodore. He was holding his stomach and pointing at us and shaking uncontrollably. His hard, dark marble face was shattered by the widest, whitest smile I had ever seen. Theodore wasn't lying. We fellows really did make him laugh.

The problem was that laughing to the Mudman was like kryptonite to Superman. Whenever Theodore laughed he lost all his strength and coordination.

This meant that if something slightly funny, weird or unexpected happened on court (which, thanks to our team, was just about every second rally) Theodore would fall apart and become as useless as a super-jumbo-sized rag doll.

And that caused another problem. Once the opposition saw the Mudman transformed from an awesome, threatening mountain of cold, black marble to a wobbly, giggling blob of chocolate sponge cake, it became almost impossible for him to work the Brown Undies Effect on them. To make matters worse, we discovered as the season wore on that our Intimidation Factor was, in fact, the nicest guy you could ever hope to meet.

After we'd lost the opening set to Harrisville in that first match and slumped to 12–nil down in the second, Mr Guthrie called a time out and gave us a pep talk. It would set the tone for the rest of our season. We grouped in a tight circle around him.

"Guys, I hate to break this to you," he said, "but I think I can hear the fat lady clearing her throat. Things are getting desperate."

"Maybe if Bill moons the opposition again, we could score a few points while they're in shock," Razz suggested.

Beside me Theodore squeaked like someone was trampolining on a mouse, and everyone, including Mr Guthrie, laughed.

"Let's keep that as our secret weapon in case we make the finals, Orazio."

"Geez, keeping Billy's butt a secret – now *there's* a challenge, Sir."

More laughing – and squeaking.

"So, sir, do you think we can actually come back from here and win this thing?"

We all looked to Mr Guthrie – St Daniel's Patron Saint of Lost Causes. His eyes shone with optimism and hope.

"Not a chance, Orazio," he said with a smile. "But that doesn't mean we shouldn't keep fighting, keep trying our best, keep encouraging each other and keep having fun. And maybe we can have some mini victories along the way. Take some baby steps."

"Baby steps? Have you been watching us play, Sir? Maybe we should start off with like embryo steps and work our way up," Razz said.

"OK, how about this, then? Harrisville need three points to win the match. Let's make our first goal stopping them from beating us to nil. Let's see if we can get at least one point. That's our first…

embryo step. If we do that, then we go for two. Who knows, maybe we can beat them to three points. What do you say?"

When there was a general rumble of agreement for this plan, Mr Guthrie reached behind him and pulled his sports bag into the centre of our circle. "And just for added incentive..." he said, unzipping his bag and holding it open.

Across from me Theodore Bungalari's eyes grew into a pair of white-walled tyres and his pink tongue poked out from between his lips. The bag was filled with mini chocolate bars.

"Okay, here's the deal. One bar each for every point we score, a bonus chocolate each if we get to three before them, and two bonus chocolates each if we outscore them."

"What if we win the set, Sir?"

"If you win the set, Orazio, I will text Willy Wonka immediately and book an all-you-can-eat tour of the factory."

Then Mr Guthrie stretched his arm into the middle of the circle and seven hands piled in a heap on top of his. We were getting pretty good at that. We gave the St Daniel's shout and filed back out onto the court.

We ended up earning four mini chocolate bars each.

And we played those last few points as we would every other point for the rest of the season – for each other, for Mr Guthrie, for St Daniel's, for the chocolates and for the fun of it. And the best thing was, because no one expected anything much from us, there was never any pressure.

Until the day there was. Then there was a truckload of it.

11.
That's What I'm Talking About

After our first volleyball defeat we managed to successfully maintain an unbroken losing streak. It matched my success with Kelly: I hadn't seen or heard from her since the Moorfield meeting.

Luckily, things were going much better in our quest for the Senior Debating Trophy. Two debates. Two victories. As for Operation Tarango, we were about to face the next big test – the Inter-house Cross-country. It was time to put Scobie's 'Saturation Participation' strategy into overdrive. To do that we had gathered at our usual lunch table. All eyes were on the door to the sports office.

"Geez, we're cutting it a bit fine, aren't we, Scobes? Hardcastle said nominations had to be on the noticeboard *before* the end of lunch, remember? And there's only ten minutes to go, man. Here, give them to me. I'll whack 'em up."

"No need," Scobie said, pointing across the playground.

Mr Hardcastle was leaving the sports office and making a beeline for the main noticeboard. It was a beeline that would take him right past our table.

"Excuse me, Mr Hardcastle."

"Yes, Mr Scobie. What can I do you for?"

"Well, I have a *few* last-minute Charlton House nominations for the cross-country. I was just about to take them over and pin them up with the others, but if you're collecting them anyway, could I just hand them straight to you?"

Mr Hardcastle checked his watch. Then he took the sheet from Scobie and studied it closely. There were about fifty names on it. A single eyebrow arched upwards on his tanned forehead.

"Call me suspicious, Mr Scobie, but my gut reaction is that the reason you've kept all these names until the very last minute and handed them to me directly, is so the other houses won't see how many runners you'll be fielding on the day and try to match you. Technically you're not breaking any rules, but some people might consider this a tad... devious."

Scobie smiled innocently but didn't reply. We all waited. Mr Hardcastle folded up the list of names, tucked it into his top pocket and gave it a pat.

"Love it. I'm going to miss you, Scobie, I really am," he said before striding happily on his way.

Not surprisingly, when the day of the cross-country arrived, Mr Hardcastle found himself surrounded by the unhappy faces of the other house leaders.

"Too late to start whingeing now, gentlemen. You had exactly the same opportunity to register runners as Charlton. Them's the rules. Sorry, fellas," he told them.

He didn't look very sorry.

Of course, just having more runners didn't really mean anything. They still had to finish within the set time limit to gain a participation point. Thankfully, three-quarters of our runners did just that. It was a great day for Charlton House as well as for our newly appointed Sports Captain.

I think Razz must have completed nearly three cross-countries by the time it was over. He spent all day charging back and forth along the course encouraging the Charlton competitors and making jokes to keep their spirits up. In the end he barely made the time limit himself. This was because he was practically dragging Ignatius along the ground behind him for the last 100 metres or so.

But Razz was well supported in his efforts. Melvin

Yip and Theodore Bungalari made the time and did a great job inspiring the stragglers with a combination of ninja moves and friendly intimidation. And our ex-captain Jimmy 'The Main Event' Mainwaring went a long way to redeeming himself by piggybacking about half a dozen struggling younger runners across the finish line. Even Bill beat the bell. All the jogging and hooping he'd been doing was really starting to tell. He was still big, but more and more of him was muscle. And believe it or not, I made it too, although it took me quite a while to put out the fireball in my lungs and to regain the power of speech.

But the biggest cheer of the afternoon was reserved for the 'runner' who came in last. Twenty minutes after the qualifying time had elapsed, the chubby form of James Scobie appeared at the end of the bush track and shuffled around the final half-circuit of the oval before collapsing across the finishing line. And when he did, it wasn't just Charlton who cheered – so did the other houses and all the teachers. I was standing beside Mr Hardcastle at the time and heard him say, "Now that's what I'm talking about," to no one in particular.

In a miraculous turnaround from the previous year, Charlton ended up winning the day. It was a win that pushed us ahead of Radley and Franklin in the overall house totals, into outright second place. In his first test as Charlton House Sports Captain, Razz had come through with flying colours and he proudly held the cross-country trophy above his head to the roar of his teammates.

But Razz was soon going to come face to face with a different kind of challenge. One that would scare the life out of him.

And it all came about because of the Courses and Careers Expo.

12.
Words in the Blood

"She asked you yet?"

Razz and I were having lunch and waiting for the others to arrive. I shook my head at him. It was the same question he'd asked just about every day for the last few weeks. He was talking about Kelly inviting me to the Lourdes College Formal.

"Don't worry, man. She'll get around to it. Sal reckons the Kelster's been real quiet since she came back. Got her head buried in the books all the time and keeping to herself. But there's still plenty of time. Probably just trying to keep you keen."

If that was true it was working a treat!

"I don't know, Razz. I'm not even sure she'll go to the Formal."

"Of course she will. Everybody goes to their Senior Formal."

I hoped that was true. Really hoped.

"Hey, boys. Recovered from our crushing cross-country victory yet?"

It was Miss Tarango on playground duty. She was wearing a blue St Daniel's sports cap and big, white-rimmed sunglasses. She could make anything look good.

"I think I'm just starting to get some feeling back in my legs," Razz informed her.

"Excellent. One point at a time," Miss said with a wink. Only she couldn't do it properly and both eyes sort of closed. Even that looked good.

"Now, what I really want to know is, have you boys worked out what talks and presentations you're going to attend next week?"

Miss was talking about the big Courses and Careers Expo at the university. The whole year group was going.

"I know James is looking into law and politics options," she said, "and Bill wants to find out about film courses and Ignatius is checking out the sciences."

Razz reeled back. "Whoa! Prindabel and science? What a shock! I had him down for interpretive dance."

"Well, what about you, then?" Miss Tarango asked. "What does the future hold for Orazio Zorzotto?"

"Not sure, Miss. I've been tossing up between plastic surgeon to the stars and playboy millionaire, but I'll probably just end up working for one of my uncles. You know, do some labouring or work in a garage.

Plus, I've still got the gig playing drums at the Italian Club. Probably try to do more of that."

"Not interested in going to uni then, Orazio, or doing more study somewhere else?"

"Me, Miss? What would I do?"

"Something with sport, I would have thought. Physiotherapy maybe, or you could become a personal trainer or even a health and physical education teacher."

"HPE teacher? That's what my girlfriend says I should do. She keeps going on about me 'wasting my potential'."

"Sounds like one very smart young lady to me," Miss said. Then she tilted her head to one side. "And you say she's *your* girlfriend, Orazio?"

"Ignatius reckons it's one of the great unexplained mysteries of the universe, Miss," I informed her.

"Hey, careful," Razz said, trying to look offended, "you could be lowering my self-esteem."

He didn't get much sympathy. Everyone knew you'd need a truckload of strategically placed plastic explosives to lower Razz's self-esteem.

"But seriously, Orazio, I want you to promise me you'll check out some of those courses."

"What's the point, Miss, with my grades?"

"You don't even know what grades you'd need.

That's what you can find out at the careers day. And anyway, if you put your mind to it, you could improve your grades. Now, promise me you won't waste your time on the day, Orazio. Promise me you'll think seriously about this and do some research. Promise me?"

Razz held up his hands in surrender. "Okay, Miss. I promise, I promise."

Miss turned to me then. It was the moment I'd been dreading. I had no idea what I was going to do when I left school.

"Ishmael, what exciting path are you going to explore after school?"

"Umm, I haven't really decided, Miss. I thought I might take a year off, maybe get a job and think about it for a while. I don't really know what I'd be good at."

"I think you'd be good at plenty of things. But have you thought about following in the footsteps of your namesake?"

Of course I knew my namesake was the Ishmael character from *Moby Dick* but I couldn't see what Miss was getting at.

"Join a whaling fleet and hunt whales, Miss?"

"Geez, Miss," Razz said, "I thought you would've been totally against all that whaling stuff. I know Mr Guthrie is. He's always going on about it..."

Razz hesitated and his eyes shifted. You could almost see an idea clawing its way to the surface of his manic brain.

"Hey, you should talk to Mr Guthrie about it, Miss. Whaling, I mean. He's really interesting and he knows tons of stuff. He's a great guy too, I reckon. You know, like how he's always trying to save the rainforests and wombats and stuff. And he's always helping people out, like us with our volleyball. He's the best. Oh, and what about him in the teachers' race at the Swimming Carnival? That was so awesome, don't you reckon, Miss? Except for the swimming trunks, of course. Maybe you two should..."

Miss Tarango's lips were squeezed together. Her eyes were narrowing and one eyebrow kept cranking higher and higher with each thing Razz said. She looked like a cobra poised, ready to strike if Razz took one more step into the no-go zone.

"... Well ...Anyway ...Ummm ...What were you saying before about Ishmael's namesake thing, Miss?"

Miss Tarango made sure Razz had plenty of opportunity to read and memorise the look on her face before turning to me.

"I definitely do *not* want you to hunt whales, Ishmael. What I was referring to was your namesake's *other* important role in the book."

I desperately tried to remember what Ishmael did before he joined Ahab and the crew of the *Pequod*. Miss Tarango finally took pity on me.

"Okay, time's up. He was the *narrator*, remember? He told the story. Perhaps you could follow in those footsteps. After all, English is your best subject, and you know how I loved those pieces you showed me from your journals."

Miss squinted and pointed a finger at me.

"Which reminds me, Mr Leseur, why haven't I seen anything from this year's effort yet? You promised me something ages ago."

"Sorry, Miss, I keep forgetting. I'll bring some stuff next week."

"Well, see that you do. And make sure you check out all the creative writing courses at the expo. Your father's a songwriter, so you've got words in the blood. Think about it."

Miss left then and headed for the staffroom. She arrived at the door just as Mr Guthrie was coming out. There was a bit of awkward shuffling about before they figured out who should go first.

Razz clicked his tongue.

"Gotta get those two together."

I stared at him in disbelief.

"Razz, didn't you see Miss Tarango's face just now when you oh-so-subtly tried to match her up with Mr Guthrie?"

Razz dismissed my concern with a wave of his hand. "Bah! That's nothing. She'll end up thanking me. You'll see."

I knew I couldn't change Razz's mind so I changed the subject instead.

"So, are you going to do what Miss suggested? Are you going to seriously look at HPE teaching?"

"Said I would, so guess I have to. But it's a bit stupid, don't you reckon? *Me* a teacher."

"I don't think it's stupid at all," I said. "You're already coaching and training junior kids plus our volleyball team. You're doing a great job as Sports Captain and Mr Murphy says you practically run those afternoon activities with the boarders. I think you'd be a great teacher."

"Really?" Razz seemed more than a little stunned.

At that point Scobie, Bill and Ignatius joined us at the table.

"Hey, guys, wanna hear something hilarious? Miss Tarango and Ishmael think I should become an HPE teacher."

"An excellent idea," Scobie said. Bill nodded.

"What, really? You too?"

Razz looked at Ignatius. "I got a feeling these guys are just being nice, Prindabuddy. I know you won't pull any punches, man. Tell me honestly – I can take it – do you really see me as an HPE teacher like Mr Hardcastle?"

Ignatius thought about it for a moment.

"No," he said.

Now it was Scobie's, Bill's and my turn to be a little stunned.

"See? I told you guys," Razz said, struggling to look pleased about being proved right. "There's no way I could..."

He was silenced by the Prindabel Power Pointer hovering in front of his face.

"I haven't finished," Ignatius said. "Mr Hardcastle could never have got me onto a volleyball court. You have. And I'm not hating it or afraid of it any more. So no, I don't see you as a HPE teacher *like* Mr Hardcastle. But – and I'll probably regret saying this – I think you could be a very different one... a better one."

"*Really?*" Razz said, completely gobsmacked. "Gee... thanks... Thanks, Ignatius... thanks, man."

The bell rang for the end of lunch then and everyone

got up to go. Razz was the last one to move. I think he was still trying to imagine a future for himself that he'd never even considered possible before.

He wasn't the only one.

13.
Operation Get Razz into Uni

Like me, Razz kept his promise to Miss Tarango and he discovered at the Courses and Careers Expo that getting into HPE at uni was at least a possibility – *if* he could improve his grades enough. And yes, when you looked at some of Razz's grades, it was a seriously big *IF*.

Razz's HPE results weren't the problem. He was getting top marks there, at least in the practical assessment part. Modern History was solid as well. Ms Heckenvaal had made sure of that. And English and Media Studies weren't *too* bad. But Maths, Multi-strand Science and particularly Economics were a real worry. Razz had a big decision to make, and for once it wasn't something he could joke his way around or rely on his natural ability to see him through.

"If you're serious about trying to get your grades up," Scobie told him, "we'll all help you. Are you serious about it?"

I'd never seen Razz look so nervous. It took a while for him to answer.

"Yeah. Yeah, I am."

It was probably the hardest thing Razz had ever had to say. And as soon as the words left his lips, we had ourselves another quest. Operation Get Razz into Uni. It was decided that Scobie would oversee everything, Ignatius would focus on Razz's performance in Multi-strand Science and Maths, I would be responsible for English and Bill would cover Media Studies. We knew that Sally was also going to be a huge help. Our first task, however, was convincing Razz to ask Mr Barker to let him drop Economics where he was really bombing out, so he could use the extra time to work on improving his remaining subjects.

"No way he'll let me do that. After that *Hamlet* thing last year, Barker thinks I'm a waste of space."

"Hey, I bet your *mother* could convince…" Prindabel's comment shrivelled up under the heat of Razz's glare.

"What if I come with you, Orazio, and help argue your case?" Scobie said.

It was turning into a time of tough decisions for Razz, but he eventually agreed. The next day when Scobie and Razz returned from their appointment they told us that Mr Barker said he would let Razz drop Economics if he could prove that he was committed to his school work. That meant he had to pass all the upcoming end of term exams and show a clear improvement in his overall grades.

"Barker reckoned it wouldn't be easy. But he said he thought I could do it. He even wished me luck." Razz shook his head in disbelief.

"Firm but fair," Ignatius said with grin. "Mr Barker would make someone a great father."

But Razz was too lost in his own thoughts to hear.

So with Operation Tarango already progressing steadily, Operation Get Razz into Uni lurched into life. If only Operation Get Kelly to Invite Ishmael to the Lourdes Formal was proceeding as strongly. And as for Operation Win at Least One Volleyball Match, that was about to come down to the final roll of the dice.

But none of us could have predicted just how much would be riding on it.

14.
The Poor
Suckers Are Us

By the time the mighty Fighting Fifths reached the final round of the volleyball season we had built a magnificent record of six losses and one forfeit.

Our last game of the season was the return match against Windermere High. The last time we were down to play them they had to forfeit after most of their team was struck down with the flu. It gave us our only points. We didn't even rate it as an embryo step since we'd done nothing to earn it. Ignatius suggested that we should mark it down as a zygote step and he was so pleased with this joke that for the next week or so he'd break into his weird hissing laugh every time he thought of it.

The Windermere High team were second-last on the points table, with a couple of very narrow victories. No prizes for guessing who was two points behind them at the bottom of the table. On the Monday before the match Ignatius caught up with us all in morning Tutor Group. He looked pretty excited. He told us that he had discovered something 'interesting'.

"A whole new level on Super Nerdio Brothers?" Razz suggested.

Ignatius ploughed on without missing a beat.

"No, something to do with volleyball. Last night I completed a thorough review of the entire season for Mr Hardcastle, checking the accuracy of all the points tables for the various age groups and analysing the position of each of the schools," Prindabel said, placing a folder on the desk and patting it gently with his bony hands. "Now, as you know, trophies are awarded for each of the five age divisions, and as the name implies, the Overall Champions Trophy is awarded to the school that performs best across all of those age groups. Now each team gets points for their age group depending on where they finish up on the table and these points contrib—"

Razz grabbed his head and crossed his eyes. "Emergency! Emergency! Boredom overload. Brain freezing. Must. Get. Help."

"Maybe you could 'cut to the chase', as they say, Ignatius?" Scobie said.

"Right. Well, as it stands, even with one round to go, St Daniel's has the Under 13 and Under 16 trophies wrapped up already and it's the same with Churchill College in the Under 14s and 15s. The only age level still in any doubt is ours – the Opens. So that means, whoever wins the Opens trophy will be crowned champion volleyball school. *Interestingly* enough, in the Open division St Daniel's and Churchill College are actually tied in first place, and according to my calculations, there's only *one* result in this weekend's Open division matches that can possibly move either a St Daniel's or a Churchill team up or down the table and break the deadlock."

"Wow, really, man?" Razz said, pushing his hands back through his hair. "You mean the whole season's championship depends on one team and one game. Why didn't you just say so? Talk about your humungous *pressure*! What game is it? Who are the poor suckers?"

Ignatius Prindabel held up Saturday's fixture schedule and pointed a long finger at the bottom of the list.

"St Daniel's versus Windermere High. The Open Fifths," Ignatius said. "The poor suckers… are us."

"What? No way! Your calculator must have Alzheimer's, Prindabel. It *can't* be us. We couldn't possibly change the Open trophy points thingy. We're last on the table. And whether we win or lose on Saturday we'll still be last."

"Not *quite*, Orazio. If we lose on Saturday we'll be last, yes. But if we *win* on Saturday, we'll be *tied* for last with Windermere."

"Tied for last?" Razz said, doing an imitation of that *Home Alone* kid. "Oh, wow! Yippie! Happy days! Yay! Notify the press! Let's declare a public holiday!"

Razz leaned forward and patted Prindabel's hand.

"P-buddy, I don't want to rain on your parade, dude, but 'tied for last' is still 'last'."

"Except," Ignatius said, pulling his hand from under Razz's, "Rule 13 Sub-section (d) Clause (vii) says that 'when teams are tied, the combined points for both positions on the table will be shared equally'. So, in our case this means you take the points for coming last, which is two, and add them to the points for coming second-last, which is four, so that makes six…"

"I'll be checking that later just in case you're trying to put one over on us," Razz said.

"… Then you share those points *equally* between both teams involved in the tie. So *each* team would receive three points."

There was no clowning from Razz this time. His eyes just grew larger and his mouth fell slowly open.

"So if we beat Windermere and tie with them on last place, we'll get one extra point for St Daniel's."

"Correct. And that extra point will win St Daniel's the Open Trophy and that will make us champion volleyball school. Isn't mathematics wonderful!"

Ignatius was beaming.

Razz was going pale. "But what happens if we don't win?"

"If we don't win, it will stay a tie in the Open division and Churchill will be awarded the Overall Championship Trophy because their Open Firsts are higher up the table than ours. That's Rule 16.8."

Everything seemed to be closing in and pushing down, like someone had turned the knob on the gravity dial up to 'crush'.

Razz reached forward and grabbed Prindabel's face in both hands.

"Ignatius, listen to me. This is serious. Whatever you do, man, don't let Hardcastle know about this, okay? 'Cause if he finds out, he'll go completely nutso and our lives will be hell."

With his face still squeezed between Razz's fingers, only Prindabel's eyes darted back and forth bouncing around the rest of us. Then a word slipped out from his squished-up fish-mouth.

Unfortunately for us, the word was "Ooops."

15.
Airy-fairy, Tree-hugging, Cheesecloth-wearing, Incense-sniffing Hippy Twaddle

Razza's plea came too late. Ignatius had given a copy of his 'findings' to Mr Hardcastle as soon as he got to school. As it turned out, Razz was right about the "completely nutso" bit.

It started that afternoon when Mr Hardcastle turned up at our training to give us "intensive, individualised instruction" for what he described as "the most important game ever in St Daniel's volleyball history". Apparently (as Mr Hardcastle was keen to remind us at every conceivable opportunity), in twenty-two years of trying, St Daniel's had never won the Overall Volleyball Trophy. Fabulous, no pressure.

Mr Hardcastle also announced that he was scheduling training sessions for us every day that week right up until the 'big game'. That's when Mr Guthrie suggested they have a "quiet word". Everyone in the gym, and possibly some people outside, ended up hearing most of those quiet words.

Mr Guthrie's quiet words included things like "over the top", "too much pressure", "just a game" and "carrying on like a lunatic" while Mr Hardcastle's quiet words were more along the lines of "character building", "do or die", "treating them like babies" and "don't give me any of your airy-fairy, tree-hugging, cheesecloth-wearing, incense-sniffing hippy twaddle".

A compromise was only reached when Mr Barker wandered into the gym to see what all the shouting was about. It was finally agreed that we'd stick to our normal two training days for the week but that Mr Hardcastle would work with us for the first day. He did, and it was pretty full on. When it was over we collapsed in an exhausted huddle on the gym floor for a Mr Hardcastle pep talk. He looked tense. After observing our team at close range all afternoon, he could probably see his dream of a first volleyball championship for St Daniel's disappearing faster than wrinkles at a Botox convention.

From what I could hear over my own wheezing lungs and pounding heart, the key message of Mr Hardcastle's pep talk appeared to be that we were going to "kick Windermere's lily white, pimply butts" and show all those "wimpy ladies" at Churchill College what "real men" were made of. (I got a feeling that Mr Hardcastle hadn't done Ms Heckenvaal's History of Feminism unit.) The rest of Mr Hardcastle's talk consisted of gems of wisdom such as "Quitters never win and winners never quit!", "Go hard or go home!", "What doesn't kill you makes you stronger!" and "Losing is NOT an option!".

Our second and final training session wasn't quite so turbo-charged. We concentrated a lot on serving practice and finished with a muck-around game with Mr Guthrie joining in. When it was almost time to head off home we got our second pep talk of the week – only this time 'Woody' Guthrie style.

"Look, guys," he said, shaking his dreadlocks, "if we win on Saturday, obviously that would be great. Amazing, in fact. But if we don't win, just remember, nobody dies and the world doesn't end. I don't want you to let other people's expectations and hang-ups weigh you down, okay? Just go out and have fun, give it one hundred per cent and play for each other. Same as you've done all year. Do that, and no matter which way the result goes, you're still winners. Any questions?"

"Did you know that Miss Tarango is anti-whaling just like you, Sir?" Razz asked.

I liked Mr Guthrie's talk much better than Mr Hardcastle's. And what he said made a lot of sense. But when game time arrived on Saturday and we saw the normally empty mezzanine level of the gym packed with St Daniel's supporters including Brother Jerome, Mr Barker, Miss Tarango and, of course, Mr Hardcastle, the only words that stuck in my brain were these:

"Losing is NOT an option!"

16.
The Razzinator

When we started our match against Windermere we had everything going for us – overwhelming home-crowd support, the incentive of a championship trophy for motivation and an opposition who had nothing much to play for.

On top of that, during Monday's training Mr Hardcastle had taken Razz aside for special tuition and made him practise his serving for ages against the Firsts. All the hard work paid off. As well as his stock serve, Razz now had a slow serve, a swinging serve, a top spin dipping serve and a bullet-out-of-a-gun serve that Scobie christened the 'Razzinator'.

Also, because of their last forfeit, Windermere had never seen Theodore morph into a giggle blob before. That meant that 'the Brown Undies Effect' was back in full swing and not only that, but the Mudman had brought along his A-game.

We had more good fortune when we won the toss. Razz's first six serves were virtually unplayable, including one plimsoll-crushing Razzinator that knocked the Windermere receiver clean off his feet. Then they finally managed a return of serve and one of the Windermere players successfully blocked one of Theodore's shots at the net. The Mudman cranked his death glare up to 'Annihilate' while Razz leaped in front of him shouting, "No, Bunga! Stay! Bad! Mustn't touch! Remember what happened last time. You don't want to get that sticky red stuff all over your clothes again, do you?" Windermere's blocking didn't seem quite as committed after that.

Unbelievably, we ended up taking the opening set easily 15–5. Our embryo steps had gone straight to puberty!

The second set was a *slightly* different story. The word had got around about why we wanted to win the match so badly. Now Windermere had something really worth playing for too – crashing our party and stopping St Daniel's winning the championship trophy. As other matches finished and more and more of their supporters and players turned up to watch our game, our overwhelming home-crowd advantage dwindled away.

But we had even more problems than that. Windermere had started to work out our strengths – i.e. Theodore and Razz – as well as our glaring weaknesses – i.e. the rest of the team. They began concentrating most of their efforts on Ignatius and Scobie and directed everything they could towards them. Scobie in particular became a very popular target for serves.

We ended up losing the second set 15–9.

It was all down to a third and final tie-breaker set. First to seven. No advantage. We had a quick break filled with tons of encouragement from Mr Guthrie and Razz and then returned to the court determined to get off to a good start, just like we did in the first set. The last thing we wanted was to find ourselves tied at six–all with all the weight of the school on our shoulders and everything hanging by a thread on the very next point.

Ten minutes later the game was tied at six–all, we had all the weight of the school on our shoulders and everything was hanging by a thread on the very next point.

Both coaches simultaneously signalled for a time out. It was looking bad for us. Windermere would be serving the last point. Their best player had the ball in his hand. Scobie was stuck in the back court. He was giving it his all but he'd hardly dug a serve out all match. He'd be in their sights for sure. Razz, Scobie, Bill, Ignatius, Theodore, Melvin and I gathered in a close circle around Mr Guthrie. We waited for his words of wisdom.

"Well, boys," he said, "you're probably wondering why I called you all here."

A circle of grim faces relaxed into smiles.

"Has it got anything to do with the possibility of all of us being exiled to Siberia if we lose this next point, Sir?" Scobie asked.

"Yes, James, I was going to touch on that very possibility," Mr Guthrie said. "Okay, look, boys, I've got no magic words. But I want you to know this: whatever happens, win or lose, being your pretend volleyball coach has been great fun… and an honour. And if things don't go our way, then I couldn't think of a better bunch of fellas to be exiled to Siberia with. So just go out there and do your best."

Mr Guthrie was wrong when he said he didn't have any magic words.

"And now," he continued, "I think I should pass you over to someone who actually knows more about the game than me. Razz, anything you want to say to the team?"

"Well, we gotta give ourselves a chance. We have to at least make these dudes fight for this point and earn it. So the first thing is, we gotta dig this next serve and get it back in play."

We all knew whose name would be on that serve and we didn't like our chances.

"They'll serve to me, won't they?" Scobie said.

Razz nodded. "Yeah, they will. Mad if they didn't – no offence, man. But don't worry, I'll take it for you, Scobes. As soon as he serves, you back off and I'll get across in front of you."

This seemed like an excellent plan and probably our only chance of staying in the game. Razz's suggestion was met by a circle of nodding heads. All except Scobie's.

"No. I'll take the serve."

We all looked at the pale, chubby figure before us blinking the sweat away from his short-sighted eyes.

"You don't have to, man. I'm pretty sure I can..."

"I'm taking the serve, Razz."

Something in James Scobie's voice told us that was the end of the discussion.

"I know you're Captain, but I'm the reason we're here. I wanted to play a sport and you all helped me out. So if anyone's going to mess up and be held responsible, it's going to be me. I'm taking the serve."

Scobie twisted his mouth defiantly to one side and held it there.

"Okay, I'm glad I sorted all *that* out then," Razz said brightly. "Now here's what I think should happen and I don't want any arguments, okay? *Scobie* here will take the serve and the rest of us will be ready to chase down anything and everything after that. It doesn't really matter how we do it, we just need to get the ball over their side as soon as possible, then we defend like crazy and hope they make a mistake."

Razz thrust his hand into the middle of the circle. We all piled ours on top.

"The quest for the volleyball championship stands upon a knife edge, dudes," he said. "Let's show 'em what the mighty Fighting Fifths are made of."

17.
A Heavily
Drugged Giraffe

We all pushed our hands down hard together and gave a rousing St Daniel's shout. Above us our supporters clapped, cheered, stamped and whistled as we took our places for the final time on the court.

Ignatius, Melvin and Theodore had the net positions. Razz and I were back on the baseline with Scobie in between us. Bill had twisted his ankle in the last set and was on the reserve bench beside Mr Guthrie. The umpire blew his whistle. My heart rate went off the scale.

The Windermere boys broke from their huddle and took up their spots. I looked across at Scobie. He was crouched over with his arms stretched out and his hands cupped in front of him waiting for the serve. He was wearing his glasses for the first time all season. They kept slipping off his sweaty button nose and he had to constantly push them back.

On the other side of the net Windermere's best player

was waiting for the umpire's signal to serve. His hair was shaved short around the sides but hung in a long fringe to his eyes. He was tall. The ball was going to spear down into our court from a great height.

I wondered what was going through his mind. He'd have to be thinking about the serve, trying to make up his mind what he'd do. Would he play safe or would he give it everything he had and go for the big hero-serve to win the match?

The umpire called play. Fringe guy flicked his head back to get the hair from his eyes. He scratched his groin for a bit, then twirled the volleyball on the tip of his finger. Definitely a big hero-serve man. We waited. Forget the knife to cut the tension. You'd need a chainsaw.

Fringe guy grabbed the spinning ball in both hands, bounced it three times then tossed it high into the air. As it came back down he bent his knees, arched backwards and with his hand cocked behind his head, launched himself up to meet it. A sound like a gunshot echoed around the gym as his open palm met the full face of the ball at maximum velocity right in the sweet spot. The serve that resulted really was a thing of beauty. Unless of course you happened to be James Scobie and you were watching an angry white sphere hurtling towards you like a runaway comet. Then it was your worst nightmare.

The ball sizzled over the middle of the net with just a few centimetres to spare then it dipped wickedly and speared towards Scobie's chest. It was on him so quickly he hardly had time to react, but he held his ground and somehow managed to get his arms up. The ball thudded into his wrists. James' head reeled backwards and his glasses flew from his face as he was sent tumbling to the floor.

All the St Daniel's supporters' hearts sank as they watched the ball fly high over Scobie's head and sail towards the back wall. All the Windermere supporters cheered. Everyone on our team took a few frantic steps after the ball and then stood mesmerised by the inevitability of our impending defeat.

Everyone except Razz.

He was now charging at full pace beneath the flight line of the ball, peering back over his shoulder as it peaked high above him and started its rapid descent. It was a race to see who would reach the back wall first. The best bet looked like a tie but then about a metre out Razz leaped up and belted the ball as hard as he could with the back of his fist. It sailed into the air at the same time as Razz sailed into the wall. There was a sickening crunch as shoulder met solid masonry. And for the second time in two years, the masonry won.

Razz bounced off the wall and landed with a thump. A sympathetic "Ooooooooo" filled the air.

Razz seemed okay but there was no time to check. Everyone's eyes, including Razz's, were back on the little white synthetic globe that was soaring its way in an arc towards the ceiling. If it touched any part of it, St Daniel's could kiss the championship goodbye. The ball edged its way closer to one of the exposed girders and began to slow. Closer. Slower. Closer. Slower. Clossssssser. Slowwwwwwwwwwwer. Clossssssssssssssssssssssssseeeeeeeeeeeeeeeeeer. Stop!

A mass moan rose from the Windermere supporters. A roar burst from St Daniel's. Miss Tarango squealed. We were still in it. But the ball was dropping and it was impossible to tell which side of the net it would fall on.

Everything I'm about to describe now happened within the space of five seconds. First, just before the ball propped and dropped from the ceiling, I began running back into the court in case I was needed. What I didn't notice, because I was watching the ball, was Scobie on his hands and knees looking for his glasses. The first sign of trouble was when I felt a crunch under one of my plimsolls. That was just before I somersaulted over the top of James and skidded on my sweaty back across the polished timber floor.

I probably would have slid right under the net and onto the opposition's side if I hadn't collided with what felt like two cement pylons. They were in fact Theodore Bungalari's legs. Now normally, me smashing into the back of Theodore's legs would have had about the same effect as a pillow smashing into a couple of giant redwoods. But not this time. This was because the Mudman's feet weren't in contact with the ground. You see, Theodore at that moment was in the process of leaping up to spike the ball (remember the ball?) to win us the match.

Well, *that* didn't happen.

Perhaps Theodore would have been able to complete the almost certain winning spike, even while I was smashing into his legs, but something else was occurring at exactly the same second. That something else came in the flying form of Melvin Yip. Yippy, who up to this point in the match had somehow been able to contain his enthusiasm to just within the bounds of sanity, suddenly snapped under the tension. When he saw the ball falling and the game hanging in the balance, he decided this was the perfect time to unleash the full fury of his inner ninja.

From a running start Melvin Yip leaped like a flying assassin at the ball. I have to admit that as leaps go, Melvin's wasn't all that bad. Sadly though, his timing, as always, was. Whereas Theodore had only just left the floor, Melvin had already flown over a metre into the air and was already on his way down when they met. So you see, while I was busily taking the Mudman's legs out from under him, Melvin Yip was landing on his chest and back-flipping him right over the top of me and onto the floor.

Afterwards Miss Tarango said the gym looked like the last scene in *Hamlet* where the stage is strewn with the dead and dying. Razz was watching everything from down by the back wall lying on his stomach and clutching his shoulder. Scobie was still scrambling around on his hands and knees trying to reassemble the various pieces of his glasses. And I was in a tangle of arms and legs with the Mudman and Nutcase Ninja.

Only one St Daniel's man was left standing.

Ignatius Albert Prindabel.

Somehow Ignatius had managed to stay out of the way as the chaos erupted around him. He was the only one who could save us and he knew it. With all the grace of a heavily drugged giraffe, he started loping in the direction of the ball. But there was no way he was going to make it in time. The ball was always going to beat him.

And it did... kind of.

But instead of coming down on one side of the net or the other, the ball took everyone by surprise and hit the edge of the tape almost dead centre. The net shook and dipped, absorbing most of the impact. The volleyball rebounded about 10 centimetres in the air. As it rose, it tilted and rotated and began to drop towards our court. At the same time Prindabel lost his footing and stumbled. The Windermere players started to raise their arms and turn to each other in triumph.

But the P-man wasn't done yet. From on his knees he made one last lunge, stretching out his thin right arm like an telescopic pole. And then, at the last moment, when it looked like he would have to fall just short, a familiar long bony finger uncoiled itself. It was the Prindabel Power Pointer! It straightened and locked firmly before jabbing into the side of the volleyball. The ball bobbed upwards, landed for a second time on the tape, balanced there for a moment, then slid off down the opposite face of the net. By the time Windermere realised what was happening it was too late. Despite desperate sprawling dives by two of their players, the ball bounced off their fingers and landed on the court.

The St Daniel's crowd went crazy. In among it all I caught glimpses of Mr Hardcastle pumping his fists like a madman, Mr Barker and Brother Jerome applauding madly and Miss Tarango doing her justifiably famous war dance. Back on the court Mr Guthrie calmed us all down and told us not to go completely crazy until we shook hands and congratulated the other team, which we did.

Then we went completely crazy.

After a lot of high five-ing, back-slapping, bear-hugging and whooping, Theodore and Razz (with a bit of a wince) hoisted Prindabel onto their shoulders and paraded him around the gym while the cheer squad up above performed a raucous version of the school song. Ignatius waved at the crowd and held high the long bony digit that had delivered the college its first ever volleyball championship – a digit referred to by an emotional Mr Hardcastle at that week's school assembly as the "Finger of God".

For the next few days at school, boys would run up to Prindabel offering their open palms for a high five. And as befitting his new standing as a St Daniel's College Volleyball Legend, Ignatius even managed to make contact with some of them.

18.
OMG! OMG! OMG!

It ended up being one of the best terms ever. Along with our victories in the cross-country and the volleyball, we also won our last two debates and qualified unbeaten for the finals. They were the big highlights. But there were two other things I don't think I'll ever forget from the first half of this year.

One was the look on Razz's face when he saw his Term One report card. I'd be guessing it matched the look on Mr Farmer's face when Razz gave him the sad news that he wouldn't be in his Economics class any more.

The second one was this phone call.

(Theme to *Mission Impossible* ring tone.)

Me: *Hello. Leseur residence. Ishmael speaking.*
       (Yes, I know. But it's what I was taught to say as a kid.)
Voice on the line: *Hi, Ishmael. It's Kelly. Kelly Faulkner.*

Me: *Hi, Kelly. How're you?* (But really – Oh my
       god! It's Kelly! OMG! OMG! OMG!)

Kelly: *I'm fine. How're you?*

Me: *Good. Fine. Great. Yeah, good.* (Had she got
       the message that I was okay?)

Kelly: *That's good. Well, why I'm ringing is... I guess
       you know about our Formal in a couple of weeks.*
       (Yes, I know and I'll come!) *Look, I realise this
       is really late to be asking* (Who cares?
       Ask away! I'll come!)... *and I feel really bad*
       (I feel great! I'll come!)... *but I wasn't sure if
       I was even going to go or not and then I thought
       you only get to do this once* (Absolutely! And by
       the way, yes, I'll come!)... *so I was hoping, you
       know, if you were free* (Are you kidding? I was
       born free! I'll come!)... *and you wanted to*
       (I do! I really do! I'll come!)... *that
       maybe you'd be my partner for the night.*
       (Hmmmmmmmmm. I might have to think
       about it. I don't want
       to rush into anything.)

Me: *That'd be great. I'd love to. Yeah, sure. Thanks.
       Great. I'd love to. Great. Great.*

Kelly: (with a giggle) *I'll take that as a 'yes' then.*

And that's how Razz, Sal, Kelly and I ended up going to the Lourdes Formal together. Razz's Uncle Georgiou chauffeured us all to the venue in a 1956 red Cadillac convertible. As well as Show Tunes, Uncle Georgiou also loved showy cars.

It turned out to be a good night with plenty of laughs. How could it not be with the Razzman there in fine form? And even if Kelly was quiet and seemed afraid to let herself be truly happy, being near her was still the best place in the world to be.

After it was all over, Razz and Sally headed off to a post-Formal party but all the Lourdes boarders had a bus waiting to take them back to the school. Kelly didn't seem to mind that much.

Outside the venue she thanked me for the "lovely night" and for being her partner on such "pathetically short notice". She also said she was lucky to have a "friend" like me who would "put up with her". Then she kissed my cheek and thanked me again for everything. She was about to board the bus and take a big chunk of my heart with her, when I managed to squeeze out the one question I'd been wanting to ask all night.

"Kelly. It's ages away yet I know, and you don't have to decide right now of course. But I was wondering… Do you want to come to our formal…

you know, with me… as my partner?"

The tiniest of smiles crept onto Kelly's face and stayed.

"I thought you'd never ask," she said.

Term Two

Those friends thou hast, and their adoption tried,
Grapple them to thy soul with hoops of steel.

William Shakespeare, *Hamlet*,
act 1 scene 3, lines 62–63

19.
Male
Chauffeuring Pigs

few weeks into the new term we were back in one of the library discussion rooms. Scobie was sitting at the end of the table with a laptop opened in front of him. I was sitting beside Razz, and across the table from us were Bill and Ignatius. Scobie was hunched forward and we could only see half of his head sticking up above the back of the computer screen.

"Anything?" I asked.

Scobie tapped on one of the keys and waited. His round pale face appeared above the screen. He adjusted his glasses.

"Nothing yet," he said.

We were waiting for the school Debating Society to post the grand final topic on their web page. That's right, we'd made it all the way! Scobie, Bill and Ignatius had won the *That We Should Re-introduce the Death Penalty* quarter-final and Scobie, Razz and I won the *Climate*

Change is the Only Issue secret subject semi-final. Now the grand final was only one week away.

The topic was scheduled to go up at noon. Mr Slattery had given us special permission to miss English so we could start our preparation as soon as it arrived. It was five past twelve already.

"Man, I can't believe we're in the final. Our last debate ever and it's the Big Kahuna! But boy, Wesley are gunna be tough. They beat Sal's team in the quarters. They were pretty deadly."

Wesley Senior College was an exclusive girls' school with a reputation for academic excellence. Razz reckoned their uniforms had higher IQs than a lot of the guys at St Daniel's. I was there when they took on Lourdes. It was the only time I'd seen Kelly since the formal. We didn't get to talk much.

Scobie pushed the *Refresh* button again. We waited. He shook his head.

"Man, the suspense is killing me!" Razz said with a slap of the table. "Gee, I hope we get something good. Remember that secret topic debate in our first year, Bilbo? No Scobes that night and we thought we'd get killed and then we scored that topic about the sci-fi fantasy stuff and you blew 'em away! Hey, maybe you'll get lucky again, Billy, and we'll be Affirmative for *That*

Hooping Should Be Made Compulsory in Schools. Or maybe we'll get a Prindabuddy special like *That the Geek Will Inherit the Earth.*"

A click came from the end of the table. Scobie's head ducked down and was almost lost behind the screen.

"Is it up, Scobes?"

We could just make out James's head bobbing up and down.

"Well what is it? What's it like? Come on, man, tell us."

Scobie slowly lowered the screen a little and sat back. His mouth was twisted off-centre.

"This is going to be *very* interesting," he said. "We're an all boys' school, we're up against an all girls' school, two of the three adjudicators including the chief adjudicator are female, and our topic is..."

Scobie clicked the lid of his laptop shut.

"*That Women Are the Weaker Sex.* We're... Affirmative."

For a moment it felt like someone had died. But it was really just our chances of winning suffering a near-fatal stroke.

"But... how are we going to argue *that*?" Bill asked.

Scobie sent his mouth on a full circumnavigation of his face then gave his considered response.

"Verwy, verwy carefullwy," he said.

"You're telling me, Scobes," Razz said. "Otherwise we're gonna come out of this looking like a bunch of male chauffeuring pigs."

Ignatius didn't even bother to object. All he said was, "Maybe you could read a passage from *The Sun Safe Adventures of Britney and Amber* to prove them wrong, Orazio?"

Razz was going to respond but then he stopped and slapped his forehead.

"Man, and I just thought of something else. The Wreckin' Ball said she was coming to the final! We're dead meat, dudes. Even if a miracle happens and we win, we'll never get out of there alive."

"Well, let's not get carried away, Orazio. We need to look at the positives. First of all, at least we know it's true, don't we? Women *are* the weaker sex, right?"

We all nodded automatically.

"Sure," said Razz.

"Absolutely," said Ignatius.

"No question," said Bill.

"It goes without saying," I added.

We'd come a long way in debating since our first competition. We never complained about a topic any more and Scobie had banned Razz from ever saying that we'd been given the "crap side" of the argument.

Now, whatever side we had, we automatically believed it with all our hearts.

"Excellent!" Scobie said. "Now that we are all agreed that women *are* in fact the weaker sex, we just have to work out *why* they are."

Everyone stared at their pens and fiddled with their notepads for a bit before Ignatius spoke up.

"Well, if we are defining weak as in 'not as powerful', then when it comes to physical strength, on average, women are not as strong as men. Statistics from various power sports will prove that."

"Thank you, Ignatius. It's a start, but we're going to need much more than that. And keep in mind that saying women are less powerful than men is not the same thing as saying that women are inferior to men or less intelligent or less capable than men."

"No, no, we're not saying that. Absolutely not," Razz said, laughing nervously as he checked quickly over both his shoulders, "because everybody knows that's so totally not true. Isn't that right, Ms Heckenvaal, just in case you're listening in on some sort of spying device?"

"Speaking of Ms Heckenvaal, Orazio, how do you think she would argue this topic?"

"What, you mean after she printed it out from the web page and shoved it down the throat of whoever wrote it? Sorry, Scobes, I can't see the Wreckin' Ball ever agreeing that women are less powerful than…"

Razz stopped as if he'd been struck on the back of the head.

"Wait on. Miss *did* say stuff about women having less power… less influence… didn't she?"

James smiled and nodded.

"Yeah, that's right. Isn't that what all those Suffering Jets chicks were going on about? Women not having the right to vote… not having the same *political* power as men. And, and remember in that feminism stuff how we looked at all those countries where women still don't have the same rights as men? We could use that, couldn't we? Like how they're sort of *weaker* that way?"

The rest of us nodded along with Scobie and started scribbling on our notepads.

"Hey, man, and I think I got another one! What about all that equal pay stuff and how women don't get the top jobs? That'd make them less powerful too wouldn't it?"

Razz was really getting excited now.

"And wait, wait, wait. There's all that cultural and religious stuff we did too. Like how women are treated as inferior to men in some places and they can't be priests and stuff. That reduces their power I reckon. I mean, didn't Wreckin' Ball say that the whole feminist thing was about women trying to get their fair share of power? And in a lot of places they still haven't got it, right? We could use some of that stuff couldn't we, Scobes?"

Scobie didn't answer immediately. He just started to clap slowly and firmly. "What a piece of work is a Razzman," he said.

The rest of us joined in the applause. While James Scobie might have been able to paraphrase *Hamlet*, Orazio Zorzotto was never one to be outdone.

"I am Razzman, hear me roar. My brain is too big to ignore!"

As a sign of our appreciation we pelted him with pens and bits of screwed-up paper.

20.
Grace Under Pressure

The debating finals for all the various year groups were hosted by Preston College in their Performing Arts theatre. The Senior final was the last debate of the evening. The theatre was jam-packed.

Both teams were lined up on opposite sides of the stage separated by the timekeeper's and chairperson's table. On the desks in front of us were pens and notepads as well as glasses and jugs of cold water. Behind us were big vases of flowers. The school banners and colours of St Daniel's and Wesley College were draped on the back wall. We'd never been in a debate quite like this one.

Scobie was sitting between Razz and me. That was our team for the Final. Bill and Ignatius were sharing timekeeping and chairperson duties with the Wesley reserves. It was great that the whole team got to be on stage together for our last-ever debate. We all looked pretty good too. We were wearing the special St Daniel's school representatives jackets, which were navy blue with red trim. Thanks to Mrs Zorzotto, we also had red carnations in our lapels.

I looked across at the Wesley girls. A single long-stemmed rose was sitting in front of each of them. The girl beside Bill was smelling hers and smiling. Those roses came from us. When we walked on stage a few minutes before, we introduced ourselves to our counterparts on the opposition team, shook hands, wished them luck and then presented them each with a rose. I don't think it won us any points with the judges but the audience liked it. So did the Wesley girls I think, and as Scobie had kept reminding us in the lead-up to the night, "It's our last debate – whatever the result, let's go out in style. Like St Daniel in the lions' den, we'll show them grace under pressure."

'Going out in style' and 'grace under pressure' had become our mantras for the night. That's why we made sure our uniforms were Gerard Carlson-Steele perfect and it was also why our index cards sat in three untouched, neat little bundles on the desks in front of us, each tied up with a thin blue ribbon. That was Scobie's idea too. He said it would send the message to the opposition that we were confident, totally in control and fully prepared.

At the last debating meeting when Scobie suggested we tie up our index cards, I almost had a panic attack. I thought I'd be so nervous on the night, I wouldn't be able to stop myself chewing off the ribbon and shuffling through my notes like a hyperventilating card shark. But it wasn't like that at all. I'm not saying I was calm, but after I accepted that I wasn't going to be able to look at my notes until the chairperson got up to start the debate, I stopped worrying about them and just let myself feel excited and happy about being there. It all seemed like a bit of a miracle, especially after my first disastrous debate when I passed out on Kelly. For the first time ever, thinking about that made me smile. When I looked around at Razz and Scobie they were smiling too. So were Bill and Ignatius. I guess I wasn't the only one feeling excited and happy.

With minutes to go before we were due to start, the audience continued to build up. Quite a few people were now standing at the back and down the sides. I looked around for familiar faces. As well as quite a few St Daniel's boys from our other debating teams and their supporters, Mum and Dad and Prue were there along with Prindabel's parents, Mrs Zorzotto, Uncle Georgiou, Mrs Kingsley and Mr Scobie. They were all sitting together. In front of them was a bunch of teachers including Brother Jerome, Mr Barker, Mr Slattery, Mr Guthrie, Ms Heckenvaal and Miss Tarango.

Razz nudged me and grinned knowingly when he saw Mr Guthrie shooting a few glances at Miss Tarango. She was a couple of seats away talking to Brother Jerome. Razz stopped grinning so much when Mr Barker leaned over the back of his chair and started chatting with his mum. Judging by the size of the smile on Mrs Zorzotto's face, I'd say *she* didn't mind in the slightest.

They weren't the only familiar faces. Sally and Kelly were there too. They were up at the back of the theatre with Sally's mum. They waved when they saw me looking. I gave them a quick wave back. I attempted to make it as stylish as possible. I even spotted Raychell Taylor, the girl who'd been my partner for last year's Semi-formal when she wasn't off talking and laughing with other people or texting on her mobile. I was still spotting other faces I knew when the three adjudicators entered the theatre and took their seats.

Razz leaned into Scobie and me. "Not long now, guys," he said. "Are you ready to rock and roll, Ishmael?"

We were Affirmative. I would be the first to speak. I nodded.

"And dude, if you're going to throw in one last

faint for old time's sake, could you make it *after* you've finished your speech this time, okay?"

"Sure thing," I said and we all smiled in a stylish kind of way.

"Oh, and I almost forgot, man. Young Prudles told me I had to give you this," he said, reaching into his jacket pocket. "She reckoned you might relax more if you knew *exactly* where it was."

He handed me an old wooden clothes peg with the head of one of the Beatles on it. The old Ringo peg person was in pretty good shape considering his last embarrassing appearance (via my shorts) was at my very first debate. I think Prue might have given his mop of hair a recent coat of black paint.

I sought my little sister out in the audience. She was watching me and laughing. She was a Senior now – not so little any more, I guess. I was smiling back at her and shaking my head when the chairperson from Wesley stood up and began officially welcoming everyone. Not long after, she was saying my name and calling upon me as first speaker for the Affirmative team to open the debate. My heart was pumping up a storm.

I stood up, undid the ribbon from my index cards, placed it on the desk and walked to the middle of the stage. When I got there I smiled at the audience, took a deep breath and began.

"Ladies and gentlemen, madam chair, tonight my team will prove to you…"

I reckon I must have looked pretty stylish standing up there, especially with the head of a Ringo peg person poking out proudly from the top pocket of my special St Daniel's school representative jacket.

21.
A Razzman
Masterclass

I definitely had the easiest job of all the speakers on the night. As First Affirmative I had nothing to rebut from the opposition. I just had to state our theme, outline our overall case and then present the first of our arguments as clearly and persuasively as possible. That, and not turn into a stumbling, bumbling freak show in front of a theatre packed with people who were intently boring their eyes into me.

It was weird. It was almost like I was someone else, listening to my speech. I kept giving myself advice while I talked – *slow down, take your time, you're doing great, look at the audience, that's it, remember to smile, speak loudly and clearly, pause and let those words sink in, use your gestures, really hit this point hard, not far to go, you're almost there, big finish now, make sure you end strongly.*

When it was all over I sat down with the sound of applause drumming in my head. Razz and Scobie shook my hand and patted my back. I held on to the desk top. I felt so light I was scared I was going to float away. Everyone told me afterwards that I'd done really well. Raychell Taylor came up and said she couldn't believe I was the same person she'd met last year. Maybe they were all just being super-nice, but I knew this much at least. I'd done my job and I'd done my best. I'd take that any day.

But we were soon reminded that the Wesley girls weren't in the grand final just to make up the numbers. Not for a second. Even though their first speaker looked like a ballerina, she came out swinging like a heavyweight. When she'd finished we weren't exactly reeling on the ropes but she had landed quite a few telling blows and had clearly established her team's claim for the title. Next up was Razz.

After he was introduced, Razz stood and pushed his chair into the desk. As he walked behind me, he pulled Ringo from my top pocket and slid him into his own. I was watching the St Daniel's supporters as he made his way to the centre of the stage. They looked tense and uneasy. Sally and Kelly were both leaning forward with their fingers covering their lips. Prue wasn't watching at all. I couldn't blame them for being nervous. It was a tricky topic, especially for Razz, and he did have a bit of a reputation for being a loose cannon. Not tonight. Tonight the Razzman was a high-tech, sophisticated piece of artillery locked on to a target. But he was still Razz.

"Ladies and gentlemen, this evening I am faced with a difficult task. I must attempt to convince you that women are the weaker sex while at the same time standing before three members of that very gender who frankly are making *me* weak at the knees."

None of us knew Razz was going to say that. But it worked. In the first few seconds of his speech he'd made the audience laugh and he'd won them over. And as much as they tried to resist, even the Wesley team weren't totally immune. Their captain rolled her eyes and gave a pained smile. Their first speaker looked down and blushed. Their second speaker stared at Razz for a moment with what I'm fairly certain was the 'game over' look before she smothered it in a frown. Then Razz continued.

"But tonight I must put my personal feelings aside, because the first speaker for the Negative team has put forward arguments that, while eloquent, clearly don't stand up to close scrutiny."

Razz then rebutted each of the opposition's arguments before showing how women often had less power and influence than men in three major areas – society as a whole, the political arena and the workplace. And he did it with oodles of charm and just the right amount of humour thrown in. It was a Razzman masterclass in style. Scobie and I applauded him to his seat. He was wearing a sizeable grin. It got even bigger when Ms Heckenvaal gave him two thumbs up.

Then, of course, Wesley's second speaker came in and threw our arguments back in our faces by saying that women had survived and flourished *despite* the inequalities and discrimination we had rightly pointed out, and that this was proof of their *strength* not their weakness.

That's how it went all night. We'd build something up that looked strong and indestructible and they'd come in and start tunnelling under the foundations and chiselling away at the brickwork and sawing through the support beams. Then they'd build something new and equally impressive in its place and we'd start on our own tunnelling, chiselling, sawing and rebuilding.

The highlight of the debate was definitely the battle of the third speakers. Scobie had saved his best till last. He was like a ball of energy on stage, using everything he had to get us over the line, including a certain peg person poking out from his pocket for good measure.

After seven and a half minutes of intense work dismantling the opposition's case and restoring ours to pristine condition, Scobie concluded with this:

"Ladies and gentlemen, madam chair – my colleagues and I have not argued here tonight that the female of the species is in any way inferior to the male of the species. How could we," Scobie said, holding his hand towards the Wesley girls, "with such *overwhelming* evidence to the contrary? And we don't deny the claims from the opposition that women have achieved great and remarkable things both as individuals and as a gender. But we still hold that they are the *weaker* sex, because as we have clearly demonstrated, in the political system, in the workplace, in the household, and in society at large, the power and influence of women have been, and continue to be, undermined and weakened by years of prejudice, discrimination and lack of opportunity. And ladies and gentlemen, my colleagues and I should know, because shamefully, it is our gender that has been largely responsible."

As final speaker for the night the Wesley captain was clinical and ruthless. She was the only debater I'd ever seen who'd even come close to matching Scobie. When it was all over, Bill and Ignatius joined us and we waited for the adjudicators' decision. Razz was making jokes as usual and we were all waving and smiling at people in the crowd. Another 'last' was almost at an end. A big one – our last debate together. I thought I might feel sad, but I didn't. I felt great. Not because it was all over, but because we got the chance to do it in the first place. And whether we won or lost, nothing was going to take that feeling away.

Just for the record, the chief adjudicator said it was a debating final of the "highest order" and that she had never heard two finer third speakers in a school contest. She also said the decision was "agonisingly close" and that in this case the old cliché was true and that "no one deserved to lose".

But of course someone did.

I kept my eye on Miss Tarango while the adjudicator was talking. She was chewing on her thumbnail and gripping onto Brother Jerome's arm. When the result was about to be read out, Miss closed her eyes and lowered her head. I saw her take a long deep breath and hold it as the winning school was announced. I really wish someone could have taken a picture of Miss Tarango right at that moment. They could have stuck it in one of those visual dictionaries – right under the word 'Joy'.

22.
Dying in Key

We were officially congratulated for our debating victory at a school assembly, but there wasn't that much time to bathe in all the glory before our next big challenge loomed large. It was the Inter-house Athletics Carnival – the last of the Big Three. If we didn't do well here, we could kiss Operation Tarango goodbye.

Scobie had the whole of Charlton House revved up for a massive effort. He wanted us all to be "point scavengers" and he enlisted Bill and Gerard Carlson-Steele, who were both Art and Design students, to create a new house T-shirt for the day. They came up with an all-gold one that had on the front the outline of a hand with the index finger pointing skyward. Circling the hand were the words *charlton house – winning the college cup – one point at a time!*

On the back was a silhouette of the cup itself with CHARLTON HOUSE SCAVENGERS at the top and WE FIGHT FOR EVERY POINT! below it. It was a big hit, and our Art and Design teacher, Ms Lagilla, agreed to print them for a cheap price as long as any profits went to her department.

Bill and Gerard also made a special shirt for Miss Tarango. It was the same design as the others but instead of CHARLTON HOUSE SCAVENGERS on the back, it had CHARLTON HOUSE PATRON, and both the drawings of the cup and the hand were decorated with red sequins. Miss Tarango loved it.

On the day of the Athletics Carnival every Charlton member was determined to at least get their 'one point' for the team total, and they couldn't wait to hold up their index finger when they did. Scobie, of course, led by example, even though he failed to reach the qualifying marks in any of the field events and on his last attempt at the high jump actually went under the bar. Razz had quite a bit more success and ended the day as runner-up Age Champion. Even Ignatius, Bill and I managed to scavenge a handful of points between us. Overall we performed solidly in both the track and field events and once again trumped the other houses with overall participation levels.

But our biggest successes came in the final event of the day, the tug of war. This was mainly due to the formidable trio of Bill, Theodore Bungalari and Jimmy 'The Main Event' Mainwaring. Even though the new improved Bill was no longer automatic choice for tug of war anchor (that honour now went to Novak 'Jabba' Jablonski), his four years of tug of war experience were invaluable. And he was still strong. So were Theodore and the Main Event. Together, with Jabba rock-solid at the end of the rope, they led the Open team to a crushing victory as well as coaching and encouraging all the other age groups to the finals, where we lost only one. When it was all over, Bill and the Main Event engaged in some enthusiastic, celebratory chest-butting, much to the delight of everyone in the stands.

Charlton House came in second, which was a huge result for us. But the following day when Ignatius sat down to give us a brief Operation Tarango update report, for some reason he didn't look overjoyed.

"What's up with you, P-man? Your subscription to *PlayGeek* magazine didn't run out, did it?"

"I'm worried about the athletics results."

"Why? We did great. Second! Woohoo! Charlton House rocks!"

"Yes," Ignatius said, "but unfortunately Creswell came first and by a good margin. So while we've moved clear of Radley and Franklin on the overall points table, Creswell has increased their lead on us."

"But we've got time to make up the points, haven't we?"

"Theoretically, yes. But our margin for error is getting alarmingly close to zero."

"What have we got left this term?" Scobie asked.

"Well, there's the six-a-side football competition."

"No worries, Scobes. Got it covered. Our Open team will blitz them and I've been working with a bunch of the younger years. Some of those little dudes are stars. And the two teams below us should go okay. We'll get points back on Creswell there. You've got the Razzman's personal guarantee on it."

When it came to football, the Razzman's personal guarantee was a blue-chip investment.

"Right," Ignatius said, placing a tick on the sheet of paper in front of him. "Then there's Mr Guthrie's Food for the Homeless appeal. Points given for the house that donates the most cans of food."

"Tick it off, Ignatius," Scobie said. "Charlton House doesn't need a points' incentive to win that."

"Well, the only other major item is Arts Week."

Not surprisingly, Arts Week was St Daniel's annual celebration of all things arty – music, drama, painting, sculpting, design, you name it. It was held in the last week of term and included displays, performances, competitions and special guests, finishing with an Open Day on the Saturday.

"What points are up for grabs, P-buddy?"

"There's some little things like a painting competition and a junior public speaking competition, but the big one's the Battle of the Bands. Quite a few points for the taking and the way things stand now, that's almost a must-win for us."

"Well, we won last year," I said, "and we've got the same guys, so they should be better. What do they call themselves again?"

Ignatius shuffled through a few sheets.

"Ah, Dusty Roads."

Beside me Razz shuddered.

"Is there a problem, Orazio?"

"Well they're good musos, Your Scobeness, but what a waste. That country and western crap they play, man, that's not music. That's just someone dying in key. Anything else in Arts Week, Prindabel?"

"Not really. Here's the draft of the programme Mr Barker gave me."

Razz took the booklet from Ignatius and began flicking through it. Then he froze.

"Aww, man!"

"Something else troubling you, Orazio?"

The booklet came spinning across the table to Scobie.

"We're stuffed, Scobes, that's all. Check out the name of the judge for the Battle of the Bands."

Scobie held up the programme and pushed his glasses back up the short bridge of his nose.

"Let's see. Guest judge – Eddie Schneider," he read out. "Says he's a past pupil."

"See! What'd I tell you?" Razz said. "We're stuffed."

Ignatius did the honours of asking the question for the rest of us.

"Who's Eddie Schneider?"

"Who's Eddie Schneider? What, seriously?" Razz said, looking around in disbelief. "You guys don't know who Eddie Schneider is? Crazy Eddie Schneider. Lead singer and guitarist for the Filthy Pigs. What rock have you guys been under? Ishmael, as a son of a Dugong you should be ashamed."

"The name sounds familiar. But so what? Eddie Schneider is the judge. What's the problem?"

"The problem, Ishmael, is that the Filthy Pigs were a heavy metal band, man. They were majorly wild. They had this thing at the end of their shows where they would attack each other with their gear because apparently they didn't get on. Most people reckoned it was an act, but one time Eddie got smashed over the head with a Fender Stratocaster and spent a week in a coma. When he woke up he couldn't remember the lyrics to any of their songs. They broke up pretty soon after that."

"A touching story, Orazio, but all this concerns us why?"

"Well, you tell me, Scobes. Does Crazy Eddie Schneider sound like the kind of guy who'll dig country and western to you? I mean, do you really think he'll get off on all that 'I love to stroke your hair, 'cause my dog's got the mange' stuff?"

Maybe Razz had a point.

"We have to do something, Scobes. You heard what the P-man said. We need to win the Battle of the Bands to give ourselves any hope of catching Creswell. We have to come up with something."

We did. Or rather Razz did. And even by his impressive standards, it was pretty bizarre.

23.
A Tsunami
Brainwave

A couple of days later in Tutor Group, Razz informed us enthusiastically that he had "kicked our Battle of the Bands problem's butt" and that all would be revealed to us at lunchtime. When the time came we gathered at our usual table in the Senior area. All that was missing was the man himself.

"What do you think it will be this time?" Ignatius asked. "Kept back after the lesson because of (a) his uniform being, damaged, worn incorrectly or missing completely (b) not handing in or completing his class work, homework and/or an assignment (c) falling asleep, talking too much, or generally displaying some sort of inappropriate behaviour in class or (d) all of the above."

We were contemplating those possibilities when Razz came jogging across the playground to join us.

"Sorry, dudes. Got held up after Science. Wanted to

check a couple of things with Mr Caskell about my draft multi-strand assignment."

We stared at him. I guess it was going to take us a while to get used to the new and improved Razz. Even though he was getting a lot of help and support from teachers and Sally and everyone around the table, what was really making the difference to his grades was Razz himself.

He looked back at us and brushed his hand over his mouth.

"What?" he said. "Is there something on my face?"

"Just the usual stuff," Scobie said. "So what's this big idea you said you had about the Battle of the Bands?"

Razz slid onto the seat.

"Not just an idea, O Cruel Wielder of Unlimited Power, but the mother of all brainwaves – an awesome tsunami brainwave, man."

I was kind of glad that the new improved Razz was basically a lot like the old Razz.

"Pray tell," Scobie said.

"Well, first up I went to see those Rusty Toads dudes or whatever they call themselves."

"Dusty Roads," Ignatius corrected.

Razz did his usual shudder at the mention of their name. "Yeah, whatever. Anyway, I told them all about

Crazy Eddie Schneider being the judge and how if they wanted to win they had to rev up their performance a bit. You know, go a bit psycho, maybe bite the head off a bat or something. And guess what they said to me? They said they couldn't do that because it would 'destroy their musical integrity'."

Razz screwed his face up in disbelief.

"Musical integrity? What musical integrity? They've got a piano accordion in their band. A piano accordion! That's not a musical instrument. That's an instrument of torture, man. You can make a better sound if you squeeze a pig and stick your fingers in its nose."

"Such a beautiful image," Scobie said. "So what do we do now?"

"*Now*, Scobes – and this is where my tsunami brainwave starts to kicks in – what we have to do is get a *second* band to represent Charlton."

"A second band?" Bill said. "Have we got one?"

"Absolutely we have, Bilbo," Razz said, looking around crazily. "We've got *us*."

"Us?" we all chimed in like backing singers.

"Yep."

"Razz," I said, trying to spell it out as gently as possible for him, "besides the very real problem that the Battle of the Bands is, what... um, *twelve* days away...

do you see the fact that none of us here is actually *in* a band as being, perhaps, a *slight* flaw in your tsunami brainwave?"

Razz shook his head sadly at me. "Man, Ishmael, you always gotta go digging for negatives, don't you, dude?"

"Actually, Razz, I didn't have to dig at all. They were right there on the surface and I sort of ploughed straight into them."

"I think Ishmael might have a valid point, Orazio."

"You too, Scobes? Look, obviously we haven't got a band *now*, but that doesn't mean we can't put one together, right? It's heavy metal, punk rock stuff. How hard can it be? Twelve days will be loads of time. You don't want to over-rehearse these things, otherwise you lose that rough edge."

I was still light years from being convinced.

"Okay, let's just say for the minute that's even vaguely possible. Who's in this band?"

"Well, I haven't had time to figure out all the *finer* details yet, but I'll be on drums…"

There was no problem with that. When Razz filled in at the Dugongs concert, Uncle Ray said that he was a natural and one of the best young drummers he'd ever seen. Of course Uncle Ray also said Razz was a "monumental pain in the arse", but I don't think that automatically counts against his musical ability.

"…and Ishmael, you'll be on guitar."

"Me?"

"Sure. You're the son of Ronnie 'the Red' Leseur aka a Dugong legend, aren't you? Rock and roll is in your blood, man. And don't try to weasel out of it because I know you play. I've seen a guitar in your room."

That was true. I'd actually learned for a couple of years in primary school but it never really interested me until after Dad got the Dugongs back together. Then for the first time I found myself picking up my old guitar and trying a few songs just because I felt like it.

"So how many chords do you know, dude?" Razz asked.

"Not sure. Twenty or thirty. Maybe more."

Razz looked a bit horrified.

"Geez, man, you might be overqualified. Doesn't matter, we can beat that out of you. But anyway, that's drums and rhythm guitar covered. Now, Iggy baby, you do some stuff with the college orchestra, right? What do you play again, man?"

"Mainly triangle."

"All riiiight! Wickeeeed!" Razz growled, giving Ignatius the devil's horns symbol with both hands. Then he sighed. "But unfortunately, Prindabuddy, even though the triangle is technically *metal*, it's not quite *heavy* enough metal for what I had in mind. Got anything else for me?"

"Five years of classical piano."

"Awesome, dude! I'll put you down for electric organ. We'll borrow one of those portable ones from the Music department."

Ignatius didn't have time to object.

"What about you, Bill? You play anything?"

Bill shook his head.

"Scobes?"

James followed Bill's lead.

"No worries. We got drums and rhythm and Iggy Pop here can add some bass and lead on the organ. *Plus* there's our secret weapon."

"We've got a secret weapon?"

"We certainly have, Ishmael my main man. According to the rules, everyone in the band has to come from the one house but you're allowed one outside person as long as they're still at school somewhere."

"So have you got a friend of yours lined up?"

"Nope. I've got a sister of *yours* lined up."

"Prue?"

"Yep, little Prudles. She plays a few things, doesn't she?"

"Violin, saxophone and piano."

"Well, we got piano covered, but sax and violin are cool. She any good?"

"She's a near-genius. Of course she's good."

"There you go. She's versatile *and* talented. *Plus* she has two other things going for her that our band desperately needs. One – she's a chick. Two – she's a hot chick. And personally, I don't think there's anything hotter than a hot chick playing sax or violin. And I'd be willing to bet my life that Crazy Eddie will totally agree with me."

"So you want to exploit my sister just to get some cheap points."

"Exactly. Okay, we've got the players all organised. All we need is a lead singer. Now, the ability to actually *sing* would be handy, but not essential. What we basically want is someone who can leap around screaming like a maniac out the front. That rules me, Ishmael, P-buddy and Prudles out because we'll be playing instruments. So what about you, Billy? You're in the college choir. Maybe you could twirl a few hoops while you sing. It'd be really cool if you could set them on fire."

"I think I'm more ABBA than heavy metal, punk rock."

Razz frowned and pointed a finger at Bill.

"Kingsley, what'd I say about never mentioning that

name in my presence? Okay, but I'm putting you down for backup singer and roadie. That leaves you, Scobes. You could do it, man. You've got the confidence. You've got the charisma. People love you. *Please*, I'm begging you, tell me you can sing."

Scobie smiled encouragingly. "Not a note," he said.

"What? You're kidding."

"Afraid not."

"Maybe you're being too hard on yourself, man. You don't have to be that great. Just loud and in tune every now and then. Sing something. Sing the college song. Go on."

Scobie shrugged his little sloping shoulders and sang.

"Into battle proudly we go
Facing every fear and foe
All men of St Daniel's know
We will fight for justice."

Razz held up a hand.

"Stop, man, you're killing the grass! I think someone might be strangling a cow in your throat."

Sadly, on this occasion Razz wasn't exaggerating.

"But fortunately, Scobes, what you have there is definitely the voice of a band manager. Apart from catering for our every whim, you may have to spend a lot of time with Prudles, because she's the only chick in the band

and she might get lonely. How does that sound to you?"

"When can I start?" Scobie said.

"That's my boy! And we'll also get you up on stage to mime some backing vocals with Bill. The crowd will love it. Still down one lead singer, but…" Razz said, scanning the tables spread around the Senior area. Suddenly he was on his feet.

"Bunga! Hey Bunga! Got a minute?"

Theodore Bungalari wandered over to us.

"Here he is," Razz said, "the man himself. Every chick's dream guy. The Smokin' Gorokan!"

Theodore's face remained unchanged.

"Anyway, Bunga, enough of this idle chit-chat. We're looking for a lead singer for our heavy metal, punk rock band and I reckon you've got 'it'. I know you're in the choir like Billy here, so how's about belting out the first verse of the college song for us?"

Theodore's head remained still but his dark eyes moved to each of us at the table.

"I will sing for you," he said.

He did. He sang the first verse of 'Men of St Daniel's' in a voice that was high and pure and perfect.

When he'd finished Razz gave his verdict.

"Bunga, this has got nothing to do with any of that cannibal crap of Wallace's, but I think you might have swallowed an angel, dude. That was rigidly beautiful, man. Which means, of course, you failed the audition miserably. Best I can offer you is the job of backup singer and roadie along with Bilbo here."

Theodore looked at Bill and gave one of his rare smiles. "I will take it," he said and wandered off.

"Man," Razz said stirring his hair up into a frenzy, "we're *soooooo* close. We just gotta find someone who's more out there. Someone who could…"

A throat-shredding cry ripped across the school yard. It was followed by a few wild yelps. Over on the tennis courts Melvin Yip was thrashing his racquet around like a weapon and attacking each shot from his opponent as if his, and every member of his family's life, depended on it. As we watched, Melvin leaped into the air to take a high bouncing return. At the peak of his leap, he shrieked like a mountain lion, performed a wild scissor kick and smashed the ball over three tennis courts and onto the roof of the science block.

Razz snapped his fingers. His face was invaded by mad scientist eyes and a wide mad scientist grin.

"Time to unleash Mel!" he said.

24.
Spawn of Bjorn

After a bit of shouting and waving Razz managed to get Melvin Yip's attention and he jogged over to us.

"Yippy, I need you to sing the first verse of the college song and I want you to give it everything you got, man. Imagine you're singing it for all your awesome ninja bros 'cause you're all about to go out and do all this awesome ninja-ing stuff."

The scary thing was that Melvin didn't even bother to ask why he was doing it – he just agreed straight away. And it was quite a performance. It went a bit like this:

Into battle (fierce grimace plus flashing hands and wild karate kicking) *proudly* (hand beating on chest) *we go* (fist punched into air plus bloodthirsty shout)

Facing (chin and bottom lip thrust out) *every fear* (disturbingly horrified expression) *and foe* (tongue out and face like a demented zombie)

All men (grabbing and shaking groin) *of St Daniel's*

know (jabbing index finger where brain is located in other people)

We will fight (more fierce grimaces plus extended version of flashing hands and karate kicks) *for justice* (recap of highlights from above, all ending in an enthusiastic but painfully awkward attempt at the splits).

Yippy got the gig.

"Bingo!" Razz said as Melvin sprinted his way, ninja-like, back to the tennis court. "The last piece of the puzzle falls into place, gentlemen. Now comes the most important part. The name. We need something that sort of sums us up. Any ideas? What about you, Scobes? You're good with words."

"How about the Debaters?"

"Well, your High and Mighty-ness, I wouldn't say that was the worst band name I've ever heard… No, wait, you know I actually would. That's the worst band name I've ever heard."

Scobie narrowed his eyes at Razz but said nothing.

"What about you, Iggy? You must have something rattling around that massive cranium of yours that could help us out. We're a heavy metal, punk rock band, man. We need something that says 'energy'."

Prindabel's brow knotted with concentration. Then it slowly relaxed.

"What about the Islets of Langerhans?"

Razz spoke behind his hand to Scobie. "Hold the presses, Herr Scobmeister, I think you may have just been pushed out of top spot in the worst-band-name-ever rankings."

Then he turned back to Ignatius.

"The Instep of Wacky *what*, Prindabel?"

"The Islets of Langerhans."

"Okay," Razz said, shaking his head, "I'll bite. Why?"

"You wanted something that said energy."

"Yeeeeeeeees."

"Well, it's obvious, isn't it? The Islets of Langerhans are regions of the pancreas responsible for the secretion of insulin. When glucose levels rise they produce more of it. Insulin makes us store glucose as an energy supply in our cells. Other parts of the Islets produce glucagon, which releases this energy supply back into our blood. You wanted something that said energy. The Islets of Langerhans are all about energy."

"Well, thanks for that, P-bud. I'll certainly give your suggestion serious consideration, just as soon as someone puts a rocket launcher to my head."

Razz patted me on the shoulder. "What about you, Ishmael? I realise the standard of competition is *incredibly* high, but would you like to have a go at naming the band?"

"Well, I did have one idea. You said the name should say something about us and I was thinking how we're all friends and everything, so I thought it could just be 'friends', but we could spell it *F-R-E-N-Z*."

"Wow," Razz said like he was in shock. I knew straightaway I was in trouble. "You don't think that might be a bit too *edgy*, man? You know, a bit too controversial? We wouldn't want to fall foul of the spelling police."

Razz didn't say any more. He just squeezed his eyes shut for a couple of seconds then snapped them open.

"Okay, Bill. I'm ready. I can take it. What's *your* suggestion? ABBArama? ABBA Dabba Doo? Spawn of Bjorn?" Razz stopped. "Actually, Spawn of Bjorn's not bad. We'll put that one aside. Come on, big guy. What have you got? Maybe something with a hoop theme?"

Bill shifted uneasily in his seat.

"Well, actually… I *have* got a hoop theme one, but you'll probably hate it and think it's crap."

"Yes, of *course* I will, but that hasn't stopped anyone else, has it?"

Bill took a deep breath and went on.

"Okay then. You remember that *Hamlet* oral I did last year?"

"What, you mean the one where I tried to stop you from coming out but just ended up making a complete idiot of myself in Mr Slattery's English class and getting ten whole days of afternoon detentions from Mr Barker? No, can't say I do."

"Well, anyway, there's this bit in that Polonius speech I thought we could use because, like Ishmael said, it's about being friends. You know that bit that goes, *'Those friends thou hast, and their adoption tried, grapple them unto thy soul with hoops of steel'?*"

Razz grimaced and put his arm around Bill's broad shoulders.

"Nice try, Hoop Boy, but it's not exactly *punchy*, is it? I mean we might have a bit of trouble fitting it all on the front of the drum kit, don't you think?"

"I didn't mean we'd use it all. Just the end part. You know, the 'hoops of steel' bit. That's what I thought the band could be called. The Hoops of Steel."

Nobody said anything for a moment. We were all running the name through our brains trying to find some reason to reject it. Finally Razz spoke.

"You know, I actually think that's pretty cool. Yeah, the Hoops of Steel, man. That's awesome. Whataya reckon, Scobes?"

"You can't beat the Bard," James said.

"Ishmael?"

"I like it."

"P-buddy?"

"Well, apart from the point I made last year about the relative strength of steel as opposed to carbon nanotubes, I'm happy with it."

"Cool!" Razz said. "Then I officially announce that the Hoops of Steel are set to rock the house!"

I looked from Razz to Bill, Scobie and Ignatius.

"What, so we're really going to do this?" I said, hoping it might still turn out to be just some kind of hidden camera stunt. "In twelve days we're going to get up and play as a heavy metal punk rock group in front of actual people?"

Razz didn't answer me but turned to Ignatius instead.

"P-buddy, how important is it for Charlton to win Battle of the Bands?"

"Well, if Creswell does better than us they'll increase their lead on the overall points table. If they do that, then as far as us winning the cup is concerned, it's all over."

"And let me remind you, Ishmael," Razz said, "Creswell at the moment has *two* bands down to play compared to our *one* and both their bands are pretty good, *plus* they're gonna play stuff Crazy Eddie might actually like."

"He might like a bit of country and western too?"

"Ishmael, the Filthy Pigs' last CD was called *Dog's*

Vomit Soup. Eddie wrote its big hit, 'You Taste Like Chicken'. Do you really think that 'down on the faaaaaarm' kind of crap that Dusty Roads play is going to appeal to him?"

"Yeah, well, okay… but even if we have a band, what would we play?"

"Ah, good question. And here's another bit of my brillo master plan. You get points for originality. Bands that play their own stuff always do better. At least that's one thing the Dusties have going for them. So we definitely have to play an original song."

"What? We've got twelve days before the competition, we've never even played together as a band and *now* we have to write an entire song as well?"

"No, not an *entire* song, Ishmael. You see, that's the real genius of my brillo master plan. The words are already written, man. They're done and dusted. We just have to add some pretty basic music and I'm thinking your dad could help us with that."

"What words are you talking about?"

Razz pulled something from his top pocket, unfolded it and slapped it dramatically on the table.

"These words."

I could see a few verses typed on an A4 page. But it was the title printed in bold capital letters at the top that sent a deathly chill through my veins.

HOT OR WHAT?!

"You've *got* to be kidding?"

I couldn't believe it. It was Razz's old love sonnet from two years ago. The one he'd wanted me to give to Kelly Faulkner. The one Ignatius described as "fourteen lines of crap" and that even Scobie crowned the "*crème* de la crap". I thought I'd got rid of it, but it kept coming back like a bad case of head lice!

"Yeah, it's pretty awesome, isn't it? I thought you'd gone and lost it on me. Lucky I made a copy, hey?"

"Yeah, think I'll buy a lottery ticket," I said.

Scobie's mouth was smudged to one side. He returned it to a central position and picked up the sheet. He read the first verse.

> *"Like a microwave on high – you're hot!*
> *Some chicks think they are – they're not!*
> *They haven't got the bod you've got!*
> *Man! Are you a total babe – or what?"*

"Ah, the memories!" Scobie sighed then looked at the rest of us. "Poetry? – doubtful. Heavy metal, punk lyrics? – just maybe."

"I'm telling you, Scobes, it'll rock big time. I reckon

it sounds even better than when I first wrote it. Must've matured with age or something."

"A bit like cheese?" Ignatius suggested helpfully. "Well, it definitely has something in common with a vintage blue vein, anyway."

"Hey, thanks, Prindabuddy! I knew you'd eventually come around. So it's all settled then. The Hoops of Steel will debut at the St Daniel's Battle of the Bands performing their original composition, 'Hot or What!'. Are we all in?"

Razz placed his hand palm down on the table. Here we go again. Scobie laid his hand on top. Bill and Ignatius looked at each other and shrugged in sync. Two more hands joined the stack. Everyone's eyes moved to me.

"It's for Miss Tarango, dude," Razz said.

I said once before that for Miss Tarango we'd coat ourselves in honey and dance in front of a pack of bears. But I never thought we'd do anything this crazy.

Reluctantly I lowered my hand to complete the pile.

25.
Hot Geek Chicks

Just as we were unstacking our hands, Miss Tarango herself came bustling in. She was carrying a big bunch of Manila folders and struggling to hold some sheets of paper in her hand.

"A bit of marking to do there, Miss?"

"Unfortunately just the tip of the iceberg, Orazio, and I'm way behind. Here, boys, take one of these forms before I drop the lot. It's for the Formal. Only a few weeks away now, and I really need to get table arrangements finalised. Here's the deal. You can have up to six couples at your table but no more. If you need a partner just indicate that on the sheet in the space provided. You must have that form completed and back to me by Monday at the latest, okay? Don't forget. Ciao."

After a quick flash of the dimples Miss Tarango bustled off.

"Man, Miss needs to chill a bit," Razz said. "I reckon it's *definitely* time I started working on getting her and Woody together."

"I think she'd be happier if you just filled out that Formal thing," I told him.

"Luckily the Razzman can multitask," he said, dragging the sheet in front of him and pulling a pen from Prindabel's top pocket. There were spaces for six couples. Razz wrote his name in the first one and added Sally's beside it.

"So Scobes, you're all fixed up with Prudles, right? And Ishmael, you're set with the Kelster?"

We both nodded happily and Razz added the four of us.

"Prindabuddy, you're still tight with Good Lordy Miss Maudie, aren't you?"

"Ah, actually, no," Ignatius said. "We've just broken up."

"Bummer, man! Got dumped, hey, dude? Did she catch you sending suggestive texts to your laptop or did she just get stronger glasses?"

"No, *I* broke off with *her*."

"What?! Are you mad? You actually had a chick who was willing to be seen in public with you. What are the chances of that ever repeating itself? What happened, man?"

"We didn't have much in common."

"You cannot be serious. You guys were like two nerds in a pod."

"Not really," Ignatius said. "She was more into physics and chemistry and I'm more into maths and biology."

"Those mixed marriages never work," Razz said. "So, I'll put you down as needing a partner then."

"No. I've already asked someone else."

Razz clutched at his heart.

"What? Who? How?"

"Her name's Lily Nguyen. I met her at the Science Expo last term."

"P-buddy, you're a chick electro-magnet! Now I know why you're so keen on all those nerdy seminar things. You just go there to pick up hot geek chicks."

A crooked smile slid on to Prindabel's face. "No," he said as he straightened his tie, "the hot geek chicks go there to pick *me* up."

Prindabel hissed out a jerky laughing fit and there were high fives all round.

"All right, that's enough hilarity for one day," Razz said, returning to the Formal sheet. "Billy Boy, I'm adding your name down at number five on this list, man. No arguments, pal. You're coming. You can't back out on us like last year. The Fab Five gotta be together for our Senior Formal. Miss Tarango can hook you up with a token partner for the night."

Bill agreed without much enthusiasm.

"Did you ever get around to having that talk with your father, Bill?" Scobie asked. It was a question I'd wanted to put to Bill for a while but had never found the right time.

Bill shook his head. "He's been overseas for ages. Only made a couple of quick trips home. He's back in about a month and then he's here for a while. I'll speak to him then. Definitely."

"Don't suppose you had anyone you wanted to bring to the Formal anyway, Bilbo," Razz said.

Bill took a moment to respond.

"I did, actually."

"*Really?*" Razz said leaning in. "Anyone we know?"

Bill nodded again.

Razz leaned further. "*Really?* What, so you mean it's someone here at St Daniel's? Someone in our year?"

"Yes," Bill said.

Razz's eyes grew large. "*Really?* Who?"

Bill shrugged. "What does it matter? I can't go with them anyway."

"I don't see why not."

Everyone turned and looked at Scobie.

"Why not?" he repeated. "You should be able to bring whoever you want – same as everyone else. If you like,

I'll go with you and we'll see Brother Jerome about it."

"Yeah, Billy Boy. We'll all back you up, man. And I reckon Ms Heckenvaal, Miss Tarango and Mr G would be on your side too. And if they don't let you take who you want I'll chain myself to the flagpole! Just like all those old Suffering Jets dudettes did."

"Thanks, Razz," Bill said, "but even if Brother Jerome was okay with it, there'd be loads of people – other students and teachers and parents – who wouldn't be. And someone'd kick up a stink and cause a lot of trouble and I don't want to do that to the school."

"Man, it's so stupid," Razz said shaking his head, "but you're right, Bilbo. Same thing happened with Sal's formal. There were these two chicks who wanted to go together and there was all this crap about it. Even made the news. In the end those two chicks just had a gutful and pulled out. Didn't go at all. Sal was really pissed that her friend missed out on going to her own Formal. She reckoned…"

Razz froze as if his power source had just shut down. Then he gazed about like he was in *The Matrix* and the world around him was finally revealing itself.

"Well, I've got it, haven't I?" he said as a disturbing smile stretched across his face. "I've figured it out and it's beautiful, man. It's beyond genius. I am donating my brain to science. It would be a crime against humanity if I didn't."

"I'm certain any scientist involved in the study of abnormal behaviour would be very grateful to have the opportunity to study your brain, Orazio," Ignatius said.

"Perhaps you could let us in on your *revelation*, Orazio?"

"Sure, Scobes. What we do is this," Razz said, pausing for dramatic effect. "We match Billy Boy and his 'preferred partner' up with those two Lourdes chicks I was telling you about. You know what Formals are like – tons of people sitting around tables and dancing in groups together. Half the time it's hard to tell who's sitting or dancing with who. See what I'm saying? So as long as no one gets too carried away on the night, who will know? Billy and his partner will be happy. The girls will be happy. It's another classic win, win, win, win situation."

That worried me a bit, but I think this time Razz might have finally got it right. He obviously thought so too. He was now bobbing his head around at all us.

"What do you reckon, dudes? Am I a genius or what?"

Scobie answered for everyone. "Orazio, I may have to download you an application form for MENSA."

"Cool!" Razz said, "I've always wanted to be an

astronaut! So, Billy Boy, what do *you* say, dude? Are you and your mystery man up for it?"

"Well, yeah," Bill said, looking the happiest I'd seen him for a while. "Yeah, if we could be at a table with all you guys and those girls are happy too, that'd be good. That'd be great."

"Awesome. I'll get on to Sally and see what those two chicks say. And even if there's some problem, we can still get Miss to find other partners for you. So don't worry, whatever happens, you and Mr X will be at our table."

Then Razz slid the sheet across to Bill and laid his pen on top of it.

"So… you want to write the name of your partner down on the sixth spot?"

Bill hesitated a moment, then printed a name carefully on the sheet and pushed it back to the middle of the table.

We all leaned in.

"*REALLY?*" we all said together.

26.
KABOOO
OOOOOOOOO
OOOOOOM!

The Hoops of Steel had their first rehearsal the following Saturday afternoon at my place. Razz got dropped off early by his mum so we could work with Dad on putting his poem to music before the others arrived. Uncle Ray was there too because he and Dad were organising some Dugongs gigs.

Razz and I were down in the basement setting up the drum kit and waiting for Uncle Ray to arrive when Prue came in. She was carrying her violin and saxophone.

"Prudles! Looking good," Razz said. "You all ready to audition?"

Prue looked from Razz to me and back again.

"Audition? I only agreed to join the band to do you all a favour. Why should I have to audition? No one else has."

"Well,' Razz said, "you *are* the only non-Charlton member of the group, and being Ishmael's little sister and a *friend* of the Scobster, some people might get the idea that there was some sort of *bias* involved in the selection process or that maybe you just got into the band because you're so hot."

Prue managed to look angry and blush at the same time.

"That's stupid. You're just being stupid. No one would think that. I'm not auditioning if no one else is."

"Fine," Razz said with a pleasant smile. "No problems. If you're worried that maybe you're not good enough, then we'll just forget all about it."

Prue glared at Razz from under her dark fringe. I was half-expecting to see smoke come from her eyes. She snapped open her violin case, pulled it out and shoved it under her chin. Then she snatched up her bow.

"Hold on a sec," Razz said, grabbing a pen and notebook and dragging a beanbag to a spot right in front of her. "Okay, whenever you're ready."

Prue proceeded to give blazing performances on both the violin and then the saxophone. When she finished she put both instruments to one side and waited while Razz continued to scribble down some final thoughts.

Eventually he slapped his notebook shut.

"Right, thank you, Prudles. We'll get back to you as soon as possible."

Prue's eyes flared.

"What? Stop being stupid, Razz. Tell me now."

"Now?" Razz said. "But I *really* should discuss your audition in detail with Ishmael here and my other colleagues. We wouldn't want to make any hasty decisions that we might regret later."

"What do you mean, regret later?"

"Well it's just that playing in the Hoops of Steel might be too much of a step up for you."

I closed my eyes. It was like watching someone tapping on a nuclear warhead with a hammer, just to test how much it could take. When I opened my eyes Prue was smouldering.

"Stop being stupid and tell me the truth – now!"

"Look, we can't all perform at our best on every occasion. Perhaps you were nervous."

Tap. Tap. Tap.

"Razz, I mean it. Stop mucking around and just tell me truly how I did."

"Well, there were obviously a few *questionable* notes, but I took into account your very tender age."

Tap. Tap. Tap.

"It was note-perfect and you know it! Tell me the truth!"

"Well, let me just say this. I thought you *tried* very hard. Couldn't fault your effort!"

Tap. Tap. Tap.

"Look, do you want me in the band or not?"

"Prudles," Razz said, looking hurt and horrified, "of *course* I do. But perhaps at this stage in your career the best way you could contribute to the band would be to wear something short and sexy and just dance around up the back *pretending* to play."

TAP.

KABOOOOOOOOOOOOOOOOOOOOOOM!

Prue moved so fast that I didn't know what was happening until she was hitting Razz with the best crash tackle I'd seen since Tommy 'Flat-liner' Manu creamed James Scobie two years ago. In a split second Razz was barrelled off his beanbag onto the carpet and Prue was perched on his chest with her knees pinning his arms to the floor.

'Really, Prudles," Razz wheezed, "Do you think this is acceptable behaviour for a young lady?"

"Tell me the *truth* about my audition," Prue growled.

"Well, I thought you showed real... *potential* and AAAAARRRRRRGH!"

Prue now had Razz firmly by both sideburns and she looked like she was determined to pull them off.

"All right! All right! All right! I'll tell you! Let go! Let go! Let go! I'll tell you!"

Prue released her grip. Razz lay sucking in a few breaths. Then he continued.

"Okay, Prudles. I'll be honest now. No joking around. I thought you had absolutely perfect… posture… and AAAAAAARRRRRRRRGH! OKAY! OKAY! OKAY! OKAY! STOP IT! STOP IT! STOP IT!"

But Prue didn't stop it. Near-geniuses learn fast. She had Razz's sideburns and she wasn't letting go till she got what she wanted.

"ALL RIGHT! YOU WERE AWESOME! YOU WERE UNBELIEVABLE! YOU'VE GOT MORE MUSICAL TALENT IN YOUR LITTLE FINGER THAN THE REST OF THE BAND COMBINED! WE'RE NOT FIT TO BE ON THE SAME PLANET AS YOU, LET ALONE THE SAME STAGE! AND NOT ONLY THAT BUT YOU PLAYING SAX IS THE COOLEST AND THE HOTTEST THING I'VE EVER SEEN IN MY ENTIRE LIFE!"

Prue opened her hands. Razz slumped back panting and groaning. He had beads of sweat on his forehead.

"Awwwww, that is so sweeeeeeeeeeet!" Prue squealed with a big smile. "And you're not just saying that?"

"Prue! What on earth are you doing?"

It was Mum. She was standing at the basement door. Dad and Uncle Ray were peering in behind her.

"What does it look like?" Prue said as she sat straddled on Razz's chest. "I'm auditioning."

Uncle Ray raised his eyebrows. "This looks like my kind of band," he drawled.

27.
The Dugongs
of Steel

"You wrote this?"

Uncle Ray was holding Razz's poem. Razz was nodding.

"And you weren't being tortured or force-fed any sort of mind-altering drug at the time? Amazing."

"Thanks! I reckon it's pretty awesome too. Now we just need some killer music – but like, nothing that's going to overpower the lyrics."

"Just a stick beating on a rock, then."

Razz looked doubtful. I don't think he quite 'got' Uncle Ray.

Writing the music for 'Hot or What?!' ended up being a lot of fun. Dad and Uncle Ray did most of the work, of course, but Razz, Prue and I threw in a few ideas. Dad said we wanted it simple, fast, loud and targeted at the inner Neanderthal. An hour or so later when he played through the final version we were pretty sure we had a caveman hit.

After lunch, Ignatius and Melvin arrived. Our backing singers – Scobie, Bill and Theodore – were going to rehearse with us back at school. The first task was to teach Yippy the song. After his initial run-through with Dad on acoustic guitar, Uncle Ray described Mel as "the love child of Johnny Rotten and Bruce Lee". The big problem was that Yippy's musical timing was about as good as his volleyball timing. Dad said he was "more your intuitive artiste". That basically meant he just sang when and how he felt like it.

On our first couple of run-throughs as a band, I doubt it would have been obvious to a casual listener that we were all in fact playing the same song. And I'm sure that most people would have just assumed that Melvin Yip was suffering from some rare musical form of Tourette's Syndrome. As for Ignatius, he seemed totally overwhelmed by the whole thing. Dad kept telling him to relax and forget everything he'd ever learned about music, while Uncle Ray just growled, "It's rock and roll, for god's sake, not Rachmaninoff!"

But then, on our third and fourth attempts, something happened. A few times, totally by accident, everything kind of clicked together, and for a few bars we found ourselves somehow all playing and singing the same thing at the same time. And it felt good. Really good. It was like we'd caught the same wave and it was driving us all along. Of course it didn't last long and we ended up being dumped head first into the musical sand, but the thrill of the ride stuck with us and we were keen for more.

After Dad did some extra work with Yippy on his timing and Uncle Ray got on guitar and ran through the music a few times with the rest of us, things really started to come together. I'm not saying we turned into the world's greatest band, but at least you could tell we *were* a band, not just a group of people standing around making noise at each other. By the end of the afternoon we'd managed to get through the song a few times with everyone in pretty good shape. We even played an extended version with Uncle Ray joining in on lead guitar, Dad sharing the vocals with Melvin and Prue doing ad lib solos on both violin and sax. We really knew we were getting somewhere when even Ignatius threw in a couple of unscripted notes. Razz claimed we were the next super-group and hailed us the Dugongs of Steel.

I went to bed that night tired but excited. For the first time I think I understood maybe just a little bit of what being in the Dugongs must have meant for my dad all those years ago and what it still meant for him now. I also started to think that maybe we could actually do it. That maybe the Hoops of Steel could play well enough to win the Battle of the Bands. And if we could do that, then maybe we could do something that at the beginning of the year seemed totally impossible. Maybe we could win the College Cup for Miss Tarango.

But there were still a lot of maybes to get through.

28.
Reverse Cool

We had two more Hoops of Steel rehearsals in the music room after school with our three backing singers. Then after a busy and successful Arts Week, Open Day arrived.

The feature event was always the Battle of the Bands. It was held on a special stage in front of the main oval grandstand. I don't know about everybody else, but for me, a slight case of total and absolute terror had started to set in over the previous couple of days.

Now there was a little over an hour to go. We'd just finished a couple of unplugged run-throughs of the song, and Razz, Prue and I were waiting in one of the spare classrooms for the others to return with some food.

I checked on Razz. I couldn't tell if he was nervous or not. He was drumming away like a maniac on his knees while his legs jumped about like pistons. But that was Razz's 'normal'. Prue, on the other hand, didn't look quite her regular confident near-genius self. She was chewing on a nail and staring at the carpet. She seemed a little on edge.

"RAZZ, FOR GOD'S SAKE! CAN YOU SIT STILL AND STOP THAT THUMPING FOR JUST A *SECOND*?!"

Okay, she sounded a little on edge as well.

"What?" Razz said, yanking out an earplug. "What's up, Prudles? Not packing it, are you?"

"No! Well . . . yeah, maybe. Just a little." Prue screwed up her mouth. "Maybe just a lot."

"Awwwwwww. Come here. What little Prudie-Wudie needs is a great big cuddle and a kiss from Uncle Wazzie."

Prue's face looked like it had been carved from stone – and by a not-very-happy chiseller.

"Then again, maybe not. Whatcha worried about, anyway?"

"Well, you know, just the usual things – playing in front of all those people after only a couple of rehearsals, being a total disaster, coming last, getting laughed off stage. I mean, we're not exactly your regular rock band, are we? We're a bit... weird."

"Weird? No way, Prudles. We've got Reverse Cool."

"Reverse Cool? What's that supposed to be?"

"Ah," Razz said, shaking his head and smiling warmly at Prue, "young kids today. You know nothing – but you're *gorgeous*!"

"Razz, if you want to keep your sideburns attached to your head, just get on with it."

"Well, listen and learn. It's like this. You've got two types of cool – your traditional Classic Cool and your Reverse Cool. Most people know Classic Cool when they see it. That's your common everyday movie star, rock god, fashion model… *me*… kind of cool."

Prue stuck her finger in her throat and pretended to throw up. Razz smiled and mumbled "Gorgeous!" but carried on regardless.

"But the old Reverse Cool is a bit trickier to recognise. To have Reverse Cool, some*thing* or some*one* has to be so uniquely *uncool* that they actually turn cool again."

"That's ridiculous," Prue said.

Razz thought for a moment and then tried to explain.

"Look, imagine there's this island, right, and it's surrounded by water."

Prue's mouth fell open. "Wow, what an *unusual* island."

"Yes, it is," Razz said, ignoring the sarcasm. "Because all the cool people in the world live on this big beach on one side of the island. Now, as it turns out, the closer you can get to that beach the cooler you are. The further off the beach you go, the less cool you are. Get it?"

Prue nodded at Razz like he was a dangerous mental patient.

"Good. So just recapping: if you're on the beach you're

way cool. If you're wading in the water you're a bit cool. If you're a couple of kilometres out to sea you're pretty lame. And if you're just barely visible on the horizon… you belong to Creswell House."

Razz stopped briefly to receive a round of applause from me and Prue.

"But here's the thing. You know how the Earth is round?"

"Well, I read *something* about that on Wikipedia," Prue said, "but I wasn't sure how accurate it was."

"Yes, good one, Prudles. Anyway, what I'm saying is, the further you go away from Cool Island beach the more uncool you become, *BUT* eventually you reach the other side of the world and then you start getting *closer* to Cool Island, but from the *reverse* side."

"And you've worked all this out by yourself?" Prue said.

"It's one hundred per cent Razz. I am the Guru of Cool!"

"So, Mr Guru, you reckon the Hoops of Steel have Reverse Cool?"

"Absolutely. Check it out. First we got Bill and young Ishmael here. They got your very subtle Corny Nice Guy Reverse Cool."

I wasn't exactly sure if I'd been complimented or insulted.

"Then you've got Bunga. He's got Reverse Cool 'cause he doesn't even know there is a Cool Island beach and if he did, he wouldn't care."

I agreed with that one. Theodore was a Cool Island entirely unto himself.

"And then of course we got our big guns. First up, Prindabel. Now the Prindabuster is your absolute cutting-edge Reverse Cool. He really pushes the envelope. Then we got Melvin, of course. He's a clear case of Extreme Reverse Cool. Either that or he's clinically insane."

Razz spread his arms wide.

"And finally there's the Scobemeister – the reigning and undisputed champeeeeeeeeeeeeeeeen of Reverse Cool. Scobes has Reverse Cool coming out of his uncool backside. He has so much Reverse Cool everyone can see it. That's why he's School Captain. Scobie has brought Reverse Cool to the masses."

Prue watched Razz closely and waited for him to continue, but he just pushed in an earplug and started to get comfortable in his chair.

"Yep, no doubt about it. The Hoops of Steel have got Reverse Cool to burn," he said as he closed his eyes.

"Yeah, well, great theory, Razz. I look forward to reading about it in more detail in all the scientific journals."

Razz grinned but remained silent as his head began bobbing to a beat. Prue watched him for a few seconds with a crooked smile fading on her face. Then she picked up a magazine and started flicking through its pages. She didn't look as if she was enjoying it much. The further into the magazine she went, the faster, louder and harder her flicks became until I was sure the pages were going to start ripping off and flying across the room. They didn't. The whole magazine did. Right into Razz's chest.

"Help! I'm under fire! Incoming!" Razz said, holding his hands in front of his face as the magazine tumbled to the floor. "Hey, what did I do?"

Prue's eyes were little pinpricks of anger.

"Well, what about *me*, then?" she snapped. "You talked about everyone else except me with your stupid theory. So what about *me*?"

Razz was a picture of innocence and confusion.

"What about you, what?"

"What about me and Reverse Cool?"

"You and Reverse Cool?"

"Stop repeating everything I say!"

"Stop repeating everything you…"

Even Razz could hear the nuclear warhead ticking this time. "Ah… What exactly would you like to know?"

"Have I got any Reverse Cool, obviously?!" Prue shouted, then added quickly, "not that I even believe in it in the first place… or I actually *care* about what you think… but you know… just for interest's sake… If the stupid thing *was* true… would I have any?"

Razz pulled on his earphone cable until it popped out from his ear. Then he stared hard at my sister. She was wearing a T-shirt with a picture of the Beatles on it. It was the one from that old album cover with the four of them on the zebra crossing. Except Prue had Photoshopped it and now two of them were floating above the ground. One was higher up as if he'd left first. She had sewn little angel wings on their backs.

Razz wrinkled up his nose.

"You? Reverse Cool?"

Prue folded her arms tightly across her chest and everything but her eyes said that she couldn't care less what Razz was going to say next.

"Sorry," Razz said, shaking his head slowly, "I thought you knew already. You're the Queen of Reverse Cool, Prudles. *You* make Reverse Cool hot."

"*Really?*" Prue said, perhaps just a little more excitedly than she intended. "Well, that's… *interesting*… you know… If there really was such a thing… Anyway, um… Hey, look at the time… I guess I'd better get myself changed…You know, for the big performance."

Prue sprang up from the desk she'd been sitting on and grabbed up a bag and a shiny black wig. She held them up.

"Show time!" she said and skipped from the room.

Razz watched her go before pushing his earplug in, closing his eyes and settling back in his chair.

"My work here is done," he said.

29.
You Da Bomb!
Da Bomb-bomb!

There were six entries in the Battle of the Bands. Two from Creswell, two from Charlton and one each from Radley and Franklin. We were the last to perform, so our nerves had plenty of time to get well and truly jangled.

Out of all the other houses' bands, the two from Creswell were clearly the best. One of their entries, Snotty and the Obnoxious Mutants, went down really well with Crazy Eddie Schneider. On the other hand it was hard to tell with Dusty Roads. They were obviously super-talented and the big crowd liked them, but all through their song Crazy Eddie just sat sprawled back on his chair with his eyes closed. Only a slight rocking of his head indicated he was still alive.

After five acts, it was our turn.

Razz was set up in centre stage at the back on drums. Prue was beside him holding her violin and bow with her saxophone on a stand. A little bit further forward on one side of the stage was Ignatius on electric organ. I was on the other side on rhythm guitar and beside me huddled around a microphone were Bill, Theodore and Scobie. Right out front and dressed in a shredded, safety-pin-encrusted, black ninja outfit courtesy of Gerard Carlson-Steele and the Art Department, was Melvin Yip.

Mr Cave, the Music Director and MC, introduced us, and a big cheer came up from the Charlton House supporters led by Miss Tarango along with some lukewarm applause from everyone else. Razz raised his drumsticks above his head and clicked them together four times as my heart was having a real crack at smashing some kind of blood-pumping record. But there was no backing out now.

After those four clicks, Razz leaped out of his seat and pounded out three thunderous beats on the drums and two ear-splitting clashes on the symbols. Then he launched into a blistering roller coaster of a beat and Prue, Ignatius and I leaped on board with electric piano, violin and guitar while Melvin, complete with distorted facial expressions and elaborate ninja moves, unleashed his machine-gun vocals.

> *Like-a-microwave-on-high-you're – hot!*
> *Some-chicks-think-they-are-they're – not!*
> *Haven't-got-the-bod-you've-got!*
> *Man-are-you-a-total-babe?*

And after a Razz drum thrashing, Melvin brought it home with a real tonsil shredder.

> *Or* WHAAAAAAAAAAAAAAAAAAAAAAAAAAAAAAAAAAAAAAAAAAT?!

That was repeated with increasing volume and craziness for the next two verses.

> *Your-bod-is-hot-but-you-are – cool!*
> *You're-deeper-than-a-swimming – pool!*
> *You're-the-hottest-chick-in – school!*
> *'Cause-you-full-y – rock!*
> *And* RUUUUUUUUUUUUUUUUUUUUUUUUUUUUULE!
> *You're-a-smokin'-babe-a-sweet-as – chick!*
> *Hot-to-trot-and-fully – sick!*
> *I'd-give-Kirsten-Dunst-the – flick!*
> *Man-of-all-the-chicks-you'd – be!*
> *My* PIIIIIIIIIIIIIIIIIIIIIIIIIIIIIIIIIIIIIIIIIIIIIIIIIIIIICK!

Then Razz pounded out a thunderous jungle beat and we all clapped along in time, while the refrain was chanted by Bill and Theodore and mimed very convincingly by Scobie.

> *You fry my brain/You turn me on/You light my fuse/*
> *'Cause you da bomb!*
> *You fry my brain/You turn me on/You light my fuse/*
> *'Cause you da bomb!*
> *You da-bomb! You da-bomb! You da-bomb-da-bomb*
> *Da-bomb-bomb!*
> *You da-bomb! You da-bomb! You da-bomb-da-bomb*
> *Da-bomb-bomb!*

With *the refrain* repeating in the background and the crowd stamping and clapping along with us, Prue danced onto centre stage waving her saxophone above her head. She was wearing a shiny black wig, heavy black eye shadow, black lipstick, a black T-shirt, a black studded jacket and chunky black lace-up boots. It was the perfect rock punk Goth outfit – except for the little pair of bright tie-dyed rainbow-coloured cotton shorts she had on.

Mad cheering and whistling erupted not just from Charlton House, but from all the St Daniel's boys in the crowd as Prue did a wild, loopy, twirling dance to the backing of *You da-bomb! You da-bomb! You da-bomb-*

da-bomb Da-bomb-bomb! Then after a few circuits of the stage the Queen of Reverse Cool unleashed an insane saxophone solo that had Crazy Eddie Schneider pumping both fists in the air and howling at the sky.

It all came to a climax when the chorus built to an ear-splitting '*DA BOMB-BOMB!*' and Melvin, much to the delight of Crazy Eddie, executed a perfect spinning karate kick and smashed a gaping hole in Razz's base drum (thanks – once again – to a fake front, courtesy of Gerard Carlson-Steele and the Art Department).

I don't think I'll ever forget the next minute or so standing on stage with the crowd cheering and laughing and making lots of noise. I just tried to take it all in, all the happy Charlton supporters and Crazy Eddie pounding on his judge's table and Miss Tarango smiling and waving. Sally was there going crazy as well. I even spotted Raychell Taylor again, bouncing up and down and woo-hooing and shouting out. She was with Gary Horsham, who didn't look very happy. It probably had something to do with him being from Creswell House.

I found Mum and Dad in the crowd too. Mrs Zorzotto was with them. So was Mr Barker. They were all on their feet waving and cheering. And Uncle Ray had turned up. He was standing beside Dad, clapping his hands above his head. That's when I noticed the other two guys next to him doing the same thing. One was dressed in black and the other one had a shaved head. I shouted at Razz and pointed them out. He took a second to see them and then his face broke into a massive smile. Mine was probably just as big. After all, it's not every day you get a standing ovation from the Dugongs.

I think the only way the day could have possibly been any better is if Kelly had been there... Oh, and if we'd won.

30.
You Are to Me

We finished up second in the Battle of the Bands just in front of Snotty and the Obnoxious Mutants. The winners on the day were Dusty Roads.

Apparently, during his days at St Daniel's, Crazy Eddie Schneider was the leading music student and after graduation he'd completed an honours degree at the Conservatorium. So he knew real musical talent when he heard it. It was still a close thing. Crazy Eddie reckoned his musical head had said Dusty Roads and his punk heart had said the Hoops of Steel. His musical head won.

We were all pretty happy with the result, although Razz still couldn't believe Dusty Roads had beaten us. He thought the Fender Stratocaster that put Crazy Eddie into hospital must have knocked his musical head completely out of tune. But the really good news was that because Charlton bands had taken out both first and second spot, we'd gained a heap of valuable points on Creswell and narrowed their overall lead in the race for the College Cup. Operation Tarango was still very much on target.

Once our heavy metal punk rock debut was out of the way, all attention focused on the next big event on the college calendar – the Formal. The two Lourdes girls had happily agreed with Razz's plan and everything was set for the night.

It kicked off with pre-Formal drinks, nibblies and photos at the Zorzottos' for everyone at our table as well as our parents. Then Uncle Georgiou chauffeured the five couples to the venue in another of his showy vehicles – an iridescent pink minibus. He even wore one of his most elaborate 'Show Tunes Serenade' costumes to celebrate the occasion. Razz's mum was right about those peacocks. Bill was impressed.

The Formal itself was great fun and Kelly seemed happier and closer than last time, but it was the way the night ended that I'll never forget.

Dad picked Kelly and me up and drove us back to Lourdes College and waited for me while I walked her to the boarding house. At the entrance of the Senior dormitory we stood together in the shadows of the old stone building and told each other how much we'd enjoyed the night and how much fun it had been. After all the easy things were said came the silence.

With Kelly standing in front of me looking so beautiful I couldn't help thinking about that moment we shared after the Dugongs' concert. Our first and only proper kiss. I wondered if it would ever be like that again. Would Kelly Faulkner's eyes ever sparkle at me the way they did that night? Were we ever going to be anything more than just friends? I knew there was only one person who could give me the answer to those questions. I had finally worked up the courage to speak when Kelly beat me to it.

"Remember that night at the Dugongs' concert?" she said.

For a second I thought I'd been speaking out loud or that Kelly had read my mind.

"Yeah… Of course."

"Remember the poem, the one you wrote about me – 'The Weatherman's Daughter' one? Remember that line you wrote… *the weatherman's daughter… makes the sun shine?*"

"Sure."

She raised her eyes and looked at me.

"Do you still think that?"

"Yeah, I do."

Kelly's forehead creased in a frown. I couldn't be certain if that was the answer she wanted to hear or not.

"I really think you're lovely, Ishmael, and I don't know what I'd do without you for a friend. But I'm worried

I'm being very selfish... and wasting your time. So I want you to know something. I want you to know that if you get sick of waiting... or if you meet someone else... or if there already *is* someone else... then I'd understand all that, I truly would."

Kelly's words made me feel good and scared all at the same time. I was glad we were friends but I didn't want her to 'understand' if there was somebody else. I wanted her to care. I watched as a tiny sad smile came to her face and she looked out into the night.

"I really do love that poem," she said. "I keep it on my noticeboard beside my desk and read it all the time. I like the girl in it. She's who I thought I was... who I want to be."

Then Kelly turned to me looking lost and tired.

"I'm trying... but I don't know if I'm that girl any more."

I wasn't sure what to say. I didn't know what words Kelly wanted or needed right then. But Mum and Dad always told me, "When in doubt, just stick with the truth". So I did that.

"Well, you are to me," I told her. "You'll *always* be that girl to me."

For a moment I thought Kelly's eyes had begun to sparkle, but it was just the lights of the boarding house reflecting in the beginnings of tears. They soon pooled and rolled down her face. Then she moved closer, wrapped her arms tightly around me and rested her head against my chest.

I've got no idea how long we stayed like that, just standing there holding each other. If it had gone on forever it would have been fine by me. But then voices and laughter began drifting up from down the drive, and I felt Kelly ease back.

"Better get inside and beat the rush," she said, and kissed me on the cheek. At the entrance to the dorm she stopped and turned.

"I owe you a poem," she added with a quick smile, then disappeared inside.

There were tons of other things that happened on the night of our Formal, but it's the time I spent holding on to Kelly and neither of us saying a word that I remember the most.

That, and the smiles on Bill Kingsley's and his 'partner' Katie's faces. The smiles that first appeared when Katie's friend Phoebe arrived at the pre-Formal party, along with her 'partner' ... Jimmy 'The Main Event' Mainwaring.

31.
Three Phone Calls and a Decision

" **I** shmael! We're all set, dude. The Big Z has come through with the goods!"

It was the Monday after the Formal and I had just arrived at school when Razz galloped over to meet me. I didn't have a clue what "goods" he had "come through" with.

"I've scored us all a beach house, dude! For one whole week at Sunshine Cove, straight after we break up. Belongs to my Uncle Sasha. And here's the best part. They're knocking the joint down soon to put up flats, so Uncle Sasha's letting us have it for nothing! I mean, it's a bit of a dump, but there's loads of space for you and me and all the guys and we don't even have to worry about wrecking it. Awesome!"

"Wow! Sounds great. By the way, Razz, how many uncles have you actually got?"

"Seven," he said as if that was the obvious number.

"Hey, and guess what, man? As an added extra special bonus, Sal and a bunch of Lourdes chicks are renting this posh unit not too far away from us. How cool is that? Maybe not that exciting for Bilbo, but awesome news for you, Ishmael, because Sal's trying to talk Kelly into coming down too, before she goes to New Zealand to see her dad. Dude, think about it. You and the Kelster together at the beach for a week. You'd have to be as excited as Prindabel at the Miss Nude Nerd finals."

Normally Razz would have been right. But to tell you the truth, I just wasn't sure any more. Don't get me wrong, I still felt exactly the same way about Kelly, but I wasn't really sure exactly how she felt about me.

"Man, can you believe it?" Razz said, scanning the yard. "In less than two months, no more school and we'll have our own house at the beach for a whole week. Does that sound totally rigid or what?"

It did sound totally rigid – and a bit scary. Soon we'd be leaving St Daniel's for good. Just five weeks of normal classes, two weeks of exams, a graduation dinner and then sun, surf and sand… and possibly Kelly Faulkner. It all seemed a bit unreal.

"Anyway, Mum and I are driving down to Sunshine Cove on Saturday to check it out. I'll call and let you know how it goes."

The following weekend I was reading on my bed and waiting for the phone call from Razz. What I ended up with was three phone calls – and a decision to make.

Phone call No 1:

Theme to *Mission Impossible* plays. I snatch up my mobile without taking my eyes off my book.

"About time. Where ya been?"

"Sorry. I had no idea you were so demanding."

"What? Kelly? Is that you?"

"Afraid so. Hope you're not too disappointed."

"No, no, I thought you were Razz."

"Do you often have trouble telling us apart?"

"Well, only in a certain light, you know, like pitch black. Oh, and sometimes when Razz tries on his Uncle Georgiou's hand-me-downs."

Kelly laughed. "Too much information. But look, what I rang for was to see if you wanted to do something Saturday week? That'd be the twentieth."

"Sure. Great. Love to."

"Terrific. I'll put your name down for the Lourdes working bee. They're cleaning the toilets."

I was trying to figure out how to sound excited when Kelly saved me.

"Gotcha. But you might want to actually hear what it is first. It's not that exciting. It's just that our dorm supervisor is taking the boarders in our year to see a local production of *Hamlet*. We're doing it in English this term. Anyway, Ms Entwhistle has generously allowed us to invite one guest if we want. I just thought you might like to come along."

"Yeah, that'd be great. We did it last year."

"Are you sure? Don't say yes just to be nice."

"No, I'd love to come. Thanks."

"Okay. But if you change your mind or you're too busy or you get a better offer just let me know, all right? That'd be no problem at all. I'm going anyway."

We spoke for a bit longer and sorted out all the details for the night. Kelly said to ring next weekend and let her know if I was definitely coming. I got off the phone feeling great. I'd only just settled back on the bed and found where I was up to in my book when my mobile went off again.

Phone call No 2:

Theme to *Mission Impossible* plays. I snatch up the phone without taking my eyes off my book.

"Hey, Razz, you'll never guess what happened."

"Ooooo, sounds exciting! What?"

It wasn't Razz. It was a girl's voice. I couldn't place it but it seemed familiar.

"Sorry I... I thought you were someone else."

"Yes, I guessed that. The Razzman, right? Remember him well from your Formal last year. Pretty smooth debater too – and a wild drummer. I saw you guys play at the Battle of the Bands. So cool. Didn't know you had all these hidden talents, Ishmael."

"Raychell?"

"Got it in one."

I had no idea why Raychell Taylor would be ringing me.

"Hope you don't think I'm stalking you or anything. You know, debating final, Battle of the Bands and now this. I'm not. I've given that sort of thing up. Found it too time-consuming. All that hiding behind bushes, phone-tapping, setting up the telescope on your bedroom every night – it just became too much."

"Yeah, good idea to cut back, what with exams coming up and everything," I said with a bit of a laugh. "I saw you at the Battle of the Bands with Gary Horsham."

"Ugh! Don't talk to me about that creep. As of two weeks ago, as far as I'm concerned, he is totally like a non-person."

"Sorry about that."

"Not a problem. Glad to get rid of him. And anyway, it's sort of why I'm ringing you. I was *won*dering if you wanted to come along to a bit of a party at my place."

Two invitations in five minutes! It had to be a dream. I looked carefully around the room. Any second I expected a runaway freight train like the one in that *Inception* movie to come ploughing through my bedroom wall. I guess I must have been taking a bit too long to reply, because Raychell went on.

"Look, I realise this is a bit out of the blue and I know we didn't get to spend that much time together at your Formal, which was my fault entirely, but if you come to the party maybe I can make it up to you. It's not going to be a big thing. Just me and some friends from school and a few guys they know. There'll be plenty of supplies too. And we'll have the whole house to ourselves because my parents are going away for a few days. It's a big house. Lots of quiet, private spots and plenty of opportunity for you and me to get to know each other better. So… are you interested?"

All sorts of things were racing through my mind.

"I… um… Yeah… Sounds good… When is it?"

"The Saturday night after this one."

"Not the twentieth?"

"Ah, let me just see… Yep, the twentieth. Is that a problem?"

"It *could* be… I *might* have something on… Some… aaah… *family* thing… I can probably get out of it… just not sure at the moment. I'll have to check. Can I ring you back and let you know?"

"Well, I suppose so, but don't keep me waiting too long, Ishmael. I can guarantee you'll have a lot more fun at my place than at your 'family thing'. I'll make it my *personal* mission."

After I took down Raychell's address and mobile number and promised I'd ring her back sometime before the end of the week, I flopped back on my bed. My head was spinning with possibilities. A minute ago everything had been simple and straightforward. I'd been so happy to go to the play with Kelly. But now…

My mobile rang a third time.

Phone call No 3:

Theme to *Mission Impossible* plays. I snatch up the phone. This time I check for a name first. Unknown number.

"Hello. Leseur residence. Ishmael speaking."

"HAHAHAHAHAHAHAHAHA! What're you doing, man? Trying out for the job as butler or something? You crack me up, dude!"

"Very funny. How come you came up as an *Unknown Number*?"

"Using Mum's phone. Took mine to the beach and forgot I had it in the back pocket of my boardies when

I went for a surf. Totally stuffed. Mum's not too happy. Also not happy about the hubcaps I scraped practising my reverse park."

Then I heard all about Uncle Sasha's place. Razz reckoned it was "totally awesome", although apparently Mrs Zorzotto rated it "*just* fit for near-human habitation". It sounded perfect. When Razz finished his usual ramblings on I told him all about Kelly's and Raychell's phone calls.

"Man, it's raining chicks!"

That was his first comment. Then I was expecting him to say something like:

"So what's the problemo, man? You got a choice between sitting in a crappy theatre watching the Chocoholic Dane with Kelly 'Let's-just-be-friends' Faulkner or spending a wild night alone with Raychell 'You-and-me-and-a-big-empty-house' Taylor. What's wrong with you? It's a no-brainer, dude!"

But Razz didn't say that. What he actually said was, "Man, that's a tough one. I guess you'd be mad not to pick Raychell. But then I keep thinking, what if it was *me* doing the picking and what if that other chick I left sitting alone in that theatre ended up being someone like Sally and I never knew? Wouldn't that be a bummer?"

I'd been sort of hoping that Razz would come to my

rescue and just tell me what I should do. But it looked as if the Lifesaver of Love was having some down time. It was all up to me. I had a decision to make. A big one.

To party with Raychell or to *Hamlet* with Kelly?

That was the question.

32.
Play or Party?

"**E**mergency Operation Tarango meeting? What are you on about, Prindabel?"

The rest of us were wondering the same thing. As well as our first and second placings in the Battle of the Bands, we'd also had good success in the inter-house football comp as Razz predicted and we'd picked up points in a few of the smaller Arts Week competitions.

"We've been going great. What are you calling an emergency meeting for, dude? We must be getting pretty close to Creswell by now."

"I've just factored in all the outstanding points and we are officially nine points behind them," Ignatius replied calmly.

"Only nine points behind! Well, geez, P-bud, if *that's* your idea of an emergency, never volunteer for Cyclone Watch, dude."

"The problem is, Orazio, we have only one event left in which to get those nine points and that's the Talent Quest."

The annual house Talent Quest was for acts of one or two people only. It was always held on the Friday afternoon of the very last day of classes for the leavers. Anyone could enter, but there was a limit of two acts from each house. At the end of it the rest of the school formed a guard of honour and the Seniors were cheered from the college before the pressure of two weeks of final exams began.

"Well, that's okay, isn't it? We usually do pretty good in that and I'm doing my drum solo again. Last year I came second and I've ramped it up a lot and added some new stuff."

"That's good to hear, Orazio. Because if we don't win the Talent Quest, we don't win the College Cup."

Razz eyed Ignatius suspiciously.

"You're not jiggling the figures, are you, Prindabuddy, just to get an exciting finish?"

"See for yourself. At the moment we're nine points behind Creswell. In the Talent Quest they give *thirty* points for first place, *fifteen* for the runner-up and *five* for third. So to make up the points needed we have to either win the Talent Quest outright or come second behind either Franklin or Radley. Whatever happens, if Creswell wins, we're sunk. And therein lies the real emergency. Because Creswell's entrant in the Talent

Quest is going to be... Slobo Bugslag."

There were blank expressions all around the tight circle of faces as our hopes commenced shutdown procedures. It was like making it right to the brink of Mount Doom only to hear someone say, "I thought *you* had the Ring."

"Slobo Bugslag," Razz repeated like a death knell.

Way back, Slobo Bugslag and I were at Moorfield Primary together. He was a grade below me. He was the most popular kid in school, which just goes to show that some people at least do rise above their names. After primary, Slobo went to another school but he'd turned up at St Daniel's this year. True to form, he was already one of the most popular kids in school and a strong tip for the next school captain. Some people were saying that Slobo was the new Scobie.

Our problem was that Slobo had one thing Scobie definitely didn't have – musical talent. Lots of it. He sang, he played the piano, he wrote his own stuff and he had a personality the size of a supertanker. Last year he made the finals of that *Search for a Star* show on TV. So if Slobo Bugslag entered our piddly little Talent Quest, he wasn't just going to win it, he was going to chew it up and spit it out.

It had now gone pretty quiet for an emergency

situation. It felt like the emergency had passed because the patient had died and we were all attending the funeral.

"Well," Razz said, trying to prod our enthusiasm back to life, "we've still got a couple of weeks. I can work more on my drum solo, I guess, and try to find something else to add."

"And we've still got the house auditions to do," Scobie added in support. "Who knows what that's going to turn up? All is not lost."

No, not lost. Maybe misplaced – like a contact lens left on a sand dune in the middle of the Gobi Desert.

That night in my room I tried to come up with a solution to our Talent Quest problem. I failed. So I decided to man up and at least do something about Kelly and Raychell. I'd made my decision and now it was time to make two phone calls – an easy one and a hard one. One to say 'Yes' and one to say 'No'.

My mum reckons that whenever you're faced with a number of things you have to do, always do the hardest one first while you're fresh, to get it out of the way. I held my mobile in my hand.

I scrolled down to Kelly's name and pushed *Call*.

33.
Lines 116 to 119

It was Saturday the twentieth. I got off a bus to walk the short distance to 72 Norwood Road. That was the address written on a slip of paper in my pocket. She was waiting for me at the front of the house. My heart jumped like it had suddenly remembered why it was beating. Those ice-blue eyes did it to me every time.

My mum's pretty smart, but I didn't always agree with her. Personally, I think it's better sometimes to do the *easy* things first, you know, to sort of help you build up some momentum for the hard ones.

Watching *Hamlet* with Kelly was great. Razz always complained about it being too long, but for me the night just rocketed by. Before I knew it, the lights were going up and everyone was filing out from the theatre and spilling out into the courtyard area just off the street. Ms Entwhistle told all the Lourdes girls to wait beside the road while she went and brought the minibus around.

"Make sure you're all ready to go," she warned them. "I don't want to be chasing anyone up".

Kelly and I moved a little away from the main group and found a quiet place to ourselves.

"You survive the night all right then?" Kelly said.

"I thought it was great. I had a great night."

Stick around – I promise I'll come up with another word besides 'great' shortly.

"Really? Me too."

"Great."

Maybe not.

Then Kelly glanced at me a few times like she was trying to make her mind up about something.

"So… you don't wish… that you'd gone to the party at Raychell Taylor's house instead?"

For a moment my brain struggled to work out exactly why those words didn't seem right. Then it knew.

"But… how did… Who…"

I didn't take long to figure it out.

"Razz has got a big mouth," I said.

"The biggest," Kelly said with a smile. "And Sally's not too far behind. You're not angry, are you?"

I shook my head. "No, I'm used to it by now."

Kelly bit her bottom lip and said, "It sounded like you could have had quite an…interesting… night over there."

"Still rather be here."

Kelly was looking straight at me now.

"You must really love *Hamlet*, huh?"

I was looking straight back at her.

"Yes. I do," I said. "Always have."

Just then a sharp beep made Kelly jump and a white minibus flashed past and parked a little way down the street. She glanced over her shoulder. The other Lourdes boarders were already saying goodbye to friends and moving off.

"Um well… I better go. Thanks again for coming. I'm really glad you did. Otherwise it could have been ugly. You know, with me turning up at Raychell Taylor's and scratching her eyes out and everything. But before I go, I just wanted…"

There was another beep. Kelly glanced around again. The last of the Lourdes girls were getting on the bus. A whole bunch of faces were looking at us through the rear window. They were smiling and laughing. Kelly turned back and shook her head.

"Great," she said, pulling one of her beautiful daggy faces. "Look, this is probably the wrong time and *definitely* the wrong place… but I just wanted to say…"

Horn again. Two blasts this time.

Kelly's shoulders slumped. Behind her the girls at the back of the bus laughed and waved. A couple of heads poked out the side windows. A beaten smile crept on to Kelly's lips.

"I better go. I…" she said.

And that's when I kissed her.

I didn't really know if she wanted me to or not. But like Hamlet had just pointed out, thinking about something too much can often be 'one part wisdom' and 'three parts coward'. I decided I'd been a coward long enough. The sound of cheering and whooping filled my ears. I wasn't sure if it was coming from the girls in the bus or from inside me. Almost immediately a horn began blaring in one long continuous *BEEEEEEEEEEEEEEP*. It didn't stop until Kelly's lips left mine. Then she stared at me for a second before hurrying off down the street to a rowdy reception.

As soon as Kelly climbed inside, the Lourdes bus pulled away from the curb, did a U-turn and headed back my way. I could see Ms Entwhistle in the driver's seat. She looked like she wanted to aim the bus at me and stamp on the accelerator. I waved as it shot past, but further down the road it veered to the kerb and jerked to a halt. A side window slid open. Kelly stuck her head out.

"Ishmael!" she called. "*Hamlet*. Act Two. Scene Two. Lines 116 to 119. Got it?"

I could only just make out what she was saying above the tinny minibus motor and the noise of the other traffic.

"Um yeah, right. Act Two. Scene Two," I called back. "Lines… um…"

The bus began to move away.

The other girls were laughing and waving. I waved back.

"Lines 116 to 119!" Kelly shouted. "Don't forget!"

"116 to 119," I shouted back. "I won't!"

Kelly fell back giggling into the bus and was caught by the other girls as Ms Entwhistle put her foot to the floor and sped off into the night.

I spent the entire trip home trying to work out what the quote could be. By the time I was back in my room, I was pretty sure I'd worked it out. It had to be the old 'hoops of steel' bit about friendship. Kelly told me that was one of her favourite parts.

When I found my copy of *Hamlet* I flicked through to Act Two, Scene Two. I ran my finger down the pages to line 116 and read to line 119. It wasn't about hoops of steel at all. Instead, Kelly had found me that poem she promised.

Being wrong had never felt so good.

34.
A Show Tunes Superman

The weeks leading up to exams came with a rush of 'lasts'. Last assignments, last house meeting, last school assembly, last regular school day, last Tutor Group (where we all put in and bought Mr Guthrie a new backpack for his upcoming holiday trip to Nepal), last lessons for each of our subjects and then, last lesson altogether. Finally, the only thing that remained was the St Daniel's Talent Quest and with it, our very last chance to make Operation Tarango a success.

The two acts representing Charlton House were Razz and a couple of guys from two years below who did comedy routines. They were pretty funny but I couldn't see them getting anywhere near topping Slobo Bugslag. As for Razz, he'd been staying back after school in one of the music rooms and working on a 'new dimension' to his drum solo. We all wanted to know what it was, but he said it was a secret and we'd just have to wait to see "how it all came out on the day".

The gym was packed and noisy. The Seniors were all up the front in the best seats. Scobie, Ignatius and I were sitting together. Bill had gone with Razz to help carry his drum equipment and get it set up backstage. Brother Jerome was the sole judge.

The first act was a magician from Franklin House. Not exactly mind-blowing. Our boys were second. They went down well because they impersonated some of the teachers, but after Slobo Bugslag performed it was depressingly obvious that whoever wanted to win the Talent Quest would need to push him into second place. A few more mediocre acts followed and then it was Razz's turn.

After a year of trying, a year where we'd dragged ourselves from laughing stock to within a handful of points of being college champions, all of Charlton House's hopes were now riding on this one performance. If ever we needed the Razzman to be a real superhero, now was the time.

After he was introduced to a wild reception from Charlton, Razz did his regular clicking of the drumsticks then launched himself into his performance.

Right from the first clattering, pulsating drum roll,

Razz was on fire. He was leaving nothing in the tank. But it still needed that 'something extra' to top Slobo. That 'something extra' came after Razz completed a thundering pass on the drums and changed into a steady, repetitive tribal beat. It didn't take long for the audience to become a little restless.

Then Bill Kingsley walked onto the stage.

The reaction to Bill was deafening – a wild mixture of laughter, whistles and jeers. It wasn't that surprising. As well as having his hair greased back and wearing heavy eyeliner, Bill had on a pair of white tights and a three-quarter length jacket that was covered in tassels and sparkles with a mass of coloured feathers exploding from each shoulder. I picked it right away as an Uncle Georgiou special. I think Bill might have finally had that talk with his father.

As the gymnasium went off, Bill just stood centre stage with his hands on his hips like a Show Tunes Superman. Then he undid his jacket to an explosion of hoots and whistles and threw it to a junior Charlton boy who had scuttled on stage to catch it. Under the jacket Bill was wearing a sleeveless skintight muscle shirt in Charlton gold that left his midriff exposed. It was amazing to see how much weight he'd lost and how much muscle had replaced it. He looked great. But the best part was the words on the front of his shirt spelled out in shiny red letters. TO THINE OWN SELF BE TRUE it said.

Then Razz cranked up the beat and Bill held out his hand and a sparkling hoop came flying in from the side of the stage. In one movement he caught it, spun it in his hand, slipped it over his head and set it twirling effortlessly on his hips. What followed was a dazzling array of tricks. I'm pretty sure I recognised the 'corkscrew', the 'vortex', the 'booty bump' and possibly the 'ninja pass' in among them. And with every twirl and pass of the hoop, the jeers were replaced by whoops and cheers.

For most St Daniel's boys, it didn't matter what you looked like, or what you were – an impressive display of motor skills and hand–eye coordination could win them over every time. So could courage. Bill was giving them a hefty dose of both.

The performance finished with an earthquake of a drum roll and Bill spinning four hoops simultaneously on his neck, knees and arms. The crowd – except for a handful of boys who had trouble raising their knuckles off the floor – went wild. But no one went wilder than Jimmy 'The Main Event' Mainwaring, who was leading the cheering from the front row. Miss Tarango might have come a close second, but I like to think that Scobie, Ignatius and I were right up there. As for Billy – he was beaming.

And the final result?

Well, you know those movies where you've got this group of people and they have to win like a horse race or a big hockey match or a football game because if they don't, the world will end or something? And you know when you're watching those kinds of movies, you sort of know all along that they'll end up doing it – winning that race or that game – because after all, it's just a movie and you have to have a happy ending, right? But then sometimes they write the story so that for a moment you start to think, hey, maybe they're not going to make it after all – maybe they're just going to try really, *really* hard and come really, *really* close and miss out, and you start getting a bit tense and worried even though you keep telling yourself you're being stupid because of course they're going to do it. And then, right at the last second, when all looks lost, they actually *do* win the horse race or the hockey match or the football match. Well, my point is this: sometimes real life is just like those movies.

And sometimes it's not.

Slobo Bugslag won the Talent Quest ahead of Razz and Bill in second place, and in our final year at

St Daniel's, Creswell won the College Cup.

Operation Tarango had failed.

But when our year group were dismissed from the gym, and Scobie, Ignatius, Razz and I made our way through the guard of honour with our friend Bill Kingsley smiling and laughing and walking proudly beside us, it really didn't seem that bad.

35.
Perfect, Just
Perfect

Ten days later our final exams were over. I was pretty happy with how they went. So were Scobie, Ignatius and Bill. And, for the first time in his life, so was Razz. Now the only thing that remained to officially mark the end of our time at St Daniel's College was the Graduation Dinner.

It was held in the school gymnasium. At one end was a stage decorated with a massive display of flowers, balloons and streamers as well as the four house banners. The rest of the floor space was filled with long tables and chairs all set out and decorated in the college colours. It looked pretty special.

At our table were Razz and Mrs Zorzotto plus special guest, Uncle Georgiou; Ignatius, his parents and his sister Cynthia; Bill and his mother but not his father (who apparently had an important business meeting that couldn't be missed); Scobie and his dad along with his mother, who had flown in especially for the night; and me, my parents and Prue.

It was a huge night. There were plenty of speeches, of course. The best one came from Scobie as the retiring School Captain. He told us that we should never be afraid of taking on impossible things. Unless we did, he said, we would never discover the amazing things we were capable of. After that Brother Jerome presented James with his College Captain plaque and described him as "the standard to which every future captain should aspire". It got the biggest cheer of the night and a standing ovation.

Then came all the other awards and presentations. After the College Cup was presented to Creswell, all the individual academic prizes were given out. By the end of the night there were quite a few trophies and plaques on our table. Scobie got Dux as well as first place in just about every subject he did, Ignatius picked up awards in Science and Maths and after a huge improvement in his theory grades, a shocked but "totally blown away" Razz took out the HPE award. Bill and I didn't miss out either. I got a third-place certificate for English plus a Conscientious Study award and Bill got a second-place certificate for Film and TV.

After dinner came the viewing of the ten-minute

videos each house had put together to sum up their year. Like other houses', Charlton's had lots of clips of Seniors involved in a whole range of college activities. Footage of Scobie dancing at the Formal got a big laugh. To put it kindly, Scobie is to dancing what a three-toed sloth is to speed skating. There was also a few fleeting seconds of fame for our debating and volleyball teams as well as the Hoops of Steel. The biggest roar of approval was a tie between a clip of Miss Tarango at the Athletics Carnival doing a wild happy dance after one of the tug of war victories and the clip of Bill keeping four hoops in motion at the Talent Quest. After that came up on the big screen, Mrs Kingsley smothered him in a bear hug.

The official part of the evening ended with the presentation of our graduation medals followed by a performance of the college song. It was led by Theodore Bungalari, and I even thought I saw Mr Hardcastle choking back the tears. The rest of the night was spent talking, laughing and telling stories. Oh, and taking plenty of photos.

Mrs Kingsley was our table's official photographer. That's what she did part-time at a local paper. We made sure we didn't miss anything. We took photos with our families, with other Seniors (even Barry Bagsley was in there somewhere) and with our subject teachers including a special one where Mr Barker and Brother Jerome were pulling stupid faces and the rest of us were giving them our best Grim Reaper looks.

But that was just the beginning. There were photos of our debating team holding the champion's trophy, and one of the Fighting Fifths volleyball team with Mr Guthrie where we recreated a shot of Ignatius and the legendary 'Finger of God' play. Then we reunited all the members of the Hoops of Steel and Mrs Kingsley took heaps of shots of us in all our Reverse Cool glory while Melvin did his best ninja moves. The last photos we took inside the gym were of Miss Tarango and the Fab Five.

Then came the hard part: saying goodbye to her.

First we gave her our presents – some flowers, a big box of chocolates and a huge, illustrated, leather-bound edition of *The Complete Works of Shakespeare*. For some reason Scobie had given me the job of writing the inscription inside the cover for all of us to sign. I kept asking, "Why me?" It took ages to come up with something that sounded anywhere near good enough. In the end I wrote, "To Miss Tarango from the Fab Five. Somewhere in here we hope might be the words to match you." When I showed it to Scobie he just said, "*That's* why you."

Miss really liked the book. When she read the inscription she stared at it for ages with her hand on her chest. Then she said, "So lovely. Thank you."

"We were supposed to get you something else as well, miss, but Operation Tarango ended up an epic fail," Razz said.

"Operation Tarango?"

"Yeah, well, we sort of had this plan, right from the beginning of the year. We were gonna win the College Cup for you. That was gonna be our big end-of-year gift. Except we blew it."

Miss Tarango looked around at all of us and frowned.

"Blew it? Epic fail? You gave me much more than a cup. You gave me this year and everything you've put into it. I've never had so much fun in my life. That's your gift to me, boys – the whole year, every day of it. And you, *all* of you, right from my very first day, that's the gift you've given me."

Miss looked at each of us in turn and unleashed the dimples.

"Best. Gift. Ever," she said.

And we thought James Scobie was the master of finding the right words.

Then Miss Tarango took a deep breath.

"I'm a terrible teacher, really I am" she said. "My father

was a teacher and he always told me that good teachers never have favourites. But I can't help it. You guys are my favourites. I'm certain you always will be."

"Hey, don't beat yourself up, Miss," Razz said. "After all, look at us. We're clearly adorable. And you're only human."

Miss Tarango laughed and wiped her eyes.

"Thank you, Orazio. I feel a lot better now that I realise I never stood a chance."

Then Miss breathed in again and threw her shoulders back.

"Right, time to say goodbye. But I refuse to blubber because I want every one of you to promise me under pain of death that you will visit St Daniel's whenever you can to let us know how you're going, and when Charlton *does* win the cup next year because of your inspiration, you will come back to celebrate with us."

No arm twisting needed for that one. Then Miss spoke to us in turn and ended each time with a hug and a kiss on the cheek. Prindabel was first in line.

"Ignatius," she said, "who am I going to turn to when I need the answer to an obscure question? I'll be lost without you. The only reason I'm letting you go is so you can use that incredible brain of yours to discover cures and other amazing things and make the world a better place. So don't let me down."

"I won't, Miss," Ignatius said as the Prindabel Power Pointer quickly brushed at his eye.

Miss Tarango moved on.

"Billy," she said, shaking her head. "Those Jedi guys are nothing compared to you. After that hooping performance, you will always be my hero. And when you're picking up your Oscars for all those brilliant movies you are going to make, remember, I'm always available for the red carpet."

"Thanks, Miss, I will," Bill said.

Scobie was next in line.

"James, what can I possibly say? You have spoiled us with your presence. You have single-handedly made St Daniel's a better place. I can't wait until you're running the country."

"Thank you, Miss," Scobie said with a quick mouth twist. "Will you be my Minister for Education?"

"Believe me, Mr Future Prime Minister," Miss Tarango replied, "it would be an absolute honour."

Then she turned to Razz.

"Orazio Victor Zorzotto – the face that launched a thousand 'awesomes'. I have two pieces of advice for you, Orazio. The first is to do everything in your power to hold on to that amazing girlfriend I chatted to at the Formal. She is gold."

"Already know that, Miss."

"Good. Well, the second piece of advice is, when you qualify for uni, which of course you will, make sure you knuckle down and study and get that degree. And after you do, apply for a job back here at St Daniel's, because there are boys here who desperately need you, and unless I am very much mistaken, as a teacher, *you* will be awesome."

"Wow, Miss... I..." Razz clamped his mouth shut and shook his head. Silencing the Razzman. Was there nothing that Miss Tarango couldn't do?

Then before I knew it, Miss was standing in front of me.

"Young Ishmael," she said. "Mr Still Waters Running Deep. I have something for you." Miss Tarango pulled a small rectangle of cardboard from her purse and waved it at me.

"What's that, Miss?"

"This, Ishmael, is a business card. But not just any business card. This belongs to a friend of a friend of mine who is a publisher – a book publisher. I hope you don't mind, but I showed her some of your journal extracts from the past few years. She liked them. Said they were very rough around the edges and needed a lot of work, particularly the earlier ones, but that they 'showed real potential' and she was 'keen' to talk with you. She said to contact her if you were *serious* about writing and were planning to do a creative writing course at uni. So, will you… call her, Ishmael?"

"I… yeah… I will… Thanks, Miss… I don't believe it."

I really couldn't. The other guys were patting me on the back and I could hear them congratulating me, but it felt so unreal. I had no idea anyone else would ever be interested in my journals when I began writing it, four years ago. I thought about the first words:

There's no easy way to put this, so I'll just say it straight out. It's time I faced up to the truth. I'm fourteen years old and I have Ishmael Leseur's Syndrome.

There is no cure.

It all seemed so long ago.

Miss Tarango's voice brought me back to the present.

"And of course when you do write your best-seller about St Daniel's, Ishmael, the most important thing is to make me look good, okay?"

"I think I'd have to tone you down, Miss – otherwise no one would believe you're real."

The other guys greeted that with a chorus of *Oooooo*s and groans. But Miss Tarango just smiled cheesily at them and said, "Told you he had a way with words." Then she turned to face me. "But mind how you use them, Ishmael, because they're powerful things, words. Remember – good, not evil."

"Got it, Miss."

Then after a hug and a kiss on the cheek she stepped back and looked at us all.

"Right, that's the lot of you, then. See, no tears. All done with a smile."

"And dimples," Razz said.

"Dimples? What are you going on about, Orazio? I don't have dimples."

We all laughed as Miss totally destroyed her own argument by breaking into a big grin.

"Now I *definitely* have to get going," Miss said, collecting up her presents. "Unlike some *lucky* people, I still have three weeks of school left and a stack of marking to get through."

"Then you'll be hitting the beach again, I bet, Miss," Razz said. "Hey, remember to wear a hat, use thirty-plus suncream, and don't stay out in the sun for more than fifteen minutes at a time. I learned that last year. I'm a Sun Safe guru, Miss."

"Sound advice, Orazio… but I'm actually not off to the beach this year."

"How come, Miss? You always hit the beach."

Miss shrugged her shoulders.

"No reason… just decided to try something different… You know… as you do."

"So where're you going, Miss?"

"Nowhere that exciting, Orazio… just somewhere to get away for a bit."

"Where's that?"

Miss gave her head a little shake as if the answer wasn't important.

"Just… you know…. Nepal."

We all looked around at each other and smiled.

"*Nepal*, Miss?"Razz said.

Miss Tarango's face hardened.

"Yes, Nepal, Orazio. Have you lot got a problem with that?"

A jumbled chorus of *No, Miss* came her way as we tried to maintain serious faces.

"Good," she said, still squinting at us suspiciously. She'd only taken a few steps away before Razz called after her.

"Hey, Miss, Nepal could be a bit more dangerous than the beach. Make sure you get yourself a good guide."

Miss Tarango froze in her tracks, then turned slowly and levelled her big brown eyes on Razz.

"Thank you for both your concern and your suggestion, Mr Zorzotto. But I've already found one.

And I've been reliably informed… that he's the best."

Miss Tarango's dimples returned then for one final curtain call.

"An assessment with which I heartily concur," she said.

36.
There's No Easy Way to Put This

We took our final photo out in the yard. It was one of the Fab Five sitting around our regular table in the Senior area. The very last, last. Then after we made sure everyone knew the arrangements for the beach, one by one Bill, Ignatius, Scobie, and their families headed off home.

That just left Razz and me sitting side by side.

Across the playground a few groups of people were still gathered outside the gym chatting. One group was made up of Mum and Dad, Mrs Zorzotto and Mr Barker. Inside we could see Mr Guthrie and Miss Tarango with a small army of boarders from the year below stacking tables and chairs and cleaning up. Prue was in there helping them. The boarders looked pretty happy about that.

"Hey, what about me getting Mr G and Miss T

together? How rigid was that? I really worked the old Razz matchmaking magic on that one."

"You? What did you have to do with it?"

"Are you kidding me? I planted the seed, dude."

"Oh right, of course, and don't tell me, let me guess. That would be because you are the… Gardener of Luuuurve… um… cultivating romance… in the… ah… barren soil… of broken hearts."

"Man," Razz said with a look of amazement on his face, "you must have been reading my CV!"

We both laughed then Razz went serious.

"Hey, man, heard any news from the Kelster? You know, about the beach or anything?"

Apart from a couple of emails wishing each other good luck with our exams I hadn't been in contact with Kelly since the night we saw *Hamlet* together.

"Nuh, nothing. Has Sal said anything to you?"

Razz squirmed a bit in his seat and wouldn't look at me. It wasn't a good sign.

"Not really, man."

That was an even worse sign. If Kelly was coming to the coast she would have said something to Sal by now and if Sally knew, Razz would know.

"You should totally ring her tomorrow, dude – that's when Lourdes finishes up. You got all Friday before we head to the beach. You should see if she wants to do something, man. Seriously."

"Yeah, I think I will."

Razz scanned the playground.

"It's so weird to think we're not coming back here. *Uni* next year. Never thought I'd be saying that. Hey, wouldn't it be awesome if we all ended up at the same place – you, me, Sal, Kelly and all the guys. How rigid would that be, dude?"

"It'd be great, but we'd have to be pretty lucky. It all depends on who gets offered what courses and what we all qualify for."

The smile on Razz's face fell a little and he picked at a loose splinter of wood on the table for a moment.

"Yeah, I suppose. But whatever happens… wherever we end up… you and me, man… we'll always be tight. We'll always be hoops of steel, right?"

I looked at the face that had been there with me through all the highs and lows of the last four mad but unmissable years.

"I don't know about that, Razz," I said.

That face was now gawking at me like I was Ignatius Prindabel explaining advanced Chaos Theory. "What? What are you talking about, dude? What don't you know?"

I gave him a classic Bill Kingsley shrug.

"About us being hoops of steel."

Razz stare crazy-eyed at me until I couldn't take it any longer. Then, Scobie-like, I hit him with just the right words.

"More like hoops of carbon nanotubes, I would've thought."

A grin the size of a crescent moon grew on Razz's face. Then he wrapped an arm around my neck and wrestled me into a headlock.

"You think you're a bit of a comedian, don't you, Ishmael? Thought you had me going there for a while, eh? Well, I wasn't fooled for a minute, you dirt bag. Let this be a warn—"

Suddenly Razz stopped and released his grip. He looked around behind him and under the table.

"Hey, where's my blazer gone? Geez, Mum'll kill me if I lose that thing. She wants to sell it. Aw, man! It's got my graduation medal on it too. Must have left it in the gym. Wait here, dude. I'll be right back."

Razz bounded from his seat and raced off a few metres before spinning round and continuing to skip backwards. He was pointing two fingers at me like a gunslinger.

"Love ya, man!" he called out. "You know, in a totally non-Hoop Boy sort of a way."

"Love you too, Razz," I laughed. "Same way."

"I'm totally cool with that!" he said, then charged off towards the gym, throwing in a few of Melvin Yip's ninja moves for good measure.

Then there was just me.

It felt so strange sitting at our regular table, without the normal chaos in the yard and without the other guys. After the pressure of exams and all the rush and excitement of the graduation, everything was now so quiet and still. Bit like I was sitting in the eye of a cyclone, and I guess in a way I was. It was a brief moment of calm between the end of school life and the beginning of whatever the future might hold. The future? For a moment I tried to picture what that might be like.

Well, if it was a perfect, happy-ending, movie kind of future, it would be like this: Miss Tarango and Mr Guthrie would stay together and eventually get married and raise the luckiest kids in the world; Mr Barker would become part of Razz and Mrs Zorzotto's little family and be the partner and father they both deserved; the Dugongs would release a brand new album and it would be a hit and win awards and my dad would keep performing and writing songs and never have to sell insurance again; the current Deputy Principal of St Daniel's would follow his heart and quit teaching for good to become manager of a legendary rock group; and Scobie, Bill, Ignatius, Razz and I would all end up at the same uni and stay friends for ever.

But sometimes life is like those kinds of movies. And sometimes it's not.

And my personal future? Well, if it was perfect, in just two days' time I would be at Sunshine Cove with Kelly Faulkner and we would be laughing and swimming together with a whole magic week stretching ahead of us. And I would go to university and become a writer, and I'd write all about my crazy, embarrassing, wonderful school days at St Daniel's and about the best friends anyone could ever have. And I would bind those friends to my soul with words, because they are stronger and more powerful than steel or even carbon nanotubes.

And that story, if I ever wrote it, would end right here – with me sitting at the table of the Fab Five, grinning like an idiot, and waiting for Cyclone Razz to come rushing back and sweep us both into the future. And with these few words.

There's no easy way to put this, so I'll just say it straight out. It's time I faced up to the truth. My name is Ishmael Leseur. I am seventeen years old. I have Ishmael Leseur's Syndrome.

There is no cure.

And do you know what?
I am *totally* cool with that.

37.
Just in Case
You're Interested

Oh, and just in case you're interested, this is how my phone call with Kelly Faulkner went the following night.

Kelly: *Hello.*

Me: *Kelly? Hi, it's me, Ishmael.*

Kelly: *Hey, Ishmael.*

Me: *How'd the exams go?*

Kelly: *Good. I was really happy with them. Hopefully, it'll get me into Journalism. How'd you go?*

Me: *Not too bad I think.*

Kelly: *Great.*

Me: *Ummm, look, I was wondering… Now that exams are over and everything… if maybe you wanted to do something tomorrow, like maybe go to the cinema?*

Kelly: *Sorry, can't. I'm busy tomorrow. I've got something on.*

Me: *Oh, right, no worries… No, that's fine. I just thought… but you know, if you're busy…*

Kelly: *Yeah, sorry I am. I'm going shopping.*

Me: *Shopping? Right. Great. That's great…*

Kelly: *With Sally.*

Me: *Oh… cool… that'll be fun… You should totally do that… You know, what I was saying before about doing something… I only meant if you didn't have anything… you know…important planned…*

Kelly: *Well, what could be more important than us buying new swimming suits?*

Me: Silence

Kelly: *For the beach.*

Me: Silence

Kelly: *You know, so we can look our best in case we meet up with a couple of hot guys when we're down at Sunshine Cove.*

Me: *You're coming?*

Kelly: *Uh-huh.*

Me: *For the whole week?*

Kelly: *Afraid so.*

Me: *Well, that's… that's great. That's really good. That's…brilliant!*

Kelly: *It was supposed to be a secret but you forced it out of me. Can't believe you didn't know already. Don't tell me Razz actually kept his mouth shut for once. I think that might qualify as a miracle.*

Me: *I agree, but it's just so great you're coming.*

Kelly: *Well, I thought I should, otherwise who'd keep an eye on the weather if I'm not there? I mean, someone has to make sure that Sunshine Cove lives up to its name, right?*

Me: *That's right!*

Kelly: *Only I'd better warn you, Ishmael, I'm a bit out of practice with the whole weather goddess thing. A few clouds might slip through every now and then… possibly even some occasional showers.*

Me: *I don't mind. Hey, maybe I can help you?*

Kelly: *What, you think together we could make the sun shine for the whole week?*

Me: *Sure. Who knows, we might even start a heat wave.*

Kelly: *Reeeeeeeally? Well, we'll just have to wait and see about that one, won't we…*

And the way Kelly Faulkner said it, I just knew she was smiling and those beautiful ice-blue eyes were sparkling like the sea.

ACKNOWLDGEMENTS

My unending thanks and gratitude go to the following:

My publisher at Omnibus Books, Dyan Blacklock, for blessing me with the opportunity to tell Ishmael's story, and to my editor, Celia Jellett, for making that telling better than it otherwise would have been without her. Love you guys.

Everyone at Scholastic Australia, with a special thanks to Claire Pretyman and the ladies in the Rights and Permissions Department for sending Ishmael overseas and helping make it possible for me to be a full-time writer.

The wonderful folk at Templar Publishing for welcoming Ishmael and his mates into the fold.

All my family, especially my wife Adriana, for being 'the very best of everything' in my life and for drawing on her maths and biology teacher background so that I could put suitably nerdy words into Ignatius Prindabel's mouth; my son Joe, for his thoughtful and helpful manuscript reading, and for his encouragement and support; and my daughter Meg, whose own wonderful writing inspires me to try harder.

My ever-supportive friends and colleagues, with a particular mention this time round to Natalie, for her assistance with all things hooping; to Ruth, for her enthusiasm for the series and for letting me borrow her surname for one of St Daniel's houses; and to Margaret, for keeping me entertained and informed on Facebook when I should be writing and for helping out with band names.

Finally, and most sincerely, thank you to every reader who has followed Ishmael from first word to last. I hope you have enjoyed the journey and had some laughs and maybe even shed a happy tear or two along the way. I know I have. It has been a joy and honour (and totally rigid!) to have had your company.

—MGB

Don't miss the first hilarious *Ishmael* book:

Don't Call Me Ishmael

by Michael Gerard Bauer

ISBN 978-1-84877-683-8

Also available as an ebook

As far as I know, I'm the only recorded case of Ishmael Leseur's Syndrome in the world. It is capable of turning an otherwise almost normal person into a walking disaster registering 9.9 on the open-ended imbecile scale. And that is why I've decided to write all this down.

'Comic genius and a great read.' *The Bookseller*

'Sharp and witty… utterly engaging.'
Marilyn Brocklehurst, Norfolk Children's Book Centre

'An extremely funny book that doesn't shy away from the inevitable growing pains of adolescence.' *Staff Picks, Foyles*

Don't miss the brilliantly funny sequel to
Don't Call Me Ishmael:

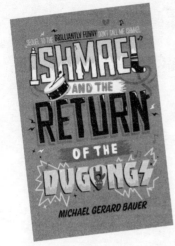

Ishmael and the Return of the Dugongs

by Michael Gerard Bauer

ISBN 978-1-84877-712-5

Also available as an ebook

Your bod is hot but you are cool
You're deeper than a swimming pool
Man, you're the hottest chick in school
You fully rock and fully rule!

Ishmael is back at St Daniel's for another year of misadventure, with his best mate Razz determined to set him up with dream girl Kelly.

Before he can win Kelly's heart, Ishmael has to overcome a mortifying pool incident, a nasty knockout and getting caught red-handed with her diary.

Ishmael's only hope lies with his Dad's rock band, but can the Dugongs set everything right?